RUIN OF THE SCARRED

STING OF LOVE BOOK 1

MEDHA NAGUR

Copyright © Medha Nagur
All Rights Reserved.

This book has been published with all efforts taken to make the material error-free after the consent of the author. However, the author and the publisher do not assume and hereby disclaim any liability to any party for any loss, damage, or disruption caused by errors or omissions, whether such errors or omissions result from negligence, accident, or any other cause.

While every effort has been made to avoid any mistake or omission, this publication is being sold on the condition and understanding that neither the author nor the publishers or printers would be liable in any manner to any person by reason of any mistake or omission in this publication or for any action taken or omitted to be taken or advice rendered or accepted on the basis of this work. For any defect in printing or binding the publishers will be liable only to replace the defective copy by another copy of this work then available.

To Basav, for his love and support.

Contents

1. Chapter 1 — 1
2. Chapter 2 — 21
3. Chapter 3 — 36
4. Chapter 4 — 50
5. Chapter 5 — 64
6. Chapter 6 — 74
7. Chapter 7 — 81
8. Chapter 8 — 90
9. Chapter 9 — 108
10. Chapter 10 — 117
11. Chapter 11 — 131
12. Chapter 12 — 145
13. Chapter 13 — 155
14. Chapter 14 — 173
15. Chapter 15 — 183
16. Chapter 16 — 194
17. Chapter 17 — 206

To Be Continued... — 223
Leave Your Feedback — 225
About The Author — 227
Glossary — 229

"The course of true love never did run smooth."
- **William Shakespeare**
"Love all, trust a few,
Do wrong to none: be able for thine enemy
Rather in power than use; and keep thy friend
Under thy own life's key: be check'd for silence,
But never tax'd for speech."
— **William Shakespeare**

CHAPTER ONE

When scars become medals and every death at your hands become pride, it gets harder to embrace love because there are eyes around waiting to prey not just on you but also on your loved ones. There were scars not just on her body but also on her soul. Bidisha was already incapable of taking care of the only person she loved more than her life, her mother. She wouldn't dare to love another and put his life in peril too. Many had told her, without even seeing her face under the veil even once, that she was of age and she needed a companion.

But little did they know that Bidisha Maitra, who always hid her face, was the daughter of Mokshita Maitra—the woman people had despised for several years and had chased her out of her village for being a royal fugitive. For years, Bidisha had been trying to free her mother from a life of hiding in the jungle. However, if only there was a way to clear her mother's name from the false conviction of killing a British officer... Mokshita Maitra was accused of stabbing the man she had loved with all her heart, the man who was also Bidisha's father.

However, her mother wanted nothing from life anymore. She only feared for her daughter's life. Though Bidisha had come up with a few plans over the years, her mother had always held her back. And the obedient daughter that Bidisha was, she wouldn't dare to hurt her mother. All that her mother wanted for her brave girl was a peaceful life. And after what happened to her, Mokshita had told her time and again that she wouldn't care much for a man in her daughter's life. Bidisha could only affirm her mother's thoughts. She had never let her heart sway for a man.

More than anything else, no man would want her for a wife. Bidisha was not a delicate woman who looked after herself and preserved her beauty for her future husband. In contrast, she battled for survival every day, mostly with wild animals but also with humans on unfortunate days. And at the moment, as she saw masked men with swords, she knew it was one of those days.

The blade hissed as Bidisha swung it. The man's white turban fell off his head and into the mud. A broad framed man slashed his sword directly at her neck. She ducked at once and as she rose back, slashed his thigh. His white *dhoti* bled in no time just like his *Panjabi*, which was laced all over in his blood. His attempt to get her out of his way and reach his target seemed far-fetched. She wouldn't allow that. The last of the three rebels, he was soon bound to fall at her hands. Just like the other two had.

'You'll die at my hands before you commit the treacherous act of killing a noble lady of this land,' Bidisha yelled, pointing to the carriage with her hazel eyes.

The blue cotton cloth that resembled a night sky and had ragged edges, slipped off of her head as she placed the tip of her long sword straight on his neck. Her loosely braided golden-brown hair shone under the rays of the sun. The wind carried her cloth with it and dropped it somewhere between the green branches of the trees. She turned her face away before anyone could see her and covered her face with her hand when her fingers touched her gold septum nose ring. Her mother's only gold asset, which was now hers.

'Wait,' a firm sound echoed in the woods straight out of the carriage, 'Don't kill him yet. This is an order.'

But Bidisha couldn't show her face to the world. She sheathed her sword. And without missing another beat, she covered her face with the extra patch of cloth she always carried with her.

When she peeped inside the carriage from afar, a pair of dark eyes met hers—a woman's eyes. She took a step back in recognition, looking at the woman's attire and decorated interiors as she lifted the *purdah* of the carriage. It was not just any noble lady. She was the queen.

Bidisha cursed her fate. Had she known who the lady was, she wouldn't have bothered to save her. Why would she? The royals were nothing but a pain for the poor. Not that she cared for the deprived. But the queen's life might not mean much after all. At least, not worth her blood that had spilled in the fight.

The man lying in the pool of his blood grunted in pain as he attempted to crawl away from the place. It would be hard not to kill him when she was skilled enough to do it. Even if there was an order, she cared the least to follow.

Bidisha had been building strength, practising with her sword every single day until her body ached, felt weak and dizzy. It was all for the moments like these.

She kicked him hard in the chest. The man had no chance against her welly. He opened his mouth to scream but her long sinewy leg threw him back in his blood. He moaned in pain as he hit the ground. And her sword met his leg and cracked open his bone. The marrow flowed out of his body, onto his *dhoti* and dripped on the ground as water being sprayed from a leaking can.

'Hold it. Do not strain yourself anymore,' a hoarse voice stopped Bidisha.

Two men on their horses stopped next to the carriage. She looked at the man, clothed in a grey *Panjabi* over a black dhoti. His curly hair reached his broad shoulders. He looked huge on his tall brown horse with his bulked-up body, firm that she could make out because his *Panjabi* hugged his body against the wind. His eyes bore into hers as she committed his chiselled face to her memory.

'Will I ever be able to take this huge man down with my sword?'

Bidisha took her position, holding her long sword firmly in both her hands. The minute she looked up, her head clear of thoughts, the man jumped from his horse and landed right before her. In reflex, she used her sword to block his, batting her eyes, her attention divided once again.

'Why didn't he jump into the carriage and finish off Her highness Durga Moni Devi instead of fighting me?'

He swiftly held her elbow with one hand and with his other hand, moved her out of his way, swirling her towards the man who was still comfortably sitting on his black horse. And then he stood still next to the half-dead person.

'Are you hurt? Who are you?' The same hoarse voice startled her; unexpectedly, the voice was not the man's she thought it was.

Bidisha had presumed it belonged to the huge man who had shaken her belief in her strength just moments back. Howbeit, it wasn't his but of the man who still sat on the horse.

Anyhow, the person in front of her looked lean and didn't have the charm to match his manly voice. But then again, she realized, he didn't care to unmount from his horse either with the chaos around him, as if the sword he carried on his waist was just an ornament to add to his rich silk and gems.

He rode a fantastic black horse—she had always dreamt of riding one just like that—which was another sign of his rich background.

She looked up at him. 'What matters at the moment is, who are you? Are you here to attack RaniMaa?' Bidisha asked, still holding the sword in her hand almost ready to pounce on him as she slowly stepped towards the man in confusion.

Suddenly, her eyes widened and her cheeks flushed with blood as her eyes followed his, which were stuck on her chest. She looked down and covered herself with her hand as she turned away from him. She hadn't realized that the fight with the rebels had ripped her *Panjabi* right on her chest exposing the white cloth she had wrapped inside.

Bidisha broke into a sweat.

Adding to her dismay, the huge man she had seen earlier walked right into her from the opposite side while dragging the traitor's half-dead body by his dress. He made a brief pause and handed over her blue cloth that had flown away with the wind. She squeezed her eyes gathering her clothing tightly together as he walked past her. In a haste, she covered herself with the blue cloth, her chest in particular, before the situation got out of hand.

But clearly, the two men were not who she had expected them to be—they weren't the companions of the dead rebels.

The queen stepped out of her beautiful carriage that had a metal rooftop, on the outside, with an intricate design. She looked nothing like what Bidisha had envisioned her to be; she'd imagined the queen to be more charismatic and delicate. However, the woman before her was huge with bulky arms and a full bust that ran down in line with her round mid-waist. Her eyes looked scary on her round face and fair skin and the thick black *kajal* did not help. Her deep red *Athpourey saree* made her look bulkier as she stepped down from the carriage with the help of a stool that her handmaiden placed for her.

'His Highness is late as always. If not for that brave girl, you two halfwits would have had to take my dead body back to the palace today. Didn't I tell you to join me from the palace?' Rani Maa gushed at the two fully grown men while her maidservant tended to her crumpled red saree, setting every pleat to perfection. 'I guess it's time for me to rely more on girls for my safety rather than a meek prince and his bulked-up hound.'

There was no answer from either of the men whose eyes were on the ground all the while till Rani Maa finished reprimanding them.

Bidisha was astonished to see the prince for the first time but what amazed her more was that he looked pale and malnourished. And his extra elegant silk clothes added little charm to his personality. Too unusual for a person of that stature. She wondered if Yuvaraja Prabir, the second son of Maharaja Mitul Singha Dev, was sick like she had heard everyone say.

On the other hand, she agreed with Rani Maa about the person accompanying the prince, the hound, who did look like one. He was tall and bulked up with muscles pushing the veins out on his skin.

Was he only addressed as a hound or was he even treated like one?

Bidisha had heard of stories and she had witnessed the British treating the poor of Bishnupur like their hounds; they were even addressed as hounds. Moreover, she had even seen these people, who the British took pride in raising, unlike the locals who took tremendous joy in looking after their cattle. And if the rumours were to be believed, then the royals were no different from the whites.

What if she was the queen of Bishnupur? She didn't have the right to mistreat people.

But unlike the animal the man was being addressed as, he didn't look scary. Rather, he looked pleasant and appealing to Bidisha, in spite of his mountainous frame. Or, perhaps because of his mountainous frame, he caught her attention. Yes, she noticed men, almost every one of them who crossed her path, but for her own motive.

Rani Maa walked towards Bidisha with a smile on her face, which didn't make much of a difference to her intimidating appearance. 'Tell me your biggest wish and I will make it come true for you as a reward for saving my life today.'

Bidisha dared to look straight into Rani Maa's eyes. 'Can you actually do that for me, Rani Maa?'

'How dare you question my offer and my calibre to make one measly wish of a petty girl like you come true? After all, what big thing would you want apart from a few gold coins or some precious gems,' Rani Maa almost bellowed.

Bidisha smiled in her mind. She knew even Rani Maa was not capable of fulfilling her wish for it had to do something with her husband, the king of this land, Maharaja Mitul Singha Dev. She wished she could ask Rani Maa for his life. If she could kill him with her own hands. After all, he was partly responsible for her mother's misery. The Maharaja was the one who had convicted Mokshita of treachery against the throne by killing its ally, a British officer. Had he tried to find out the truth, her mother wouldn't have had to suffer all her life. However, after all these years, the Maharaja could do good to at least one person in his kingdom—her mother.

Bidisha smiled at the queen.

'Parden me Rani Maa. I was too foolish to say those words to you. But can I ask you to give me a sustainable job in the palace so that I can earn my living without worrying about losing my livelihood ever again?'

'Is that what you truly want? A job and not gold.' Rani Maa's tone softened and the wrinkles on her forehead vanished. 'Think again if you want to.'

'Gold will last for only as long as I want it to, Rani Maa, and will soon exhaust even if I am wise in spending it. But a job will earn me my life.'

'Well then, come to the palace tomorrow. Debesh will take care of your entry into the palace.' Rani Maa walked back to her majestic carriage but then, halfway through, turned around, gazing at Bidisha from top to bottom. 'Don't forget to wear some clean clothes, if not silk.'

'The name of the hound is Debesh.'

Bidisha looked at herself; her mud-stained *Panjabi* was worse than rags. And the blotches of the blood of her enemies, which she had imagined as the motifs on her plain clothes, glittered as the stains dried.

The *Panjabi* was no good even in comparison with the rich embroidered maroon velvet cloth that covered the bullocks. Bidisha then looked at the rich green velvet curtains used for the carriage to keep the queen under covers; they could easily be used by at least four people to hide their skeletal bodies. The king had happily accepted all those riches from the British in exchange for the livelihood of the people of his kingdom, and this made her blood boil.

But then, come to think of it, they were the same people who had forced her mother out of the village years back without caring for her sorry state. Just like the Maharaja, even the people, whom Mokshita had known all her life, had convicted her of murder. They stood against her.

Why should I even bother about these spineless people in Bishnupur?

The queen's carriage rolled further and the prince followed her on horseback.

'Come to the palace east gate tomorrow when the sun is on the head,' Debesh said, slitting the traitor's throat.

'I thought you'd take him to the palace dungeons and interrogate him,' Bidisha said, sliding her sword back into the scabbard that was suspended from her waist using a worn-out baldric.

'The symphony of your voice doesn't match your personality. What a pity, you could have become a fine singer instead!' Debesh remarked, his eyes scanning her from head to toe, without caring to answer her question.

Bidisha took a step closer to Debesh and whispered in his ear, 'And what a jest! The strong hoarse voice belongs to the meek prince and not the hound.' Bidisha turned away from him before she said, 'I can't make it to the east gate; see you on the north instead.'

And she walked into the jungle, her home, before Debesh could answer.

'What did you do today? Was it an animal or a man?' Bidisha's mother asked, her eyes on Bidisha's blood-stained clothes, as she put more wood into the fire under the huge copper container filled with water.

'I had to kill only three, to save one life that mattered. I am going to the palace tomorrow,' Bidisha said, unfastening her baldric, waiting for her mother to retort.

'Washup and eat your meat. I am going to barter this deer for some decent clothes for you. I know how much you like to dress up,' Mokshita said, ignoring the words she had just heard.

'Selling it to Lady Agnes again?' Bidisha grinned as she checked the temperature of the water for her bath.

Lady Agnes was one among the many English families that bought animal skin from Mokshita. She was also one of those few people who relished wild meat. She was their regular customer who never hesitated to barter good stuff in exchange for fresh meat. And that was profitable for Bidisha's mother who usually had a hard time negotiating with the English. They mostly used their power even while dealing with a lonely woman and hardly made a fair deal with anybody in the market.

'Who else? The woman has a fetish for wild meat and skin,' Bidisha's mother replied, tying the legs of the wounded deer that struggled to breathe.

'The English!' Bidisha sighed. 'And that Mr James who likes to share his bed with men, he is another unusual man.' Bidisha took out her dagger from the sheath and slit the deer's throat. 'Let it rest now.'

'There are men like that I have seen in *jomidaar* families too. It's known to everyone. But nobody dares to talk about it.'

'Hmmm... You indeed have seen a lot, Maa,' Bidisha said, her eyes on the scar on her mother's face as she touched its uneven and hardened skin. 'I'll be taking a long bath, Maa.'

'The small pleasures we can afford in this forest...'

Mokshita, who was once accustomed to all luxuries, had made a small bathtub with stones and wood. Of all the riches her mother once had before falling straight into a pit of despair and hiding after trusting an English man, she still couldn't let go of a good bathing place and a cotton stuffed bed, which she had managed to make over the years.

'I will be back before the sun goes down,' Mokshita said, using a veil to cover her head and face before she ventured outside their safe territory.

In all her years, Bidisha did not remember going out with her mother even once. Mokshita had made it clear that Bidisha could never be seen with her. That way, she could keep her identity as Mokshita Maitra's daughter a secret from the world that had chased Mokshita into the jungle when she was pregnant.

Bidisha upbraided her long hair and unfurled the patchy curtain her mother had made out of rags as she entered the secret bath in the middle of the forest. It was part of the ruins of an old terracotta temple, once a sacred home for the Goddess worshipped by the royals. But now it was her home, far away from the place caged by the walls that were built by the royals of Bishnupur but ruled by the British.

It was said that, one night, exactly a hundred years ago, Goddess BipottariniDevi appeared in Abhoy Malla's dream, the then king of Bishnupur, to relocate the temple near the palace. The king had made sure to find a place like what he had seen in his dream. It is believed that he even had a specific design in mind and overlooked the temple construction until it was built as per his requirements. It was the same place where Rani Durga Moni Devi was ambushed on her way back from the temple.

Whatever the story that was associated with the temple, the remains of the old place were her home now. The good part of the ruins turned out to be their home and the remnants of the entrance served as an open bath.

Access to good food, at least once in a while, was not a problem depending on their hunt and her mother's negotiation skills for coins or barter for exotic spices. If they got lucky, Mokshita sometimes even brought home-cooked delicacies and *misti* too.

Bidisha looked up at the sky as she stretched her arms, trying to ease the ache in her back. She undressed and stepped in the bath, a small round pit dug in the ground, laid with uneven stones in the base. As the warm water touched her bare skin, Bidisha moaned, part in pain but mostly because of the comfort it brought even in distress. Her cuts and bruises seared with the touch of water.

'Ow!' Bidisha clenched her hands.

But she got in further and sat on the wooden plank placed over the stones. The pain settled just like it always did. She closed her eyes seeping in the fresh air after a morning of an intense fight that was no less a fatal one.

She scrubbed her skin with an old piece of cloth. The dirt and the bloodstains washed in the water. Bidisha slid further down, and her chest, back and shoulders thanked her for the warmth.

'Am I really going to the palace tomorrow?'

Mokshita wouldn't be happy about Bidisha going to the palace. Though she wouldn't mind her daughter killing men. Howbeit, she would never tell her not to. She had never told Bidisha anything. A mother's guidance was never there for her. Sometimes it was convenient that way. Bidisha need not worry about anything and could do just like she pleased. But there were times she wished her mother would tell her things like that. To do or not do certain things. Help her make decisions she was not sure about.

The only promise she had made to her mother was that she wouldn't risk her life to free her mother from the royal conviction. Mokshita had always told Bidisha that she was happy, away from the two-faced people. And she had always seen her mother happy, she couldn't deny that. But Mokshita had spent all her life in hiding and had told Bidisha that she would continue to be good that way if her daughter was by her side, safe and happy. If only her mother showed courage and agreed to it, Bidisha would do what she should to free Mokshita from a life of running.

Bidisha was light-hearted, unlike the restless nights she had spent for days trying to find a way to get into the palace. Perhaps the reason was that one of her wishes had come true. And she had found her way inside the palace without even executing her plans.

She was relaxed at the moment. And in no time, she fell asleep.

She woke up to the sound of a blade clanking against the terracotta bricks on the wall.

'Are you awake yet?'

The voice of a man startled Bidisha. Her eyes were on the wall, the place where she had hung her clothes that were nowhere to be seen. Bidisha's sword was gone too. She pulled her legs to her chest. How could she not hear him sneak inside? She had always been wary of her surroundings, having lived in the jungle for years since her childhood. Bidisha could not only hear the tiniest sound but was also sensitive to movements around her.

That man had taken Bidisha's sword and clothes. And she had been sound asleep through it. The clothes could be pulled from outside. But her sword? Her mind denied the possibility that he could have seen her naked. But deep down, Bidisha knew whoever it was had stepped in. Her heart pounded. He knew she was asleep.

She was capable of doing so much at that moment. And yet she couldn't, in that state, except stay put in the place where she had dozed off.

'Who... Who are you?' Bidisha asked, her eyes scanning the edges of the walls around her.

'Don't you recognize my voice? I thought we met earlier today.'

'I am not good at playing twisted games. Give back my clothes. Whatever it is, we can talk.'

'Should I come in and show myself?'

The man was still as stone, she could sense. He hadn't moved a muscle other than his tongue.

'That's enough. Are we going to continue our conversation like this?' Bidisha let out a sigh after hurling the words in one breath. 'If you think you can force me to talk by putting me in this position, then hear me out clearly—you are wrong.'

'Alright then. Let me show up in front of you.'

'You would have done that already if you really could.'

'You win. For now. Not after you're out of the bath. Let's have a fair conversation then and if needed, we can use our swords too.'

Bidisha saw a pair of dark hands sliding her clothes back on the uneven wall. She stood up, still uncertain, water dripping down from her bare body as she knotted her wet hair up and grabbed her saree.

'Are you still there?' Bidisha asked, scrutinizing closely as her ears pricked up.

Bidisha was boiling with rage at the thought of a man around her. Particularly when she was naked.

She wasn't a warrior or a brave heart who could crush her limits and pound the man with her fists. Men, she had seen them. They were all eyes whenever they were near her. And then they would grow tentacles like the sea creatures at any chance to touch and feel her even when she was fully clothed.

But this man didn't show up before her.

'Do you think I am here to play some sort of a game and then leave without getting the answers I am looking for?'

'What answers?' Bidisha asked, taking the *Pallav* on her right shoulder after wrapping the saree around her chest firmly.

'Since you got your saree back, why don't we talk face to face?'

Bidisha walked out of the old ruins. There was no one around and the voice had magically disappeared too. She took a few cautious and calculated steps forward. Suddenly a pair of hands grabbed her from behind. He held her hands at her back, grasping them together. Bidisha's heart skipped a beat as she slipped in the muddy silt near the lake. She struggled to break free.

'Prove you are not a coward. Stand before me,' Bidisha challenged, still grappling, 'Is this all you can do? Are you even a man?'

Bidisha was in his arms the next moment as he lowered his hand, taking her weight on his arms. She dropped her head back to look at the man and her eyes met a pair of black eyes that stared down at her. His face was straight above hers, a familiar face. And then a smirk appeared on his face.

'You? What are you doing here?' Bidisha yelped, attempting to straighten up from her awkward bending position, as he still held her hands together.

Debesh bent over, 'Did you pull together a ruse so you could pretend to win by killing your partners? Why do you want to get into the palace? Or, is your aim to get close to Rani Maa?'

'Hold on to your baseless thoughts and your irrational questions!' Bidisha said, her temper calm and her voice mocking, as she attempted to get up right back in his face.

Howbeit, Debesh slid her further down, and her back rested on his hands, her wrists still clutched together. The sudden jerk startled Bidisha; her breathing became rapid and she struggled to not let him see it. Bidisha's wet hair rolled open on his hands. His arms swelled up and the veins popped up over his muscles right before her eyes as he tugged her hands and held her dead weight. She was engulfed by him. Bidisha shuddered when his hands touched the bare damp skin at her back and his warm breath caressed her chest.

'Talk. Tell me what you are planning. I don't have all day and I won't go easy on you. Speak now.'

'Why do you think I have hidden motives? I need money, as you can see. We can't even afford to live in the village. I was looking for a way to earn some... Aaugh!'

Debesh tightened his grip. 'Lie to me and I will make you pay for it. This is not where a girl would prefer to live. Tell me everything about yourself. Everything I need to know.'

'Can you first let go of my hands? You're hurting me.'

'Can't believe my grip can hurt a girl who killed a group of men all by herself.'

'That doesn't mean my body is made of rock.'

Debesh suddenly let go of Bidisha's hands and she fell flat on her back. 'Ah!' She ground her teeth and stared at him as she lay flat on her back. She sat upright immediately, however, and covered her back with the extra fabric of her *pallav*.

'What are you waiting for?' Debesh asked as he walked towards the lake.

'I am famished,' Bidisha said, walking towards her home.

Her mind was hard at work trying to understand the man with her. Nobody had ever come to that place. Nobody. Even animals seldom made it to that part of the jungle. Sometimes a bear or a boar would roam around at night, and there were snakes she could see on the trees during the day. But nothing other than that in all the years they had lived there.

This man must have followed her. And for the first time, someone had scared her. Bidisha wasn't able to sense his footsteps when he had shadowed her home. And she wasn't able to feel the presence of a man when she had gone to bathe.

'How can someone be so light on their feet?'

Debesh barged in after Bidisha. She was serving herself some rice on a clay plate along with some fish curry her mother had cooked.

'*Gondhoraj Maachh*?' Debesh said and let out a smile. 'And you said you were so deprived that you couldn't afford to live in the village.'

'I get to eat this because I am not in the village. You see that lake you were headed to earlier, yes, the home for these fishes.'

'Hmmm... So you get to eat fresh fish whenever you please,' Debesh said, his eyes still set on the plate, 'Are you not concerned that I saw your face? Don't you hide behind your veil all the time?'

'Is that why you suspect me so much? Did Rani Maa ask you to follow me?'

Bidisha dreaded him. He was interested in her affairs. And that didn't sit well with her. He was the first person to have ever seen her home. She was not sure if Debesh was acting on his own or if Rani Maa had anything to do with it. Either way, it was not looking good.

She was stiff at the sudden touch of Debesh as he startled her by snatching the plate from her hand.

'Uh... Shameless!' Bidisha commented and turned around to grab another plate for herself.

'But I have heard that the waters here are poisoned.'

Animals had stopped coming to the lake behind the temple to quench their thirst, which eventually had led to the rumours that the waters were poisoned. People started to believe that the Goddess had left the temple but Bidisha and her mother still worshipped Goddess BipottariniDevi's idol, grateful for blessing them with a safe home.

'Then why are you eating it?'

'Because I had to follow you, I missed my royal meals.'

Bidisha laughed. 'Royal meals for the prince's hound?'

'You... You'll see it when you come to the palace,' Debesh said, gulping the morsel. 'Let us hear your depressing story first.'

It was a better option to give him some information that wouldn't harm her instead of raising his suspicion.

'People are scared of this place because of the rumours of the poisoned waters. That turned out to be a boon for us,' Bidisha said as she tried to read his mind.

His suspicious look didn't settle well with Bidisha. Debesh had not only seen their hiding but was also interested in her life. He was a man who could crush her chances of entering the palace and could also put Bidisha and her mother's life in danger. She was cautious with her actions and even more careful with her words as, over the next hour, Bidisha told him their story in parts.

But Bidisha didn't tell him the real reason they had been living in the jungle for the past eleven years. Mokshita had been on the move every few months, going from village to village as soon as she feared her identity would be revealed. Sometimes, her mother would come across a person who had seen her before. Or worse, a person who was aware of her crime and knew she was a fugitive.

She couldn't let anyone know that they were running away from the British. They were safe in their hiding as long as the mother and daughter were not revealed to the whites. And the Maharaja—if he got a clue of Mokshita's whereabouts, he would personally hand her over to the British to garner their trust.

Bidisha was eight when she had not only made a strong resolve to solve the problem of moving often but also convinced her mother to do the impossible. To find a place where no one lived. A place where no one would dare to even pass by. She had not only thought about living in the jungle at a tender age but also had gone with her mother to look for a place. And the best they could find was the cursed temple deep in the jungle near the poisoned lake.

All that she wanted was to live free, do anything and go anywhere at her free will. Just like she had been living with the animals for so many years. But she wished she could move in and out of the jungle along with her mother without the fear of being recognized and punished. Or, even get killed.

But Bidisha only told Debesh of their everyday struggle to meet ends. She told him about her father's untimely death but left out his identity and the real cause. She told him how a widow, her mother, was outcasted by the village blaming her for her father's death, tagging her as an unlucky witch. Bidisha even made-up parts of the story that Mokshita was shunned by her maiden family too.

'So, you have been leading a safe life thus far, at least safe from humans, if not from animals.'

'Yes, you can say that. But more than anything, we have enough to eat. Meat and fish anytime we want.'

'Not everybody, especially a girl, would want to learn and master sword fighting unless they have a dangerous goal in mind, deadly revenge to seek, an impossible quest to achieve. What's your plan?' Debesh asked, a frown on his forehead as he washed the plate near the lake.

Bidisha laughed. 'First, tell me, Debesh, are you struggling to judge the truth or is that face because I asked you to wash your plate?'

'I have never done anything like this in my life before.'

'And I have never had an uninvited guest before.'

Bidisha learnt her own form of martial arts without any guidance from a trained guru, who anyway seldom imparted their skills to a girl. But her mother's grit and stern resolve to hone her daughter's self-defence skills for her safety led Bidisha to master her fight skills. The tough life in the jungle and the need to be vigilant at all times had thought Bidisha things that a normal martial arts trainee would miss out on.

Bidisha was a natural and her lessons were imparted by nature, influenced by hunting animals and sharpened by the calmness of the wild.

She had strengthened herself by chopping wood for fire. Bidisha mastered her aim by hunting her prey with a bow and arrow for survival. Her precision with the sword was honed as she learnt to chop the meat in exotic cuts to meet the needs of the British palette. Because some of the whites would give them extra coins in exchange for meeting their specific needs of exotic meat and precise cuts.

'If at all I decide to believe your story as I get to know more about you in the future, I will acknowledge your strength and skills. But till then, you're an eyesore I would want cured.'

'And what about you? Who are you working for? The prince or the queen? Or for the king himself? Could it be possible that you're acting on your own and spying on me for your selfish motives?' Bidisha said, crossing her arms and squinting her eyes.

'You don't have the authority to question me. Try and save your head first,' Debesh said by way of answer as he took a few long strides, walking away from her.

'But why are you so interested in me? I am just a regular girl trying to make a living and finding a way to earn some money.'

At that, Debesh smirked and walked back towards her and stood right before her, towering over her. 'Don't fool yourself with that thought. Because anybody who has seen you cross swords with a group of men wouldn't believe your lie.'

'And how do you think I was supposed to survive here in this jungle without those skills? I don't live in the palace like you.'

'Palace. Yes. You have lived here in the jungle. And you want to work in the palace. You will see it for yourself. How different it is. Or, perhaps, how same the two are.'

'Wait. You did not return my sword.'

'It's right above the wall. Take it if you can reach it.'

'Can I ask you something? Did you peep on me while I was in there?'

'What if I did?'

Bidisha looked down and took a deep breath before glaring up at him. 'Don't ever come here again. And do no talk about this place to anyone.'

'Do you think I will heed your request?' Debesh said, his dark eyes narrowing on her.

'It is not a request. I demand it after you saw me in my most vulnerable state.'

'What does that mean? Are you bartering with me in return for what I might have witnessed?' Debesh took a few steps away from her on the path that would lead him out of that place before he shouted, 'Just to make it clear, I have not seen what I should have. So, don't trust me to keep your little secret.'

Bidisha didn't know if she should be happy that she was spared the embarrassment or worry that a third person was now aware of their safe home.

Loons warbled back to their nest as the sun rays lost the strength to brighten the lake. Crickets chirped as Bidisha pulled the clothes hung on the tree branches. Her ears pricked up at the sound of shuffling footsteps. Bidisha kept the clothes on the tree stump.

'Here it is. Your dress.' Mokshita gasped for air as she sat on the rock resting her back on the tree behind it.

Bidisha took the bag from her mother as she handed her a glass of water.

'Did you run all the way here, Maa?'

Mokshita gulped the water. 'A bear...bear chased me. You won't believe how huge it was.'

'Again? Why are there so many of them around this place recently?' Bidisha asked as she removed the veil from her mother's face. 'Are you hurt?'

Every time she saw the scar on her mother's face, her heart twitched in pain. Mokshita had burnt her own face with hot coal that had left a huge scar. It started from the right side of her forehead and ran down across her nose to her left jaw. She not only covered her face with a veil to conceal her identity but also made the pretext for doing so a believable truth. People had stopped asking her the reason for covering her face once they got a glimpse of the mark on her forehead over the veil.

'I am alright.'

'Let us get inside.' Bidisha gave her a hand. 'You're getting old. See, you struggle to run these days.'

'Don't start that again. I am still capable of killing just like you. Running is an everyday task. Don't worry much about that.'

'And tomorrow, let's go hunt together. Lady Agnes has a feast at night and has asked for more rabbit and deer meat.'

Bidisha stopped right in front of the steps. 'Why don't you tell me not to go to the palace instead?'

'The palace is not a place for us to take up any kind of work. You know it's not safe for us to show up to the royals. What if they recognize you, Bidisha? Give up on that idea. I am happy hiding in the jungle rather than living without you all my life.'

'Didn't I promise you I won't do anything in haste, Maa? I am only going to the palace once. I will never step in there again.' Bidisha picked up the clothes from the tree stump.

Bidisha's ears pricked up when she heard twigs snap behind the temple. She looked around as she walked inside after her mother taking cautious steps. Bidisha dumped the clothes on the floor in haste. And her hand went straight to her sword as she walked out. She closed the door behind her and latched it from the outside. Bidisha stepped out in the twilight and walked to behind the temple.

'Could it be a bear?'

Howbeit, it was not an animal but a man fully clothed in black, his back to her. Bidisha held the sword straight at his neck even before he realised her presence. But in an instant, the man turned around and pulled his sword out. The two blades clanked.

'Not bad. You sensed my presence,' he said, his sword moving against her steel as he closed in on her.

'You'll be sorry for that soon,' Bidisha sneered wrapping fingers around her worn hilt as she lurched back against his move, her nose just an inch away from his blade.

The man cut again. She scrambled back. But Bidisha came hard at him as she cut and thrust her sword against his. The two closed in on. Their swords clanked. His deeply set intense dark eyes peeked out at her from under his mask as their blades locked.

'He is not the same man. He is not Debesh.'

Just when Bidisha aimed at his head, the man suddenly lunged. He caught her wrist and twisted it till she dropped her sword. He picked up her sword before he let go of her hand. Bidisha aimed her fist at his jaw and connected. But he moved back just in time, so she was barely able to touch him.

'Hold on. We can talk,' he said, taking a step back.

Bidisha advanced, her hand headed straight to his mask. But he dodged her, stepping back into the bush and onto a snake that hissed back at him. To protect himself, he ran ahead and landed on her, losing his balance. Even as he tried to get a hold, Bidisha was on the ground, on her back, groaning. His face above hers, their breath hitched. The man was stiff on his fours as if he was desperately avoiding her touch.

And just when he tried to get up, her eyes widened as the cobra struck right at her face, making it through the gap between the two. She held it and, in an instant, threw it away while the man in the mask slid off her. Bidisha bounced back on her feet when he had already grabbed the two swords he had dropped on the ground. She shuddered as the open mouth of the snake made it again before her eyes.

'Can we talk now?'

His deep voice reverberated in her chest.

The cool breeze from the lake brought the musk of the mud and the touch of the dew in the dusk moving her out of her thoughts.

Bidisha pulled herself together, 'Why should I when you are still behind the mask.'

She took a few steps away from him, climbed up on a tree and jumped on a branch. Bidisha was on the ground in the next moment with a sturdy branch in her hands, breaking one, off from the bough. It made a good weapon, better than her bare hands against the two swords he held.

'Nice weapon but I trust your wits. Hope you wouldn't dare to use it against me,' he said, spinning the swords on either side as they whistled in the air.

'I just need my blade; your trust has no use to me.'

Bidisha broke the branch on her knee and threw away the useless thin part making it apt for her use.

'Why do you think I will let you have it back?' the man said, his husky voice loud in the calm of the falling darkness in the jungle that faded the hissing and chirping sounds.

She wasn't bad, not bad at all in her skills. Most men wouldn't be able to stand before her for more than a few—daunting—minutes. But she couldn't tell the same about this man. He was an exception. She wouldn't try him again unless there wasn't another way for her.

'Stop wasting my time. Tell me who are you? And what are you doing here?'

'Who am I? Let's just move beyond that. But for your other question, I am here to keep an eye on you.'

Her home was not all that safe anymore. Not the way she had always believed. She was being watched. And more people knew about the place. But how much does he know? And from how long has he been spying on her? Or her mother?

Bidisha held her exploding head for an instant, her brows farrowed into one as lines of suspicion and fear appeared on her forehead. 'Was it you behind the trees in the morning? Keeping an eye on me?'

The leaves rustled behind the man and Bidisha heard another pair of footsteps approaching them, piercing the darkness behind the huge man. He was quick on his feet and the swords in his hands came to his rescue. His stupendous frame added to his advantage as he crossed the blades and attacked the animal coming through the bushes.

But the light squeal sounded familiar. Bidisha's heart thudded and her foot took longer than usual to displace. She went further towards the man who had just attacked something or perhaps someone.

Bidisha lost her balance as her eyes caught a clear glimpse in the dark.

'Maa!' Bidisha shouted as she rushed towards Mokshita. 'Hold, hold it.' Bidisha removed her dupatta and tied it on her mother's hand that bled.

The man lifted Mokshita in his arms, taking Bidisha by surprise, as she fell unconscious on the ground. Bidisha ran after him as he stepped inside their home. He slowly put Mokshita on the bed and sprinkled water on her face, tapping her cheeks in an attempt to bring her back to her conscious state.

Bidisha pressed her mother's arm trying to stop the bleeding. Just as Mokshita opened her eyes, Bidisha could hear the man letting out a sigh from even under that cloth on his face.

'This was not something I intended to do. You must believe me.'

'But you wounded my mother!' Bidisha glared at him, her hands still helping her mother.

'It felt like there was an animal behind me. And the darkness around this place is blinding.'

The man picked a clay glass and fetched some water from the *matka* next to him. He held Mokshita in his arms as he helped her drink the water.

Bidisha relieved the pressure carefully and untied the dupatta on her mother's hand. She looked away as her tears spilled out. The bleeding had finally stopped and the tightness in her chest eased. Though the wound didn't look deep, it was a long cross-cut on Mokshita's arm, showing the white tissue, visible on the inside of her fragile arm.

'I am alright, Bidisha. Don't worry,' Mokshita murmured as she tried to get up, her voice frail.

The man stood up too, ready to leave without uttering another word and seeking no apologies from an elderly woman he had hurt so badly in his haste.

'Wait,' Bidisha said, wiping her tears. 'You can't just come into my home, hurt my mother and leave.'

'Stop me if you can,' he said as he walked to the door.

Bidisha picked her dagger from one of the empty *matkas* and swung it hard aiming for his arm. The man moved just in time and the dagger made it out through the door ripping his cloth and scratching his skin just a little.

The man went back to where Bidisha was standing and, in front of her mother, held her jaw, his fingers digging into her skin. 'If you think you can dart any metal at me and have my blood on your hands the way you want, you are mistaken. I am letting this slide just for once. But there will not be the next time.' The man snarled at her, his eyes piercing her soul.

'You don't scare me. Not one bit. I will find you.'

'I will wait for that moment when you find out who I am.'

'Who are you?' Mokshita stood up. 'What do you know about us?'

'Nothing. But now, I am sure there is a lot I need to know about you two.'

The enraged man left the place, drops of blood from his arm spilling on the ground.

'We will leave this place immediately at the break of the dawn,' Mokshita Maitra said, holding her arm and clenching her face in pain.

CHAPTER TWO

The safest place in the world wasn't that safe after all. Not anymore. Two men on the same day had made it to her home. Bidisha looked at her mother who wouldn't rest at night even with her wounded arm. Rather, she was packing essentials to carry on their journey to their next hideout, God knows where.

People don't abandon their homes. But Bidisha and her mother had done it several times in the past. And Mokshita was determined to do the same again.

But Bidisha was done moving in fear and hiding away from people. Not this time. She wouldn't leave her home. Moreover, even if they did move, they would always encounter people like the man in the mask who would barge inside their home anytime and harm them any way they wanted. She had to take care of it. For the sake of her mother. Make their home safe again. And this time, it wouldn't be a hiding but a real home where they could even invite people without fear.

People like that crook who hurt her mother needed to be taught a lesson so that they'd let others live. Mokshita had stopped Bidisha all her life from taking the risk but she wouldn't budge to that idea anymore. She'd suffered many slanders. But how long would Bidisha let it happen? This time, she wouldn't let her mother play with her emotions and manipulate her into moving or giving up on the thought of leading a free life.

Mokshita Maitra had done everything she could to keep Bidisha safe since the time she was in her womb. Her mother was slandered and shunned away from her home, her village. She was convicted of killing a British officer, the man she had loved. The same man who had betrayed her without thinking twice.

Mokshita's family was implicated for treachery against the British, hence against the king who was swathed in the self-proclaimed English aristocracy. Her father was executed for his involvement in his daughter's act. Her brothers were brutally killed. Mokshita's family was destroyed.

Her mother was the youngest of the six and the only daughter who was loved and brought up like a princess on the flower bed. But everything was snatched away from her. A high born, once the daughter of a jomidaar, was forced to lead a life of a fugitive in a place far away from her home under the roof of fear and dressed in disguise.

Her mother had shown the courage to escape in the dark of a rainy night while she was pregnant. No man had had the steel to follow her on that path even to punish her as they had planned before. Everybody was under the impression that she wouldn't survive the harshness of the weather with a baby due to be born soon. And even if she did, she wouldn't be able to get past the wild animals.

But Mokshita had survived the odds and the dread in the wilderness while protecting young Bidisha. Now it was her turn as a daughter to fulfil her duty. Moreover, it was the right time and she wouldn't look back again.

After Bidisha had the opportunity to see Rani Maa and get acquainted, she hoped that the queen could make way for her to realise her mother's freedom. But first and foremost, it was important for her to protect her mother's identity till she decided on a plan.

'Stop tying those things, Maa. We are not going anywhere. We will not leave our home,' Bidisha declared, snatching the clothes from her mother and putting them back in their place.

'We don't have any other way out from this. Learn to be safe, Bidisha,' Mokshita shouted as she glared at her daughter.

'You mean continue to be a coward and run away like we have always done?'

'Look for ways to survive rather than fight with the powerful and end up losing even the little you are left with.'

'That's not even living if I can't do the things that I want, the way I want. I will not lead a life as you did. I can't.'

Debesh raised his eyebrows as he looked at Bidisha from head to toe. She squinted, her gaze steady on him. He cleared his throat and stopped glaring at once. Bidisha was used to that kind of a stare from men all her life even though she covered her face with a veil. Some looked down on her for being half British and half Indian while others pitied her. At best, men loathed her and at worst, they lusted after her striking non-native charm.

Debesh's impudence was the same. Nothing that could bother her though. She was in his arms just the previous day and his touch on her bareback had given her goose pimples. And the very thought tingled her skin again. And for the first time, she admired a man instead of glaring back at him.

The bystanders near the huge palace gate gazed at her, men and women alike. She was looking nothing like what Debesh had seen her earlier—first in muddy rags with a veil covering her face and then in a bland white saree and damp golden-brown hair as she indulged in a fight both the times.

She was adorned in new clothes her mother had bought after bartering the kill. The clothes were not a match for her personality and were nothing close to what she could see women wearing near the north gate. Hers were made from plain cotton while the women around her carried embroidered silks graciously.

Yet, there was no one around who matched her tall gait. Her large deep-set eyes were enough for any man to get attracted to her. And she managed to pull off even the simplest of clothes with ease and elegance. Unlike other girls of her age, Bidisha dressed more for a fight rather than to draw eyes. That was a requirement she couldn't afford to overlook. But given a chance, Bidisha always loved to adorn colourful garments. Just like the one she was wearing at that moment.

Her long red flared *Panjabi* accentuated her curves as the strings were neatly tied on the left of her chest covering her full bust. The extra flare not only gave her freedom to move with ease but added more weight to her slender lower body. The white fitted pyjama was perfect to give her the comfort she needed for kicking the crap out of her enemies. The striking deep red hue of the *Panjabi* contrasted with her radiant skin. The white *dupatta* that she tied on her waist held her worn baldric in place while the long loose ends of the dupatta swayed in the breeze. The messy golden-brown locks lingering on her face added to her charm even as her long thick plait bounced on her shoulder as she walked swiftly. Even without any jewellery except for the tiny gold septum ring on her sharp nose, she had always looked pleasing, her face resembling her mother's.

Debesh cleared his throat. 'Looks like you have come prepared to impress Rani Maa into believing your sad little story. And that bruise around your lips will add a nice sympathetic touch to the drama,' Debesh mocked, gesturing at her clothes.

'You mean these second hand rags will do it for me?' Bidisha chided, her hands crossed in front of her chest.

Debesh took a look at her again, as if he had not seen her before, his eyes on the faded patches and the sewn cuts on her *Panjabi*. It was better than what she was wearing the previous day but nothing fit for a person entering the palace.

'Didn't you think of covering your face today?'

'Thought of leaving it behind as I enter a new world.'

Debesh began to walk. 'The east gate is definitely the closest to the place you're coming from. And I already knew you were simply satisfying your ego asking me to come this far.'

'And you thought it would do to massage my ego just a little. I am glad.'

Debesh kept walking without looking back and she walked with him at the same pace, matching his long strides. Bidisha didn't miss out on a glimpse of the beautiful garden. But the sight before her eyes twitched her heart. It ached for all the people who were deprived of many things. The blossoms were grown by feeding them the suffering of the innocent in Bishnupur. The maharaja had been sucking the blood of the poor, like the bees swarming over the vibrant flowers for the nectar, and caulked the wealth in his treasure.

Every view that seeped into her mind and every image that crossed her eyes added to her rage. The beautiful terracotta walls of the palace stood erect against the contrasting broken huts in the village. The silk that was hung on the huge doors reminded Bidisha of unclothed children in the streets. The exquisite imports from England and the gifts red-coats had adorned the king with testified that he ditched his subjects ripping them off their rights.

The walk through the hallway surprised her. She had heard the tales from her mother and the commoners about how the royal women are isolated in the harem and no men are allowed to enter it. But unlike what she was told, the things she witnessed were different.

Debesh freely walked past the eunuchs positioned at the entrance of the harem and there was no reaction whatsoever. A few steps ahead, female guards were posted at another entrance. She could hear the voices of women, giggles and loud waves of laughter. A peek inside gave her a glimpse of women clad in silks and pearls. They were holding glasses of *madira* and ogled at Debesh.

He halted suddenly after they had started walking from the north gate inside the walls of the small fort.

'Just a few more steps and you'll wait outside. It's not a place for just anyone to enter.'

'Not even you?' Bidisha mocked, raising her dark brown eyebrows hoping for once that he would be stopped before he entered the queen's chamber.

Debesh's eyes widened as he hushed her. He took a few steps closer to her, bending a little as his face got closer to her ear. 'You're expected to lay low in the palace or else you'll face consequences.'

He stepped back and turned left even before she could reply. Bidisha rolled her eyes and let out a sigh before following him.

As she turned left, she realized she had stepped into a world unlike anything she had seen before. Unlike any other place and corner in the palace on her way, she had suddenly walked into a dream of sorts. However, she was taken aback when a tall person dressed in a shiny bright yellow saree blocked her path. A eunuch stood like a barrier between her and Debesh, who had, by the way, walked straight inside the chamber.

Bidisha stared as she stood quietly for more than a few minutes. None broke the silence until the words came from within the queen's chamber.

'Bring her to me after some time.'

The words made it to her ears. The eunuch and Bidisha were still staring at each other when Debesh came out. 'Come with me.'

Debesh led her away from the queen's chamber, which didn't seem like a part of the women's world in the palace; it stood secluded from the harem.

Walking through a colonnaded veranda guarded by pillars that met grand arches, they entered the cloistered courtyard. As they walked further, Bidisha heard the loud cries of women. A few more steps later, she could see two maidservants hitting each other with wooden swords while a eunuch watched over them. With every hit they got, the women screamed and struck back with more strength even as they continued to growl.

'What is happening there?' Bidisha asked, trying to get a better look.

'They are ordered to fight with wooden swords as punishment for both till one hits the ground unconscious.'

'But why? Did they violate any rules or did they—'

'They were caught receiving silk in exchange for giving the youngest queen information about Rani Maa,' Debesh interrupted her. 'You'll meet the same fate if you do not abide by the rules.'

'Even if I did, I know I will escape without a scratch on my body.'

'That you might, considering your skills. But do you think you could hit another person you have worked with for years?'

'That's nothing. One of us has to fall. And I never will. Moreover, guilt has not stopped those women from attacking each other. Instead, just like Rani Maa had wished for, both are getting equally hurt. We all want to survive and do so with as little pain as possible.'

'You're not only intelligent, but you're also cunning. I need to be wary of you.'

Bidisha's eyes went to his bulged arms visible through his thin white *Panjabi* as he walked in front of her. He held the sword hilt, as he walked, that hung on his waist by his baldric. His other hand swung free in tandem with his footsteps and his curled-up hair waved over his wrestler-like shoulders that spoke of strength.

'You have to be. I am not an easy woman.'

Debesh turned back abruptly in the middle of the garden, a bad habit of sorts, forcing Bidisha to step back. Every time he did that, she told herself not to be startled and then there she was again, thinking about him, when Debesh managed to scare her again.

'You'll wait here in this garden till I come back for you. You'll avoid talking to strangers and refrain from wandering around outside this garden,' Debesh instructed, his face grim as he walked away.

'Wait. How long am I supposed to wait?' Bidisha shouted back. 'You can't just bark out orders and leave without giving me answers.'

She took off her baldric that was digging into her shoulder. Bidisha hadn't got a wink of sleep after her mother was hurt the previous evening. The wound on her mother's arm had scared her like the one on her face had done long back. And the disturbing decision she had to make overnight, to break her mother's trust and risk going to the palace, had made her head heavy. Moreover, she had no plan for her next steps after entering the palace.

The only thought that kept creeping up in Bidisha's mind was to force herself inside the harem and into the queen's chamber. She couldn't take it any longer. The pain of waiting just to meet Rani Maa was unsettling. She had better things to do—help her mother in the market to sell the freshwater fish they had managed to catch. Or, better yet, sneak around and spy in the palace. Why not? That sounded better than anything else. She let out a sigh. If only she could! Bidisha couldn't afford to miss this kind of an opportunity. She had already fared well in impressing the queen. And it was time to reap the benefit.

'Patience, Bidisha, patience,' Bidisha preached to herself as she took deep breaths in the freshness of the beautiful garden.

It was a breezy afternoon. The sun was bright but the trees made it pleasant by offering shade. The air she breathed in had a subtle scent like the ones she had sniffed from the bodies of the royals and the *Goras*. The abundance of flowers around her was like a treat to the eyes but she couldn't appreciate it with all her heart. The prosperity was testimony to the maharaja's selfishness.

Bidisha sat under one of the bougainvillaea trees on a bed of pink flowers. She leaned back and closed her eyes. Her mind wandered taking her into her past, bringing back unpleasant memories. There was a time when, as an eleven-year-old girl, Bidisha wanted to stay far away from all humans. She wanted to go somewhere she could live free without covering her brown hair and her face.

But now as a 17-year-old girl, she didn't want to belong in the forest anymore. And she was trying to find a way for her mother and herself, out of the forest into the so-called civilization.

The sudden clank of a blade and a cold touch on her neck woke her from her slumber. Bidisha knew at that moment the things that were to follow.

She sat still as dead, careful enough not to cut herself and slowly opened her eyes. Her gaze followed the steel that was held at her neck and then the hand holding it, his left hand. She tilted her head just a bit to take a look at his face though her neck was stuck in the same position. Bidisha's eyes met a pair of black marble-like eyeballs. Half of his face was covered, exposing only his rugged forehead. His charcoal black hair rolled up in waves; she could see them from under the black cloth just below his jewelled ears. He stood tall and broad, hovering over Bidisha. Her hand slowly moved towards her sword that she had placed on the ground.

'I don't like people acting smart against my will,' the man said, his face still covered. 'Now will you take the pain to stand up?'

His husky voice... She had heard it before.

'But I can't hold back my wits. I always like to outsmart men like you who chase after women for no good reason,' Bidisha said as she rose, steady and careful.

'Is that right? If that's a challenge then why don't you try and take your sword first?' he mocked, the tip of his sword still at her neck.

'May I have the privilege of knowing the identity of the person I am going to fight? Moreover, for what?' Bidisha asked, her voice calm.

'I have never come across a woman who can hold her composure in a situation like this. That I have certainly come to admire about you.'

His voice had finally ignited her memory. Bidisha was certain about who the masked man was.

'But, who could it be? What is he doing in the palace, masked up like that?'

How could this man, she wondered, make his way inside the palace? Perhaps, he had managed to sneak in? Or, was he an insider? But the biggest puzzle for Bidisha was that he had shown up, risking the possibility of getting caught, punished or worse, being interrogated in a dungeon.

It struck her as she looked around. There were no guards or maids. It was suspicious. Bidisha had walked past at least a dozen guards only a while ago.

She didn't want any trouble. Not when she was so close to securing a job in the palace.

Bidisha looked for Debesh. But she couldn't find him either. If only he'd show up and handle the situation tactfully. Bidisha contemplated if she should address the matter her way, given the time and the place.

In a split second, she decided to take charge. Bidisha dodged the sword that was ready to slit her neck. Turned around and kicked straight into the man's chest, thrusting him with force. The mountain of a man that he was, he simply took a step back and in no time he was back on his feet. His eyes looked fierce, red, like her dress, that swirled as she found back her ground. Bidisha had barely touched the sword when he attacked her. She blocked his steel with her sheathed sword, trying to regain her balance.

Her eyes went wide when the man pushed his sword against hers, pushing her straight to the ground. Bidisha fell on her back. It spasmed painfully as she tried to stand. But she pulled herself together and unsheathed her sword.

The two swords clanked and the eyes of their handlers locked. She held her long sword firmly with both hands and tried to push his shiny steel away from herself. Even before she realized it, he had twirled her blade with his. And then they clashed uninterrupted with a steady rhythm. Like the music of sorts. Bidisha overpowered him as he retreated. Their arms still moved seamlessly and their swords jangled. And then he turned around and came back with force. This time, she retreated. She realized for the first time that the opponent fighting with his left hand could hinder her capability. On the other hand, the man looked quite comfortable fighting a righthanded sword's person. Of course, that was only what he expected, didn't he after fighting her in the darkness of night.

Bidisha's eyes moved away from the sword and to his face. Surprisingly, she couldn't see a trace of the fierce glare he had directed at her earlier. He raised a single eyebrow as he locked his eyes with hers.

Bidisha was puzzled.

She had no idea what was going on. Who was she fighting with? And, for what? Was it ok to hurt him? Or get hurt for nothing? She didn't have answers. This was not part of her plan. Nothing that was happening was, as a matter of fact.

Moreover, that man was a skilled sword fighter. Unlike the thugs, she had saved Rani Maa from the ambush. Bidisha could fight a dozen of such unskilled men. But a man like the one who stood before her at that moment, she feared, would not be an easy opponent.

His eyes...they were getting in her way. He squinted, even as his blade still moved against hers. Bidisha didn't want to hurt some random person inside the palace and invite unwanted trouble. It didn't seem like he was trying to hurt her either. On the contrary, it looked like he was practising his skill or testing hers.

'You are good...' he commented, dodging her attack.

'I don't need validation from a man who has snuck into the palace,' Bidisha said as she attempted to target his legs.

'Not so quick,' he proclaimed, jumping up on the terracotta brick fence, challenging her move as he landed back on the ground.

It was surprising. The intricately designed fence stood tall and intact even after bearing the man's weight. A man so large was so light on his feet, it was unbelievable.

'How is the wound on your mother's arm?' he dared to ask without faltering on his movements.

'Your cheap compassion won't change anything between us,' Bidisha said as she jumped up on the stump, gaining the height equal to him.

Bidisha was enraged by his false façade. She had to take off his mask.

'And you think I care about your approval of me?'

She jumped on him in an attempt to unmask the crook. He backed, hitting the wall behind him. Bidisha was on her toes, very close to grabbing the cloth from his face. The man caught her hand and pulled on it. Bidisha lost her balance. Their eyes locked and her pulse raced. Both their swords were on the ground. The man swirled her. She landed on her back and on top of him. His warm breath tingled on her nape.

Bidisha's breath quickened. She fisted her hands and her body stiffened.

He held her by the shoulders and nudged her forward. Bidisha took a deep breath as the fresh cold breeze hit her in the face trying to calm herself down. And then she was back on her feet and her mind out of the mystic moment she thought she would never have.

'Come on. Let's finish it. Pick up your sword,' he said, unfazed.

And as they continued, the swords clanked again. None of them budged before the other. But it was getting difficult for her to keep up with his strength. He was now getting on her nerves as she tried harder to block his sword. And then he found an open spot between the movements of her tired arm. The man thrust her in the chest with his open palm. Bidisha lost her balance but she held on to her sword. She gasped for breath, her hand on her chest and suddenly felt darkness clouding before her eyes. Shaking her head was of little help. And when she came back to her senses and opened her eyes, the man had disappeared. Bidisha looked around. The guards had returned to their positions.

'You look terrible. What happened to you? Did you roll in the mud? And your hair!' Debesh examined Bidisha, just like he had done earlier at the palace gate only she looked the opposite. 'Good thing that you didn't rip your clothes as you did...'

Debesh stopped abruptly and paced again like he had done earlier in the day.

Bidisha looked away from him as her ears blazed and she clenched her jaw. 'You...you were gone for long... I'll have to think twice before I trust you again,' Bidisha said as she walked towards the harem alongside Debesh, matching his long strides effortlessly.

'I don't remember asking you to trust me.'

Bidisha blocked his way. 'What took you so long? Do you even have the slightest idea about what I had to go through?' Bidisha fumed. 'I could lose my only chance to earn my living or worse, I could have been dragged away and punished for killing someone on the palace grounds.'

Debesh let out a sigh. 'But you're safe. And there is no dead body. Calm down.'

He moved aside and walked past her as if it wasn't anything serious. Bidisha's ears were hot. She took a moment before following Debesh as he deposited his sword near the lady guard who stood outside the queen's chamber. Bidisha followed suit.

As soon as she entered the chamber, Bidisha stepped on the carpet with a floral design in rich green and royal blue. There were extravagant motifs painted on the terracotta walls. Sunlight beamed in through the small windows and lit the place with its golden hues.

Debesh had walked behind the intricately carved see-through wooden partition. Bidisha was unsure if she had to follow him for she got a glimpse of Rani Maa behind the screen.

Just when she was thinking about a suitable way to greet the queen, her eyes fell on the lean person sitting on an elegantly carved wooden chair next to one of the wooden tables. Yuvaraja Prabir was staring directly at her. Bidisha bowed to him before she looked away.

Debesh suddenly emerged out from behind the wooden screen and a man, much taller than Debesh, followed him. She was taken aback and felt parched all of a sudden. The man was clad in black and his mask was off his face. Her eyes met his, the same black eyes she had seen a while ago. It was him, the person she had duelled just before coming to Rani Maa's chamber. The same man who had hurt her mother. And the person who had tormented her heart, for the first time in a long time. Her eyes widened as he smirked.

'You?' Bidisha's voice faded as she squeezed her eyes shut and fisted her hands in an attempt to control her temper, lest she ended up doing something terrible in the presence of Rani Maa.

'Aren't you going to greet me yet?' The voice startled Bidisha. 'Is this how you show respect to your queen?'

'Rani Maa, I... I was just...'

'You were what? Pretending to be a fool? I know exactly what you're capable of. Don't even try to act otherwise. And never bother to justify or explain yourself to me. Or, there will never be a next time,' Rani Maa said.

'Please pardon me, Rani Maa,' Bidisha said, looking through the immaculate workmanship on the partition.

'Don't be under the impression that you are an exception because you saved my life,' Rani Durga Moni Devicontinued. 'Didn't I tell you yesterday that you need to be at least clean if not anything else? But look at you.'

Bidisha's forehead scrunched even as she fisted her hands part in disappointment in herself and part in anger towards the man who was responsible for her current state. Bidisha looked at the man before her in annoyance. Her anger amplified when he gave her a smug smile even as the queen continued her tirade.

Nobody had ever spoken to her like that. Though Bidisha had encountered rude men and women, she had always taught them a lesson if they crossed the line she had drawn. Bidisha was already having a one-on-one combat with Rani Durga Moni Devi in her mind and was mincing the queen with her sword in her world. She smiled at her thoughts, hiding her face when, in their imaginary battle, Rani Maa fell carrying her huge body weight.

Suddenly, a pair of legs appeared before her and she knew instantly that it was none other than the mysterious man. Bidisha lifted her head.

'Did he see me smiling? This is not good. I should have been more careful before mocking the queen.'

The man took her in from top to bottom, then stretched a hand and moved her out of his way. He then walked out of Rani Maa's chamber as if nothing had happened. The huge man in black was not only mysterious and rude but was also indecent, she concluded.

Bidisha felt a flash of irritation and she glared at his retreating form. Her first mission, she thought, would be to dig out all the information she could about that man, once she got into the palace.

The maidens in the chamber moved the partition. It was atypical of any royal ladies to get their hair done before others. It was considered indecent. They were expected to be modest, presentable and dignified at all times. Or, at least that was what she had heard about the royal etiquettes.

However, as was this case, Rani Durga Moni Devi turned out to be precisely what Bidisha was aware of her personality. The queen didn't care much for *izzat* or societal rules. She had always done things her way. And there was gossip about her ever since her firstborn had died. It seemed she had stopped caring for the superficial etiquette imposed on women after that. Now that Bidisha had got the chance to witness it, Rani Maa had not abided by the Harem rules either.

After the death of her elder son, Prince Man Singha Dev, all she wanted was for her younger son, Trinabh Singha Dev, to ascend the throne. Her reputation preceded her everywhere; she was known to be as cunning as a fox! It was also believed that she was the brain that controlled the actions of King Mitul Singha Dev. She was a woman with a heart made of stone who enjoyed crushing others under her authority. Rani Maa was the most dreaded and the most hated person in the whole Bishnupur kingdom.

There were stories about Rani Durga Moni Devi that were hard to surmise about any human being. She was believed to be a shrewd woman who wouldn't spare anyone for her benefit especially if it concerned her younger son, Yuvaraja Trinabh Singha Dev.

Rani Maa's harsh tone broke the silence in the chamber and the noise of the thoughts in Bidisha's head.

'Prabir could use some extra assistance since he is dealing with the *Goras* these days. Even with a person as fierce as Debesh to guard the prince, another one would be an asset. A skilled person like you will be helpful to guard the Yuvaraja's delicate body. You will listen to him as if they were my words,' Durga Moni Devi commanded as she sat on her dressing chair, her belly hanging over her upper thighs.

Her huge forearm bore the weight of heavy ivory bangles cased in gold. The thick golden *bajuband*, studded with rubies and diamonds, dug into her upper arm as her maid tried to hook it together in place. Yet another woman, dressed in a plain white cotton saree just like the other maidens, helped Durga Moni Devi with her big ear *bali* as the queen moved her sunlit round face in admiration in the mirror. Her neck was decked fully in gold, the spiky design of her necklace almost digging into her double chin.

'Is Yuvaraja Prabir that delicate? Does he really need another bodyguard for support? But, why me for that job?'

The Yuvaraja, Prabir Singha Dev, seated in Rani Maa's chamber, indeed looked weak. In fact, weaker than when she had seen him on the horse the previous day. Perhaps, Bidisha hadn't observed him closely. He was the well-known ill-fated man born in the royal family. Yuvaraja Prabir had lost his mother soon after his birth. And he was the much talked about prince who could never ascend the throne given his calibre of knowing nothing, and being good at nothing and good for nothing.

Yuvaraja Prabir still sat in the same spot and like a statue looking outside the door that was decorated with *resham pardas* as he listened to his stepmother, Her Highness, speak for him. It must have been a splendid view for him or at least a better one than inside the chamber where all one could do was glare at the terracotta walls decorated with colourful mirrors.

'You must drink this *sarbath* before you leave, Prabir. My maid, Aarini, makes the best *sarbath*,' Rani Maa said. 'As a woman, I wonder how Bidisha could have been so brave yesterday. You witnessed it yourself, Prabir. She is capable of doing things that even some men cannot. She dared to risk her life.'

There was the hint of a taunt directed towards the prince in everything she said. But unsurprisingly, the man said nothing and Debesh, his bodyguard, stood like a pillar next to him without an expression on his face. But her words were clear and anyone could interpret them very well.

'I will have it when I visit you next time, Rani Maa,' Yuvaraja Prabir said as he walked out of the chamber and Debesh followed him after bowing to Rani Maa.

Bidisha rejoiced in her small victory. After all, as the queen said, she had risked her life to win her trust. With her actions and words. And it had paid off for her. She had achieved a leap in her mission unexpectedly by bagging a chance to work for the Yuvaraja who dealt directly with the British traders. Perhaps, she could chance upon something to impress the queen yet again. Everyone knew how much the queen despised the *Goras*. And Yuvaraja Trinabh Singha Dev was no different either. It was only the maharaja who upheld their interests and lived on a stipend from the British. He had no other way but to be an emeritus to the British who had annexed the glory of Bishnupur.

As Bidisha bowed to the queen before she took her leave, Rani Durga Moni Devi solved Bidisha's dilemma on whether she should follow the prince or wait for the queen's further orders.

'Remember, Bidisha, you're working for me, not for Prabir. You'll report his every move to me. And hereafter, you'll never step in my chamber again unless you're asked to. One of these three maidens will reach out to you when necessary. You'll have to be ready with answers at all times.'

Bidisha understood her job very well. She could even spy on other people using the pretentious cover blessed by the queen herself. She could find a way to help her mother, by the grace of Goddess Bipottarini Devi.

Bidisha bowed to the queen again. 'As you say, Rani Maa. I understand. I'll be your ears.' Then she added, 'only.'

'That's not all. You'll try and win his heart. And...'

'What?' Bidisha blurted.

'You dare interrupt me, girl?!'

Bidisha went quiet, cast her eyes down. She understood what the queen meant. She had fallen into a trap she couldn't dare escape.

'You are learning. At least you didn't justify your mistake. Like I said, you'll win Prabir's heart, get close to him, read his mind and tell me about his plans.'

'What are you waiting for? Go follow him now.'

Bidisha contemplated a reply but she couldn't think of anything other than a meek 'yes'. There couldn't be another answer Rani maa would have accepted. She took Her Highness' leave and walked out with her heart thudding against her ribs.

Bidisha saw the tallest of those three maidens bring a plate full of dry red chillies. And even before Bidisha had left the chamber, the maiden uttered a few words holding the chillies in her left hand to ward away any negative vibes the queen may have caught. Then the maid paced out of the chamber pushing Bidisha aside and burnt the chillies in a clay pot full of hot coal that was placed right outside the door. The sentry moved far away. The maiden shut the chamber doors. And Bidisha rushed out but the smoke had engulfed the walkway already. She coughed and rubbed her eyes as tears poured out and her eyes burned. Bidisha cursed the maidservant in her mind. If only the witch could wait for a moment, she would be saved from this horrific beginning to her new life.

CHAPTER THREE

'Let me help you,' a voice as meek as that of a dying man greeted Bidisha. 'You should rinse your eyes with milk. It will soothe the pain.'

'Aaaahhhh! Give me something. Help me please.' Bidisha sniffed loudly, her hands waving around, searching for help. 'It's stinging.'

The man held her hand and guided her as she struggled to open her eyes. His hands were softer than her calloused palms. Bidisha followed him, the breeze swaying her hair into her burning eyes and making her uneasy. The soft hands caressed her skin as he tried to dab milk onto her eyes. The urge to rub her eyes was becoming unbearable. And the tears wouldn't stop flowing from her eyes. She was drenched in sweat and she could sense people watching her.

'Don't even think of touching your eyes. Come and sit here,' the man commanded, holding her shoulder with his other hand.

Bidisha was in no state to comprehend anything. Her nose tingled and it felt like a thousand needles were pricking her eyes. The pungent smoke had made it impossible for her to even open her eyes. Moreover, she had no idea about the person helping her but she was glad that someone had offered to help her. She hadn't expected any assistance, especially in the palace where people expected her to be of assistance.

The sudden cold touch of the wet cloth on her eyes gave her goosebumps.

'I can do it myself.' Bidisha said, holding her hand out, her eyes still closed.

'Let me do it,' he said, with a flat tone.

Bidisha didn't insist. What mattered to her the most at that time was relieving the pain and the burning sensation in her eyes. The dabbing was helping. She sat sniffing and felt messy because of her tears and the milk dripping on her dress. Her running nose added to her misery but she sat there patiently.

She was feeling much better after a while. And then she washed her face with the water from the fish pond that was in the small garden they were sitting in. Bidisha opened her eyes to a blurred world before her. The milk worked its magic and then the water did its job too. Relieved a little, Bidisha was finally able to grasp her surroundings.

She stood up at his sight. It was Yuvaraja Prabir who had assuaged her pain. It was him of all the people. Bidisha was there to serve the prince on Rani Durga Moni Devi's orders. Instead, she had been on the receiving end on their first encounter. And to her shock, Debesh was right there, standing like a statue while his master did the job.

How could she not recognize his voice? She had heard it earlier, hadn't she?

'I am told that you are to stay by my side at all times. I trust in Rani Maa and, therefore, in you. I am sure the queen has made arrangements for you to stay here in the palace.'

'Yes, Yuvaraja,' Bidisha whispered. 'I will be moving in along with one of the maidens in the rooms provided.'

'What a fox?' Debesh mocked. 'You are a fast learner. Befitting your employer.'

Prince Prabir hushed Debesh and said, 'You may leave now, Bidisha.'

What does this innocent man even have to hide? He was known to be kind, obedient and a loyal son whom Maharaja Mitul Singha Dev treasured. Yuvaraja Prabir was like an open book who always minded his own business. Rani Maa had nothing to worry about where Yuvaraja Prabir was concerned. He wouldn't possibly be plotting against the queen.

But Durga Moni Devi's desperate intention to see her son on the throne made her insecure about her stepson, who, ironically, didn't seem to harbour the intentions to ascend the throne. He couldn't possibly challenge a strong person, his stepbrother Trinabh, going against the will of the selfish queen.

Moreover, rumours were that Yuvaraja Trinabh would be soon declared the crown prince of Bishnupur. And that's what Maharaja Mitul Singha Dev wanted too. His strong son to rule and the younger one to enjoy the riches of the kingdom. Rani Maa had no reason to be suspicious of Yuvaraja Prabir. And the King's other sons, with his 3 younger wives, were not even in the position to challenge Yuvaraja Trinabh as they were too young. Rani Durga Moni Devi had made sure of it in her own cunning way. She had been meticulously planning it all since the time she had married and stepped into the palace.

How could she not take precaution now when it was almost time for her son to ascend the throne?

Whatever her big plan was against Yuvaraja Prabir, Rani Maa had already made it clear to Bidisha and she had to do something to win his heart and seduce the prince. The very thought made her cringe. It was the worst thing she could ever do to a person who is so kind to her.

'You reek of milk!' Debesh frowned and covered his nose.

'You didn't have to accompany me. I can find the maidens' home myself,' Bidisha said disgusted by the smell herself.

She was much worse than she had been in the jungle. Her clothes were muddy, her eyes were swollen and she smelled terrible. Her clothes were sticky too and needed to get out of them as soon as was possible.

'First, you put the Yuvaraja in a situation where he can only offer you more help. And then you're complaining that he asked me to help you. Go on now. There is the place you'll be staying hereafter.'

'Why are you acting so strange all of a sudden? I don't think I did anything that could have offended you.'

'Of all places, you had to come to the palace in search of a job. And now, you'll be sticking your nose in Yuvaraja Prabir's affairs stuck to his side day and night.'

'I can't help if you are not pleased by what I am asked to do,' Bidisha said as she walked inside the maidens' home to change.

'I have no time for your nonsense. If you don't make it to the Yuvaraja Prabir's chamber quickly, we will leave for the *darbar* without you. Also, remember that women can't enter the *darbar* without someone higher up putting in a word for them. And by that, I mean you can only wait outside the darbar without Prince Prabir's influence. So, you better make it fast before he goes in leaving you behind.'

It was a pity that she had to work with people she hated and do a job she disliked. But she had to do something to keep herself safe and stay in the palace for as long as needed so that she could find a way to accomplish her goal. To free her mother of the false conviction so that they both could lead a free life just like everybody else.

Bidisha entered the maidens' accommodation, which was nothing but a big disorganised room. There were a dozen maidens doing their thing—cleaning the room, changing their clothes, giggling and gossiping.

She quickly grabbed a white saree from the stack that was placed on one of the shelves on the tall wooden rack. She couldn't care less about the person it belonged to. All she focussed on was to clean herself and be present there in the *darbar* to see the man on the throne, the Maharaja.

Bidisha rushed past the guards in the long veranda that headed straight to the fish pond right in front of Yuvaraja Prabir's chamber. She got a glimpse of both, Prabir as well as Debesh, as they stepped out of his chamber. Bidisha hurried feeling light without her sword and the baldric on her waist. She had left it back in her quarters, as she was asked to, since weapons were not allowed in and around the *darbar*.

She walked like a servant, dressed in a plain white saree over a deep green blouse. Bidisha had braided her hair; her plait, that reached her hips swayed with her long and hurried steps.

She managed to almost catch up with the Yuvaraja's pace who was walking out of the fish pond courtyard. Debesh didn't take the pain to notice her presence and followed the Yuvaraja. Prince Prabir didn't bother to acknowledge her presence either.

The courtyard leading to the *darbar* was bustling and was far from the quiet ambience in the parts of the palace Bidisha had visited so far. People were moving in and out of the heavily guarded premises. There were a handful of Britishers who stood in a group conversing among themselves. But they took notice and greeted Yuvaraja Prabir unlike the other ministers who didn't bother much for his presence. Indeed, there was favouritism in their demeanour. As was the rumour, the *goras* seemed to be supporting Prabir while the Bishnupur locals looked up to Trinabh as their next king.

She was mesmerised by the gathering in the *darbar* which wasn't a big one. What made it exceptional was that, Bidisha was seeing all the prominent faces she had only heard of under one roof. The dignified ministers and the British officers she had seen earlier from far, were all together in the same grand majestic hall.

She looked at Debesh who stood next to her like a warrior for no particular reason, as if he would take down someone soon, in the peaceful assembly. Though he looked at her for an instant, his stone-cold expression stayed.

And suddenly there was a commotion as the king made it inside the *darbar* and graced the throne.

'Sir Oliver Watts, welcome to Bishnupur,' greeted Maharaja Mitul Singha Dev as he stepped down from his throne but not for long.

The handful of attendees in the *Byaktigata darbar*, the Maharaja's private assemblage, stood up, including Prince Prabir, as His Majesty stepped down.

Bidisha was spellbound and didn't quite believe what she was seeing. She was aware of the ties between the kingdom and the Britishers but hadn't expected the king to be a *gora*'s pet. Maybe this was new only to her, the king greeting a foreigner in person and exhibiting his obsequious behaviour with confidence par excellence.

Sir Oliver took off his black hat and held it under his arm. Maharaja Mitul Singha Dev hugged Sir Oliver and patted his back. The king looked oversized and short in front of the fit and large stature of the British trader.

His Majesty was all shining in his silk robe, dhoti and a flashy pink turban on his head along with the glittery crown studded with precious gems.

On the contrary, the English man wore a muted black sack suit with a black vest and a black tie over his white ruffled collar.

She had no idea why oil and water had to attempt to mix and make such a ruckus in a country that was free once upon a time. Couldn't Goras just live in their country and let others live in peace?

The darbar, she was witnessing it for the first time. Men in gold and pearls, their silk and the velvets, the loud laughs but only of the important British and the king himself, everything astonished her. There were few other people seated in their extravagant chairs but either with frown on their forehead or with hung faces. There was a stark difference in the way people behaved as if they belonged to two different worlds or were divided into two parties.

Bidisha was a girl who lived in the jungle away from the civilization. She had always relied on the information that reached her in the form of gossip in the market. And through the rumours among the women who sometimes even made up things for their lack of exposure to the palatial environment.

Some of the things she had heard were true above all. But most of it was not the same as people on the streets had made it up. There was no *madira* in the darbar after all like many other things that were assumed to be like the exuberant entertainment.

Bidisha, however, was disgusted by the whole exhibitionism.

'Sir Oliver Watts!' An orotund sound pierced through the king's laughter as a man paced in and barged between His majesty and Sir Oliver.

It was him. Bidisha couldn't trust her eyes. The man who had attacked her mother even had the authority to cut through the king's words. Bidisha gaped at him trying to trust her eyes.

He had the audacity to hurt her mother in the quiet of the dark in her own home.

He had the rudeness to attack a girl for reasons unknown, in broad daylight that too in the palace grounds.

He had the boldness to greet a British officer out of turn when everybody else in the king's court was mindful of their behaviour.

Even Yuvaraja Prabir acted with utmost decorum in the presence of the Maharaja and other dignitaries.

Nobody, but that man had crossed the line of etiquette.

'Who is he?'

Sir Oliver bowed just a bit in acknowledgement. 'Prince Trinabh,' he greeted before straightening.

'Trinabh!' Bidisha repeated the name in her mind just as his eyes met hers for a brief moment in the *darbar* full of men. Bidisha stood in shock. A prince. Rather, the prince. The heir of the Bishnupur kingdom.

But the first thing that struck her was, why would he attack her and that too masked and disguised. It didn't make any sense. Nothing that he did make anyway.

The same way as she witnessed his impudence in the presence of the king himself when he had dared to cut the king's words a while back. Perhaps this was the result of the extraordinary benevolence showered upon Prince Trinabh, the heir apparent.

King Mitul Singha Dev returned to his throne, which was a spectacle in itself. She had heard people talking about the opulent silver throne and now, she got to see it with her own eyes. The intricate Indian motifs on it took her breath away. The feet of the throne were shaped like the paws of a lion and the arms ended with lion heads. The chair had golden and deep green tissue drapery around the inside. But how she pitied the fate of Bishnupur, the very marvellous throne was now used to curry favour with the British sovereign.

The assemblage was only a formality more than a discussion where every minister was assigned a task with due diligence by Yuvaraja Trinabh without consulting anybody present in the *darbar*. And Yuvaraja Prabir was asked to deal with Sir Oliver directly to close the cotton trade deal in a fruitful way better than his previous deal.

'Prabir, you know how important Sir Oliver is to his Majesty and me, don't you?' Yuvaraja Trinabh said, a scowl on his face as he looked at the king rather than making eye contact with the person to whom his words were directed to. 'I hope you will uplift the honour of Bishnupur hospitality and take care of our guest.'

'Like always, Yuvaraja,' Yuvaraja Prabir said and graced his wooden seat placed away from the throne and after the ministers' seats.

After all the formal talks and the usual affairs, the *darbar* was dismissed and the ministers left. Bidisha, however, looked in all the directions taking in all that she could as she witnessed her surroundings.

White pillars stood erect not only bearing the load of the roof but also the weight of the king's betrayal to his own country. The magnificent art on the ceiling told her the tale of the kingdom's ancestors while the chipping floor uncovering the terracotta begged her to free the place from the king's incompetence.

She took a mental note of every possible detail and the passages that went out in different directions. And just before they stepped out of the hall, the glint of the semi-precious stones above the beautifully chiselled door left her with more disgust and a sense of betrayal. Walking with her eyes narrowed from the glare, she thumped right into Prince Prabir who stood there noticing her.

Prabir had been watching her every move and he had made it obvious with his stares and glares for many days now. Just like Rani Durga Moni Devi, who had planted Bidisha next to Prabir as a warning to him to be wary of his actions, he had given Bidisha signs to be cautious of her actions.

Debesh placed a wooden stool in front of the *gadda*. The carvings on its legs decorated with bronze intricacies caught Bidisha's eyes as she placed a bowl of warm water for Prabir to wash his hands. And then she handed him a small embroidered cotton cloth, too delicate and exquisite, to clean his hands. Another maid kept a big copper *thali* in front of him, which held small copper bowls for the side dishes to be served.

Bidisha started serving him dishes from the tray full of scrumptious food. The Yuvaraja sat tall, his wrists resting on his knees. He looked at her and then at his food. There was *phulkori singara, begun bhaja, aloo chorchori, chingri malai, shorshe bata ilish maach, tok maach, nolen gurer payesh* and piping hot *luchi*. The aroma made her stomach growl as she walked towards the door.

'Stop. Where are you going? Did you forget again that the same food is always served to Debesh along with me?' Yuvaraja said, crinkling his eyes as he made stern eye contact with her and continued, 'It has been days you are here and yet you dare to ignore the customs I set?'

His fierce almond eyes had made things that he didn't say clear to Bidisha and she didn't delay in serving the food to Debesh. No matter how much attention she tried to pay, she was simply not made for such chores; this was the third time she had messed up by not serving Debesh. She always got distracted. Sometimes she worried about her mother and at times about Yuvaraja Trinabh's motives and his purpose behind his actions against her. Moreover, she had not seen him in the palace for days to confront him.

'Forgive me, Yuvaraja Prabir...' Bidisha mumbled.

In the few weeks she had worked for the Yuvaraja, Bidisha had managed to get some information on all the members of the royal family. And it turned out that Yuvaraja Prabir's only well-wisher was Debesh. Nobody else was as important to him as Debesh, whom the queen always addressed as the hound. Perhaps to demean Prabir's morale and look down on his only support, Debesh. But she hadn't seen Debesh reacting to those insulting words. Not once.

Yuvaraja had insisted on eating with Debesh since his childhood even though it was objected to many times as they grew up. It got worse, his insistence. Yuvaraja wished to eat with Debesh and even at gatherings and on special occasions. Debesh couldn't disobey his master and despite hating to be the matter of the argument, especially over food, he continued to wait like other servants till he was served. However, it was unacceptable to Yuvaraja Prabir; he had once left a meal with a British envoy, his food untouched, because Debesh was not allowed to sit with him.

Debesh was sitting on the floor with a stool in front of him and a wooden *thali* before him as big as that of the prince. Bidisha served every dish that was on the Yuvaraja's *thali* and then bowed to take a leave.

'Wait...' the Yuvaraja ordered, 'come and taste the food for me.'

His broad forehead was wrinkled and his wide face didn't look very pleasant. Bidisha didn't utter a single word and promptly started tasting the food, starting with a small morsel of the *luchi* and *tok maach*.

Unlike the food that is served to the other royalties, Prince Prabir's food didn't go through much of a safety check. It was done only when he explicitly needed one. His safety meant nothing much to anyone in the palace except for Debesh, who insisted on checking the food every time. He even checked the *thali* for contamination before serving the food.

'Yuvaraja, it's safe.'

'Not yet. Taste each one of the dishes served on my plate and eat a mouth full,' the Yuvaraja insisted and looked at the maid Janaki, whose eyes were wide open. 'What are you looking at? Leave.'

Debesh's stone-cold expression had changed and his mouth was curled up. He looked away, unable to hold his chuckle that made to the Yuvaraja's ears anyway.

'Hmmm...' Prince Prabir squawked as his square jawline looked prominent.

Bidisha couldn't understand any of the things that were going on at that moment. It had been weeks and this was a new development she had seen. Prince Prabir was not his usual self and neither was Debesh, who wore a stern face almost always. She failed to understand if the two were chiding her or something else was going on. At times both Prabir and Debesh warned her to watch her actions which could harm them knowing she worked for the queen. And other times they were amiable which was least expected from Prabir in particular.

Bidisha had seen the drama in the palace for many days now.

Like everybody else, Debesh too was mysterious. His words were polite and his actions fit the demeanour of a servant in the palace. But his intentions... Bidisha couldn't tell. Especially when it came to Rani Maa and Prince Trinabh.

Debesh paced towards Yuvaraja Trinabh's chamber and Bidisha matched his stride. She took a glance at him every so often. His chiselled jawline drew her attention to his face and then she took note of his skin. Bidisha had not noticed him closely in all these days. She was curious, about his skin, which looked unusually smooth for a Prince's hound who otherwise looked like a warrior.

He was good with the sword she could tell by the way he practiced every day. And yet there was no trace of tan on his dark even skin tone. And just like his strong body contrasting his even skin, he seemed aggressive at times and then empathetic and dependable otherwise.

And there was a different side to him as they walked together. He seemed resolute when he was about to barge into his enemy, Yuvaraja Trinabh Singha Dev's chamber.

Debesh was more than just loyal to his master Yuvaraja Prabir. Their bond was much deeper which Bidisha was unable to gauge. Not yet. But anybody plotting against his master was his enemy for sure.

Bidisha had learnt a little about the royal family in the past few days. And just like everyone in the palace, she was aware of the situation between Yuvaraja Trinabh and Yuvaraja Prabir. Though the latter was kind and soft-hearted, he was considered to be the British's favourite for the next in line to ascend the throne. However, this didn't sink in well with Yuvaraja Trinabh and Rani Durga Moni Devi.

It was believed that, though Yuvaraja Prabir's mother was the eldest queen, she couldn't bear a child again for years after giving birth to a princess. Rani Durga Moni Devi was the one who had his majesty's full attention every single night till she gave birth to Prince Trinabh. His Majesty, they said, used to visit her chamber even when she was carrying the prince. Rumours were that all other queens wanted to teach her a lesson and joined hands since they too wanted to make their place in Maharaja Mitul Singha Dev's heart by giving him the heir he could consider for the throne. And strangely, since the day prince Trinabh was born, his majesty never once made it to the queen Durga Moni Devi's chamber. What was even more surprising, they say, was that Rani Maa didn't take it to heart nor did she do anything about it. However, none of the queens succeeded in bearing a prince for the king for years until Subhashree Moni Devi gave birth to Prince Prabir 3 years after Prince Trinabh was born.

The guard stopped them. Debesh and Bidisha were asked to wait outside since Yuvaraja Trinabh was busy. Everyone in the palace knew what it meant. He was with a woman.

Debesh strolled in the corridor. He was there for an important matter. Debesh and Bidisha were asked to overlook the arrangements for the hunting event that was organized to entertain the British merchants, primarily Sir Oliver Watts, who would be leaving soon to England after months of his stay in Bishnupur.

Bidisha was getting equally restless as Debesh. She had been working on a plan, a better one than seducing Yuvaraja Prabir, for the queen. And she needed to prepare for the same before leaving for the hunting. There was information that had to be collected and things that had to be bought to execute her plan. But Yuvaraja Trinabh had been wasting all her time.

Just then a woman walked out of his chamber. Debesh rushed back to the door and the guard went in to seek permission for their entry.

Bidisha fidgeted as she stood beside Debesh, their heads bowed.

Trinabh was wearing nothing but a dhoti and held a *hookah* in his hand. He was seated on his bed. He pushed his thick hair away from his forehead and ran his fingers into his dishevelled mane. His ear stud shone in the bright sunlight from the small window behind him. He stretched his leg on the beautiful carpet and his arms on the bed.

'What news do you bring today, Debesh?' the Yuvaraja asked, puffing the *hookah*.

'Yuvaraja Prabir has organized a hunting event for Sir Oliver over the next two days and has requested your presence, Yuvaraja Trinabh,' Debesh informed, his hands behind his back.

'Did he ask me before fixing the day? I am too busy with work in the palace to be running around behind animals. And why hunting of all the things to please the guest when Prabir can hardly lift his bow let alone shooting an arrow?'

Prabir hardly had the authority to even decide on the date to organise something. He was expected to overlook everything related to cotton trading but didn't even have the power to take matters in hand. Prabir was expected to report everything to Trinabh who had the final say. Hence, Trinabh's presence would help finalize the matters pertaining to the cotton trade for the year without going in circles for his approval.

'But Yuvaraja Prabir said this is important as there will be pressing matters discussed over cotton trading for the next year. Your presence would mean sealing the deal officially.' Debesh finally looked directly at Trinabh, who was focused on pouring a glass of *sharaab* from the brass *aftaba* in the broad daylight.

Bidisha was astonished, to say the least. If the future of the kingdom looked like that, it was a ratification of her plans to destroy the selfish royals. But she had nothing to add to their conversation. She not only wanted to get out of the chamber at the earliest but also didn't want to look at the man who had hurt her mother for another second.

'Didn't you hear me? Or is it that your master has arranged for a bandwagon of beauties to host that English friend and me in the forest? In that case, I wouldn't give it a miss,' Trinabh mocked. 'Ask your master not to fret over my presence. Remind him who is the next king of the Malla dynasty. The day is not too far for me to ascend the throne. I will check with the ministers if there is a possibility of leisure to hunt and send in a word. I have more pressing issues to take care of.'

'And you,' Prince Trinabh turned towards Bidisha, 'Why did Prabir send you along with Debesh? You seem to be quiet. Didn't he ask you to coax me into giving a nod to his plan? But you rather look pale and tongue-tied to do anything. You wait up. And you can leave, Debesh. Relay my message to your Yuvaraja.'

Bidisha rubbed her palms as Debesh took the Yuvaraja's leave and left the chamber. She couldn't come to lift her head and look at the man before her. Not because she wasn't expected in the first place, as a servant in the palace, but she didn't want to or else her politeness would evade her in an instant.

'Bidisha,' the Yuvaraja said, as he got up from the bed and walked towards her. 'It's been months now since you started working in the palace. What have you done to side Prabir?'

Bidisha bit her lips, still not looking at the Yuvaraja.

'Don't you have anything to say?' the Yuvaraja came closer.

'Yuvaraja, I... I have been trying.' Bidisha took a step back from the smell of the hookah that reeked from Trinabh.

'How? You haven't put even the slightest of efforts to even steal his glance leave alone gain his entire attention.'

Yuvaraja Trinabh grabbed some bangles from the tall table next to him. It was a deck of women's accessories that had everything a woman would want to beautify herself. Many women had entered his chamber and had left some pieces of accessories back, just like the lady who had walked out before her sometime back. Bidisha had seen only one of her earrings dangling as the lady went past her a while ago. The other earring would have fallen around in the chamber. And it was a pity, some of those women had not even made it again to his bed for the second time to collect their belongings.

But Trinabh took Bidisha's hand in his unexpectedly.

'Yuvaraja...' Bidisha said pulling her hand back as her heart raced.

'Just stay still and do not interrupt me till I finish.'

Bidisha was finding it difficult to control her rage that was rising with his every action. She fisted her hand, the one which he held, hoping he would get the signal and stop sliding the bangles.

Instead, he closed in on her and held her hand firmly.

He slid the green glass bangles in both her hands. He took a silver necklace and moving her plait, clipped it at her nape. His touch sent a shudder down her spine. She swiftly turned around, her face in his bare chest and her plait still in his hand. She moved back trying to pull her hair out of his hand. But he held it firmly, tugging on it, and she was forced to lean towards him due to the pull. He untied her plait and ran his fingers through the hair as it swirled open.

Bidisha pulled her hair back and moved away from him, 'I... I must head back to my job Yuvaraja. There's a lot of preparations that need to be done for the hunting event.'

'That's what I am doing right now. Preparation.'

Trinabh pulled her towards him again and put big dangling silver earrings on her ears.

She wanted to show him what she was capable of by fisting him in the face. But his touch on her neck had petrified her will. Moreover, she was in the palace and on a purpose. How could she ruin it all by punching the Yuvaraja?

And before she realised, he took some *kumkum* on his finger and made a round dot between her eyebrows. He held her shoulders. And Bidisha let out a gasp.

'I never thought you could be afraid of someone or even nervous around a man,' Yuvaraja Trinabh remarked as he moved her towards the mirror.

She had never seen herself like that before. Not dressed like that and not in a mirror so big. The red *bindi* and the dangling earrings made her look different from what she saw every day in the small mirror in her home. The only thing she recognized was the ring on her septum.

She had always wanted to wear such luxury but not something that was given by a man like him.

Trinabh moved behind her, his image reflecting in the mirror as he towered over her, his rugged face, broad forehead, the stubble that added charm to his already appealing face. She had not seen him so closely before. His broad chest extended into strong arms, which were rested on his waist, and looked as if they were her wings because of the way he was standing.

Bidisha shook her head in disbelief. 'What am I thinking?' she murmured to herself.

'Did you say something?'

'Hmmm... No, Yuvaraja.'

'Now you look like you're even trying. This is the first step. Let me know if you need more help in getting to his heart. You know it very well that I can help you with that.'

CHAPTER FOUR

The first rays of the sun were starting to break the darkness of the night. The white flares of Bidisha's *kurta*, which ran down her long frame and reached to below her knees, danced to the tunes of the wind as she took long strides in a rush. Her arms, a little too strong and muscular for a girl, were covered underneath her cotton fitted sleeves. She walked tall, as usual, with her slender shoulders rolled back and chin up. Her shoulder bones, befitting for the fighter she was, peeked out of the blue *dupatta*. Bidisha's eyes peered through the wild golden brown tresses that waved on her face in the pleasant windy morning.

The stench of the horse dung didn't seem to bother Yuvaraja Prabir as it had always done. The dry hay on the ground underneath his feet seemed to have stopped messing with his comfort instantly at the sight of Bidisha walking towards him through the stone arches of the stable. His constant complaints to Debesh about the lack of facilities in the horse stable were silenced in no time. Yuvaraja Prabir's attention seemed to be less on the reins and his black beauty, Bhrithi. He had eyes only for Bidisha as his gaze settled on her unaware of the people around him.

She was conscious as the Yuvaraja stole glances at her. She hadn't seen him like that before. Staring at her even when their eyes met. She clutched the sword on her waist.

'Not him. Not like everyone else.'

'Yuvaraja,' Bidisha greeted, bowing before him, 'Pardon my tardiness.'

His eyes made her conscious, more than any man's gaze had ever made. Perhaps, because she hadn't expected him to notice her much for all that she had known about him in months. Prabir hardly looked at women, leave alone ogling at them. But he was behaving strangely today.

'Shall I help you with the saddle Yuvaraja?' Debesh asked, as if attempting to bring him back from the world he had travelled in his mind.

'Hah!' Prabir gaped, his face blank.

'Yuvaraja, can I?' Debesh whispered, his words directed straight into the prince's ears as he leaned forward.

'Hah! What? No...' Yuvaraja Prabir muttered as his hands went back to where he had stopped earlier, to the saddle. 'Go on with your work. We need to leave at the earliest.'

Bidisha's anticipation heightened at the thought of riding a horse as she followed Debesh into the stables. Just as she passed the food trough, tasting the chaff in the air, rustling through the hay, the snorts and the stamping thumps made it to her ears. Her lips widened at the sight before her as she got accustomed to the dark. Her hand reached the velvet of the horse skin as she touched one for the first time in a very long time.

'That beast of a stallion belongs to Yuvaraja Trinabh. Don't even think of going close to it,' Debesh warned her even as he walked a horse towards her. 'This one is for you.'

Bidisha's hand moved away from the horse as if the words 'Yuvaraja Trinabh' had stung her hand.

She took over the ropes Debesh passed to her. The temporary possession of a horse, borrowed from the royal stables, she hoped to ride. Bidisha stroked its neck and then its forehead. Its withers, just about her shoulder height could easily be 2 hands shorter than the well-bred Yuvaraja Trinabh's chestnut-coloured horse. Its brown skin, however, matched with that of his stallion, although it was nowhere close in the shine. But the joy it brought to her, for she would be the one riding on his back, had her head dazed.

Out in the open, even as Yuvaraja Prabir stole a glance at her every so often and watched her with his curious eyes, she caressed the horse. Bidisha gently rubbed its chin. Her long fingers brushed its ears and then stroked its crest softly.

However, in no time she got back to work and fastened the saddle with the help of the girth seamlessly and soon the bridle was in place attached to the reins through horse bits. She was all set to ride the horse and to fulfil her desire to hunt, the hunt no one would have expected, the head that would free her mother. Bidisha had her plan in place.

'So far, it's all going good for you. Come on now, show your horse who the master is,' Debesh mocked.

'I will show you who the master is on the hunting ground, Debesh,' Bidisha replied attempting to climb the horse and ride around a little before they left to the forest for hunting.

'Debesh, won't you give her a hand?' Yuvaraja Prabir said as he settled on the horse ready to ride.

Bidisha, though a timid rider, didn't wait for any assistance. And by the time Prince Prabir turned back to her, she was already on the horse.

'Do you think women are allowed to hunt?' Debesh asked and patted on the horse's rump carelessly. 'Come on now. What are you waiting for?'

To Bidisha's dismay, the horse neighed and lifted its forelegs. Bidisha lost her balance and fell.

'Aaah!'

'Aaaw!'

There was a loud cry. Bidisha had thumped on Debesh as he took the blow of her fall but she wasn't spared of the pain either as she hit the ground and hurt her arm. Her hair was all over Debesh's face. Both were on the ground, her body flat against him as they attempted to get up. She hurried and rolled over to the ground in the rush to get away from him. And then his gaze met her large eyes as if he was ready to get lost in her hazel glistening coin-like eyeballs.

Yuvaraja Prabir, the horse caregivers and a few sentries posted in the stables surrounded them as Debesh stood up and dusted himself. Bidisha held her head low and gaped at her feet, shaking her head and then squeezing her eyes in pain.

'Now back to work,' Prabir ordered the horse caregivers before Debesh could say anything.

'You. You said you know horse riding.' Debesh pointed at her.

'But who asked you to startle the horse when I wasn't ready yet,' Bidisha murmured without giving in to the burning rage, respecting the Yuvaraja's presence.

She stood with grime on her fair face, still looking at her feet. Her hair was loose and whipped in the harsh breeze. Debesh came closer and she clenched her fists in anger trying to refrain herself from doing anything untoward in the presence of the prince.

'Here, take it. Clean your face. I hope there's no serious injury,' Yuvaraja Prabir said offering her a piece of machine woven cotton fabric, pulling it out from his silk *panjabi* pocket.

She bowed just a little, as she accepted it and crumpled the cloth in her fist and headed inside the stable to calm her temper and clean herself. Bidisha felt a heaviness in her chest along with the throb in her arm. Just when she was seeing a ray of hope for her plan, the darkness seemed to engulf it all.

Bidisha was already in a dilemma over the matter of riding for half a day with her less than average horse-riding skills. To make the matter worse, she now had an aching arm. She had to think of something to sail through this newly formed filth that was overpowering her resolve.

Who could help her survive the situation so that she could make it?

Bidisha looked at the men before her. A man dressed in silk for hunting with neither a heart nor the courage to pull an arrow. And then there was the other one, who disliked her for keeping an eye on his master for his enemies in the palace.

In truth, both, Yuvaraja Prabir and Debesh, would find it as an excuse to leave her behind. When push came to shove, they both would protect their affairs from Bidisha, the person planted by Rani Maa in their life.

Bidisha's ears pricked up when she heard hushed voices from outside where she had tied her horse to the wooden rails. Bidisha pressed an ear to the wall.

'Yuvaraja, do you still think Yuvaraja Trinabh will be here?' Debesh asked.

'He likes to show his authority over me. And I am sure he will be here to please father. We can't leave without him or else we will have to face his fury later.'

'And you would best avoid the friction with Yuvaraja Trinabh. I understand, Yuvaraja,' Debesh said.

Yuvaraja Trinabh!

Why didn't she think of that name earlier to help her get into the hunting encampment?

He could be of help and she needn't bear the inconvenience of riding the horse. After all, it was his mother she was working for.

And she was sure he would have a wagon full of women that he might want to indulge in at leisure in the cold jungle. Perhaps she could travel with the women if not on the horse.

But then, she couldn't risk being seen with those women. She would put her reputation at stake and be seen as one of his women.

Bidisha didn't belong to anyone. Least of all to Trinabh. Besides, that bloody womanizer couldn't be trusted.

The cavalcade of men on horseback entered the forest. Sir Oliver Watts along with his entourage, Yuvaraja Prabir and Debesh formed a group and trotted ahead of everyone with a few soldiers accompanying them. The cart with royal chefs and female attendants rolled as the soldiers made their way cutting the branches ahead of the horses that dragged the wheels. Another cart with a woman followed suit as she peeped in and out of the *parda* ogling at Yuvaraja Trinabh, who was following on his horse.

Bidisha had managed to convince Yuvaraja Prabir with a smile and a fake brave front even as her right arm throbbed in pain. She had finally made a choice to ride the horse along with Prabir and Debesh than ask for any help from Trinabh. The constant movement on the horse had made it worse after cantering through halfway from the palace. There was still a long way to go but she had to steel her will in pursuit of her imminent goal.

Bidisha had not only concealed her subpar horse-riding skills but also showed that she could use her left hand with the same efficiency. However, it had caused her to become the last person in the troop heading to their adventurous game of killing animals.

The thick canopy of trees made it difficult for the hunting party to navigate their way through the approaching darkness as dusk began setting in. It was getting colder as they climbed up the hilly forest making their way through the dense fauna.

Trinabh suddenly halted and yelled at Bidisha, 'I have been watching you and noticing your incompetence. You were supposed to be with Prabir. But look at you, slacking from your responsibilities. What are you doing here? Let's go and stay close. Don't let your inefficiency hinder my plan.'

As Bidisha tried and paced on her horse, Yuvaraja Trinabh stopped again when she got closer to him.

'Do you ever wear washed clothes? What is wrong with you? Is this how you're going to win Prabir's heart?'

Bidisha let out a sigh. She had neither the will nor the energy to answer Yuvaraja Trinabh's pointless questions. If only she had the strength to tell him how Debesh was responsible for her ruined clothes and her shattering resolve to execute her plan. She mustered all the strength she had left as she quivered in the cold. The ache in her arm was worsening and Yuvaraja was adding more fuel to her rising temper. They made it past the carts and she was losing her courage to hold up against the growing pain. But they had caught up with the troop.

'Prabir, I had no idea that your choice in women was so brilliant,' Prince Trinabh commented and continued, 'Isn't Bidisha a little too good to be just a help?'

Prince Prabir continued to ride without responding. Bidisha frowned and clasped the reins tighter.

'She is a great sword fighter I was told. Isn't she exotic, even for her British face?'

'As I was told? He even indulged in fights with me in disguise. Both mother and son are such dreadful actors.'

Bidisha wanted to say those words to the Yuvaraja's face. Instead, she looked straight ahead pretending to have heard nothing.

'Her mother might have enjoyed having an Englishman in her bed.'

That was the tipping point for Bidisha.

Her hand reached for her sword. But Debesh held her hand giving her a stern look, instantly stopping her. Bidisha swallowed and let out a heavy sigh. She felt a strange heaviness in her heart and all the nonsense made her suffocate even amidst the greenery and fresh air around her. She lacked the wherewithal at that moment but she would someday make Trinabh pay for the nonsense he was spewing.

'So, Sir Oliver, when are you planning to leave for England?' Yuvaraja Prabir beseeched, bringing it up as if it was a matter of urgency.

'Well, in the next three weeks. The ship is being readied. I have received the cotton from all the villages in Bishnupur for this year just like His Majesty promised me.'

Her breath came heavy as she wheezed in rage. Bidisha's temper rose on hearing those words. The Britishers and the Maharaja were sucking the blood of the weavers and farmers of Bishnupur. And just like they had executed their plan all these years against the people of her land including her mother, she would show them what they could receive in return from a common person like her. It was time for her to execute her plan against them.

'I will never let you set your foot back in your country, Sir Oliver Watts. Your last days are here. Talk all you want while you can and wait for the night sky to take your soul to hell,' Bidisha told him albeit in her head.

The wrath of the British on the subjects of Bishnupur had been beyond her imagination. And one of the sufferers had been her mother who suffered for their wrongdoings after being unjustly accused of killing one of them. And the coward kings of that land in the past who had joined hands with the *goras* had not left any chance to exploit their people either. Maharaja Mitul Singha Dev's reign had only made the situation worse.

The condition of the farmers who were forced to grow more cotton and Indigo, the primary raw materials required by the industries in England, had deteriorated. Worse was the situation of the people who were left with no choice but to grow tobacco and poppy after their fields became barren from continuously growing the cotton crop.

The British exploited farmers by buying the raw material at lower prices and the Maharaja had been the middleman acting without qualms in trading the cotton with the British. The mill cloth made in England was in turn sold for a cheaper rate to the people of the kingdom. This had led to the downfall of the handloom in Bishnupur and the weavers were getting poorer.

One such skilful weaver family was her maternal kin who fought back after her grandfather took the hit for years. It wasn't much about the business itself that he had cared for. Being a *jomidaar* with a huge inheritance, he could still lead a comfortable life. But he couldn't let the injustice continue.

However, it was her mother's love affair with the white that came to light at a reproving time. The family had been stripped of their property and blamed for conspiring the death of the man Mokshita had loved. The king, who had just ascended the throne then, took no risk and joined hands with the *goras* to prove the family guilty and sentenced them to death. Bidisha, who never got a chance to see her grandparents and her uncles, had grieved all her life for her mother's ill fate.

Sir Oliver had been one of those wealthy merchants from England who had been trading cotton since he was just a young boy. He used to accompany his father before their family's tragic death in a fire accident when they had decided to stay put in Bishnupur for a few years and carry out business without having to travel for months on the ship. Sir Oliver's parents and his two younger brothers were burnt to ashes when their home, once a *Jomidaar Boro Bari*, was set on fire.

Since then, Sir Oliver, now in his late 30s, had taken over his family affairs and had been keeping up with the trade from England, travelling back and forth once every couple of years.

Bidisha shook her head and blinked rapidly in an attempt to stay alert as the constant pain in her arm and the exhaustion had taken a toll on her. She didn't have a very good feeling about it as her body was on the verge of giving up.

She was once again left behind. But the whole hunting drama was the perfect opportunity she had been looking for. She couldn't let one simple mishap and the measly pain ruin everything. This was also one of the best chances to gain Rani Durga Moni Devi's trust and get closer to her and she wouldn't give it up.

If things went as per her plan, she could pin the murder of a royal guest on Yuvaraja Prabir. Finding the true culprit would be the last thing on Rani Maa's mind if one obstacle between her son and the throne was removed. And when she learnt that Bidisha had a hand in making her wish come true, Durga Moni Devi's faith in her spy would be solidified.

Although the king had promised the throne to Trinabh, Durga Moni Devi's only living son, Rani Maa would gladly remove all the possible threats capable of challenging her beloved son. Their suspicion towards Yuvaraja Prabir, about him seeking the aegis of the whites to make it to the crown, had been undeniable. And in turn, the interests of the British to see Yuvaraja Prabir on the throne were unnerving for Rani Maa.

Yuvaraja Prabir was the only eminent threat even if he was a good for nothing man in Rani Maa's eyes. The king's other four sons, from his other wives, were too young for Rani Maa to be worried about them.

If at all Bidisha succeeded in killing Oliver Watts, that would put Rani Maa's heart at ease. Bidisha was hoping Sir Oliver's death would become her stepping stone and make all the things she had dreamt of come true. It could open up two ways for Bidisha and take her a step closer to seeing her mother walk free.

She could seek the Maharaja's favour without putting Yuvaraja Prabir's life and reputation at stake by uprooting the one obstacle named Oliver who was stuck in his throat like a bone for a very long time.

During all those months in the palace, Bidisha had snuck into places that were restricted for the outsiders. She had gathered information useful for her to work on a plan to free her mother. Though she operated as eyes and ears for Rani Maa, she had an opportunity to spy for herself as well. In doing all that she did by taking immense risks, the one most important fact she had learnt was that, Oliver was an unwanted person for Maharaja Mitul Singha Dev which she hadn't expected earlier.

Maharaja had an eye for another trader who had promised him more profit than Oliver, the stingiest man Bidisha had ever seen, had been offering the king over the years. She had even eavesdropped over a conversation with one of his ministers talking about the difficulties they would have to face if they killed Oliver. The British wouldn't take it lightly and the maharaja was not in the condition to face their fury. But his words had hinted that he would be thankful to a person who would dare kill Oliver.

Bidisha's one right move would allow her to curry favour with the Maharaja which she was aware was a big leap of faith. It would be a huge risk but it would also be worth it if he agrees to even turn a blind eye to her mother's existence and allow her to lead a free life without having to hide in the jungle under the mask. As far as clearing her name with a royal edict was concerned, she would wait for the right time to earn a respectable life for her mother. Maharaja wouldn't do it openly. He was too faint-hearted for that.

Or, she could go to Rani Maa and help her erase the existence of one of the possible heirs to the throne. Neither the British nor the Maharaja would be able to put Prabir on the throne once he is convicted of murdering a white. And then Bidisha would ask for Rani Maa's kindness in return.

She had been vexed on her actions and plans after leaving behind her mother alone in the jungle, only to visit her and see her from afar. And Oliver's death could mean her mother's freedom.

Bidisha's drooping eyes had caught the sight of Trinabh. The otherwise aggressive leader had somehow lagged behind the hunting party. Or maybe, he had purposely let all the carts get ahead of him.

'I wonder what is wrong with the lioness today. How is it possible that you're tailing the group and not leading with your master Prabir?' Trinabh asked as she walked her horse further towards him.

'Yuvaraja,' Bidisha said politely, 'I just wanted to see if the people in the horse cart needed any help since they were left behind by the troop without any guards to protect the women.'

'That's so good of you to think about them. Let me join you. I can be of some assistance if the need arises,' Trinabh said, riding beside Bidisha. 'But are you sure you can protect others while you are struggling to make it through the jungle given that you look so pale and weak?'

'I don't understand what are you implying Yu...'

'Pretend all you can, but you can barely manage to sit on the horse let alone do anything for those women travelling comfortably in the cart,' Prince Trinabh said cutting her words.

Bidisha smiled. 'Can I dare ask you something, Yuvaraja?'

She had been sitting on the questions that had been killing her peace for months. But the rare encounters with Yuvaraja Trinabh and his evil eyes had kept her wary of the possible mayhem that could follow if she dared to lose her temper before him. And now that she was in a distressful situation, battling to make it to the encamp, the words had escaped even before she could think about them.

'Why not?'

'Yuvaraja, why did you sneak into our home that night? And how did you know the place?' Bidisha asked, mustering the courage as she fisted her hands, and the reins dug into her palms.

'Hmmm... So the lady here is trying to dodge my question with another one. Or should I say two?' Trinabh said. 'Do you think that was our first encounter?'

'Was it not, Yuvaraja?' Bidisha replied in a feeble tone.

'Not your mistake. You had hardly seen me before. But I can't say the same about myself. Because I had chased you for months by then.'

Bidisha was taken aback. Suddenly, he had her full attention and she couldn't care less about her throbbing arm.

'Why? Why would you chase me Yuvaraja?'

'I first saw you in the jungle when I was out hunting. It was the day when you ran into a bear and got yourself a permanent mark on your back. I was astonished by your courage and the way you duelled with it even after getting your back ripped open by its claws,' Trinabh said, suddenly blocking her path and looking into her eyes. 'I clearly remember that day. The animal was huge—monstrous. Your clothes were drenched in blood and the pain was visible on your face but didn't reach your eyes. You still managed to look into its ferocious eyes. Just like the way you're hitting daggers at me with your gaze right now.'

Bidisha batted her eyelids and looked away. 'Pardon me, Yuvaraja. I didn't mean to.'

The reins slipped from her sweating hands and she moistened her dry lips as her stomach fluttered. He had seen her fight the bear, an episode that had taken place more than two summers ago. Instantly, Bidisha started recalling the day. She had cried in pain lying under the beast and then she had woken up at her home. Ever since she had wondered who had rescued her. When she hadn't been able to find an answer, she had given up and eventually forgotten about it.

'Oh! You didn't. I wasn't complaining. Rather, it was pleasing to be under your gaze,' Trinabh said, his voice mellow and his eyes still set on her. 'That day, I was close enough to offer you any help that you could use. But Rani Maa wanted to see it all to the end.'

'Rani... Rani Maa?'

'Yes. She likes to be part of the hunting games at times. And she was with me that fateful day when we witnessed your true mettle.'

Bidisha felt uneasy and was grappled by an unknown fear as she heard Yuvaraja Trinabh recount the events of that day.

'Shouldn't we keep pace with the others, Yuvaraja?' Bidisha said, her breath shallow and beads of sweat trickling down her forehead.

'Why? Don't you like my company? Women in Bishnupur feel honoured to speak with me. But you are trying to run away from me. Anyway, we are not done talking yet. You better get off the horse.'

Bidisha was trapped and tense as her head ached in panic. She couldn't tell how long he had been following her or sneaking into their house, eavesdropping on her conversations with her mother.

Bidisha's voice grew shrill. 'But Yuvaraja, it's da...dark already. The moon is getting clearer. Shouldn't we be in groups in jungles like this?'

'Aren't you a huntress? What do you have to fear? Or, is it that you want to go against me for no reason?'

Bidisha got off the horseback and squealed when she landed on the ground. She didn't want to make it obvious by holding her arm. But the pain was making it difficult for her in every way possible. However, her weakness could turn into her enemy's strength and she couldn't let that happen.

'Maybe we can walk the horses. That will give us some time to talk as well as cover some distance at the least,' Bidisha suggested.

'You better tie your horse now. And then let me tell you a story.'

'Yuvaraja? Here, in the middle of nowhere?'

'Your tall gait, your moves, strength and the fierce posture with which you held on to the bear... It was all too robust. Your hair was all tied up and tucked inside your turban. I remember, the patch on your face, the dirty brown mask, just like the dirty clothes that you are wearing right now,' the Yuvaraja narrated, his eyes hovering over her. 'And your clothes on that day were more manly than what you're wearing now. They didn't give up either. Nothing about you even once hinted that you might be a girl when I saw you from far.'

Bidisha's eyes glanced around as she blinked excessively to fend off the fear from showing in her eyes. She wriggled her hands as she paced.

'You seem too shocked to speak. I know you have a lot of questions. So let me help you here. I will answer them without you taking the trouble to question me.'

Bidisha looked at him as she stopped fidgeting. An errant strand of his hair behaved just like him—unpredictably. The cool breeze brought murk before her eyes, rustles in her ears, and the dampness and fragrance of the wood hit her nostrils together. She took a deep breath trying to calm her nerves.

'That day, I couldn't believe what my eyes witnessed. When I walked closer to check if the man was dead, to my astonishment, I realized it was a woman lying under the huge bear. You were unconscious, bearing the weight of half its body. Only. Luckily. That black bear was easily 5 times heavier than you.'

'Was it... Was it you who...'

'Save it. I am coming to that question. Yes, it was I who lifted you from that misery. And I mean it literally. You're heavier than you look. Even for a man of my size to carry.'

'Stop sitting on the fence and come to the point.' Bidisha turned away from him, pressing her temples no longer concerned about her tone towards the Yuvaraja.

'To answer your question, yes. It was I who treated your wound. And it was I who took the pain to help you out of your torn and blood-stained dress when you were unconscious.' Trinabh stepped towards her. 'Let me guess, you are burning with rage right now. Or, could it be that you are blushing with embarrassment?'

Bidisha felt the warmth of his breath on her shoulder. Her cheeks turned warm. She could just run away. And save herself and not face him. Or better, use her sword and finish it off once for all. Her mind was giving her hints one after the other but she couldn't decide on one or even turn back to face the man behind her. But then it was not her fault. None of it was. He had been in the wrong. It was him who had hurt her mother.

However, lost in thought, she had turned before she was fully aware of what she was doing. 'Save your worthless...' Her face met his chest. She held her breath. Bidisha stood, petrified, and only a thin stick's distance away from him. She gasped for air as she stepped back. Beads of sweat trickled down into her cleavage and more followed from her temple.

'I can give you more details if you are interested.'

'Save it, Yuvaraja,' Bidisha said as she walked further away from him.

'I also know where else the bear attacked you. There are marks on your chest.'

Bidisha shuddered. 'Shall we go now, Yuvaraja?'

Bidisha turned around and took a step away from him but the sudden whistle of his sword made it to her ears just before the blade met her waist as he blocked her way.

'I was told you were hurt on your chest too,' the Yuvaraja corrected himself as he stepped towards her.

Bidisha turned as she heard those words and looked him in his eyes.

'It was Rani Maa's maid servants who changed your clothes. How could I disrespect a woman in her unconscious state? Rani Maa wouldn't let me carry you in that state.'

'You are a scary person. How can you try to sneak into other people's lives?'

'I know. It scares me too. And Rani Maa even more. Because there are eyes and ears everywhere around us. But the irony is that you're doing the same with Prabir, aren't you? Do you think you're any different?'

Her heart ached. Wasn't he telling the truth? But before she could collect her thoughts and reply, Trinabh spoke again. 'Do you think the attack on Rani Maa's chariot the other day was just a coincidence? And do you believe that Rani Maa would let just anybody work for her?'

'What do you mean?' Bidisha asked, her nerves ticking.

Bidisha had been rejoicing over her small victory ever since she had managed to get into the palace and stay close to her enemies. But her beliefs had turned upside down in no time. She was being watched over and she had been tricked. Bidisha was not the smartest one after all. The minds of the people she would fight in the future were capable of more than she had thought.

'We wouldn't sacrifice our people without a purpose. Not just to test the abilities of a person. You're more important to us than you think, dear Bidisha,' Trinabh said, walking around her on his horse as she stood in the middle of nowhere, his eyes devouring her. 'I have been watching you since then, as per Rani Maa's orders. And for some reason, you have been waiting to get inside the palace. I am curious about why.'

Bidisha broke into a sweat and the ache in her arm was taken over by an ache in her stomach.

'*What else does he know about me? And about my plans?*'

'Did I manage to touch a dark side of your plan? Other than you trying to make a living as you claimed?' Trinabh said, almost in her ears, leaning over her even as he sat on the horse.

Goose pimples erupted all over her body and she went cold. Bidisha cleared her throat before speaking. 'Wha... What are you trying to tell, Yuvaraja? I... I... I don't understand.'

'Relax. My mother doesn't need to know everything. So, you're safe as of now. But remember, I am still watching you. And as long as I don't see any threat from your affairs, your secrets are safe with me,' Trinabh said in an assuring tone, slowly riding ahead of her, picking up pace again. 'And as far as your question about fighting you, it was nothing. Just an indulgence. You have a long way to go if you want to match me in sword fighting.'

Yuvaraja Trinabh was an arrogant and dangerous thug who wouldn't back when it came to making a sport out of someone. However, he had been different when he duelled with her. Not too tough. Bidisha was astonished by the mastery of his skills. He was easily the most difficult swordsman she had encountered. However, she had sensed, as she had countered his moves, that he was holding himself back and wasn't giving his full. If he hadn't decided to give up, she couldn't tell for sure what her fate would be like.

And then what he had told her about their first encounter she didn't know, she felt...something...for him. But she couldn't let that happen. No. Bidisha couldn't do that. Her heart could not feel anything except anger and hatred for him.

CHAPTER FIVE

On a warm summer, in the forest with campfires lit all around and with an aching arm that was ready to put her in misery at a crucial time, Bidisha sat on a thin bed made of cotton, that only royals had access to, on the ground, quivering under the blanket as the chuckles and murmurs of the whites and royals made it to her ears.

Even though the trees were now sparse in number, most of them chopped to make space for the tents, Bidisha couldn't feel at ease. She had lived in a jungle since her childhood. But not with apes that drank wine and *madira*, laughing vociferously.

'Ah!' Bidisha sighed in pain as she pressed the warm sandbag against her swollen arm to alleviate her discomfort.

A cold-water bath would help her bring down the fever so that she could gain back the strength to execute her plan. But that had to wait until dawn, until the men slipped into a deep slumber. It was past midnight already but the chaos outside the tent said otherwise.

The whistling wind made waves on the tent and the shadows of the roaring blaze of fire danced in fury putting up a fight against the wind. Bidisha covered herself with another blanket as she trembled in chills. The wet piece of cloth on her forehead was not helping much. No matter how tolerant she was to the pains and the aches, the fever had always told her otherwise whenever she had her warrior wounds. But it would all pass in a day, just like it always did.

With just a handful of maidservants to take care of the chores, there was none she could ask for any help. Bidisha took a few tardy steps and peeped outside her tent in the hope to ask someone who could bring her something hot to drink. She pulled the blanket snuggly around her as her eyes searched for a free hand.

The fiery campfire beckoned her promising to offer the warmth she needed. However, all her enemies, the royals and the *goras* had claimed it already. Most of the other sources of heat, the hot coal and the cooking fire, in the breezy night were taken by the soldiers and other servants who took refuge away from the nobles whenever their work permitted.

If only she could light up something inside the small tent but she couldn't be so foolish. Bidisha rubbed her palms, still looking for a helping hand. Prabir and Sir Oliver were busy in their discussion away from the campfire. Her eyes caught a glimpse of the man who stood like a stone next to Yuvaraja Prabir like always, Debesh. He was looking straight at her and didn't bother to take his eyes off of her even when she gave him a long and stern look. Bidisha rolled her eyes and sighed. She was growing restless by the second. The sound of the liquor sloshing, the whispers and the constant chuckles were making her more agitated.

Yuvaraja Trinabh had settled on a sturdy block of wood, just like many others, with a *hookah* in his hand. He had put his legs up on a rock and was holding a glass of *sharab* in one hand. The maidservants poured him wine, the one the English had brought from their country, with a shiny brass *aftaba* that irritated her already burning eyes. The red coats were immersed in colluding their next coup she guessed. They were hushing each other and whispering in Trinabh's ears, who pretended to show interest.

Bidisha smirked to herself before moving back inside the tent. 'You'll all have it from me someday,' she muttered walking back to her thin bedding, spread on the rough carpet.

'Who? And what?'

A familiar voice startled her. Bidisha pressed her lips together over her stupidity. She pulled over the blanket and turned around slowly using some energy from her depleting reserve. Debesh stood in front of her in a wide stance and his arms crossed. His blank face greeted her as she looked at him with intent. Even after months, he was one person she could not accurately read. Neither his eyes nor his face gave away his thoughts. Not one bit. She couldn't tell how much he heard or what he made of her foolish words.

'It's nothing.'

'And you want me to believe it?'

'Can you spare me a fight just this once?' Bidisha said with effort as she walked closer to where he stood.

Just then, a maid barged inside the tent with a hot clay pot in her hand almost walking into Debesh, who stood right at the entrance.

'Here, take this. Our share of the *khichodi*. You go ahead and have some before it gets cold and then take rest. Save some for me. I am going to be late,' the maid said, carefully handing over the pot to Bidisha before she rushed outside.

The cloth on the pot slipped a little as Bidisha held the pot in haste dropping down the thick blanket she held dearly at that moment. Debesh was quick to catch the pot with his bare hands.

Bidisha picked it up at once and immediately held it with the cloth and placed it on the ground.

'Why are you all cooped up inside, under a blanket?' Debesh asked pulling his hands back, looking unaffected as she managed to hold it firmly by then.

'It's hot. Did it burn your palm?'

'Nothing that you need to worry about.'

A gush of wind blew inside the tent. Bidisha slumped down on the ground covering herself with her hands. The severe chills made her insides shake and her teeth chattered.

'Are you sick?' Debesh asked.

Bidisha shivered as her teeth clattered. The stone of a man finally moved and touched her forehead.

'You're burning,' Debesh remarked, adjusting the blanket on her.

He lifted her in his arms and tucked her carefully in her bed. Bidisha was in no condition to stop him. Instead, she was thankful that there was someone around who could attend to her weak body.

Debesh looked around, pulled another blanket from the other bed and covered her. He placed his sword on a small wooden block that served as a table. His hands moved quickly towards the bowl of water and cloth near her. Debesh tore the cloth and dipped it in the water before putting it on her forehead and used another one to wipe her face and neck.

'Is it because of the fall you took in the stable?' Debesh asked, his face as expressionless as it always was. 'Look now what you have done. There's no one here who can help you in this condition. You should have been honest when Yuvaraja Prabir checked on you in the morning. Where does it hurt exactly?' Debesh closed his eyes and a thoughtful frown appeared on his forehead. 'Your hand, I think. Right hand, isn't it?'

Bidisha continued to shiver uncontrollably under the blankets. Debesh took her hand out of the blanket and checked it with care as he felt her arm under the sleeves. 'Here, your arm is swollen like plump papaya. Don't you understand what this means? Are you a fool to travel in such a condition? I can't believe you rode on a bloody horse all day hiding your pain and fever.'

Bidisha was clueless about how she was supposed to react. This was the closest any man had come to her in several years with her approval. She was a nervous wreck. His touch on her swollen and tender arm made her moan in pain. However, it also gave her an unknown pleasure to be touched by someone with care in her mother's absence. She needed some warmth and a few comforting words at that moment. But that would be expecting too much from the stone-faced man sitting next to her.

Debesh rushed outside and then came back again in no time. He changed the damp cloth on her forehead. 'Nothing much can be done right now. You need to bear it. I have asked one of the maids to help you with a cold water bath once the chills reduce. That should help bring down the fever.'

'What's going on Debesh? Whose tent is this? I saw you going in and out in haste,' Yuvaraja Prabir questioned, his tone meek, as he peeped in from behind Debesh.

Debesh, the moron, explained the situation to the Yuvaraja and held Bidisha responsible for her condition. He had probably forgotten who had instigated the horse to throw her off its back. Yuvaraja Prabir didn't speak a word and walked out. It was late night and people outside the tent had mostly dispersed to rest.

Soon, two maidservants walked in. One held a bowl with a hot and spicy herbal concoction. The other, young and charming, rushed towards Debesh, a smile lighting her face. 'If you can leave us for a while, we will take care of Bidisha. Yuvaraja Prabir has ordered us to sponge her so that the fever breaks at the earliest,' she told him bringing her hand to her lips, her eyes running all over his body.

Debesh rolled his eyes and walked out.

Bidisha's chills had lessened but she still felt the need to stay under the blanket. The cold breeze of the calm night was not helping. Her senses had grown extra sensitive as her ears constantly buzzed with the sounds of fire crackles, chirping crickets and rustling bushes. The spicy aroma from the glass tingled her nostril, suddenly giving her goosebumps.

'You should have stayed back in the palace if you were so sick. What makes you think we would enjoy hopeless chores in the middle of the night after a day-long journey?' the maid murmured as she attended to Bidisha.

'Ah!' Bidisha groaned, pulling back her hand as the maid touched her swollen arm.

'What is it? I was only trying to help you,' the maid said, supporting Bidisha as she sat up.

'Here, have some *kaada*. This will help break the fever,' offered another maid handing her an earthen glass and a cloth underneath to hold it.

Bidisha felt good instantly as the warmth of the cloth wrapped on the hot glass transferred to her cold palms. The steam rose to her nostrils, soothing her for a moment.

She had just enough of that bitter, throat burning concoction when she wanted to slump back in her bed. But the maids insisted she undress and let them sponge her. It brought her comfort. Though the maids did it out of obligation towards Prabir, she was thankful to them. They had done it repeatedly taking turns while compromising on their resting hours.

Dawn was setting in and the maids had magically disappeared when Bidisha woke up feeling better. Their bedding was neatly stacked in a corner of the small tent that housed four of them including Bidisha. She looked at her arm as she sat up, covering her bare breasts with the blanket. Her servant friends were too busy to help her back into clothes and she had dozed off after an eventful day's burnout.

The purple blotches were spread out on her pale white skin and a nasty big green patch right in the centre made her swollen arm look even bigger.

Bidisha sighed, letting the blanket slide off her chest and sat upright. She gathered all her hair and tied them up and secured it with a wooden stick. Just when her hands reached the cloth in the bowl of water, she heard footsteps closing in on. She pulled the blanket to cover herself and held it onto her chest.

Her heart raced and a bead of sweat slowly made it down from her neck onto her chest. She turned around exposing her bare back to the visitor. Bidisha had not felt so vulnerable before. She clenched onto the blanket and swallowed dry as her eyes fell on Trinabh. Her heart thudded as the footsteps closed in on.

She took an awkward turn trying to reach the clothes behind her, hoping to shield herself from the embarrassment.

'Ah! Hmmm...'

Trinabh was not someone who would walk away and spare the pride of a young girl. The very thought petrified her.

'Ahem ahem...' Yuvaraja Trinabh cleared his throat. 'You need not shy away from asking for help. I am not exactly the brute everybody thinks I am. Look, I have the strength to take my eyes off a beautiful body like yours. I can even resist the temptation to touch an exposed woman's back right before me. I can prove that.'

Bidisha removed the wooden stick and her hair unfurled down covering her back down until her hips. She grabbed the blanket and struggled to pull it over. But Trinabh held her hand, stopping her abruptly.

He moved her hair and felt the scar that ran down to her hip. 'I am glad I know the tale behind this scar. And more than anything, I am fortunate to see this beauty with my own eyes...' Trinabh said moving his fingers onto her bruised arm.

Bidisha quivered at his touch on her bare skin. But she was more surprised at his words. She had never thought anybody, a man, in particular, would be capable of praising a scar on a woman's body. Least of all, a beast of a man who couldn't even possibly appreciate the beauty in its purest foam let alone an ugly scar.

Trinabh picked up her clothes and veiled her as she tried to bury her face bringing her knees closer to her chest. She cursed him in her mind for his audacity to barge in, without notice. However, there was a reason Bidisha was tolerating this man who was growing on her nerves.

'You have a very important role to play in our plan. And Rani Maa has a special place for you in her mind. I have been asked to take extra care of you. But look at you. How can you be sick on an important day like this? You were supposed to be out there in the jungle rubbing shoulders with my fragile brother. This was a one-of-a-kind opportunity to gain his trust and get close to him. Instead, as soon as I woke up, I get to hear that you had a fever all night.' Trinabh made himself comfortable right next to her.

Bidisha went cold. She gathered the blanket tighter. 'Yuvaraja, can we talk outside in a while about this once I am appropriately dressed?' Bidisha asked, looking away from him.

'I am not here on this bloody hunting game for no reason. Everyone knows how much I hate entertaining Prabir's requests, who likes to lick the boots of those good for nothing red coats. But this time it's different...' Trinabh aggressively bent towards Bidisha trying to look at her face. 'I am not sure how you are going to make up for this, but let me make it very clear. I need another plan soon. We are not here in this jungle forever. You better take care of things that are slipping away from your hands.'

Bidisha moved her face farther away trying to avoid any eye contact. 'I assure you, Yuvaraja, I will take care of it.'

'What plan does he want me to make? To seduce a man? How dare the mother and son think I will even do it?'

However, all that she wished for at that time was for him to get lost. She couldn't stay half-naked before him any longer.

'Talking about the other aspect of our friendship, you don't have to worry about Rani Maa's warnings to stay away from me. She tells that to every girl she finds appealing in the palace. We can always hatch a plan and enjoy each other's company in secret. Nobody has to know. Think about it,' Trinabh said as a smirk lurked on his face.

Bidisha clenched her teeth in disgust and looked into his eyes. If only she had a sword in her hand or at least was clothed enough to give him an answer befitting his vulgar proposition.

'This attitude is much better. I have not seen many women stand before me with fire in their eyes. But you're different. Shy and submissive doesn't suit you...' Trinabh winked at her before he walked out.

Bidisha grabbed her clothes the moment he left. She was confused at his behaviour.

He said her scar was beautiful. He had saved her that day when she was stuck under the bear's body after killing it. He even abstained from disgracing her when she was unconscious going against his reputation as a man of loose character.

'How can he be a devil one moment and a gallant the other?'

But he was right, though not for the reasons in his head. She had to think about another way, yes, but to make up for the lost opportunity to kill Sir Oliver. She had to execute her plan at night and go for the kill to set things in motion for her future goals.

'Sir Oliver Watts, be ready to embrace your fate tonight...' Bidisha announced to the walls of her empty tent as she slipped into a long *kurta*.

A day's rest had replenished Bidisha's energy. The fever couldn't meddle in her path anymore and sabotage her plan. The hunting party had returned with their bounty from the first day of their hunt. Some were celebrating their kill while others were tending to their wounds and cuts.

Debesh was busy with Yuvaraja Prabir's black mare, Bhrithi, while Bidisha was lending a hand to serve the supper on time. The woollen shawl that she had put on was of little help as the night went by and it became colder. The dew in the forest was setting in thicker, making it difficult for her to bear the chill without a fire. While everybody else kept themselves away from the heat on the hot summer night, she could use the campfire but if only she was not tied up with the chores.

The maidservants and the royal chef, who had cooked the food for the night, did all the tasing and declared it was safe for consumption. The live goats they had brought from the palace were now on their plates along with the meat from their hunt after it was roasted to perfection on the fire. Sir Oliver, in particular, was all praise for the taste the spices had brought out of the regular meat.

'I would rather enjoy bear-spearing or pig-sticking than hunting them down with arrows or killing them with bullets. That's no fun just to kill,' Sir Oliver boasted rolling his golden-brown moustache.

'I agree,' an Englishman added.

'But fresh meat charred in fresh spices along with a glass of wine... What more can a man ask for in this jungle after a long day?' Oliver Watts cheered as he removed his coat finally.

'Yes, that was meant for you. Don't you know that an animal is always fed good stuff just before it is sacrificed?'

Three days later, Bidisha was still looking for a chance to work her plan out. She had all but one last chance before they returned to the palace and she was getting restless.

Bidisha was the only woman to accompany the hunting party on Trinabh's insistence. It felt odd to her. But nothing he did made sense to anyone anyway. She had decided to follow his orders and go with the flow. As a fact of the matter, it was not an unknown territory for her to her waste time brooding over the idea.

Bidisha had taken her position to jump on the horse as she placed her foot in the stirrup. But to her dismay, a pair of hands held onto her waist and lifted her in the air only to mount her on Bhrithi, Yuvaraja Prabir's mare. Bhrithi neighed and suddenly became restless. Prabir stroked her neck and gently kissed her muzzle.

Bidisha took in a deep breath and held on to the reins tightly while bending forward as Bhrithi lifted her forelegs in the air.

'Alright! Finally, we get to see you with a girl, Yuvaraja Prabir. Hope now Debesh is free to choose his life companion,' Sir Oliver joked. 'Debesh, leave your master alone for once. He must be happy to ride with a girl after all these years,' Sir Oliver mounted his horse, 'Why don't you join us instead'?

'That's what the hound needs to understand, Oliver,' Trinabh remarked before turning to Bidisha. 'You're not planning on riding a horse yourself with that damaged hand of yours, are you? Go along with Prabir. This black beauty is strong enough to hold the weight of two,' Trinabh announced, patting the horse.

'But she is Bhrithi. Not any ordinary horse. She can have none other than her master on her back, Yuvaraja Trinabh,' Debesh said his eyes cast down, but his tone firm.

Trinabh gave him a mocking smile as he placed a hand on Debesh's shoulder. 'I wonder what Prabir will do without you. You always speak for your voiceless master without hesitation. But you know what, your master always nods to my words, don't you?' Trinabh said looking at Prabir.

'Yuvaraja Trinabh, I can manage on my own. Kindly let me ride the other horse,' Bidisha said attempting to unmount Bhrithi.

But Prabir held the reins blocking her passage. Even before she could react, he had control over the stirrup leaving her legs hanging loose. And in the next instant, he was on Bhrithi sitting behind her, his hands on the reins, trapping Bidisha in his embrace. Bidisha was aware of his chest brushing against her back.

It was getting harder to swallow her anger towards Trinabh but she closed her eyes and took a deep breath as she let herself calm down.

'Yuvaraja, please don't mind me. Let me get down.'

'Let's leave,' Prabir said and steered his horse who started trotting into the woods.

Bidisha couldn't stop bouncing, feeling embarrassed as her back kept hitting Yuvaraja Prabir's chest. That was something she was yet to learn, to move along with the horse. It was frustrating and she couldn't wait to get down as she thought of her companion's frail condition.

She couldn't even vent out her anger towards Yuvaraja Trinabh who was incapable of minding his own matters. He always had to interfere in her affairs and cause her unbearable pain. She was already struggling to hold in her rage towards him so that she could protect her mother and also try to accomplish what she truly needed to.

They were approaching the open land and had to pass it to reach the other end of the forest to find their hunt. Soon, Debesh joined them and rode beside Bhrithi.

'She need not ride on Bhrithi along with you, Yuvaraja. Let her join me,' Debesh said as they trotted fast.

'Debesh, let her be,' Yuvaraja Prabir said.

Bidisha didn't even bother to look at Debesh who was worried mad about his master and his childhood friend as if she would end up killing his weak friend.

They were now on the open land that was covered with grass and small bushes. Yuvaraja Trinabh sped past them. He raced Yuvaraja Prabir like a mad man. Yuvaraja Prabir, on the other hand, took his time. But when he pulled the reins, his Bhrithi didn't hold back. They were piercing through the air and the horse flew them to their destination as her steady hooves made a rhythmic sound.

For Bidisha, it was far from a smooth ride, for she continued to bounce up and down vigorously as the horse galloped. But the ride had cast a new light on her impression of Yuvaraja Prabir who was not the man he appeared to be. Though he looked meek, he was much stronger than she had believed. Her back kept ramming into his chest from the impact of the ride, but he never once showed his discomfort.

Prabir looked skinny from afar but she could comfortably fit between his arms. And despite her tall frame, he could see the view before them without once asking her to adjust for a better vision. Yuvaraja Prabir could manage to hold her between his arms for that long and didn't seem to be bothered at all. At times she was all over the place, going up and down, losing her balance as Bhrithi galloped. Moreover, her hair gave in to the wind and swayed in his face obstructing his free ride, adding to his difficult situation. This was the closest she had ever gotten to him and he was clearly broader, taller and much more vigilant than what she had known.

Her bruised arm smarted as his arm came in contact over and over again. She clenched her jaw and swallowed the pain along with her pride. The Yuvaraja's silk attire with heavy embroidery made it worse and her hair was tangled in his ornaments. He was dressed for a walk on the palace grounds than for the hunt. If only he had taken a cue from the others.

CHAPTER SIX

Yuvaraja Trinabh had rushed it all. They were just back to the camp after an exhausting day and he wanted to head back to the palace the next day. There was disruption as men tended to their wounds, some indulged in drinking, and others gathered the essentials for the day's journey that was to follow.

Yuvaraja Prabir and Sir Oliver Watts were glued to each other, like they were every night. Bidisha couldn't gather much information on anything that was happening around them amidst the chaos. She wondered if she could hold on to Rani Maa's trust for long. There was hardly anything of value she could share with the queen that could benefit her. She had lurked enough, attending to their needs and serving them. But she couldn't risk overdoing it.

It was no secret that she was appointed to look after Yuvaraja Prabir by the queen herself. She had commanded her right before him after all. There was no way he would take a chance when Bidisha was around. Even for a person as humble as him, he would definitely watch his mouth and gauge his actions when she was around.

She failed to understand Rani Maa's intentions behind taking chance and doing it openly right in front of the Yuvaraja. The queen could have done it in secret and asked Bidisha to get her way in without raising suspicion.

On the other hand, Debesh gave Bidisha a tough time trying to protect his master. Riding on Bhrithi along with Yuvaraja Prabir had made things much worse between them. After all, the horse was his master's beloved. Yuvaraja cared for Bhrithi like his child and he had a special place for her in his heart.

Everything around Bidisha was straining her. Moreover, it was also the last night they would spend in the camp. If she wanted to see her mother free then she had to take charge of the situation and do the one thing she had come to the forest to accomplish—kill Oliver Watts. And tonight would be her only chance.

It was dark and Bidisha was out of energy, like everyone else, after the day-long hunt. But the stiffness in her arm irked her more. However, she had decided to take one last chance and see her plan through in the night.

Yuvaraja Trinabh, on the other hand, appeared to be worrying more about the women. He couldn't peacefully wait for another day for the troop to recover. Meanwhile, he had the biggest kill among all; a Bengal tiger was the target of his arrow. In addition, he had killed gaurs, deer and a few birds. He had more than he could show off and return to the palace with glory.

Sir Oliver was getting mad since he could kill only a deer, two boars and a rabbit, which everybody laughed about.

On the other hand, Yuvaraja Prabir had hovered more around Bidisha in the wilderness rather than getting deeper into the forest to find his hunt. All he had managed to take down was a boar that was first injured by Debesh's arrow. However, it neither mattered to him nor did anyone else expect much from him.

Bidisha was disheartened. After all, hunting was her forte. Without any regard for her wish, Trinabh had refrained her from exhibiting her skills, especially in the presence of Prabir and Debesh. He wanted her to be as secretive as possible. 'Your skills can be displayed when they are required. Until then, you better heed my words,' he had instructed. Yuvaraja Trinabh even threatened her in the name of the queen. Not that Bidisha was frightened but she had to stay calm and lay low until her time came. She couldn't risk her mission. Whatever their goal was, however, she had to look out for her advantage.

'Tonight, is the night,' Bidisha said to herself resting in the tent along with other maidservants, her heart pounding and hands sweating as she stared at the roof.

She had worked out a plan for herself. Just like everyone else, she would be questioned too once Oliver's death comes to light and the slightest doubt could endanger her life.

The bathing water was ready. She would quickly scrub her hands and body for any blood stains that would give her away. She had managed to dig a small pit to bury her blood-stained clothes and dagger. She would then burn them at the right opportunity. She had killed men and animals, many of them before but never fretted like this before. And she had always attacked them bravely looking into their eyes. But too much was at stake to be doing a flagrant violation of the law and kill an Englishman out in open.

Bidisha had to prove her innocence, like everybody else, after the final drama was over and come out clean.

'You can't be caught. You have more people to hunt before you sacrifice yourself,' Bidisha told herself before peeping out of her tent to check on the sentries stationed outside Sir Oliver's tent.

They looked exhausted and were almost asleep. Their energy, most likely, was spent in digesting the fatty meat they had for dinner.

Her breathing went erratic as the thought of getting caught crossed her mind. She couldn't let anything of that sort happen. Her mother's safety depended on her action.

The campfire was still burning wildly as the wind got strong. The sputtering of the furious flames could be heard at a distance in the quiet of the night. She took light steps towards Oliver's tent stepping away from the skate that supported the tent and the twigs that could snap under her feet. And yet, the gravel crunched as she went behind Oliver's tent. She hid in the dark. There was the hooting of the owl and the fluttering of the bats that scared her.

Bidisha stood behind Sir Oliver's tent holding a dagger in her hand covering her head and face with the black dupatta like a yashmak. She walked past the sentries and made it inside the tent. She let her eyes adjust to the darkness and then she spotted Oliver who was in blissful sleep.

The rage inside her was burning wilder than the fire that was furiously dancing outside the tent. Killing a man in his sleep was a sin she would have to live with. But she would, if that meant doing something for her mother.

'In one breath. Go.'

Bidisha took a deep breath and held it in so that the warmth wouldn't wake up Sir Oliver while she was in action. She brought her hand closer to Oliver's face to hold his mouth and nose together and brought the dagger to his neck with her other hand.

'At a time. Do it.'

Just then, she heard footsteps in the bushes nearby and in an instant, there were cries outside. Oliver opened his eyes before she could slice his throat. He pushed her away in panic.

'Who are you?' Oliver screamed alarming the sentries.

She cut the tent at the back and paced out. Bidisha made her way into the dark and ran into the bathing tent. Her legs trembled as she stood near the water storage, ripping her clothes. She quickly changed into a fresh pink flared kurta. Nobody would find the woman in black anymore. She hurried and hid her black dress behind the big wooden bucket. There was no need for her to bath anyway. There was no blood. She splashed some water on her face and moistened her hair a little. Bidisha looked around in panic, wringing her hands.

She cursed herself for not being quick enough. Sir Oliver had seen the dagger over his neck but she wondered if he noticed in the dark that a woman had held the weapon. However, she couldn't afford to be under his suspicion. Sir Oliver would bring it up soon after the ruckus subsided. Bidisha had no idea about the commotion that had sparked in the camp. Nevertheless, she had to act like she got out in haste after hearing the noise. It would all work out fine and she just had to go with the flow.

The moment she was ready to run outside, a boar made its way inside the tent running right into her. Debesh followed it in and then came Yuvaraja Prabir. Bidisha's face went pale looking at the two men who glared at her for a long moment even while the boar created a ruckus.

The women outside the tent were still yelping and running around.

Debesh chased the boar that went wild not knowing the way out and ran into the cane basket scattering the clothes all over the place. And then it barrelled over them soiling them. Debesh was after the boar but didn't seem to be focused as he tried to shoot an arrow at it and for the first time, he missed his shot. It bolted and entangled in Bidisha's veil that was on the ground.

She looked around and picked up the dagger that was kept near the water storage tub. The boar ran towards her and Debesh ran after it. She stepped back to dodge it and held the dagger to go for a stab. The huge animal pounced over her but her dagger sliced through the boar. The animal grunted in pain. But to her stark shock, she had slipped and fallen straight into the tub full of cold water. And the boar had landed over her.

The water splashed out. Bidisha bore the impact of the fall on her back and the thwacking of the beast on her body. The enormous weight had sent her to the bottom of the huge water storage tub. Bidisha felt like she'd be killed anytime now. Though the tub wasn't too deep, the weight of the boar made it impossible for her to move. The dagger was still stuck in the boar's chest and she had not let it go either. She twisted it to stop the beast from moving. In no time, the water turned bloody red. Bidisha finally got a chance to hunt but not quite what she had hoped for. Rather, the animal had ruined every part of her plan.

She let out a choking gasp under the water as the weight of the boar crushed her. Debesh and Prabir attempted to get the animal off of her. Finally, Debesh managed to lift it just enough for her to feel light under the water but she still struggled to rise above the water. She was losing it, all ready to give up and opened her mouth to take it all in before letting go of everything.

But the next instant, she was out of the water as she opened her eyes gasping for air. He held her by her shoulder and lifted her enough to bring her head to the surface. She coughed and panted, struggling to breathe.

The soldiers rushed in but by then Debesh had lifted the creature off of Bidisha. And to her shock, it was Trinabh who had helped her out not Prabir. He held her, helped her sit upright in the tub. She gasped and then sucked in all the air she could. Bidisha scrunched her face and struggled to sit.

'Hmmm...ah!' Bidisha moaned holding her stomach, 'my...my...stomach hurts.'

'Debesh, help her!' Yuvaraja Prabir instructed, looking away from her before he walked out.

'Debesh, leave her. Why don't you go after your master? And take those soldiers along with you,' Trinabh said helping Bidisha gain her balance as she swayed in his hands.

Debesh looked at Yuvaraja Trinabh and then at her lying in the pool of blood, giving her a concerned look, something she had seen on his chivalrous face for the first time. He kicked the dead boar in its head kicking it to the muddy ground in the bathing tent.

Yuvaraja Trinabh held her firmly and lifted her out of the bloody water. Bidisha groaned softly in pain as she snuggly held on to him, her hands wrapped around his neck, closing her eyes. He walked a few steps before stopping at the entrance of the bath tent.

'I see that you're feeling better now. Let me ask you a question.'

'Hmmm...' Bidisha mumbled.

'Did you see a strange reaction from Prabir or Debesh when they saw you?' Trinabh looked straight as he took slow small steps.

Bidisha batted her eyes, struggling to keep them open. 'What? Hmmm...'

'Do you want to know a secret?'

Bidisha stared at him. His words didn't make any sense. Not at a time when she was in pain.

'I think you were in shock when the boar had bolted into the tent that you didn't even tie the strings of your *Panjabi*,' Trinabh said still not looking at her.

Bidisha's heart skipped a beat. She pulled her clothing together, looking away from him. Trinabh walked out, towards the maidens' tent. Her heart was beating in her ears and the pain had lost its strength in front of what she had just heard. She had not tied the strings of her dress together over her bosom.

Everything had happened so suddenly that she couldn't even ponder over yet another failed attempt to kill the bastard. Yuvaraja Prabir and Debesh were stunned to see her but she hadn't realized it at that moment when the two men stood before her. And she had forgotten to even hide the dagger.

She squeezed her eyes in nervousness and disappointment.

Bidisha suddenly let out a gasp. 'My dagger!'

'Dagger!' Trinabh looked at her and then looked way again. 'What dagger?'

'Oh...nothing.'

But it was too late and the words were already out of her mouth. All she could hope was that he would not find the dagger and no one would ever connect the missing pieces. She tightened her grip around his neck thinking about the mishap, the dagger and her black clothes behind the wooden bucket.

Yuvaraja Trinabh adjusted her in his arms. His heart thudded against her ears and she felt the warmth of his body against her cold self. He held his head high up and walked straight.

Water dripped from her dress and soaked Trinabh's clothes. She needed to be cleaned urgently, maybe take a bath again! But her condition said otherwise. He placed her carefully on the bed as she moaned in pain while holding her dress together firmly on her chest.

'Clean her and change her clothes first. It's the blood of that beast. Her wound might get infected. Treat the cut on her stomach. It doesn't look deep but I don't want any negligence,' Trinabh instructed the maidens firmly, his voice deep.

The sudden thrust of the animal on her stomach had left it sore and the boar's tusks had cut her skin. Bidisha was lucky to have survived it all without much injury.

'How is it that only you manage to get caught up in the same position with all those ferocious animals over you? First the bear and now the boar!'

CHAPTER SEVEN

'Alright! Now that you all are here, after chasing that stupid swine to its death, let's talk about what happened with me tonight. I must accept, the animal was my saviour. If not for the boar, I would be in my coffin right now,' Sir Oliver Watts derided as he paced up and down in the dark of the night.

'What went wrong, Sir Oliver? We were all startled by the ruckus in the middle of the night. I apologize for the mishap the boar caused. But why do you say it saved your life?' Yuvaraja Prabir said apologetically standing up, a frown pleating his dark eyebrows.

'Why are you sorry? My prince, do you think I would make a hill out of a mole if it was just a hospitality issue? I was attacked by someone. Do you hear me? Somebody tried to slit my throat. Tried to kill me!' Sir Oliver shouted, coming to stand close to Yuvaraja Prabir, looking into his eyes.

'Pardon us, Sir. This...this is unbelievable. How could anybody attack you? What reason could they have? You are an honest man who has always been generous to us. I don't see any possibility that you could have enemies. And that too so close, here, today?' Yuvaraja Prabir uttered endlessly worrying as he sat down on a wooden bark, his face hung in shame.

An attack on an officer was not a small crime. It would come with consequences. If things got out of hand and Sir Oliver decided to escalate the issue, it could turn out to be ugly for everyone. He had the security that was accorded to the higher British authorities and everyone knew such an act on his life was like a threat to the king himself. His Majesty would have to give in to the unreasonable demands of the British for such a crime—like pay for it with gold or end up signing more treaties of understanding unwillingly.

Above all, Sir Oliver Watts was an important man who had earned business and contributed towards the prosperity of England. He had always boasted about his achievements, especially an appreciation letter from Queen Victoria's office. It had praised his family's contribution towards the growth of England's industrialization and cotton mills expansion. He was one of the biggest cotton merchants in England who provided the raw material for factories to make cheap machine cloth.

Bidisha was attentive to their conversation even from her tent, from her bed where she was resting with wounds and pain. She frowned on hearing Sir Oliver's words.

'Yuvaraja Trinabh, you are the only person capable of finding the culprit. I can't even think of sleeping well at night with a threat to my life. My money is for nothing if it can't buy me peace.'

Though Prabir tailed Oliver day and night, it was Trinabh who could get to the root of such a crime. He had his twisted ways to figure out things, unlike Prabir who would be too straightforward to solve any felony. And Debesh, he hardly had any power to question people around or meddle with the higher-ups in case of any involvement. Moreover, he wouldn't go against Prabir if it was not an order from him.

But the fact that Trinabh would be responsible for handling the investigation filled Bidisha with dread and anxiety.

'You have my word, Sir Oliver,' Yuvaraja Trinabh spoke casually, 'Give me two days and I will give you a name.'

'That's what I wanted to hear, and not just some lame words of worry. You're a man of action and here, I have to give you an important clue,' Sir Oliver said, walking towards prince Trinabh.

Bidisha went numb.

'What does he have?'

But Oliver whispered in Yuvaraja Trinabh's ears rather than announcing it and alerting the culprit.

Bidisha's heartbeat increased to a crescendo. Whispers began among men. Everyone was looking at each other in astonishment.

'This will make for an interesting case, Yuvaraja Trinabh commented, his tone calm and devoid of any surprise.

'Did you already know that?' Sir Oliver questioned.

'No. Not till you said it. But what you just said is not impossible. Let's get back now. Rest. We'll leave before sunrise,' Yuvaraja Trinabh announced as he walked inside his tent. Perhaps, to the bawd who waited inside for him.

Yuvaraja Trinabh would be one of those few in the palace, after Maharaja Mitul Singha Dev, who would be happy to see Sir Oliver dead. Signing another treaty or paying a hefty penalty wouldn't harm them much in comparison to what Sir Oliver was stealing. But he had to put up an act, sweat over finding the culprit for committing a capital crime. And Yuvaraja Trinabh was doing great at pretending.

Yuvaraja Prabir sat on a fallen tree trunk holding a glass of *madira* in his hand and wearing a frown on his forehead, staring into the fire, not adding a word to the conversation happening between Trinabh and Sir Oliver. Debesh stood behind him on guard, his face flat and his stance ready to protect his master.

The vivid shades of the fire brought out different colours on each of their faces as they sat around the campfire after what had happened. Nobody had a clue who attacked Sir Oliver. Was it someone from the troop? Or, was anyone else out there who wanted to kill him? The murmurs got louder as the maidens walked towards Bidisha's tent. But she pretended to have fallen asleep.

The boar had not only taken away her golden chance to end Sir Oliver's life but had also ruined her plan to hide the evidence. She wondered if she would get a chance to bury the dagger and her clothes before they all left the forest in the morning. More importantly, she prayed that no one got their hands on them. Bidisha tossed and turned in her bed not able to get a wink of sleep, waiting for a chance to make it to the bathing tent in the late hours.

Bidisha's eyes were moist and her heart ached at her failure. She laid on her back without a shawl or a *chaddar*, oblivious to the chill and the dew in the dense forest. Her jaw quivered but not a drop of tear rolled out. She held it all in not bringing anything to the notice of maidens who were fast asleep.

The troop had started early at the break of the dawn and headed to the palace. Trinabh had muddled in Bidisha's otherwise straightforward plan to ride the horse slow along with the carriage and rest once she reached the palace. He had blown the situation more than required and insisted that Bidisha travel in the carriage instead of riding the horse. He not only professed the consequences of straining her body with a wound on her stomach but almost forced her into the carriage.

The heartless crook, Yuvaraja Trinabh had coerced the bawd to ride on the horse and took over her transport, her carriage. It came out as a surprise not only to Bidisha but also to everyone else when he declared he would instead travel in the carriage. It was embarrassing, to say the least when everyone let out an 'oh' as they learnt Bidisha would be travelling safely in the carriage instead of riding due to the wound she had suffered. To be alone with a man like him was to put one's reputation at stake. He wouldn't leave a chance to make out with any woman who was willing to submit to him. She wondered what the journey had in store for her.

Bidisha sat behind a thick cotton *parda*, unlike a fancy velvety one she had seen on the queen's carriage. She wished it didn't conceal the driver and partitioned their space. That would make for a more comfortable ride for her.

The bushes rustled as the wheels of the carriage rolled on the uneven path. The wooden frames of the carriage hurt Bidisha's back. Though riding on a horse was not advised owing to the risk of bleeding from her freshly inflicted cut, she would have preferred that. Just like other men who were riding their horses as they wore their glorious wounds as their prize after hunting.

The rhythm of the horse cart had started acting upon her, calming her mind and soothing her nerves despite the bouncing. And her over exhausted body had started to give in. Her eyes drooped even as she felt Trinabh's eyes on her. And that didn't make her any alert. After a few failed attempts, she finally closed her eyes.

'We have a long journey ahead of us. And we will be the last ones to reach the palace at the speed of this carriage. I don't mind if you want to rest. You can sleep all you want,' Yuvaraja Trinabh said crossing his hands across his chest as he stretched his legs further straight.

Bidisha didn't feel the need to answer. If he was just a common man and not a royal, she would have seen his end already.

'You were bathing in the middle of the night when everybody else felt the need to rest. Does that make sense?' Trinabh asked, his eyes closed and arms still crisscrossed.

'Hmmm...' Bidisha straightened herself. 'That... Yuvaraja, I decided to take a bath because everyone was asleep.'

'Yeah, I get it. Privacy and all that. But couldn't you wait till we reached the palace?'

'Arr! Fever. Fever, Yuvaraja. Because of the fever and then yesterday's hunting, I felt drained. Yeah. The sweat and the stickiness... I felt terrible.'

Trinabh came closer to her and sniffed her like an animal. Bidisha's heart skipped a beat. She leaned back.

'But you don't particularly smell good. Just like all of us, you still stink.'

Bidisha looked away, pulling her dupatta as she tried to cover her neck, hoping to mask the obvious odour. Trinabh moved back to his seat in the rear end of the carriage.

'What do you think about this dagger?' Trinabh asked pulling it out from its sheath, from behind his back, where she guessed it was held in his waist tie.

She gasped and suddenly coughed. 'I... I... It's good. It's also beautiful.'

Bidisha could hear her heartbeat in her ears and feel the sweat forming on her forehead. She held onto her sword that was placed next to her and then she tightened her grip.

'Indeed. It's a beautiful dagger. I want to get one too. Will you get one for me?' Trinabh looked at it carefully, turning it around and feeling the sharpness of the blade.

'Me? I have no idea. I mean... It's not mine, Yuvaraja. I thought it was yours.'

'And I thought it was yours.'

'What makes you think so, Yuvaraja? I... This is the first time I am seeing it.'

'But you've used it before,' Trinabh affirmed.

'That's not possible. I would know if I did.'

'To kill the boar...' Yuvaraja Trinabh glared into her eyes forcing her to look away.

'Oh! Ahem! Arr... I...didn't realize. I must've picked it up then from the ground I think,' Bidisha replied, trying her best to hold on to her disbelieving facial expression.

'May I ask what you were wearing before bathing?'

'I was... I think I was wearing...' Bidisha looked at him, quickly changing her expression from confused to alarmed. 'Yuvaraja, why are you questioning me so much? If you have anything to ask, you can directly ask me.'

'And you think I need your permission to do so?'

'Pardon me, Yuvaraja. That's not what I meant.'

'Don't this dress and the dagger belong to you? Didn't you try to kill Sir Oliver yesterday night? Don't you dare deny it. Now, tell me why did you try to kill him.'

'Yuvaraja, what are you talking about? I swear on Goddess BipottariniDevi.'

'Do you think you can be saved with those eyes of yours? Oliver clearly remembers looking into a woman's eyes.'

Bidisha was taken aback. The knots in her stomach added to the discomfort her wound was still giving.

How? How could Oliver see my eyes so clearly in the dark of the night? Does he remember me? He has seen me with Yuvaraja Prabir before! What if he recognizes me?'

'You'll not go anywhere close to Oliver. You'll also stay away from Prabir and his hound who could go to any lengths to please Oliver. And they won't hesitate to hand you over to the English. You better get this right. I will not tolerate it if anyone dares to hold Rani Maa responsible for your reckless actions.'

'Yuvaraja, I really don't understand what are you talking about. It wasn't me,' Bidisha explained as her heart beat faster and her stomach heaved.

Trinabh moved forward and pulled her arm looking into her eyes as if he was trying to read her. 'I will make you an example and show others that I don't forget. Those who mock or betray me will have to hide until the end of time. Because I will not stop chasing them. Even if they are insignificant or trivial things, I don't make any exceptions. Not for anything or anyone. You understand.'

'Yuvaraja, you can talk all you want. And if words are not enough, you can talk to my sword.' Bidisha pulled herself out of his grip and reached for her sword. 'Let's get on with it. But I am warning you, don't you dare touch me without a reason. I will not allow that. And you have no reason to accuse me of such a thing.'

'So you say. What about yesterday? I carried you in my arms, in your damp clothes. You were snuggly hugging me. Don't you remember that?'

'I said, without any reason. And let me make it clear. Being in your arms didn't make me feel any good.'

'Now listen to me very carefully,' Yuvaraja Trinabh fumed as he widened his eyes, 'I don't respond well to threats and I don't like repeating myself. An attack on Sir Oliver means trouble for the Bishnupur throne, which will soon be mine. And I don't like it when somebody tries to muddle in my affairs. You better watch your place. And one more thing, this will be your last time talking to me in that tone. And now I want to hear your reason for attempting to kill Oliver. You can't escape with any excuses.'

Bidisha took a deep breath. She had been weak for a while and had given up to her rising temper. That could be a fatal blow to her mission. She was supposed to gain the queen's trust. Instead, she had lost Rani Maa's only son's faith. Her anger had nearly given her away. Bidisha had to come up with something. She had to mend this crack at the earliest.

Bidisha peeped inside the court from afar standing behind the silk curtains that hung loosely from the roof between the pillars. Her blood boiled as she looked at Sir Oliver who had the audacity to show his temper in the court. And the coward Maharaja sat up there in his shiny clothes on his majestic silver throne, being the supreme in the court only in name.

Bidisha's eyes scrutinized the royal *darbar* in search of that one person who had threatened her, Yuvaraja Trinabh. But he was nowhere to be seen. He was not a man she could trust. She couldn't make up her mind about him if he was helping her or planning against her. Yuvaraja Trinabh could disclose the truth and hand over the proofs, her dagger and her clothes, he had found against her. And Oliver would testify to seeing a woman holding the dagger to his throat.

Though he claimed Yuvaraja Prabir would be the one to take advantage of the situation and put his life at stake to win the credence of the English, Bidisha doubted if Yuvaraja Trinabh was any different. The revelation of the truth could be equally beneficial for him.

Her insides rumbled at the thought of how the events could turn against her.

Sir Oliver was seated in a chair close to the throne. The Maharaja's face had turned pale and there were wrinkles of worry on young Sir Oliver's forehead. His Majesty was slouched while the foreigner sat upright with authority, along with other British officials and dignitaries next to him. Since things had taken a turn, His Majesty paid extra attention to Sir Oliver. The whites would not consider an attack on their patron's life as a trivial matter.

Cutting through the tension in the *darbar*, a eunuch announced that Yuvaraja Trinabh would like to rest and wouldn't be able to attend the court. Although the king didn't look pleased with the Yuvaraja's absence, he was quick to make excuses on behalf of the Yuvaraja to save face in the *darbar*.

Bidisha's nerves calmed and she swallowed the lump in her throat even as she was taken by the surprise. Yuvaraja Trinabh wouldn't let go of a chance like this one to impress the king if not the Britishers. Moreover, he had promised Sir Oliver that he would find the felon in two days.

'What is he thinking?'

The English comrades, the ministers present in the court and all the other intellects put their best thoughts out in accusing rival kingdoms and fellow court members of their grudges. After all the arguments and the finger-pointing along with the facts provided by the spies was, it was mutually decided that the one who tried to kill Sir Oliver must be a rebel—a freedom fighter—from the Khadi Andolan group.

Bidisha wasn't surprised. As expected, they had to find someone to sacrifice. But what Bidisha couldn't do at that moment was admit her doing. Someone would be declared the culprit soon so that the king could protect his selfish interests. But the truth was that she felt ashamed of herself for being selfish just like others in the court. She too played the rules to protect her whims and motive.

She tried to convince her heart that she was doing the right thing. Her mother had suffered enough because of the *goras* and the blind king had washed his hands off by punishing an innocent. It had to stop. Mokshita Maitra deserved to be happy and be free.

Though Yuvaraja Trinabh didn't show up in the court, he had taken care of matters regarding the attack on Sir Oliver's life. A woman's dead body, similar in height and built as Bidisha, dressed in the same black clothes, was presented before Sir Oliver and His Majesty as the culprit. The dagger came in handy, which was first planted and then retrieved from her home in the presence of English soldiers. The woman and her family had suffered the same fate as many other weavers in Bishnupur. The very reason that was the motive for the murder attempt on Oliver Watts in the first place.

However, the truth was that the woman had died due to illness and her husband had fled as soon as the news about his wife's felony was proved in court. Though it was all mundane for Yuvaraja Trinabh since he had handled similar situations before on various occasions, he had planned it meticulously. Everything had worked exactly the way he had planned and with great effort. He had facts and evidence to prove his story right.

Moreover, the soldiers who carried the body were trained to carry out their duty just as perfectly as their master, Yuvaraja Trinabh. In a matter of minutes, as the argument heated up and the *Goras* tried to examine the body, they hushed up the process. As per Oliver's instructions, when one of the Englishman came closer to the body, covering his nose with a piece of cloth, to open the body's eyes, a soldier quickly did it for him and immediately closed it. And before any unforeseen occurred, the body was taken away.

Days had passed after the incident and Oliver seemed to be satisfied with Trinabh for finding the culprit in just two days as he had promised.

Trinabh was not a person who would take any chance if there was the possibility of his mother's name being connected to a crime. And since Bidisha was brought inside the palace by his mother, Bidisha was secluded. She was not allowed to move around in the palace let alone participating in anything. Everything was controlled by the queen and Bidisha was watched over day in and day out without making things obvious to Prabir and Debesh. Only she knew that she was under house arrest under the pretence that she was recovering from her infected wounds. There was something about the queen and her son who did everything possible to keep her away from Oliver and safe from every possible problem she could encounter.

The minor cut on her stomach was turned into a brave warrior's wound through gossip. She was even spared from the interrogation as her heroic story was blown out of proportion and spread like wildfire to avoid any accusations of discrimination.

She was bound by Rani Maa's keen eyes spread all over the palace. Bidisha herself had worked with a few whenever there was a need to exchange messages with Rani Maa without directly contacting her. And them being around her was an indication that they have been watching her for the queen. But Bidisha had little idea about the queen's earnest interest in her. She failed to understand the reason behind the mother and son's motivation in not only sparing her life but also protecting her thus far from any allegations.

Yuvaraja Trinabh had visited her once just before settling things with Sir Oliver. He had strictly warned her of the consequences if she failed to adhere to the queen's commands and lay low. However, Rani Durga Moni Devi herself never asked to see her in person.

This was a new lease of life for Bidisha and in a matter of days, she had learnt to live with the guilt that she was turning into the very monster she had come to kill. She was doing things to survive, staining her soul, something she never thought she would do.

CHAPTER EIGHT

Sir Oliver Watts was to leave Bishnupur in less than a week. Meanwhile, Yuvaraja Trinabh made sure Bidisha stayed away from Oliver's eyes. And he had been successful in taking advantage of the fact that he had saved her despite being caught with evidence. She didn't have a choice but to nod to all his reasonable and unreasonable demands. Though she never accepted the fact that she was indeed the person who attacked Oliver Watts, she couldn't risk instigating the Yuvaraja.

But it had all been too burdensome. She had lost a good opportunity and she was back to where she had started. Things weren't the same anymore for Bidisha. Neither was she to get another chance to win favour from the Maharaja nor was it going to be easy to please Rani Maa after what she'd done. It was a great blessing that Rani Maa had decided to turn a blind eye to her unsolicited actions that could have ruined Rani Maa's ploy. And not to mention, Bidisha's actions could lead right back to Rani Maa and Yuvaraja Trinabh.

However, Bidisha was not a woman to obey commands quietly and do as she was told. She had a mind of her own and didn't hesitate to take chances. The need to see her mother had grown deep and she had decided to sneak out to her home for a quick glimpse of her mother. Just one look at her mother would strengthen her resolve to figure out another way to deal with Oliver Watts.

She had stepped out in the calm of the wee hours and made her way through the jungle. It was dangerous to walk out in the dark, under the thick canopy of trees that blocked even the faint light of the full moon. Bidisha had never done it before in all the years she had lived in the jungle—wander in the dark outside her lonely house. The lantern in her hand shook every time she had a feeling of trampling a snake under her feet or her mind screamed a false bear growl. But she steeled her heart and threaded through the bushes. And finally, when she arrived home, she let out a sign of relief.

Bidisha helped herself with water in a big wooden tumbler. Her mother had not stopped keeping the *matka* in the exact same stop and she was thankful for that. She gulped it all, her senses woke up to the soothing sounds of the chirping birds as they flew out of their nests with the first rays of sun. She had missed it all dearly as her days passed like months bound in the palace. Her lips widened and her eyes sparkled at the break of the dawn.

But the next moment she rushed to behind the temple and hid in the cover of the temple walls. She couldn't show herself to her mother or else there was no going back to the palace. Mokshita would never let her go again. Bidisha was getting restless as she waited for her mother to step out of the temple house. She had to return to the palace before anyone found out that she wasn't there. The sun was about to rise but there was no sign of her mother who was supposed to be out cooking in the open by then. It would soon be time for Mokshita Maitra to leave for the morning market.

The sound of shuffling footsteps distracted Bidisha and just before she turned to look back, a whoosh gushed in her ears. It didn't sound like an animal. She was certain of it.

'Who—'

A hand covered her mouth, tugging her back to his chest. 'Shh! Do you want to put your mother in danger too?'

She looked up at him, the masked man. Yuvaraja Trinabh! She jerked herself free from his hold. 'What are you doing here? Can't I even visit my home? I will be back in the palace soon,' Bidisha raged in a hushed voice but a firm tone as she glared at him.

'You were instructed to stay put inside in your quarters in the palace. How dare you disobey my orders?' Trinabh scorned, his hand firm on her elbow, pinning her to the terracotta wall.

Bidisha hushed Yuvaraja Trinabh, covering his mouth in desperation. His face was right before her, separated by her hand on his mouth. His eyes narrowed and his frown disappeared. Bidisha's eyes widened.

Just then Mokshita came out of the temple, finally, as the early dawn gave way to a bright day. Bidisha peeped around the wall to get a glimpse of her mother who was all set to leave for the village. Her mother looked haggard and her face was devoid of a smile, unlike how she'd be with Bidisha around helping her every morning.

And while her eyes were fixed on her mother, her heart sinking, Bidisha's hold on Trinabh's mouth loosened. Her hand slid down his stubbled jaws as she tiptoed to get a last glimpse of her mother before she vanished into the woods.

Bidisha turned, her little finger still on his mouth and his eyes on her lips. Her other hand was still pinned on the wall under his firm grip and her heart raced at a frantic pace drumming in her ears. She pulled her hand away from his mouth as if he was a burning ball of fire. And he let her hand go in an instant. Bidisha quivered even as she leaned back on the wall and he stepped back tripping over a stone behind him.

'Let's leave before you create more problems,' Yuvaraja Trinabh said as he walked past the bushes.

Bidisha's legs swerved, her hand on her chest, her eyes fixed on her home as she followed Yuvaraja Trinabh with a heavy heart. Her tears, just like her, wouldn't listen to her and for the first time in a long time, she wanted to be back home, her home, in the jungle where her mother still lived but all alone.

The more she tried to hold herself back, the more she gave in to her tears that wouldn't stop rolling out of her eyes. And in no time, her soft sniffles turned into sobs. Nonetheless, she put her head down and caught up with Yuvaraja Trinabh's pace, who seemed to be oblivious to her. But then, he suddenly stopped and stood right before Bidisha as he turned towards her. She wiped her face with her *dupatta* rapidly blinking her eyes to cleanse off the uncontrollable grief. Her finger felt her septum ring as she always did when she missed her mother.

'After all that you have done, if you flinch now, you're dead. I hope you understand that. It's not the time to give up,' Yuvaraja Trinabh said as he adjusted the saddle and his horse neighed on his master's touch.

Bidisha was too soaked up in her thoughts to even notice the presence of the horse right behind Yuvaraja. His words had made it to her ears but sounded too heavy to put them to action. 'Hmmm...' Bidisha answered, taking shallow breaths.

'Did you even hear me?' the Yuvaraja said, pinching her cheek.

Bidisha looked up at him, her eyes red and swollen and her cheek rosy pink. She was confused by his actions that didn't go well with his harsh words. He had pinched her, softly, as if with affection, like trying to console a crying child. But he wasn't a man who was capable of showing warmth. And she wasn't a girl who was fragile enough to shed tears in front of a man, no less than her enemy.

But it had happened.

'I thought you needed a warm touch to calm you down. You looked like a girl wanting to be loved and embraced. I can even give you a hug, if you want one,' the Yuvaraja winked but his eyes gleamed with an affection she could use at that moment.

Bidisha swallowed and her finger feeling her septum ring, her eyes trying to read Trinabh. He was giving her a mixed idea about himself. He couldn't promptly mean it when he said 'a warm touch'. And he could very well play her into hugging him. That, she was sure. She had to be cautious about him. How could she trust a man like him? He was capable of many things but being kind was not one of them for sure.

'Hmmm! I have no idea...,' the Yuvaraja murmured as he looked up at the sky scratching his neck as his words faded even before she could hear it completely. 'Let's just forget that I pinched your cheek. You are not a child.'

Bidisha cringed at his words even as her cheeks warmed up. Looked like he was not even remotely clear of his own actions, just like she was not certain about him.

'But let me tell you something. If you keep touching your nose pin so often, your big nose will grow even bigger.'

She frowned at him and then fisted her hands till her knuckles turned pale even as her anger towards him turned into an embarrassment that she couldn't put into words.

Yuvaraja Trinabh stepped closer to her, the reins still in his hand, as he glared at her. 'But you dare ignore my words and take me for granted. Don't forget who you are talking to.'

Bidisha was already heartbroken and the man had made the whole thing an uncomfortable affair. And he was back to commanding her again as he did always.

'Do you still want to not say something?' the Yuvaraja took another step towards her forcing her to recede. 'I think you have forgotten what I hold against you.'

'I...' Bidisha swallowed the lump in her throat, 'Yuvaraja... I...need some time alone.'

'For what? To cry?' Trinabh asked as he walked further towards her.

Bidisha stepped back as the huge man grew on her. Suddenly, she tripped on a root that had grown huge on the ground. He let go of the reins and caught her from falling straight on the rocky ground.

'Who said you can't cry in front of me?' the Yuvaraja said, looking straight into her eyes.

Bidisha struggled to gain her footing on the ground even as the Yuvaraja continued to hold her.

'My preceptor always taught me that the brave cry and move ahead. Only the weak hold it in and give up.'

Their eyes locked for a long moment, while she was intimidated trapped in his strong arms against his hard chest. She tried to read the man before her who sometimes took her by surprise. His words, at times, questioned her beliefs about him as if he was not what she had known him to be all that while. Bidisha regained her balance, both emotional and physical, and slowly moved away from Trinabh.

'I hope you'll ruminate on what I said and come out strong.'

'What about you, Yuvaraja? Have you cried in front of anyone?'

'Many times, in presence of my guru who told me it was alright to cry and at times before Rani Maa too. And I think I've found another person to show that I am not weak,' the Yuvaraja said, his eyes fixated on her and his lips curled up as if it happened without his knowledge.

How could a man, no less the one who would rule Bishnupur in future, acknowledge that, shedding tears?'

Bidisha was getting pulled in by the smile that she had never seen before. She could use that hug he had offered her earlier and feel the warmth of a man that she hadn't felt before all her life. But how could she be so selfish and let him in her heart? He was the one who had hurt her mother. Moreover, he was a master player when it came to swindling a woman's heart. He had done it all his life.

'How much more are you willing to stretch your struggle pretending to be alright? Yuvaraja Trinabh asked as he walked the horse through the trees. 'Will you continue till you break apart?'

'How about you? Aren't you the same, Yuvaraja?' Bidisha said as she followed him in the narrow space between the trees.

'No. There's one difference. I am extremely selfish, unlike you. And I can go to any extent to save myself if I am unable to withstand it anymore. Can you do that?'

Bidisha's heart rejected his words. They were not true.

At least he would never give up on his mother for anything. Just like Bidisha who would never give up on her resolve to see her mother walk free.

The only difference was that she was going against her mother's will and struggling to help her. While Yuvaraja Trinabh walked on the path laid by his mother to fulfil her wish.

'Quiet again? You don't seem to stop otherwise. I wonder what's going on today,' Yuvaraja Trinabh remarked stroking the horse, feeling its shiny chestnut hair. 'Let us leave. Get on the horseback now.'

'Yuvaraja, you please leave, I will walk to the palace. It might not be convenient for the two of us on your horse,' Bidisha replied, her eyes lowered.

'And you only open your mouth to deny what I have to say. You better get up on the horse and leave with me right away.'

'Yuvaraja, I promise, I will head straight to the palace. You please...'

'Enough, Bidisha. It's not just the question of your safety alone. Rani Maa's life and reputation are at stake here. Should you be caught, you'll drag her down and hence, me along too. You better follow my words.'

Bidisha wiped her sweaty palms on her kurta, held onto the reins and fisted her hand in the horse's mane. The height of the horse added to her fear. But she took a deep breath and slid her leg into the stirrup, raised to its height and tried to gain her balance. When she made it on the horse, she heaved a sigh of relief.

It had been an embarrassment to ride with Yuvaraja Prabir in the forest. And here she was, yet again, ready to ride on horseback with another man. The very thought of riding with Yuvaraja Trinabh put her in a frenzy. She shrugged as he got onto the horseback and made himself comfortable right behind her. She was already growing weak in her legs and was a nervous wreck. And the touch of his arms against hers as he held on to the reins made it worse for her. Her heart had gone erratic, beating at a frantic pace, going out of her control as the horse started to walk. His thighs rubbed against her legs with the horse's gait even as she tried to hold herself together as he enfolded her.

The horse trotted as if it knew that she was scared and yet excited to ride the large beast that he was. The sound of the hooves bought her a sense of joy she couldn't understand. The soft touch of the Yuvaraja's chest on her back as he leaned forward nudging her to do the same, gave her flutters in the stomach. Soon the horse broke into a canter. She moved in unison with the Yuvaraja and in sync with the beast's movements as they rode on a path that didn't lead to the palace.

'Where are you taking me Yuvaraja?'

There was no answer and he continued to ride.

Her heart thudded in her ears. But she wasn't sure if she should try and stop the angry Yuvaraja.

The trees were speedily left behind as the horse took to a furious gallop. The sky was lit with a colourful hue of the fire rainbow[1] that gave her an unusual apprehension. The colourful flames that spread across the blue horizon looked like the fire that was lit within her at that moment.

Her dupatta slipped off her head and her long braided silky hair shone under the rays of the sun as they tried to peek at the beautiful sky. Their path was nestled with huge rocks and the terracotta temples on either side that she had grown up marvelling at their structures.

'Where are we going, Yuvaraja?' Bidisha shouted, as they pierced the wind and moved ahead.

'Turn back if you want to say something,' Yuvaraja Trinabh said as he leaned over her.

His breath caressed her ears, giving her goose pimples.

'I said, why are we not heading straight to the palace...' Bidisha turned around directing the words into his ear against the whooshing breeze.

'This horse has a backbone too. Don't you think it could use some rest after carrying the two of us? If we don't care for him, he could falter or worse, start to buck or bolt throwing us both in the air. Would you enjoy that?' the Yuvaraja replied, bringing the horse back to trot, as he adjusted the reins.

Bidisha could see the Kesta Rai temple at a distance, which was almost deserted in the early morning hours. The horse came to a halt and Yuvaraja Trinabh got off.

'Take the horse to the lake and let it drink its fill. We will soon leave before anybody comes to this place. Let me rest for a while.'

When Bidisha was unmounting the horse, it jerked unexpectedly. The sun had only risen and he wanted to rest. It was the most absurd thing a responsible prince could say. She let out a sigh as she headed to the lake. The water looked refreshing and the horse took to it as she stroked it in admiration. She let go of the reins and made herself comfortable on a rock, soaking her legs in the water. The clear water looked beckoning, and if it was just another day like the old times, she would have jumped in the lake. But all she could do was splash water on her face and revive herself for the tough journey she had embarked on.

Her ears pricked up at the sudden swoosh of air and the approaching footsteps. She was not expecting anybody or anything around in the morning hours. Bidisha was on her toes as she stood upon the rock, ready to punch whoever it was in the face. The hand was gone just in time. It was Trinabh. She attempted to get a hold of herself before her hand actually made it in his face as intended. She lost her balance from being startled by him yet again and, yet again, he attempted to hold her. But she fell in the water splashing it over Trinabh. The horse neighed and trotted away from the lake.

She stood up trying to breathe with ease as she glared at him struggling to swallow her anger. He had done it many times, sneaking on her from behind.

Trinabh looked at her with an equally annoying stare as he ruffled his wet clothes.

Bidisha turned away and squeezed her wet hair. Her dupatta, she noticed was floating away from her. She took a few steps in the water and grabbed it before it made any further. Bidisha wrung it with rage as if she would do the same to Trinabh and took a deep breath.

And just when she looked back at him, still standing in the water, their eyes locked. Her pulse raced at the sudden change of his gaze. She walked out of the water slowly, looking away from him. His eyes were still fixed on her, she was getting more and more aware of her clothes sticking to her body.

Her chest heaved in rhythm as she breathed heavy. Bidisha walked towards the horse which was busy eating the green grass on the banks. She rushed behind it and let out deep breaths trying to hide away from him. She hid her face with her hands. Trinabh had stirred her emotions with his gaze. Bidisha had never thought she would ever feel like that towards a man. In fact, she had never let desire bloom in her heart. She never wanted a man in her life leave alone an enemy at that.

The horse moved jerking her.

'Hurry, we have to leave.'

His voice, she was being pulled towards him. She was scared of what was happening to her. More because she was letting it happen to her. Her dupatta slipped and fell on the ground.

'There are a few English soldiers around. You never know what are they up to. They might even have a drawing of your masked face.'

His words disturbed her. She was trying to get out of her unsettling feelings and there he was giving her completely opposite agony. Bidisha picked up her dupatta and put it on her head and covered herself. The water was dripping from her clothes and she bend down to squeeze her kurta.

It didn't make sense. Though the British would look for her based on Oliver's description, they wouldn't search for her frantically like Yuvaraja Trinabh suspected. He was just frantic about the whole thing because he was worried about Rani Maa.

'Let's move. Cover your face, those eyes especially,' the Yuvaraja commanded as he held the reins and walked the horse away from the lake.

Bidisha let out a chuckle under her *dupatta*, trying hard to hold herself back from laughing at his panic stricken face. She almost got over her own mixed emotions and horrible things that could happen if his words were to come true and the soldiers were actually after her.

'How can you laugh in a situation like this?' Yuvaraja Trinabh said as he walked towards the temple, 'You must have gone crazy to take this whole thing as some kind of a blague.'

'Not many would be interested in Oliver's affairs to such an extent that every English solider is put on the duty to find the culprit who tried to kill him.' Bidisha said, holding her *dupatta* over her face against the breeze.

Trinabh turned around, right at the entrance of the temple. 'You don't understand...'

He stopped abruptly, his eyes fixed on her lips that he could see through her flying pink *dupatta*. She held her breath, as her eyes fixed on his face. She couldn't hold her stare for too long for she felt like she was burning under his gaze. The statues on the terracotta walls, depicting intimacy in a wholesome and beautiful way, only added to her yearning for his touch.

The moment, however, was broken when she heard leaves rustle and the sound of footsteps approaching them.

Yuvaraja Trinabh caught her shoulder in a firm grip, his fingers almost digging into her skin and in a smooth shift, pinned her against the horse. In the process, his face came to be only a hair's breadth away from hers, his lips almost touching hers. Her insides shook at his sudden advancement. She closed her eyes under the cover on her face.

'Ahem! Pardon us, Yuvaraja, we were just crossing by in search of a wanted criminal who stole a gold necklace from an official's house. Can we dare ask you if you have seen a man in his forties, a fair and limping dwarf, cross this path?'

The Yuvaraja loosened his grip and let out a sigh of relief, leaving her in a state of haze.

'Was it just an act to fend off the British soldiers or was it an excuse to get closer to her?'

She had seen his gaze earlier. It was as if he could devour her through his eyes alone. There was a burning desire in his demeanour that had left her fazed.

'Don't you see I am too busy to notice a man around?' Yuvaraja Trinabh said with a wink.

'Pardon us, Yuvaraja. It was actually a precious diamond-studded gold necklace and we are desperate to find the thief. We will leave you two alone.'

The soldiers were out of sight and Bidisha tried to step away from the man who had churned her sleeping desires. But his gaze shifted back on her and froze on her lips again. He blocked her and his hand slowly moved towards her shoulder away from the horse that stood as a barrier behind her. His other hand slowly slid to her waist. Her damp clothes gave her a cold touch as his hand held her in a firm grip giving her sudden shivers.

But her gaze lingered on his lips then on his moustache and then onto his neatly done stubble. There again, she couldn't take her eyes off of his lips. He took a step closer to her leaving no space as their clothes made their first union. Bidisha's palms turned moist even as the breeze made her quiver in her wet dress. Her hand took off to reach her septum ring in a nervous tick. He held her hand stopping it from making it to her nose. Instead, his finger ran over her cheek softly and then touched her nose ring tracing to her mouth in a steady touch. His face closed in and their lips touched but her face cover acted as a barrier between them. Bidisha shuddered and took a step back, bumping into the horse. It neighed and took off, pushing her straight into Trinabh's arms. Her lips pressed hard onto his. And Yuvaraja Trinabh didn't waste another moment before he embosomed her in his firm embrace.

She held her breath as he uncovered her face. Her eyes batted as his fingers moved to her head and ran through her hair gently. The grip on her waist tightened as his other hand made it on her back running down her hair. The long press on her lips turned into a soft envelope on her lower lip as he parted his mouth. Her hand traced the rough black garment on his back while the other hand tugged onto his clothes on the side of his waist. Bidisha was hot all over and her breathing was haywire. She closed her eyes as her heart went wild inside her chest and goose pimples erupted on her skin. And just when she was losing control over herself, her hand felt the sword hilt on his waist. She loosened her grip on his clothes and her other hand moved away from the hilt. They were bound to be enemies and bound by the sword and not by their hearts.

In the next instant, she opened her eyes to wake up to reality. He was the person who had hurt her mother and the one who wanted her to seduce his stepbrother. Yuvaraja Trinabh was the most cunning man she had ever seen and a womanizer who couldn't be trusted. All that she could mean to a man like him was another body to gain pleasure. How could she fall for him?

She pushed him away and slumped on the ground. The first man she had ever wanted to be with was a man she could neither trust nor have. He was the future Maharaja of Bishnupur, who she couldn't dare covet. And he was the man she must only hate.

Bidisha's mind was colluded after what had happened between Yuvaraja Trinabh and her.

And to add it to all, he had been putting her in difficult situations since the time she ran away from the temple without heeding his words. Yuvaraja had been asking her to visit him in his chambers often and not only question her motives but also to interrogate her for the truth. He had this bad hunch that she was in the palace with a motive of her own. No matter how much she tried convincing him otherwise, he wouldn't believe her.

He had questioned her earlier, about her illicit aspirations ever since she tried to kill Oliver. But lately, his authoritative actions and brazen words had turned even more unbearable, if that was even possible.

Yuvaraja Trinabh was not only looking aggressively into her background but also trying to understand her feelings for him. But Bidisha couldn't take a firm stand on her own swaying heart.

On the other hand, Sir Oliver would leave for England in two days and she couldn't do anything yet to realise her mission. Yuvaraja Trinabh had made things more difficult for her by keeping a watch on her in the palace. Though he would benefit from Oliver's death, he didn't trust her anymore after she failed the attempt. Moreover, he had always done things on his own and in his own way.

The least she could do was to get more information about Sir Oliver's ship and the port. But all that she could gather was that he had already left Bishnupur and had reached the place he was preparing his ship for the departure, Calcutta. He was to take tonnes of cotton as consignment along with the months-long supplies required for the journey and the loot the goras won't hesitate to hoard back to their land. It wasn't easy to manage it all unless he overlooked the preparations.

Bidisha had gathered quite a bit of information about it but didn't know a way to accomplish her mission.

It was a day-long journey from Bishnupur to reach the port in Calcutta. She was told that there was a change of plans and the ship would leave early in the morning exactly three days later.

It was only Maharaja Mitul Singha Dev who could help her. And for that, she had to show her sincerity by relieving him of his biggest pain, Sir Oliver Watts. He was the person who had been depriving His Highness of the true benefits he expected from the cotton trade. Oliver Watts was downright cunning and greedy than his father once was. He took great advantage of the Maharaja's perilous situation and looted cotton from Bishnupur by offering nothing but pieces of gold worthy of half the load he took back to England.

However, Yuvaraja Trinabh had kept Bidisha on her toes and she had no plan of action despite being enraged about the whole situation. All she had was a day to come up with a plan, escape from the palace and get out of Bishnupur to chase after Oliver. And as expected, she was summoned by Yuvaraja Trinabh yet again who, she knew, would be ready with another useless task for her.

Her heart was split into two halves. Bidisha's endearment towards Trinabh and her love for her mother pulled her in opposite directions. As much as she wished to be around Yuvaraja Trinabh, she couldn't dare and she knew she shouldn't. Her heart was ripped at the very thought of going to meet him and her legs refused to move.

She had work to do, not the one given by the Yuvaraja but the one she had to do for the sake of her mother. However, she dragged herself to his chamber, her mind cluttered with possible plans she could execute to kill Oliver, more failproof than her last one.

'I see that mere words are not helping me off late,' Yuvaraja Trinabh said, a hookah in one hand and his quill feather in another as he wrote in a ledger. 'I think you have gotten over my authority in the palace to take my orders seriously.'

'I was just finishing something, Yuvaraja. Forgive my tardiness.'

'So you say. Alright. Let me see what will be your excuse next time. And thereafter, before I lose my patience with you as I do with everyone else,' Trinabh said, his eyes focussed on the ledger, as the hookah gurgled with another drag.

Bidisha's cheeks burnt in embarrassment. 'Yuvaraja, what I wanted to say was…'

'Save your words. Haven't I made myself clear already that you will, one day, be Rani Maa's scapegoat? You're more useful to me alive than dead. And so, as per Rani Maa's orders, I am tolerating you. Moreover, I have decided to get all the answers from you today. Enough of this cat and mouse play.'

'Who does he think he can make a scapegoat of? That too declaring it on the face. I will be the one to take advantage of you and your mother Trinabh Singha Dev. You wait and watch.'

'Rogue!' Bidisha mumbled, looking away, wishing she could tell it to his face.

'That's right. I am one, and I will show you that today.'

Bidisha jerked.

'Rules and laws do not imply for a Yuvaraja. Don't you know that? At least not to me. I can't say the same about Prabir though. Now come on, and do as I say.' Yuvaraja Trinabh placed the feather in the inkpot and kept the hookah aside.

He looked determined to show Bidisha what it meant to disobey him, the Yuvaraja. If he wanted something, anything, it would be taken care of.

Yuvaraja Trinabh had assigned her a new task for the day—to run his royal bath. He was in no mood for a regular wash since his body needed extra attention, per his claim. It was all a punishment for her impudence towards him since the time she kissed him and then backed off denying his advancement.

He was already hell-bent on figuring out her motives, and now this.

Bidisha went to the royal bathing pond. She had brought in all the essentials to go into the bathing tub that was attached to the large common bathing pond. The other maidens had already filled it with warm water. A few special bathing scents, gifts from the British officers, were added to the water.

Yuvaraja Trinabh rarely used the bathing tub and the bathing luxuries, unlike Yuvaraja Prabir. But today, he was about to waste a pot full of milk that she held in her hands. It was supposed to go in too but her temper was giving in. In her anger, Bidisha's chest rose and sank at a frantic pace.

The hungry kids on the streets and the faces of people responsible for their state enraged Bidisha. She hated herself for falling for a man like him.

But her heart ached the next instant for he was before her eyes and it took her a lot of effort to harbour hate towards him and suppress the growing affection.

'How important is it for the royals to bathe in milk.'

Prince Trinabh snatched the pot from her.

'I will make you an example and show the others that I don't forget. Those who mock or betray me will have to hide until the end of time. Because I will not stop chasing them. Even if it is for insignificant or trivial things; I don't make any exceptions. Not for anything, not for anybody,' the Yuvaraja declared, his tone soft unlike the glare in his eyes.

He took another step and before she said anything, he poured the milk on her head. Bidisha stood still and closed her eyes as she tried to hold on to her temper. But the brute wouldn't stop there. He lifted her and flung her into the tub. She gasped in disbelief, struggling to stabilize herself after the unforeseen splash of water cut her breath. Her body was alarmed as she struggled to gain balance.

'Look, I made your job easy. The milk is in the pool and your scent has added that extra essence to the water making it fit for me to plunge in,' Yuvaraja Trinabh said removing his cotton robe and exposing his half-naked body ready to get in the bath.

She looked at him for a long moment. The huge cut on his abdomen crossed four waves of muscles on the right. And the scars on his back told a tale she had only heard of. The wounds and the pain he had suffered had forged him into the man he had turned out to be. And to believe that he was made stronger by none other than his mother who put him in constant pain and tested his endurance was frightening. A mother who wanted the throne even at the cost of her own son's suffering was spine-tingling and beyond Bidisha's imagination.

Rani Maa had raised him tough, making sure he learnt how to survive amidst the cruel people both inside the palace and outside. Rani Maa had learnt it the hard way after the death of her first son, an incident that Bidisha knew little about. She had not sought much information about Rani Maa's first son's death. But she was not sure if that would help her in any way for that matter.

She collected herself and tried to wend her way out but he made it in and grabbed her hand, stopping Bidisha from moving any further.

'Don't worry. You are safe with me. If you promise to be honest and answer all my questions, you'll walk out without a scratch on your body. I've never wanted to deal with a woman in this way and neither will Rani Maa be happy when she hears about it,' Trinabh said, locking her hands behind her back pulling her close to him, his hands wrapped around her waist, her face close to his and a glare that frightened her. 'Shall we start now? My questions and your answers.'

'Yuvaraja, I have nothing more to say than what I have told you earlier. But since you insist, let's finish this once and for all. Promise me, Yuvaraja, you will fight me like I am a man and your equal. And I promise that I will not consider you a royal and hold back myself either. And whatever happens today, one of us has to take the fall sportingly,' Bidisha said before she suddenly bent over and turned around, freeing herself from his grip.

A part of her wanted to embrace his warmth and didn't want to get out of his strong grasp. The tiny water drops on his rugged bare chest muddled her resolve to stay bold before him. And his breath, just like hers, went erratic sending her into a joyous swoon.

'I didn't mean a fight when I said let's start. But let me grant you that wish. And be aware, I have always considered a woman as an equal when it comes to fighting one. If you win, I will never ask you about your intentions and your motives. But if I win, I will not let you slide away with any lies,' Trinabh growled, shaking the water off his hair. 'Get started then. Pick up the sword.'

Bidisha shook her head out of her indulgent thoughts, 'But you made it clear about the fight when you promised I'll walk out without a scratch on my body.'

Bidisha grabbed her dripping *Pallav* and squeezed the water out of it, her eyes set on Trinabh as she tied her *pallav* around her waist. She gathered her hair, sticky from the milk, and tied them into a manageable bun. Either Trinabh had tricked her into a fight, for the swords were ready near the bath, or he knew her too well. Whatever it was, Bidisha would give her all. She picked up the sword placed on the stairs of the bath. It was much heavier than her sword but she could work with that.

However, tears stung her eyes as she held herself back from showing her heart to the man.

'You're a sight for my eyes even when you're staring daggers at me,' Trinabh said, twirling around his blade.

'Enough of your banter, Yuvaraja. Let's get to it.' She stood in knee-deep waters, holding on to her balance, ready to take on the man who had titillated her heart and was also her worst enemy.

'So you have decided to see my bad side.' Yuvaraja Trinabh said as his eyebrows furrowed on his rugged forehead.

'Do you even have a good side?' Bidisha countered as she readied herself for the unknown unwillingly.

'Believe me, whatever you have seen so far is my best. You don't want to see the worst side of me.'

'Show me, Yuvaraja. Let's see the true side of each other today,' Bidisha said as she narrowed her eyes.

'Don't look at me like that. I know you hate me. But guess what, everyone hates me. So, I don't care,' the Yuvaraja said with a stare that pierced through her. 'And do me a favour, don't let those tears roll out. You look hideous when you cry.'

Bidisha's face had gone bloodless and her heart was sieged by the mard.

She raised her sword and the blades clanked.

Bidisha moved back and forth for a tardy moment in the waters as her sword worked against Yuvaraja Trinabh's sharp blade. He ducked as her sword went for his throat and immediately took his blade to her waist. Bidisha was quick and receded but the sharp edge had touched her skin. Drops of blood trickled down her damp white saree. His eyes on her cut and the trickling blood, Trinabh swallowed a lump she saw. But her fierce eyes were on his leg as her hand made it to his thigh as the sword swept on the surface splashing water along. He bled, just a little, as her metal made it through his white *dhoti* and cut his skin. There was a twitch in her heart. Just like all the other scars on his body, she had marked one of hers on him too.

'Hope you'll not complain about this to your mother, Yuvaraja.' Bidisha sneered. Trying to conceal her aching heart, while her hands still worked.

Yuvaraja Trinabh dodged her attack, held her hand and turned her around causing her sword to slip and fall.

'It's always advised to talk less when in action, Bidisha,' Trinabh mocked her, griping her hand over her chest and pressing her back against his nude front.

Bidisha sensed a strange hurt on her nose, her septum, in the scrimmage but she didn't stop. She jabbed him in his gut with her elbow and then lunged pulling his leg. Trinabh lost his balance and she retrieved her sword and jumped out of the bath.

'And the same goes for you, Yuvaraja.'

He took his stance right before her. Out of the bath. Attacked her right on her head. Bidisha blocked his blow and the blades clanked again.

'What is going on here? Stop it right now,' raged a familiar voice.

Bidisha was startled and Trinabh lost his attention. His hand, which was intended to block her punch, had directly hit her jaw. And in the fit of the moment, Bidisha's hand gave in and her sword hastened as it cut his thumb off. The sword slid down from his hand and his thumb flung into the bath. There was colour in the waters and gore on the ground.

'Ahhhh!'

A long wild cry escaped his mouth and he howled in pain.

His royal bath! Not many have the privilege to bathe in their own blood.

Guilt engulfed Bidisha at the sight before her. She felt dizzy and the world before her eyes spun. Bidisha closed her eyes and wrapped her arms around herself as her insides tightened.

She opened her eyes to the thick scarlet red that flowed like water from his hand. If only it knew how precious it was...

'What did you do? You witch!' Rani Durga Moni Devi rushed on her bulky legs.

'Ahhhh! My thumb!' Trinabh looked at the blood that gushed from his thumb, horrified at the obvious consequences of the injury. His face clenched in pain and the veins popped out on his forehead as he bared his teeth. Fixing her with a stare that she was sure could burn her, he bellowed, 'My sword hand...!'

Bidisha stood still, tears glittering in her eyes as she looked at the Yuvaraja holding his wrist in his other hand. 'Run!' he mouthed.

She stood confused. Bidisha could read his lips when he said the same thing again.

'Why would he ask me to run after what I did? And doesn't he hate me?'

A sentry stationed near the bathing pool came in running. The maidens screamed and rushed to help the Yuvaraja.

'Run!' Trinabh mouthed again even as his face scrunched in pain.

Tears trickled down her cheeks. She moved away slowly, her eyes still fixed on him. He had kept everyone's attention on him and she didn't get another look from him. Her head was too full to hear anything more.

And then she ran.

Bidisha made her way out through the small passage. She was cold and shocked but ran as fast as she could.

She could see it in his eyes, his affection for her even as he held his shivering hand together. Bidisha after all had his heart but it had taken his flesh and blood to prove that. Despite being in pain and losing his thumb, he had tried to save her from his mother. And she had not only messed with the royal heir, but she had also taken away any chances for their union as soulmates in the future.

Trinabh had a heart, after all, one that nobody knew about. Unfortunately, she had a strong feeling that now it was not only stolen by her but also crushed into pieces.

[1] A Fire Rainbow is an ice halo having a flame like appearance with brilliant pastel colours. It is technically known as circumhorizontal arc. They are formed by hexagonal, plate-shaped ice crystals in high level cirrus clouds.

CHAPTER NINE

Bidisha gasped for air after the long run, stunned at what she had run into.

Debesh Das and Yuvaraja Prabir Singha Dev stood afar, their swords pointing at each other. She had never even pictured Yuvaraja Prabir holding a weapon but here, she was witnessing him skilfully giving Debesh a tough time.

They halted abruptly, equally stunned by her presence. Rather, nervous. As if they had seen the very ghost they were running away from. She was a spy planted by Rani Maa after all.

She had never seen that part of the palace, an unguarded open ground surrounded by high walls on three sides and the palace on the fourth. Bidisha paced towards them unable to find a way out from the huge area. The soldiers could reach there any moment chasing after her and all that was before her was a blocked open space.

Bidisha walked faster towards Debesh as he approached her. But then again, she changed her direction. Gathering all the strength she was left with, she started running away from them. But soon she was lost. Debesh chased after her and she ran frantically.

He finally caught Bidisha, held her arm and pulled her towards him. 'What are you trying to do? Why are you here?'

His eyes ran over her and he let her hand go. He touched her face and then her bruised lips. Debesh's eyes travelled down to her waist. But she pulled her *pallav* and covered her wound.

'Did you bathe in blood? Why is your face bruised and why are you wounded everywhere?' Debesh said in a single breath.

Bidisha's eyes welled up with tears. She didn't think of running anymore.

'I... I...' Bidisha choked on her words, 'I...accidentally cut off Yuvaraja Trinabh's thumb...from his right hand. His sword hand.'

'You did what? What are you saying? Are you alright? Are you even thinking?' Debesh shook her shoulders.

'The soldiers will be here any moment. They... They will...'

Debesh slapped a hand to his head. 'Did you? Really? We need to get out of here soon. Now.'

'I don't know how far I can run. That too from...'

'Yuvaraja?' Debesh called out. 'We need to...'

'I heard her. Let's take her away from here. Hurry.'

'Run, Bidisha,' Debesh said holding her hand as they ran towards one of the walls.

'Why are we heading towards that wall? There is no way out.'

'Yuvaraja, are we taking the...' Debesh looked at Yuvaraja Prabir.

'Yes,' Yuvaraja Prabir said even before Debesh finished his question.

'Where? What?' Bidisha asked unable to understand.

Bidisha found it difficult to put her trust in the people she had spied on. She preferred to trust her eyes that saw nothing before her but a wall.

Yuvaraja Prabir went close to the stone structure and slid a small narrow door no one could tell existed. It looked exactly like the stone wall and was painted red, just like the rest of the structure. It opened up to a narrow passage. Bidisha was relieved as Yuvaraja Prabir entered the hidden tunnel behind the walls.

'What are you waiting for Bidisha? Hurry!' Debesh said, pointing towards the passage.

Bidisha looked back. There was no one behind her, not yet. But her legs refused to move. Yuvaraja Trinabh was going through it all because of her. When she had first entered the palace months ago, her motive was to free her mother and see the downfall of the royals, if possible, for what the Maharaja had done to her mother. Though that particular move to harm Yuvaraja Trinabh wasn't planned, the result was something to be happy about. Any harm to the king and his lineage was something to rejoice in.

But there was tightness in her chest and a lump in her throat. Her thoughts were blocked and she was numb to her surroundings.

'Bidisha? Come on!' Debesh dragged her along with him and closed the door behind him.

Darkness engulfed the passage, just like her mind had told her to escape safely leaving behind the man who seemed to care more for her than his thumb.

Bidisha took a deep breath, though she felt the lack of air. She closed her eyes. Bidisha couldn't just let things happen to her. She had to make a choice. She had to either go back pretending not to care about her mother but about Yuvaraja Trinabh and get punished for what she had done. Or, look ahead of her, escape the situation, wait for the right time to return and start afresh.

'Where does this tunnel lead?' Bidisha asked, gathering herself.

'Sssh! Don't talk yet. Trust me. Just hold my hand and follow me,' Yuvaraja Prabir said and guided them through the tunnel as they formed a chain, holding each other.

'Now it's safe to light the torch,' Debesh said, using stones to spark a flame and light a wooden torch they found in the tunnel.

Drops of sweat trickled down her face and then her cleavage that was left exposed by her wet *pallav* sticking over her bosom.

Yuvaraja Prabir's eyes were glued on Bidisha for as long as Debesh was busy with the torch. She felt his eyes on her as she lowered her head and covered herself pulling her *pallav* in place staring at the flaky rough ground. The salty beads on her forehead glittered as the flame of the torch danced. Her damp golden-brown hair was plastered in waves on her cheek and ran down under her blouse.

'Are you alright? And how could you dare cut Yuvaraja Trinabh's thumb? What were you thinking?' Debesh asked taking a deep breath trying to draw in all the air that was possibly available in the narrow space that had brought all the three close enough to feel the warmth of their breath. 'And your clothes? What exactly happened?'

'Actually, I had no time to think and it was an act of reflex. I mean... Yuvaraja Prabir, please forgive me. I didn't do it on purpose,' Bidisha pleaded, her hazel eyes welling up with tears.

'There's no need to explain. This is a chance to escape and stay alive. Never come back again,' Yuvaraja Prabir said as he cocked his head and narrowed his eyes.

It was as if Prabir was trying to gauge the impact of his words on her. He was deliberately pushing her to make a choice and run away from the palace. But she wasn't sure of it yet. Not sure if she could stay away from Trinabh anymore or if she was capable of denying the lurking danger over her mother's life because of her actions.

Bidisha was at a loss for words and she couldn't dare make eye contact with Yuvaraja Prabir, who seemed to put her interests first before his stepbrother. Not that it surprised her knowing they were rivals, but her rue left her paralyzed for words.

Debesh held the torch and led them. They continued to walk gasping for breath.

'Let us forget about what happened back there. Let me tell you about this secret little tunnel not many know to exists. Although we are not far from its entrance, the secret lies here in this spot. It was built in a way that neither the light from a torch nor a sound can travel back to the door we just entered.' Yuvaraja Prabir boasted trying to divert the topic of their conversation. 'Isn't it interesting?'

Bidisha had never seen Yuvaraja Prabir speak so much. He went on as they walked along the path in the dark in the narrow space, staying close to each other. Debesh didn't utter a word. But the Yuvaraja told them everything about the passage that was like a lifeline for Bidisha.

It led to the river that trailed all the way to join the sea, which was close to the harbour. Bidisha had already collected her thoughts and cracked a plan to hide and make her way out to freedom through the jungle adjacent to the port. All she had to do was safely reach the end of the river where it would merge into the sea and then walk away into the forest.

The problem, however, was that the journey was at least a day and a nightlong. She knew she couldn't row the boat alone to safety. Her knuckle went to her nose. She tried to touch her septum ring. She stopped and felt her nose again and again.

'What's wrong? Keep going.' Yuvaraja said as he stopped behind her.

'My ring. My nose ring. It's gone.'

'You're worried about your nose ring? Your life is at stake! Come on now,' Debesh hurled at her shifting the torch to his other hand.

Bidisha dropped the sword suddenly and slumped down on the ground, struggling to keep her eyes open. The odd rotten murky smell and the lack of fresh air had drained her, giving her a nauseous feeling. The heat from the torch had only worsened her dry throat. But who was she to complain to?

'Bidisha, stay awake. We will get you out of this place soon.' Debesh patted her cheeks.

'Before we suffocate here, we have to find our way out to the river,' the Yuvaraja added as he took the torch from Debesh.

'Stay awake, Bidisha,' Debesh mumbled again.

'My...my ring,' Bidisha murmured, struggling to open her eyes.

'Debesh, come on, help her, let's move.'

Debesh tried to help her back on her feet. But she was too weak to stand let alone walk. He grabbed her sword and put it through the baldric and moved it back letting the sword hang loosely on his hip. He lifted her off the ground and into his arms. She quivered and clasped her hands around his neck.

The narrow space made it difficult for Debesh to move while carrying Bidisha who was slowly losing her consciousness. The Yuvaraja led the way with caution breaking through the darkness that greeted them at every inch. After an arduous journey, they finally reached the end of the tunnel.

Debesh carefully laid her down and patted her cheeks. Yuvaraja Prabir hurried and opened the door letting out a sigh. The sudden gush of fresh air instantly brought Bidisha back to her senses. She took a heavy breath as the green greeted her eyes. The croaking of the frogs and the cooing of the birds sounded like music to her ears. The sight of the water that was crystal clear felt like heaven after the long ordeal of sweat and suffocation. However, she was parched and felt weak.

Yuvaraja Prabir stepped out into the bushes. Debesh rushed to the river, removed his *Panjabi* and dipped it in the water. He ran back towards the tunnel holding the cloth in his hands, trying to prevent the water from draining out. He squeezed the cloth in one palm and splashed the water on Bidisha's face.

Bidisha was sitting on the banks of the river, encapsulated by guilt. She had run away without any concern for Yuvaraja Trinabh while he cared for her safe escape even in his pain and disappointment. She had not only brought him physical agony but had also handicapped him. Sword fighting was not just a skill required for his livelihood as an heir to the throne but it also was his life. It was more than warcraft or a survival mechanism for him. Tears gushed out as the gravity of her horrific action sunk into her.

Her eyes blankly staring into the river water as she vent it all out. The stream burbled as it bubbled over the rocks flowing in peace to join its much-desired destination, to become one with the ocean. Bidisha wanted to run to her mother too and bury herself in her embrace.

She touched her nose only to reaffirm that she had indeed lost her ring. The ring was the last thing her mother had treasured from her maiden home but no longer existed. The tiny ornament had brought Bidisha solace even in distress and gave her the courage to fight and move on. She needed it now more than ever since she didn't know how long it would take to even get a glimpse of her mother.

She guzzled down the water and then splashed some on her face, washing off her tears. It was already late in the evening and the sun was high just before setting. She was washing off the bloodstains from her clothes and her hands. Bidisha grimaced at her own touch as she attempted to wash the dirt off her sweaty hands.

The purple blotches on her arms were wounds given by not just anyone but Trinabh, the person who had her heart. The swollen lip and the bruised jaw were the prizes she had received for slicing the Yuvaraja's thumb. But then, it was nothing in comparison to what she had taken away from him.

Her subdued stature at that moment, as she pleated her dishevelled hair, told a contrasting story against the strong-willed offence she was actually running away from. Her hair flickered in the sunlight and her not so white saree, covered with black grim, was nothing suitable for a woman to even cover herself, let alone to look presentable.

Yuvaraja Prabir rested under a tree, after helping himself with fresh river water to quench his thirst, stealing a glance at Bidisha every so often, pretending to instruct Debesh on the next steps.

Debesh was on his toes, debarking a couple of boats that he found covered under the bushes. He had chopped out all the fauna with his sword that had engulfed the true utility of the boat.

Unexpectedly, Yuvaraja Prabir joined forces with him and together they pulled a boat to the river.

Bidisha walked towards them, struggling to keep her saree put against the will of the wind, in the twilight that had stolen the colours of the day. Prince Prabir looked at her as if he was lost in the enigma she was in the moonlight. Debesh, on the other hand, was acting weird as if he was trying hard not to give in to temptation. As if his heart ached. The kind of ache that comes when you are forbidden from taking a second glance. Just like she had felt many times around Trinabh. Perhaps, she was weird too in others' eyes.

'Yuvaraja, I owe you so much that I can't repay you all my life. I don't know any way to thank you. But I do not wish to cause you any more trouble than I already have.' Bidisha begged, bringing her palms together as a mark of respect, 'I should be on my own now. Yuvaraja, you must please head back to the palace before there is any commotion over your long absence.'

'So, we must seek your advice on our duties now, is it Bidisha?' Yuvaraja Prabir snapped.

'Please forgive me, Yuvaraja. What I...'

'Debesh is my most trusted companion. He will take you to safety,' the Yuvaraja interrupted her and squeezed Debesh's shoulder. 'Take care of her and yourself. Go now.'

'But, Yuvaraja, I cannot accept this. And how can he accompany me? Debesh is the only person who has pledged his loyalty to you.'

'Hmmm, you mean to say I don't have many people by my side and I am a lonely soul?'

'Yuvaraja and I have never been apart even for a day all our lives. And today, only because of you, I had to leave him by himself,' Debesh spat as he arched his brows and clenched his jaws, holding an oar in his hands.

'You don't have to remind me of your compromises or your sacrifices if that's how you want to look at them. I am very well aware of what's happening.'

'You could have escaped from within the forest here. But I don't know why the Yuvaraja insisted otherwise.'

'Just like you are bound by his orders, I am bound by his orders too. And you're not going to leave his side forever. It's only a matter of two nights before you return. And then we don't have to see each other ever again,' Bidisha said, looking away from Debesh into the darkness of the world around her.

'If only you knew the meaning of two nights alone for him.'

The depth of the twinkling waters under the full moon couldn't uncover the blindness of the ghostly night. They had been rowing the boat without rest, so they could reach the port sooner than later. The river was the quickest way they could make it to their destination. And more than her, it was Debesh who was in a rush to reach the end of the river so he could return at the earliest.

She sat at the other end of the boat as she looked up at the night sky and pressed her sore arms.

'I am famished.'

'Even the crocodiles in this river are. Better I feed you to them. If not for the Yuvaraja's fondness and affection for you, I would have drowned...'

'What?' Bidisha asked interrupting Debesh rubbing her palms and her upper arms.

'So, you save yourself from the wind while I do the donkey work all night and safely take you to the port,' Debesh said instead, rowing the boat steadily, causing his muscles to bulge out while in action.

His bare dusky arms shone from the sweat. His thick brown *kurta,* long enough to cover his burly torso bared his arms exposing his veins that ran in branches just beneath his skin.

'You're too quick to change the matter of discussion at hand. Anyway, nothing about the palace matters anymore, does it?' Bidisha said, her eyes on him and her lips curved downwards.

He abruptly pushed the oars into the boat and dipped his hands in the water. Raking his fingers through his long and dark curly hair, he slid to the floor of the boat.

'You takeover now. I need to rest. Row it or leave it. And yes, stop staring at me. I wonder what you are trying to see in this darkness.'

'My hands are sore but I won't give up like you. I have no idea why Yuvaraja Prabir even trusts you,' Bidisha growled, swallowing dry, looking pale and wan, and struggling with the hooked oar.

It felt like the sun was blooming far on the horizon, its unique golden, pink and orange rays coming to life. Bidisha was almost out of breath, her eyes drooping and her arms giving up. But she kept doing what she had to. Pushing herself out of her bounds and rowing like she was getting away from a frantic water animal chasing her. As dawn broke into the day, spreading the hues of hope and the promise of new a beginning, she had also cracked a plan overnight.

But she couldn't go on rowing any further and Bidisha shut her eyes as if her body was not in her control anymore. She plonked into the river and the water splashed on Debesh as the boat shook, waking him up from his deep slumber. Her tongue was tied with shock but her eyes were screaming for help. Debesh looked around as he woke up alarmed. He stood up in the boat and his eyes were on her the next moment, in the water, struggling and beating her hands. Debesh rushed and grabbed her hand pulling her towards him as she panted. He pulled her with all his force and then held her waist trying to lift her from the water. The boat tilted almost throwing him out along with Bidisha but he stepped back and gained balance just in time to prevent the boat from toppling.

Bidisha slumped on the boat floor and Debesh supported her. She wheezed in his arms dropping all her weight on him.

'Bidisha, Bidisha...' Debesh patted her cheeks, '... you foolish girl, rowing the boat nonstop all night.'

Bidisha had no idea if she had slipped into a slumber or simply lost her balance. Nothing her mind said made sense. She struggled to keep her eyes open, glancing at Debesh's worried face but she slipped back into her weary world the next.

Debesh's gaze settled on her face, still holding her in his arms. The water settled in the wrinkles of her full lips and trickled from the corners and his gaze followed its trail to her neck.

Debesh suddenly shook his head and Bidisha became conscious of his touch, his arms holding her waist, smooth and wet. Her bare midriff managed to get his unabridged attention. His gaze lasted for more seconds. She tried to move away from him and he pulled his arm with a jerk, letting Bidisha's body on the floor, turned around and grabbed the oars.

'I should not...' Bidisha heard him say.

CHAPTER TEN

Bidisha opened her eyes, feeling hot, parched and with a sense of her skin burning under the sun.

She stood up shading her eyes with her hands from the scorching sun rays. Bidisha pulled her gaunt self out of the boat and tried to steady herself on the sand. She slumped after a few steps and guzzled the river water but then she immediately spat out the last of the brackish water. Bidisha felt something build up in her stomach and she gagged. The water was too salty to drink and she had gulped quite a handful without a second thought.

She looked around, baffled. The waters had no end unlike the visible banks on both sides before she had slumped into a deep slumber. There was sand all around on the shore that faded her memories of green edges on the river. Her heart blossomed.

'The seashore. End of the river.'

She was back to her senses. Bidisha should have felt safer in that place, away from the palace, but she was also farther away from her mother. She let out a deep sigh, parched and famished as she paced towards Debesh. Her eyes opened wide at the sight of fish and the aroma tingled her taste buds as her mouth watered. Her dry and chapped lips curled up.

'How could you leave me in the boat to die under the scorching sun? I have never seen anybody as coldhearted as you,' Bidisha shouted as soon as her eyes caught sight of him at a distance on the banks.

But Debesh continued to roast the fish under the shade of the mangroves.

'Is there no difference between this fish and me? You left me in the blazing hot sun to roast!' Bidisha rushed closing in on him.

'Thank me, you are at least dry and won't fall sick after what happened earlier.'

'Really? I could have died from sunstroke while you enjoyed your fish.' Bidisha grabbed some roasted fish and started to devour it.

'You need to catch your share before you eat.' Debesh extended a stick tied to a plant tendril, 'Here, take this. Help yourself. And if you want fresh water, walk to the other side.'

Her eyes followed his directions at the very thought of freshwater. She could see a peculiar mark, a distinctive line in the waters. The visible difference in the pattern of the waves created a demarcation between the river and the sea waters as the two met. She placed her half-eaten fish on a leaf and immediately rushed to quench her thirst. She drank her fill as the water tasted so much better on the other side.

She gazed into the marvel of nature she hadn't seen before. The Ganga flowed into the sea, just like herself, walking towards an unknown destination away from her birthplace.

Bidisha rested under the trees farther away from the beach. Though Debesh lay on the sand, his hands under his head, away from her, the young hearts indulged in arguments. Dusk had set in and she had regained her strength. It was time for her to be courageous and do that one thing that could set her free despite what she had done to Yuvaraja Trinabh. Kill Oliver Watts.

She couldn't possibly run all her life. That would be worse than what her mother had to endure. Bidisha had already hurt her mother, the one thing she hated doing the most, when she had left home. It was time for her to return and seek Mokshita's forgiveness.

But first she had to carve out a way for herself to even return to Bishnupur. The circumstances were already bad for her and her mother. And with the grave mistake Bidisha had made, it would only ruin them if she didn't even try to compensate for her crime. She wasn't sure how Rani Maa would react to Oliver's death this time, if Bidisha succeeded in killing him at all. But she didn't see any other way out of the perilous situation.

She would go after Oliver.

The port was nearby and she would do what was needed to be done.

'That's all. I am free from my duty. You made it to the end of the river. I can go back to Yuvaraja Prabir,' Debesh said as he stretched his arms getting ready to row again after a day-long rest.

'Let's not meet again even after things settle,' Bidisha said as she stood up, picking up the sword that was stained with Yuvaraja Trinabh's blood, the one that had managed to get her into the hopeless situation she was running away from.

To her surprise, there was no snarky reply. She turned back to look at the serene sea. At least he wouldn't be around to nag on her actions every now and then. Debesh was already gone. The boat, however, was still on the shore.

Bidisha rolled the thick dry spathe she had managed to find from a tree. A sheath would be much better but then the very weapon meant for her protection had become a threat without its cover. Just like she had become for her mother.

She walked along the seashore. Sooner or later, she would reach the port. It was getting dark but the full moon in the sky smiled at her and showered all the light she needed. The sand underneath her feet provided the warmth she needed. And the cool breeze kissed her in the face and held her in its embrace. Bidisha walked farther and farther away from the Ganga towards the port to realize her goal. She had to seek his Majesty's forgiveness and if possible, beg for her mother's freedom along with a pardon for herself, no matter how daunting and impossible the prospects looked.

Bidisha had already reached the port and to her good fortune, she had located the exact spot where Oliver's ship was docked. She was busy watching the activities around and observing men working hard to load the ship with goods. It was dark and the fire lanterns were all that were lit sparingly.

'Have you completely lost your mind?'

She was startled at the voice and turned back. Her hand went to her chest as her eyes fell on Debesh.

'What are you doing here?' Bidisha faltered and turned around, away from him and continued to peep from behind the rocks where men were at work loading a ship with raw cotton bales, huge wooden chests, barrels and whatnot.

'What are you up to?' Debesh whispered holding her by her shoulders as his stare pierced her. 'Why did you come to the port instead of hiding away someplace safe?'

'Didn't you walk away? Why are you even here?' Bidisha asked as she shrugged his hands off her shoulders and took a peek again at the ship.

'I sensed it. You're up to something. A woman running away from her mother, leaving her alone in the jungle wouldn't be as calm as you were.'

'And so you are here to stop me from doing that 'something'?' Bidisha retorted glaring at him, 'It's all in your head. I came across the ship while I was walking away from my misfortune to find a safe place.'

'I am glad I followed you. You're so not trustworthy!' Debesh said instantly grabbing her by her elbow, 'And now we are walking away from here. That must be Oliver's ship since it is the only ship on the port.'

'Try and stop me if you can,' Bidisha challenged him as she pulled her arm from his grip and moved towards the ship, crouching behind the large wooden crates.

'What do you mean? Stop at once.' Debesh raged, taking his steps further with caution.

'Keep your voice down. There are men around,' Bidisha whispered in his ears, 'You better leave me alone.'

Footsteps crunched on gravel and sand as the men approached them. She crouched down further and Debesh moved closer towards her as they hid behind a huge wooden chest. Bidisha was close enough to feel the warmth of his breath. Debesh's eyes went wide, just like the owl's that hooted in the dark.

The silver stud in his left ear glittered in the moonlight. His two-day-old stubble, on his otherwise clean-shaven face, did not do justice to his well-defined jawline. And just as her eyes moved away from his face, she caught a glimpse of a shapeless blue shiny metal tied to a black string around his neck. It looked like a talisman with some inscription, and was worn and chipped. She looked at it for a long, and then her eyes fixed on his honeyed perfectly tanned skin. Unlike Yuvaraja Trinabh's rough and scarred skin, Debesh's was too good for a warrior who played with weapons every day.

Debesh was busy assessing the mens' movements, looking like a statue. Bidisha mocked him as she cocked her head and squinted at him. When he looked back at her, she shifted her attention back to the *goras*.

The men grunted as they lifted a heavy bale off the ground and carried it to the ship.

She took note of the soldiers in the red coats guarding the loot and the huge wooden chests on the ship, with their muskets, hung on their drooping shoulders and their eyes were ready to shut. When the cargo was loaded, the soldiers sat down on the small wooden stools on the entryway to quench their thirst and rest.

Bidisha hid behind the rocks and bales as she walked towards the ship, dodging their drained eyes.

'Come back!' Debesh murmured after a long moment as he followed her in a vain attempt to stop her.

Bidisha turned around and mouthed a 'sssh' placing a finger on her pouting lips. And then she sauntered carefully inside the ship making her way into the bales storage area. Debesh followed her, still whispering to her to return.

'You don't have to follow me. Why don't you go back?' Bidisha said when Debesh pulled her by her elbow. 'It's the right time to get in and hide. There are no guards in this part of the ship.'

Bidisha loosened herself from his grip and moved faster. She had found a safe place to hide and Debesh went after her.

'We have to get out of here right now,' Debesh tried to convince her again as she got comfortable amidst the cotton bales.

'You leave. I can't. You have to go. Prince Prabir needs you. Hurry now!'

'I can't let you do something stupid again, like what you ended up doing in the palace. What are you thinking? You'll ruin it for everybody. What are you up to?' Debesh raised his voice, irked and helplessly scratching his head. 'I have no idea what your intentions are. But seeing you risk your life like this often, I have a hunch that you've approached Rani Maa with an ulterior motive. But whatever you plan to do, I am telling you, I will make every attempt to stop you. You're not only putting our lives in danger here but you are also going to pose a bigger problem for the king and Yuvaraja Prabir. We need to get out now.'

'Sssshhhh! Quiet. I am telling you. You should go right away if you don't want to get stuck here with me,' Bidisha said as she scanned the outside for any movement.

Bidisha's heart skipped a beat at the sudden appearance of the same two red coats who made themselves comfortable on the wooden stools in front of the storage now.

Debesh's stony face was right behind her and he gave her a fierce and cold look. She could sense his rage, like that of a smouldering cheetah ready to prey on her.

She was aware of what it meant for Debesh to stick by Yuvaraja Prabir's side like a shadow. He had already stayed away for more than a day just to follow the Yuvaraja's order to help her. Bidisha couldn't ask anything more from him. However, it wasn't her fault. He had made it inside the ship despite her warning. And it was not in her power anymore to stop herself from accomplishing what she was there for, to hunt a Britisher so she could please the Maharaja. She bit her nails as her veins pulsated in her neck.

It was important that Debesh somehow made it out of the ship, for the sake of Yuvaraja Prabir, who was always in the eye of lurking dangers. She had always hated the royals of Bishnupur, but only after she set her foot inside the palace had she got to see their real faces.

Yuvaraja Prabir was like a good soul stuck in a rotten body. She couldn't understand if she felt empathy or pity for his state. But all she wanted was for him to be safe and that meant Debesh had to make it back to his master, safe and sound.

But the guards hadn't moved an inch as they discussed and laughed at the Indian whores they bedded on their trip. It was too much to bear for her to constantly listen to their demeaning conversation about the people of Bishnupur and their disgracing prattle about women. Debesh's presence made it all the more embarrassing when the two guards spoke the unspeakable in lewd language. Bidisha could understand them only to an extent. Some of their words boiled her blood while others caused her extreme pain and shame even without them being directed at her.

Debesh, on the other hand, avoided any eye contact with her as he silently tried to vent his anger by rubbing and griping the sheathe till his nails and knuckles turned pale. There was nothing he could do, just like her, but listen to them.

However, their laughs and giggles faded into the dark as they slipped into their slumber and the chirping of crickets sounded louder. The lint around the bales caused Bidisha's nose to tingle and made it even more difficult to stay calm. And Debesh's face made it obvious about his struggle with the same.

To add to everything, the awkwardness between Bidisha and Debesh had compounded into a silent war.

Suddenly, she sensed a movement she had not expected. The ship had set sail. And she hadn't even figured out Oliver's whereabouts, let alone kill him. Fear beat a loud pulse in her ears and blocked all other sounds. The fine hair on her nape rose. She wanted to scream out the terror that was stuck in her chest, tightening the insides. But the cold nerves had embalmed her voice and wouldn't make it out.

Fury and hatred towards her were evident in Debesh's narrowed, bloodshot eyes as the ship embarked. She couldn't exact his escape plan and neither could he think of anything to get out of the ship. That was not what she had planned for. The only thing she wanted badly at the moment was for him to move out from there and go to his safety.

Every wave the ship passed, she was moving closer towards the hell the English called their land. The farther the ship took her, the tougher it would get to escape. Moreover, it meant going away from her mother to a faraway land and never returning. There was a high probability that Oliver or one of the owners of the ship would kill her if they found her.

Bidisha's palms broke into a sweat as the thought of leaving her mother behind, all alone, crept into her mind. She slumped down on the floor and her heart sunk. She wrapped her arms around her knees and buried her face in the bale next to Debesh.

'Wasn't the ship supposed to sail at the break of dawn?' Bidisha mumbled with effort.

'Every nerve and bone in my body is screaming and killing me right now for my stupidity because I followed you. I should have left when I had the chance,' Debesh said as he hunched closer to her ear, 'You have ruined everything for me.' He raked his hair and squeezed his eyes shut. His hands were locked on his head.

Bidisha wasn't sure if he was regretting following her or was thinking of a plan.

Bidisha fought the rising panic that threatened to cloud her mind. 'First, you're not helping me with your blabber. Second, it was your foolish decision to stay back even when I asked you to leave. And, third,' Bidisha leaned forward trying to suppress a shiver, 'I still have good chances to see my plan through.'

'First, if we keep talking like this, the soldiers stationed out will come and grab our necks. Second, I don't even know what are you up to. Why should I help you? And third, was it you who attacked Sir Oliver Watts during the hunting expedition?'

Her throat went dry and she swallowed. 'Why would you say such a thing?!'

'I had felt it odd when I saw you half-dressed, standing in the bathing tent, in the middle of the night when everyone was exhausted. I am telling you, Bidisha, if you don't confess what's in your heart, I will make sure to get the truth out from you,' Debesh whispered and his tone pierced her like a jagged knife. 'I am in a rush to get the hell out of here first and then I will take care of you.'

'Rush?' Bidisha tried to change the topic of their conversation, 'Are you planning to jump in the sea? Do you think you're a shark to stay safe till you make it to the shore?'

'Or, what? Is your plan to hide in here and do nothing till you're caught and transported magically to another world when you're hung for your offence?'

'Stop talking, will...ah...you?'

Rats squeaked as they ran around the crannies between the bales. It disgusted her and interrupted her busy mind that was trying to figure a way out. The darkness of the night had perhaps seeped into her head too, not letting her think. For all she knew, she'd committed yet another blunder.

Her finger went to her nose but the septum ring had long gone. Bidisha might never make it back to Bishnupur. She was losing hold on her thoughts and on her emotions. Her eyes welled up. She covered her face with her *pallav* and looked away from Debesh. Nonetheless, she couldn't help her sniffles and then, to her utter shock, she sneezed before she could stop herself.

'Who is it?' one of the guards shouted. 'Show yourself this instant.'

Debesh shook his head and reached for his sword.

Footsteps fast approached them. Bidisha and Debesh took positions to defend themselves, still ducking behind the bales. Together.

'Aren't you the one who slit Trinabh's thumb? What on earth are you doing here on my ship?' Sir Oliver enquired as he strode towards Bidisha, his extra-long legs covered a lot of ground with every step. He fastened his grey night robe on his waist and stood a foot away.

A guard clasped her hands behind her back and held her in his best grip. The British messenger was quick enough to bring the news from the palace to Oliver and her reputation had preceded her.

'But how did he know it was me?'

She was captured even before she had taken the first step towards her plan.

'And you, Debesh, what brings you here?', Sir Oliver said, pronouncing his name as Dabe, 'I have never seen you alone, away from Prabir. I wonder if he is on the ship too...'

'It's her. I was chasing her on the orders of Yuvaraja Prabir so that we could bring her to justice for the crime, the treachery she has committed.' Debesh replied, his bloodshot eyes looking at Bidisha while two guards held him tight.

'But my guards said you were hiding with her.'

'Had I known this ship belonged to you, Sir Oliver, I wouldn't have made that mistake! Yuvaraja Prabir asked me to get her alive to him. And I had to protect myself and her from the unknown people the ship belonged to.'

'I don't believe this. You nasty little bitch, why did you come to the port from the palace? I don't see a need for that, if you were only trying to escape Trinabh and his men.' Sir Oliver slapped Bidisha hard enough to leave an imprint of his hand on her fair skin.

A squeak escaped her and Bidisha's eyes welled up with tears but refused to let them out.

'And you, Debesh. Am I to believe that you chased her like a hound until you reached the harbour but you couldn't catch hold of this wench till she made it inside the ship? How difficult is it for a strong brawny man like you?'

'You have no idea of this woman, Sir Oliver. I did not, either. She was not alone and I was attacked by a group of men. I had to deal with those thugs and then track her down, which led me to the port. In fact, she boarded your ship in an attempt to escape me.'

Bidisha never thought Debesh could be that good a liar. But he went overboard in improvising and tried to plaster his deceit on her head all for the sake of Yuvaraja Prabir.

'Is that right? I don't see any sign of distress on your body. Not a single bruise or a wound.' Sir Oliver walked towards Debesh and in no time, his fist had met Debesh's chest.

Debesh groaned. 'Believe me... Err... There were only two men whose whole intention was to keep me distracted. But I managed to get rid of them.'

'Hmmm...I can believe that. I have seen you taking on men like wooden stems. Two, if it's true, are flies to smash for you. I trust Prabir more than anybody in Bishnupur and he has his trust in you. I will let you be for now. Though I have my doubts that you are in cahoots with her.' Sir Oliver said with a calm face as he headed towards Bidisha rubbing his blue glassy eyes.

'I owe you my loyalty, Sir Oliver. I will never dare to disappoint you...' Debesh blurted even as he tried to lose the hold on his hands.

'Let him,' Sir Oliver ordered even as he held Bidisha by her jaw. 'Tell me, why did you come so far to the port? Tell me your real intention, will you?'

'Can I first get some water please?' Bidisha requested.

'Do you think you're in a position to demand anything right now? I could throw you out of my ship right this moment. We are far away from the land.

You will be gone without any trace.'

And even before Oliver finished his words, his hand met her cheek with yet another blow and her head turned towards her north due to the impact. Her already red cheek was bruised and a single drop of blood trickled out from her nose. There was a clang in her ear, a loud one, and even before it settled, the sting on her cheek goaded her to smack him back. But she dismissed the thought before it brought her more trouble.

'Go on. Tell me. Why are you here?' Sir Oliver raised his golden brows, the act causing wrinkles on his forehead.

'There is no other intention. I... I am telling you the truth. I had to get out of the kingdom, far away. Yuv... Yuvaraja Trinabh would hunt me if I stayed. Please trust me,' Bidisha said, breathing heavy, swinging her head in an attempt to finish her words and then she crashed down on the floor as the guards let go of her arms.

Debesh took a step towards her but then he stopped and left the chamber they were being interrogated in.

'Let her be. And also keep a watch on him,' Oliver instructed as he took a full circle around her weak body on the floor.

Bidisha still laid down on the floor, feeling sick in the stomach, occasionally looking outside. Debesh stood on the deck right outside Oliver's chamber where she was left to deal with her hopeless agony. He was busy trying to get any information he could on what was to come, for himself and for Bidisha.

'What do you think will be Bidisha's fate like in his den? Is Oliver going to prey on her?' Debesh asked the red-uniformed guard, rubbing the dorsum of his nose with his thumb. He chugged water from his metal mug and looked straight into the guard's eyes.

'You Indian bastard, what do you really want to know? Will Sir Oliver violate that wench? If only he'd have. We'd be lucky too, if we had our chance with that exotic lass,' the guard commented as he closed his eyes for a moment as if he was already living it.

Debesh was close to punching the guard in his face but then he let it go, because of the obvious repercussions, and sighed.

'What do you mean?' Debesh asked instead.

'Sir Oliver can see only gold and money, not women. He believes that lust can corrupt a man's ambition and hinder their growth. He is a businessman, a real trader, nothing more and nothing less. '

'So, what is he going to do with her? Kill her?'

'Should he not? Of course, yes. But he will first torture her to get the information he wants. His only concern is to see if somebody has planted her to destroy his business. Other traders want him gone and he can't stand it when it comes to business.'

It was dawn and the ship was well on its journey; no land was visible from any side. The deep blue waters rose in tiny waves with the sun's rays sparkling on its surface. There was no green or brown whatsoever on the far horizon. It was eerie how the only earthen colour was of the deck of the ship and that oak was home to everyone on the ship for many months to come.

Debesh looked into the void, his hand on his stomach. He was beginning to feel sick Bidisha guessed just like she was having sea sickness. He held a wooden pole that seemed to be bearing too much of a load, his dead weight along with the sails of the ship.

Bidisha moaned in hopelessness as she turned towards Debesh for his words didn't reach her anymore. She raised her trembling hand to hold the pole, pleading for water. Her dry mouth made it impossible for her to keep going.

Just then, water gushed on her face, leaving her breathless. She gasped from the onslaught of the water. The water trickled down her face, washing her hair away from her face due to the force. She struggled to open her eyes.

'Is that enough?' Sir Oliver asked after splashing a bucket full of seawater on her face, dressed in his black frock coat over black pants, his butt comfortable on his bed.

Bidisha limped towards the wooden pole that stood erect in the middle of Oliver's chamber. She leaned against it, looking straight at Sir Oliver from under her half open eyes.

'Wa...water... please...'

'Tell me why you are here on this ship and I will give you all the food and water you want.'

Sir Oliver kicked the empty wooden bucket that had dared to be in his path and walked towards her. He held her by her shoulders and shook her hard, causing her to scream in pain. His eyes were wide and clear about his resolve to get her to speak.

'You'll speak. Now.' Oliver fumed and his grip tightened as he shook her further.

Bidisha yelped. 'I was not aware that the ship... that it was your ship. I... I was only, ah, trying to escape. Water... Water, please.'

Suddenly, Debesh barged in and his face turned pale instantly as his eyes fell on her. He looked at her with an intensity as if trying to heal her with his stare. The bruises on her cheek, her bleached skin and her pale cracked lips certainly would wrench anybody's heart. Except Oliver's. And then his fiery glare turned on Sir Oliver's fingers that almost dug into her skin.

'Ah! Water...' Bidisha cried again in a voice so feeble that Debesh had to read her lips to understand what she was saying.

The waves lapped consistently and at times the sea was harsh too. The vessel surged and even swayed occasionally, making her dizzy and her insides rumbled ready to throw up.

Debesh hung his face and watched helplessly as she suffered in the hands of the white demon.

'Sir Oliver, pardon me but I think you'll lose her if you don't give her water. She looks dehydrated.'

'Get her some water,' Oliver ordered immediately as if he was waiting for someone to reaffirm this. 'She needs to be alive for me to get the information. She might be working for a group. I need to know everything I can.'

'Do you think she is a spy? She can't be. Bidisha has been working in the palace for over a year.'

'Only a year. That says a lot. But why are you so worried for her, Debesh?'

Debesh's gaze was fixed on her face even as he pretended to stand strong, his arms crossed over his chest.

'I have promised Yuvaraja Prabir to keep her alive. I... I have to get her back to Yuvaraja Trinabh alive,' Debesh faltered, 'Let me take her out from here so that she gets some rest and recovers. If she dies, then we both will pay for it, Sir Oliver. You will never be able to get the information you want to.'

Bidisha was groggy and unable to comprehend anything that was happening around her. It was as if she was suspended in the air all of a sudden. She squinted her eyes to look into a blurry man's face who was carrying her in his arms. Debesh, it was him. It was then she tried looking around. He walked behind a guard as he took them to a corner space, a size of a hole with nothing but a wooden bench.

The moon was right above the ship. Its silver light sparkled on her skin and the beads of sweat on her forehead shone under the dark sky. Her lips quivered as the breeze caressed her damp body. The calm of the night felt pleasant after the suffocation inside Oliver's chamber.

'Yuvaraja Trinabh...' Bidisha murmured.

Bidisha's back suddenly touched the hardwood and her legs stretched on the bench. She opened her eyes to witness Debesh as she came out of the trans. His hand trembled as he raised her head and held her in his arms. His chest rose and sank against her ear. She heard it, the thudding of the soft fury deep inside his chest. He got a wooden mug full of water close to her and helped her drink. Bidisha finally closed her eyes after quenching her thirst and rested her cheek on his shoulder.

'I don't like it,' Debesh stated as he pulled his arm away.

'Ouch!' Bidisha squeaked. 'Do you always have to be so rash, so...so erratic? What don't you like?'

'The things happening right now. I can't leave Yuvaraja alone. He needs me.'

'And you think I like it! But wh...what are you going to do about it?'

'This is all because of you, Bidisha. If Yuvaraja Prabir didn't have feelings for you, he would have never sent me with you. I would be in the palace next to him right now, not in this damn ship away from him.'

'Watch your tongue...' Bidisha tried to shout at him, collecting all her strength, but only a feeble sound escaped her mouth. 'Don't you dare say that. He is a Yuvaraja and I am a nobody. I don't like it when somebody links my name with a man so casually.'

'Have you not noticed the way he looks at you? Do you know how much you mean to him? Have you thought, why would he help you and risk everything? Can't you see he sent his only friend and support, me, to protect you?' Debesh said as he held her by her shoulders while she still laid on the bench.

'No. I have not. It has nothing to do with me. I am grateful for his help and I will try to repay him in every possible way. But, not like you think.'

'No matter how many times I tell you, you wouldn't even consider Yuvaraja Prabir's feelings for you. Rather, you are happy dreaming about that monster of a man, Trinabh. You even took his name with such sincerity just a while back. I can't believe a brave and intelligent woman like you would fall for a man like him. In fact, I can't accept any woman liking that man.'

'You don't know a thing about him. It clearly shows in your words. You have no right to talk about him, the man who saved my life despite what I did to him in that spiteful moment.'

'You think that man loves you? Bidisha, I never thought you could fall for his pretences. Everybody knows he is a masked man. And trust me, he is much scarier behind it than he is to your eyes.'

'I pity you, Debesh. Leave alone sensing the feelings of any other man towards me, you would even crush your feelings for me for the sake of your master. You're so blinded. You wouldn't even acknowledge your love for a girl because you think your master might hold her dearly in his heart. Coward! You have no right to talk about Yuvaraja Trinabh.'

'What did you just say?' Debesh grimaced, 'Who told you I have anything in my heart for you?'

'You did. Through your face and your eyes. The way you look at me and then the way you try to hide it from me.'

'That's your illusion. And never, ever dare to call me a coward. You don't know anything about me,' Debesh said and walked out of that hole of a space.

Debesh had always stood like a pillar with Yuvaraja Prabir through thick and thin. And the Yuvaraja was no different when it came to honouring their friendship. Despite being a royal, he treated Debesh like the light that had illuminated his pitiful life. She had also heard stories about Debesh's loyalty and their unbreakable bond. But that didn't give him any authority to push her to accept Yuvaraja's heart. And it was not for him to speak on his behalf either. And nobody knew what the Yuvaraja himself wanted. It was all insane to even talk about it when nothing was clear to anybody. Debesh was just acting up, perhaps because she had unknowingly taken Yuvaraja Trinabh's name and he despised him.

CHAPTER ELEVEN

'I thought you enjoyed seeing me in distress as Sir Oliver's captive. What made you help me? Don't say it's for Yuvaraja Prabir,' Bidisha asked Debesh, her eyebrows laced with salty beads and her lips quivering as she held the blanket from slipping down, pulling her legs towards her chest.

Debesh came closer to Bidisha and stood only inches away from her. 'I don't know what I am doing anymore. Another day has passed. We are going farther away from our land with each passing day. I have no idea where are we heading and why Sir Oliver is not ready to let me go!' He bent over to look straight into her eyes and continued, 'More than anything, I don't understand what were you thinking when you got into this ship knowing the consequences. And because of you, I am stuck here like a fool.'

'First of all, Debesh, I am grateful for whatever you did for me in the last few days. And second, I am sorry you ended up in trouble because...'

'I have no interest in your speech. Save your words for later, when Sir Oliver will torture the crap out of you to confirm something that he is suspecting. And come to think of it, even I believe there is more to you than I could ever see from the day you came to the palace.' Debesh spat pulling down his dirty *Panjabi* with one swift stroke, venting his rage on the garment that clung to his chest in an attempt to hold himself back from harming Bidisha.

'Then, why help me, why care for me?' Bidisha asked as she stood up and washed her hands after eating a weird rice porridge she had never tasted before.

'Do you think I did it for you? Don't you still get it? I hate you for all that you have done in the past few days,' Debesh growled rattling her by her shoulders, pushing her down on the wooden bench.

He moved away from her and fisted the oak pillar that stood right in the middle of the mess holding all the weight of the roof. Debesh snarled.

'Yuvaraja Prabir wanted to keep you safe and I followed his orders. I can do anything for him, even a mistake like this one, which has ultimately forced me to leave my Yuvaraja stranded alone.'

'Really? As if the Yuvaraja is in grave danger in his own luxurious abode, all guarded by his father, the Maharaja himself. How can he be...'

'You dare.' Debesh was suddenly all over her as he clasped her hands behind her back and pulled her closer, his chest brushing against hers.

Bidisha's ears were hot and her cheeks were on fire. His deep dark eyes stared into her tired ones. He let her loose, his eyes set on her quivering full lips as she let out a sob.

'You know nothing about Yuvaraja Prabir even though you should be the one knowing him more than anybody else,' Debesh said and moved away from her.

'Why should I know anything about him?' Bidisha asked him without any shift in her expression as she sat down on the bench unable to stand.

'Because he cares for you. You are the only woman he has loved after his sick wife's untimely death.'

'Don't give me this gibberish. Love? A Yuvaraja will marry only for politics. A random woman is for a passing affair only. Maharajas and Yuvarajas don't love a soul, at least not someone as unimportant as me. He couldn't have possibly loved his wife even, let alone me. Do you really want me to believe that he has been alone without laying his hands on any woman for all these years?'

Debesh held her arms, tight enough to dig his fingers into her skin, and pinned her hard on the bench. 'Just like you think I don't know Trinabh, you have no idea what Yuvaraja Prabir has gone through all his life. Don't you dare speak so lightly about him when you know nothing.'

Bidisha looked frail and meek as his huge frame towered over her. She was overwhelmed for an instant and in the next moment, she groaned.

Her face went red for she could no longer hold it in. 'Let go. Ah!'

Debesh suddenly loosened his grip when he saw the impression of his fingers on her pale skin. He moved away from her.

'You're right. He didn't love his wife. But he cared for her knowing she was in an equally helpless position as he was,' Debesh snarled at her. 'The Yuvaraja was a pawn in a game played by the man you're upholding, Trinabh and his mother, Rani Durga Moni Devi. The Yuvaraja had to marry a sick Yuvarani as part of the dealings between the two kingdoms'

'What good a Yuvaraja is for his Kingdom when he is not even capable to stand for himself? He let others treat him like that. That's nobody's mistake but his own,' Bidisha rasped before she rolled her eyes and walked out of the hole.

'You are prejudiced. Unfortunately, it was you who brought him peace, at least for some time. He knew it very well that nothing could ever happen between a woman with no royal blood and the Yuvaraja except maybe physical encounters, which he doesn't believe in anyway. But he always longed for your presence around him.'

And in the next few minutes, which felt like eons to Bidisha, her heart clenched for Yuvaraja Prabir as Debesh spoke about his master's dismal story.

The sudden demise of Prabir's mother, Subhashree Moni Devi, the first wife of Maharaja Mitul Singha Dev, had left the newborn Yuvaraja stranded. Thereafter, he had clung to the only support he had growing up, his father.

The politics in the kingdom, in his own family, which included the other three wives of Raja Mitul Singha Dev and his half-brothers and half-sisters, who were supported unconditionally by their mothers, left the Yuvaraja with little choice but to accept the unjust behaviour towards him.

His Majesty was too caught up with his royal business and trading his motherland with the foreigners who had left the people in the kingdom to starve. And yet Prabir had no one but his father to look up to as his role model. He trusted him even if he had little attention to spare for his son.

Debesh's mother, Janaki, was the only person who preserved Yuvaraja Prabir's heart with her love and affection. She cooked for him without taking her eyes off the food being prepared knowing how unsafe Prabir's life was without his mother to tend to him. As the second eldest son of King Mitul Singha Dev, he was meant to grow up into a warrior prince. But his health hadn't permitted that as he continued to be weak throughout as a result of his untimely birth.

It so happened that Janaki had unexpected labour contractions, when Debesh was on his way into the world, while attending to Rani Subhashree Moni Devi as they strolled in the garden together. Janaki had slumped down inadvertently in pain and she took Rani's hand and pulled her along.

Rani, who herself was pregnant with Prabir, but several weeks away from delivering the baby, lost her balance and fell from the slope rolling on her stomach twice before falling unconscious on the grass. Consequently, the Rani delivered a premature baby, Yuvaraja Prabir, who was born weak. Days later, the Rani took her last breath due to heavy bleeding.

Subhashree Moni Devi and Janaki had shared a strong bond despite the vast difference in their social status. Rani Subhashree Devi's last wish was to forgive Janaki who was held prisoner along with her newborn, Debesh. She had also taken a promise from Janaki that she would raise Prabir like her own son, like Debesh. The Maharaja had gathered himself and granted his wife her death wish, and let Janaki raise his fragile son, seeing no other way out.

Janaki had constantly reminded Debesh of his duties towards Yuvaraja Prabir, whose mother had saved Janaki's life from the wrath of the Maharaja after what had happened on that fateful day.

'Yuvaraja Prabir and I are exactly of the same age, born on the same day, loved and raised by the same mother. This is the only time in all these years that I am away from my friend, my brother, and I can't bear the feeling of leaving him alone to face the people in the palace,' Debesh said holding his head in his hands.

'I am happy to know that you considered me worthy of telling me your story,' Bidisha said as she moved towards Debesh and stood next to him, her eyes looking along the blue waves. 'But I can only ask for your forgiveness for putting you and the Yuvaraja through all this.'

'I see you have fully recovered now. It will be fun to put you in pain all over again. Bring her,' Sir Oliver ended his mockery with a command to his guards as he walked out of the resting hole provided to Bidisha. 'I wanted to tar and feather you. That will be fun to watch but too easy for someone who is more than just a stowaway.'

'*What does he mean?*'

Debesh was away, busy attending to his duties on the ship befitting his strength but not his interest. He was to assist the sailmaker as one of the common sailors and also be available for various other jobs on demand. Bidisha had no clue about Debesh's whereabouts when she was being taken away.

She braced herself to face the unknown as she sat on the chair with two guards standing right behind her. Sir Oliver's eyes were glued to hers but he didn't make any attempt to question her, not yet. His continuous stare had not only started making her feel uncomfortable but also apprehensive about his intentions. His blue gaze bore into her hazel eyes, sending waves of distress down her spine.

It was long past a few minutes and he hadn't spoken a word. But she was done burning under his gaze.

'Sir Oliver, is there anything you want to ask me?' Bidisha spoke with a soft but firm voice pretending to be all well and unaware of the situation that might drag her down further if he had recognized her.

'You are such an innocent maiden, aren't you?' Sir Oliver derided, as he walked towards his desk.

He made himself comfortable behind a desk, his elbows placed on the table and his hands supporting his chin. The calm on his face scared her and his words didn't make sense.

'So, tell me why did you try to kill me back in the forest?'

'What?' Bidisha let out a squeal as fear clawed up her throat.

She couldn't believe he had asked her that question. She had hoped he would never recognize her but there she was, in the face of her worst nightmare. That was not the question she had expected.

She was only prepared to answer one question: why did she board the ship? Bidisha had a story in her mind.

'Wasn't it you who tried to kill me? Now I want to know why.' Sir Oliver walked towards her, his eyes cold and his lips curled up unexpectedly.

Her breath raced and put her brain to a halt as her eyes froze open. That mockery on his face didn't sink well with her. But in an instant, she collected herself before her face made it obvious.

'I don't understand. Why would I attempt to kill you?' Bidisha stood up only to be pushed back in her chair by the guards behind her.

'Either you tell me or I will make you spill the truth my way.'

'Are you trying to scare me into accepting something I never did?' Bidisha pulled herself away from the soldiers' hold.

'Okay. It's my way then,' Sir Oliver said and left without uttering another word.

Beads of sweat flushed on her forehead as four fiends' hands grabbed her and dragged her out of Sir Oliver's chamber and bound her to the base of the foremast. And just like Oliver, the guards didn't care to utter a single word before leaving.

She knew at that point what her fate would be like. She'd die taking her secret to the grave or die confessing her plan. Either way, death was her destiny and it was not too far. In a matter of hours, she would be salt-roasted like fish under the sun.

Being bound to the foremast meant the tempestuous wind hitting her the first thing on the ship as it sailed towards its destination, the ship took her closer to hers.

It felt like she was already in heaven although Sir Oliver intended to send her to hell. She could barely squint to soak in the view of the deep blue sea as her eyes shuttered against the brazen wind hitting her. And then, in minutes, the wind started piercing her skin and clobbering her body. Her skin was soon covered with salt as the wind beat her to thrash.

Her hands tied behind her to the strong foremast, there was nothing she could do to help herself, not even jump into the sea and end her pain as she would reach the bottom of the ocean in minutes.

Every man around took a chance to spectate at her. The cook, the boatswain, the quartermaster and even the parson. And their intent didn't seem very good. It never had been. She had seen such ogling eyes many times before. And in her present state, it was only difficult to put them off.

The harsh mid-noon sun had already started burning her salty skin as she gave in all her strength to resist her growing urge to itch. The sun had kissed her face red and the exposed skin was turning adust under the scorching sun and hot wind. Bidisha panted, her lips cracked, pale and powdered at the ends. She had grown exhausted after trying to wiggle herself loose from the rope bindings.

The consistent creaking of crates added an unbearable noise to her already chaotic mind. And the violent rattling of goods on the deck as the exhausted men laboured through the day under the hot sun had left her exasperated.

Moreover, the constant clattering of chains near the mast and the wind had lashed her deaf thereafter.

'Enjoying the serenity! Let's hear what you got to say now,' Sir Oliver showed up.

He stood before her with a smirk that vanished away from his face in the next instant as his eyebrows pulled together at the sight of her face—burnt and almost blistered.

His eyes followed the drop of sweat rolling down her neck. Sir Oliver took a step back, perhaps because he had deciphered the condition of the woman who clung to the foremast. Her worn-out clothes, the frills on the rim of her blouse that hung loose, everything that stood the test of the harsh hot wind spoke in unison.

'Does my state and my exposed skin twinge your eyes yet? And did a sharp piece of ice stab your heart yet?'

If only she was in a condition to throw out those words at him.

Sir Oliver shut his eyes and looked away from her at once.

Bidisha's eyes fell on Debesh who had appeared before her like a God sent soul to pacify her. If only he wasn't away in the lower deck on work, he could have been her saviour. Or, at least he would have tried to protect her.

'Wouldn't he?'

'What have you done to her?' Debesh scorned as he ran towards her suddenly. 'If you intended to kill her, then you should have done it days before. She would die in peace and would be spared the pain at the least,' Debesh shouted as he started to untie her hands. 'She was not even close to your tent when you were attacked that night. Bidisha was in the bathing tent. Go and clear it out with your guards before getting a false impression and punishing somebody in an inhumane way, especially a woman!' Debesh barked working on the ligature that had turned her bare waist purple.

Bidisha was taking slow and shallow breaths. Her eyes were fully shut now, unable to take in any more. Every breath felt like her innards were being twisted and squeezed hard causing a throbbing in her gut.

But Debesh gave her a hand and she slowly walked towards the resting hole the two were in earlier.

Sir Oliver stood expressionless on the deck. His ever-pinkish complexion had turned red under the sun. His eyes fixated on Bidisha, no words escaped his mouth. He looked unlike his usual arrogant self, as if he was contemplating his actions.

But, did he?

The night had brought in a new worry as Bidisha's condition went from bad to worse with her rising body temperature. Debesh paced in and out of the hole as he tried his best to elevate her condition with limited access to the required supplies. And the most distressing situation of all was the availability of fresh water as he was denied access to the limited drinking water on board. But he couldn't possibly use saltwater from the sea on her bruised skin torturing her all the more.

He had done everything possible with the mug of fresh water kept in the hole, including wiping her forehead and arms with a damp cloth in an attempt to bring her body temperature down. But despite Debesh's best efforts, Oliver hadn't bothered to send any help or herbs let alone a qualified person to check on her. Moreover, her eyes had rolled back into her head and he had panicked his guts out. However, Bidisha had finally come back to her senses though she still suffered from fever and chills.

It was late at night when Oliver barged in. 'I heard you were alarmed about the woman's condition. Is she all right? I have asked the guard to fetch the physician accompanying us on this ship.'

'Sir Oliver, she means something to Yuvaraja Prabir. What...what I meant to say was, she needs to reach the palace alive. Why do things have to take an unfortunate turn for you to wake up?'

The physician rushed in then. An Englishman, in a red frock coat and white pants, paced inside the chamber.

'Are you kidding me, Sir Oliver?' the doctor barked and gave a half-smile as he looked at Oliver. 'You want me to treat this Indian bitch.'

'She needs to stay alive for me to get the information I am looking for. And she is also wanted by Prabir, actually by Yuvaraja Trinabh,' Oliver said and looked at Debesh as he put his hands in his pockets.

'I don't care who needs her. Bloody Indians.'

'Alright. Just tell us what needs to be done to keep her alive,' Sir Oliver requested as he took a few steps towards Debesh.

The physician was too headstrong to even touch her but took the pain to explain the next steps before he walked out.

'You better follow the instructions and take care of her. I will arrange for steady servings of the liquids and semi-solids she needs to consume,' Sir Oliver said, his eyes on Debesh as if he was trying to study the Indian warrior before he patted Debesh's back.

Bidisha slept on the hard wooden bench without any reaction even when Debesh tried to sponge her exposed arms and legs that her sari failed to cover without her intervention. She shivered as the chills took her over and shuddered when the cold cloth touched her exposed midriff.

He was persistent and, on his toes, to change the damp cloth on her forehead, which helped in maintaining a steady temperature. He fed her with all the weird soups that were given to him as per Sir Oliver's instructions.

'What does Oliver want from her?' Debesh murmured to nobody in particular as he washed his hands after eating some bland fish and a small serving of rice. 'He seems to be concerned about Bidisha's recovery.'

Bidisha had never experienced such strong emotions that could hinder her actions and cloud her mind. However, she didn't feel the same anymore like she once did. She was getting washed away by the surge of unreliable ardour that she could neither accept nor recognize.

But the unexpected clamour brought her back from her deep ethereal abode.

'You can't wait to torment her again, can you?' Debesh, standing guard over Bidisha, spat at Oliver.

Sir Oliver's eyes rolled away from Debesh and towards Bidisha who had shut her eyes on his arrival pretending to be asleep in peace. Her skin was better and she looked more like a British woman in her long black cotton dress with frills on the neck. He stood there next to her across from Debesh, his eyes travelling the length of her body, as if he was meticulously looking at every inch of her body. Oliver let out a sigh, his hands still clasped behind his back.

'She is getting better,' Sir Oliver remarked as he headed out.

'So, when do you plan to drag her out for the next round of torture?' Debesh blurted forcing Sir Oliver to turn back.

'Just because you're Prabir's right-hand man, don't be under the impression that you'll be spared for your attitude while you are here on the ship. My ship.'

'Sir Oliver, since when have you become an interrogator from a merchant? You were never so cold.'

'Debesh, if you intend to stay alive, you have to forget who you were earlier in some Goddamn kingdom back in India. We are headed towards Lancashire and that's in my country. You will obey me and never question me.' Sir Oliver's eyes blazed as he walked towards his chamber, his shoes clacking in rhythm against the wooden deck in the dark of the night. 'Give them some food and find her a bunk. And that lad there...'

Debesh ran behind Oliver, as he tried to convince him to lend a boat. 'Sir Oliver, I thought once this is all over, you will let us go back. What do you mean by assigning a bunk?' Debesh's voice faded as they walked out of the hole.

It was yet another way Oliver had made it clear that Bidisha had to cramp up in the living quarters along with Debesh and the situation was far from her hopes. Any other person on the ship would have rejoiced for having secured a bunk but not her. It was a confirmation that she wouldn't be going back home. Instead, she would sail away, far away, from her mother. Oliver wouldn't let them both off the ship. She had hoped, at least Debesh stood a chance to return, but Oliver's words had dashed all her hopes.

Bidisha, just like the rest of the crew, had made it through the storm of a journey. Sometimes crying in her coop and at times enjoying games of cards and dice. The rains had washed her tears at times and Debesh came for her aid when it didn't. She even held her sword against him when it was time to play the dumb blame game out of frustration. But she had made it through it all labouring on the deck and in the kitchen, running on her toes behind Oliver and at times, singing sea shanties along while they hauled the ropes. And above all, she had survived the ship yawing, which had given a new lease of life to everyone on the ship just like her.

They had sailed for months and all the while, Bidisha had even indulged in activities that were forbidden on the ship. She had come across chests of gold, statues and artefacts stored safely. She eavesdropped ever so often and found out that it was all the coins they had collected from taxation and Sir Oliver was in charge of moving the chests to London along with his loot of rare and precious commodities. Her heart went out to her people who had to suffer while the *goras* snatched their share of wealth leaving the people in poor conditions.

It had started raining again. And every time it did, people rejoiced as they danced in rain. And luckily, there wasn't much lightning and thunder in the sky like it did sometimes. Some of the men undressed on the deck, they always did under the rain, and washed themselves for nobody knows when they would get a chance again.

Bidisha was now used to it and she continued to do her work without looking at the naked men and a few women who tried to clean themselves half-dressed.

Bidisha was drenched as she moved barrels of water with the help of Debesh as they collected rainwater and stored them for later use. Sir Oliver was busy in his chamber talking to the captain referring to a map as only weeks were left before they made it to the Lancashire port.

The lanterns clattered as the clouds thickened unexpectedly and the wind was getting harsh showing the signs of a storm just when she thought it was a beautiful night. The night sky had gone wild with thunders and lightning that threatened to hit the ship anytime. And amidst nature's fury, there was another commotion created by men.

'Lock him up in the brig and let him starve for three days before he comes to his senses,' the keeper of the little ale corner the folks called a tavern shouted at a man who had chugged an extra mug of ale.

It was the same baldy who had repeatedly violated Bidisha with his filthy eyes. He deserved a good punishment, more than just starvation she thought. Flogging with 'cat o' nine tails' would serve him well for she had suffered the humiliation of his stares for months.

Everything on the ship was rationed, from the freshly roasted fish caught directly from the ocean to the biscuits and even water. And that man had broken yet another rule onboard and drank extra ale going against the rationing policy. Ale was supposed to be a substitute in dire situations when the fresh water goes out of stock. No one was allowed to break that one cardinal rule.

And to survive such everyday situations, people on the ship traded with others for their preferred food and sometimes drinks that included water and ale. Debesh and Bidisha too did the same. She mostly traded her portion of dried beef and pork for an extra mug of water or ale to wash the inedible food down her throat. In fact, none of the people from Bishnupur dared to touch the beef and they were happy to give it away for extra something they wanted instead.

Though it was a horrendous experience, she had pulled through the days as they sailed on high tides, doing odd jobs assigned to her and bearing the consequences of being a woman on the ship.

And finally, the day that everyone looked forward to for reaching their home or even seeing the land after a long sail had arrived.

The last of the ale was being served generously and Bidisha didn't hold herself back either. Sir Oliver, for a change, had joined the celebration. Some of the men had dozed off on the deck after taking in their fill while others puked their guts out after overindulgence.

All through the journey, Bidisha had tried to make sense of Sir Oliver's generosity, who had not bothered her with questions about that night in the forest again. She had even contemplated asking him directly but was stopped by Debesh just like he had managed to convince her against attempting on Oliver's life. And she didn't try it again either. She after all had to make it back home safely again. No matter how long it took.

Bidisha had finished her fourth mug of ale and Debesh stopped her from having anymore when the tavern keeper was offering the last of what was left for the day's consumption.

She pushed him away. 'Don't you try to stop me. You are always in my way, Debesh,' Bidisha said as she swayed trying to move away from him.

'Let us leave. It's better if you go settle in your bunk before you do something,' Debesh said as he supported her and took her away from the deck.

'Wait. Is that Oliver?' Bidisha asked and freed herself from Debesh's grip. 'I need to talk to him.'

Bidisha climbed up the wooden steps trying to hold her balance. Sir Oliver sat alone with a smoking pipe in his mouth and an ale mug in his hand.

She went to him even as Debesh tried to stop her. 'You know you are a good man, Sir Oliver. But not good enough to see people's suff...suffering.' Bidisha batted her eyes. 'But still, I would like to give you a chance since you let me go.'

'Are you out of your mind? What are you blabbering? Come on now. Let us go back, Bidisha.' Debesh grabbed her hand.

'Let me go, Debesh. Who are you to stop me?' Bidisha looked back at Sir Oliver. 'What was I telling? Hmmm... Yes, about that night. That night in the forest. You were right. It was I who attacked you, Sir Oliver. And I regret that I couldn't slit your throat all because that stupid boar created a ruckus.'

Debesh stood still. Bidisha made herself comfortable next to Sir Oliver Watts himself. She didn't feel anything much at that moment. All divisions that separated an Englishman from an Indian stowaway were thrown out of the window.

'What makes you think I wasn't aware of that?' Sir Oliver asked letting out smoke from his mouth, looking at her intently. 'Your eyes, I can never forget them.'

'Look, Debesh. Didn't I tell you he was a good man? He let it slide away...' Bidisha said, leaning forward as she looked at Oliver in his eyes and her lips curled up.

'Stop your nonsense and get down from there, Bidisha.'

'Let her be, Debesh. I would have punished her the day I saw her on the ship if I had to. She is only confessing to what I already knew.' Sir Oliver chugged down his ale and plonked his mug on the wooden plank that served as a makeshift table.

'But that's...that's not even true.' Debesh took a step forward.

Sir Oliver gestured for Debesh to stop. 'Tell me, why did you try to kill me?'

'That is a secret I will never tell you, Oliver. And so, you won't be able to hang me, right?' Bidisha said, putting her head down on the wooden plank before her.

'That's enough, let us leave now.' Debesh tried to lift her in his arms.

'If Oliver is a good man, you, Debesh...' Bidisha stopped abruptly and got down from the stool.

She hugged him, wrapping her arms around his neck, 'You are the best man I have ever met. But only second to Trinabh.'

Bidisha pulled Debesh closer and suddenly pressed her lips against his. And then she gave him a tight hug almost choking him with her strong arms. She enveloped him like a human shield, her neck over his shoulder and her chest pressed against his.

Debesh stood petrified as she held him in her arms for a long moment.

'You two can leave now if you are done with all the hugs and kisses.' Oliver grabbed the mug and looked inside it, disappointed that his share of the ale was finished.

Bidisha glanced at Sir Oliver. 'Goodman,' she remarked pointing at him and then waving her hand even as she held on to Debesh's neck who carried her in his arms gently.

'Land ho! Land ho!'

The screams made it to Bidisha's ears. People shouted and the handful of women on the ship danced in a rhythm. The tippy-ti-tap against the wooden floor was heard everywhere on the ship.

Bidisha struggled to open her eyes even as her head felt as heavy as a huge rock. She looked around, pressing her temples as she got down from her bunk and walked out.

'Land ho! Land ho! Land ho!'

The chant sounded like a song as the people uttered it in unison.

Bidisha covered her eyes as the first rays of the rising sun fell on her. Her red hair was dishevelled and her black dress was crumpled. The deck was packed with men who cheered and a handful of women who sang and danced with them. She couldn't relate to that new kind of fervour on the ship early in the morning. It was a celebration bigger than what it was like the previous night, the food and the ale that they had devoured.

The ale, it struck her. She had swayed her way up the stairs. And then she was sitting with Sir Oliver... Bidisha squealed. She slapped her hand on her head and shook her fear off. Bidisha turned around and, in the crowd, she spotted Debesh who looked away from her at once. She took a few steps towards him and then she touched her lips.

'The kiss!' Bidisha mumbled as she stopped.

She turned around, hesitated, and then, unable to deny her heart what it wanted, she walked back in Debesh's direction. Just a few steps farther and her downcast eyes met a pair of black shiny shoes. The white giant stood before her dressed in his black frock coat and black hat as if he'd be stepping out for a formal event. She gaped at him, her feet glued to the wooden floor and her body stiff.

Sir Oliver caressed her chin with his thumb. 'We are home.'

He excused himself and went past her.

Bidisha could make sense neither of his action nor of his words.

'Didn't I confess that I was the one who attacked him? That I tried to kill him.'

'Get back to work. Come on everyone,' a man shouted.

Let's get the hell out of this shit!' another man added.

The crowd slowly dispersed and, and its hurry, the shock-stricken Bidisha was pushed all around. She then looked at the horizon. The land. There, she could see it too. A smile broke free on her face and her eyes were filled with delight.

She could see large ships looking tiny from the deck. The line-up of boats and several wooden docks made her feel lighter than she had in days. More than anything, the sight of trees pleased her. She had missed her home for long, the jungle and the green canopy of huge trees. She took a deep breath. At least she would get off on some land, even though it was not her motherland.

Bidisha turned around, and there Debesh stood, afar, his gaze fixated on her. Her heart skipped a beat and she felt her body go warm. She broke into a sweat as she recollected, with clarity, the kiss she had planted on his lips.

CHAPTER TWELVE

Bidisha had set her feet on land that she never imagined she would. Call it the land of enemies or the land from where she had inherited some of her traits or even the place where her sword was believed to be wielded once upon a time, over and above everything, it was the land she had hated. And now, God knew for how long she'd have to call it home.

The four-wheeled carriage that was drawn by four beautiful brown horses was loaded with Oliver's belongings and ready to leave. Some of the expensive goods and exotic Indian artifacts were placed inside the couch box. The rest of Oliver's luggage was stacked under the dickey box at the rear of the carriage. Bidisha and Debesh sat over the detachable seat placed over the box.

Sir Oliver Watts settled down in his artistically bewitching couch box along with his luggage that was carefully loaded by his subordinates. Bidisha and Debesh sat in the rear seat of the carriage after alighting from a long hideous journey.

Debesh was stuck at one end of the rear seat, which was already a compact one for two. The seat had no hood to protect them from the scorching summer heat but that was not the problem, yet. Rather the hitch was in the distance between them owing to the awkwardness after the kiss. And she was to make it till Oliver's house alongside the man she had kissed in a drunken state. Moreover, despite being a warrior whose every drop of blood was sworn to fight for Yuvaraja Prabir, Debesh could turn into a timorous heart in situations like that. Though she had worked hand-in-hand with him for hours while unloading the loot and the crates from the ship, the weirdness persisted between them.

As the charioteer drove the majestic carriage, on the even but muddy roads, every house she saw on the way was more mesmerising than what she could have imagined. The city, Lancashire, was prosperous, abundant with huge villas and two-storied bungalows, rich in nature with glorious gardens that were filled with vibrant colours. Even the path that led to the mansions, as they called them, was beautified with lush green grass and stone laid walkways inside their premises. The only thing in common with Bishnupur was the muddy pathways. But they were a little better and cleaner here, just like the ones that led to the palace back home.

Women were dressed in elaborate clothing, more beautiful than what she had seen in British households back in Bishnupur. The feathers on their hats, the frills on their summer parasols and more than anything, their shoes with floral designs and laces fascinated her. Unfortunately, all that the common people of Bishnupur could afford for their sole was a *kapula* at best, or they simply walked bare feet.

Oliver seemed to be a lonelier person than he appeared just like on the ship she had observed. Even back in Bishnupur, he only met people for trade and she had not seen him much otherwise. He spent most of his time in his chamber on the ship or perhaps on the open deck upstairs under the sky all by himself with a mug of ale at his disposal. She had never seen him with the other officers who played cards or indulged in lame banter and political discussions.

His home too, as it appeared, was far away, seemingly, located in the middle of nowhere! As they went farther, the number of houses and the mansions reduced to one in acres. There were open stables guarded by fences. Streams of water burbled as the waterfall tumbled down into the river. The houses were separated by patches of trees that ran for acres before she could spot another building on the way.

But soon the carriage made it through a huge steel gate into an open garden with a lush green lawn. And in a lonely abode, a bungalow built with stones and having a white facade stood far away in a no man's land where she couldn't see another building as far as her vision ended.

The maidens were already waiting at the entrance of the house to welcome Sir Oliver Watts. But their faces knotted as soon as their eyes caught sight of Bidisha. She was aware of her state and what she might have looked like to them after a long sail of more than four full moons.

Though they had stopped several times during their journey to refill the coal and food supplies on the borders of different countries, it was not easy being a woman on the ship. She couldn't remember the last time she had had a chance to clean herself properly. She knew that she must look dreadful and smell awful.

'Take the woman to your quarters and help her with the essentials. And the man, show him the way to his bed,' Sir Oliver instructed and walked straight inside the home.

One of the maidens started to unload Oliver's luggage while the other two gaped at Debesh as he walked towards Bidisha. He looked at Bidisha with a puzzled face; the expression reflected on her face too when their eyes met.

'Don't do anything that you'll regret later. Remember, this is not our home. We have only so much knowledge about their life and rules,' Debesh instructed as he narrowed his eyes in anticipation of the acknowledgement.

'Do I look like an insane person to you? Don't you think I can understand and act according to the gravity of the situation?' Bidisha retorted as she presumed the real matter he hinted at was her urge to kill Oliver.

'If that's what you say. I am trusting you this time, Bidisha.'

Dusk had set in and the stares from the maids continued. While one of the women walked to Debesh with a stark grin plastered on her face, the other one went to Bidisha with a frown on her forehead.

They were walked to a cottage behind the mansion. It was small in comparison to the main building, but a beautiful one nonetheless. The climbers over the stones on the walls made it all the more appealing. The stem had spread over the roof and the blooming flowers hung across the single-storied cottage.

It had three big rooms with three steel beds in each. She'd be sleeping on a proper bed for the first time in her life. It reminded her of her accommodation in the palace, where the maidens still slept on the floor. She marvelled at how Oliver was living a king-sized life that also included a separate quarter for the stay-in maidens and house help.

The woman had helped her with all the essentials but at the same time, she made it clear that Bidisha was an outsider. Rather an outlander. One of the rooms was taken by the three women and she was told that they liked to be together. The second room would be occupied by Debesh and one other male help in the household. The third room was at her disposal and completely free for her use alone which she rather acknowledged with a wide grin.

She laid down on the bed, closed her eyes and let out a comfortable moon as she felt the fluffy cotton mattress. Bidisha was in no hurry to do anything else. Not even bathe or eat a hearty meal despite the aroma of fresh mouth-watering food teased her nostrils.

Just then Debesh showed up dressed in a white ruffled buttondown and a pair of black pantaloons. He leaned on the door and crossed his legs. And

Bidisha's eyes fixed on him for a long second.

'So you're still enjoying the warmth of the bed! Don't you know the kitchen closes early here in English land?'

She got out of the bed instantly and cleared her throat, 'And how do you know about that.'

'The maidens seem to be impressed by me. Didn't you see them hovering around? They gave me more information than needed including the bathroom etiquette considering it the only option available for all of us here in the cottage. I hope you will hurry.'

Just as Bidisha turned up on the table, the grin on the maidens' faces was a constant as they served Debesh his first meal in the cottage. Even while she was clean and dressed fresh, Bidisha could only receive unwelcoming stares from them as she helped herself with the food.

She had a chance to eat food followed by fruits to her heart's content after a long time but nothing like what she was used to eating back home. The night was setting in and the weather was much more pleasant compared to the summers in Bishnupur. It wasn't too humid either. And then she settled down on the wooden porch next to Debesh who perhaps felt the same as her.

'Looks like someone has admirers in this new place.' Bidisha smirked looking at the dark sky with no sign of the moon as they sat next to each other before settling in for the night. 'And these clothes that you're wearing, not bad.'

'Of course, they wouldn't have seen a man like me before,' Debesh whispered as he leaned forward, his hand over his mouth, 'I am unlike their master, Sir Oliver, who has not a muscle to show.'

'From when did you start enjoying such banter about women and their interests in a man's body?'

'You look different too. Beautiful...' Debesh said as he cleared his throat and looked up at the sky.

'What do you know about this? The dress is not something I can wear for too long and the layers of clothing the maidens forced me to wear are making me uncomfortable; they are a mighty inconvenience. Leave alone running around or holding a sword in my hand, this wouldn't even let me walk or sit comfortably,' Bidisha said rolling her eyes as she gathered her hair into a knot on the crown of her head.

'You'll get used to it soon.'

If only he could understand what she was talking about.

The long cotton dress was manageable but what she wore inside dug into her skin. The bodice was intolerable and far too inconvenient to even wear without assistance. A piece of cotton cloth wrapped around her chest would not only hold her breasts in place but also allow her to move freely. And she would stick to that no matter what women were expected to wear in this land. But what irked her the most was the clumsy giggle of the maidens, for no apparent reason, after they handed the bodice, or the corset, as they called it, to her.

'How long do you think we will be stuck here, Debesh?'

'That's not important right now. You should be asking, what will happen once you go back to Bishnupur. It was Yuvaraja Trinabh, after all, who lost his thumb. We don't even know what has happened there in the palace in all these months.'

'I might never walk around in Bishnupur again even with my face covered. The Yuvaraja and Rani Maa will hunt me down no matter where I go.'

'Or, perhaps just Rani Maa!'

'That's your fate. You're only lucky to be here. At least Sir Oliver doesn't look like he is going to hurt you for trying to murder him.'

Bidisha couldn't give him as much ear as she paid attention to his warm breath on her cheeks, which in the face, made her long for Yuvaraja Trinabh. She sighed and tried to let go of her thoughts that thirsted for the Yuvaraja's touch. But the more she forced herself to not think, the harder her urges became. A throbbing ache took over her chest and she softly squeezed her eyes shut.

'I can't even think about how Yuvaraja Prabir is surviving without anybody on his side.' Debesh looked far away in the darkness.

She gazed at the night sky as she sat next to Debesh for a long, long time. Her knuckle made it to her nose and then everything came back rushing to her mind. The rustling of the leaves and the chirping of the crickets seemed to evade her exhaustion but her worry for her mother wouldn't leave her for a moment.

Debesh moved back and laid down on the wooden porch, his hand making for a fine pillow under his head. Bidisha joined him and relaxed on her back under the dark sky as the shiny silver stars twinkled in their eyes.

'She is a shameless whore!'

'Enough, get back to work.'

She was awoken by a disturbance, of which the sound of snores right in her ear was the wildest. Her eyes still shut, Bidisha tried to stretch but was cocooned in a warm embrace. She heard feeble voices and then a harsh one amidst the rhythmic snoring sound. Bidisha turned around and opened her eyes to an unbelievable visual. Sir Oliver Watts towered her even as she laid down on the porch. Dressed in his night robe and pants, the pipe in his mouth, she could see his legs first.

And then when she looked away from him, trying to decipher the situation, she got the shock of her life. The rock-solid chest that was pressed against her bosom, her hand over him and his hand under her head. Bidisha sat up in shock. She had slept next to a man, hugging him all night.

The chirping of birds and the cool summer breeze would have otherwise been blissful. But now she had put up a spectacle for everyone.

Sir Oliver kicked Debesh in his back and the snores stopped. Bidisha stood up, and Debesh looked around still trying to come to his senses.

'See me in 30 minutes,' Sir Oliver said and walked away.

While Debesh was still waking up, Bidisha ran inside the cottage even before Oliver had completely stepped down the porch. She stood before the mirror in the bathroom. Her cheeks were flushed pink and her hand was on her pounding heart. She took deep breaths. His touch lingered as she closed her eyes.

'But it was Trinabh in my dreams all the while.'

Bidisha patted her cheeks and tried to slip out of her thoughts. And then she splashed water on her face, trying to cool herself down. She breathed heavy and her corset made it worse. The very pleasant moment had turned into a poking pain inside and even out of her chest. She unzipped her dress and contorted her arms to access the lace at the back. Though she was lucky enough to unlace the easily sliding satin through the holes and finally could breathe easy, she was stuck and couldn't go any further.

She called for help as she peeped out from the bathroom but the maidens only laughed and walked past. She couldn't explain the rage she felt at that moment.

Oliver had asked both Debesh and Bidisha to meet him in thirty minutes. She pulled her hair in a fit of anger towards the mean woman who had given her the whole set of dresses. She shouldn't have worn the corset in the first place.

The door latch clicked and Bidisha was alarmed. She had left the bathroom door open. The door opened and she had come face-to-face with Debesh. He gaped at her and then his eyes fell on the mirror behind her. Bidisha stiffened and her hands went cold. He closed the door behind him and he left at once.

The zipper. It was down. Her hand went back to clutch her dress together.

'Can't I ask him for help? If not him, who else?'

'Debesh, wait,' Bidisha yelped on an impulse and fisted her hands.

'Hmmm...'

'Can you... Can you please help me with this?' Bidisha asked as she jumped in circles behind the door in the little space just enough for her to throw out her embarrassment even as she clenched her mouth.

'What?' Debesh asked, 'I mean what help...'

She opened the door and stood behind it as the words failed to escape her mouth.

There was no sound for a long moment on either side.

'Ahhh! You want me to... Should... Should I come in?'

'Yes.'

Debesh stepped inside. And Bidisha stood behind the door without any movement trying to hide her face from him as she sensed his gaze on her back. He looked at her and then stepped out immediately.

'Wait,' Bidisha said as she gripped onto the doorknob, 'I need your help with my corset. It's stuck.'

Debesh went to her and stood dumbfounded.

'The lace, just... just pull it and loosen it. Or, forget it. Just pull the darn thing out,' Bidisha said as she let go of her dress.

She faced the wall, hiding his face from her, and fisted her hands, her nails digging into her palms. The satin slid smoothly out of the holes and her breathing became normal.

'Enough,' Bidisha yelped turning around all of a sudden as she sensed the lace was out in his hand and her hand went behind her back to hold the corset together from opening up.

Their eyes locked for longer than intended before she looked away. Debesh cleared his throat as he scratched his nape and left.

Bidisha marvelled at the steep walls and the dominating appearance of the three-storied mansion. When she stepped inside the house on the beautiful carpet that adorned the wooden floor, it evoked her memories of the Rani Maa's chamber. The artistic motifs on the roof were welcoming but if only that was the case with the owner of the house. The intricate designs on the curtains and the floral patterns on the chairs complemented the colours on the walls, unlike the various striking colours she had seen in the Rani Maa's chamber.

As her eyes followed the extravagant displays, some rustic and Indian, a sardonic smile appeared on her face. But it vanished at the sight of Sir Oliver who stood near the fireplace that was now covered with a steel mesh for the summers.

Bidisha's heart thudded as Debesh barged in and made himself comfortable next to her. Her eyes took note of everything in the living room as she tried to avoid eye contact with him. Only a while back she had been in a cumbrous situation she wouldn't want to be in with a man. Any man.

'Ahem, ahem...' Debesh cleared his throat.

She still did not look at him. Clearing his throat at an inappropriate time was one of his worst habits that made her aware of any inappropriate circumstances they had encountered together. And every time, it made her more conscious than she had already been.

'You, Debesh, get ready. You're coming with me,' Sir Oliver said as he walked towards Debesh though his eyes were fixated on Bidisha. 'Mr Philip will assist you with a pair of shoes from my collection. You may leave now.'

'Did Oliver offer his shoes to Debesh?'

A deep frown appeared on her forehead.

'Bidisha, there you are,' Oliver said as he played with his pipe over his lips, his eyes still glued on her, 'I hope you can tend to my horses in the stable till I find you a suitable job.'

'I can, Sir Oliver,' Bidisha said confused because his weird expression didn't sink in well with her.

'And would it be a problem if I ask you to heave a few buckets of hot water into my bathtub?'

'No, not at all. But before that, may I have a word with you?' Bidisha said trying to make sense of his weird behaviour as his gaze and polite words made her all the more uncomfortable.

'If it's anything related to that night in the forest, please don't bother. Don't bring it up and ruin your chances at a good life as long as you stay here.'

Bidisha didn't dare to utter another word. She headed straight to the kitchen where the water in the kitchen range boiler was ready. Unlike the fire, smoke and ashes she had seen everywhere in the cooking place, even in the palace, she stood in an artistic and hygienic kitchen. The aroma from the teapot hit her nose and she sniffed it with great pleasure. The smell of the scorched fat from the kitchen range, though, annoyed her. The fumes rose to the chimney above the kitchen range as the oil spluttered in the cooking pot placed neatly over the coal fire.

Bidisha contemplated if she should take down the teapot hung from the rod over the heat. The tea was rising and boiling it anymore would only burn it. But then she let it be. The mean maiden would do it.

There was nothing much she could do other than follow the orders of the man she had been longing to kill until she stayed under his roof.

The maiden had gone to the scullery to clean the meat and it was time Bidisha learnt the life in Lancashire. She had to figure out and access the hot water in the boiler so that she could follow the orders of the white giant. She took a closer look and after a couple of attempts she finally figured out the way to operate the boiler which wasn't very complex after all.

Bidisha effortlessly filled the tub with warm water after a few trips to and fro from the kitchen to the bathroom. The last time she had seen Yuvaraja Trinabh was in the same situation while she prepared a bath for him. Her heart sank as she recalled the sight of his blood oozing from his hand.

'Is it ready?' Sir Oliver asked as he started to untie his bathrobe.

'Hmmm...' Bidisha answered in a feeble voice, startled by the sudden approach of an arrogant voice, as she dropped the bucket in the tub.

'The tub. Is it ready?' Oliver asked as he took off his robe and stood before her in his white pants and bare chest.

'Yes. I shall leave you now,' Bidisha said as she picked the bucket from the tub and walked away from him.

'Stay away from Debesh. What happened this morning shouldn't happen again.'

'What happened today anyway? And why does it matter to you?' Bidisha asked as she turned around.

He was already in the tub, all soaked in the water. Naked. She turned away at once and left the place. She was taken by surprise by his authoritative approach.

What does it matter to him?

'Stay away from Debesh?' she smirked at the idea, 'Why should I?!'

CHAPTER THIRTEEN

Weeks passed by and Oliver had something new up his sleeve. He had asked Bidisha to join him as he went on his usual visit to his textile mill on the outskirts of Lancashire. They had started early in the morning and it was her first time visiting the mill. But she didn't know if the change in Oliver's idea of moving her from the work in the stables to the mill was good for her or was there something bad or even terrible things in store for her.

They were already there, in front of Oliver's mill. And she didn't like the place one bit.

Bidisha looked up at the sky as she stepped down from the dickey box at the rear end while trying to get a hold of her nauseous feeling. She opened the heavy door for Oliver as the driver took his time to get off of his high box seat. Her eyes, thankfully, were unaffected by the smoke-filled air though everything around looked hazy. She couldn't see any fire around but there was thick smoke gushing from the pipes above the large sheds, as they were called.

'Don't be so surprised. That's just smoke from the smokestacks,' Sir Oliver said as he adjusted his coat and then walked towards the mill.

Bidisha had seen smoke coming out of the kiln in Bishnupur but it wasn't anything like this. All through their way, since she first spotted a mill from far away, she had been breathing heavy. The smoky smell made her giddy by the time they reached Sir Oliver's workplace. They had passed what looked like a town of mills and she hated to be there.

On the other hand, Sir Oliver walked with his chest out, back erect and chin high, a confident posture she hadn't seen him assume before. She was looking at the harsh reality of the business empire that the likes of Sir Oliver Watts had established for themselves.

The workers in the mill looked terrible, their faces hung in despair. There were mostly women standing for hours, Bidisha learnt, carding, drawing and roving to produce cotton thread. What wrenched her heart was that even children were slogging, working with the huge machines. The

British, as they claimed to be caring for their people back in Bishnupur, didn't after all.

Every day, as she accompanied Sir Oliver to the mill, she was exposed to the truth the English had successfully concealed about themselves back in Bishnupur. Not only did their workers suffer from long working hours in the mill but were also subjected to harsh working conditions. The labour class was equally helpless in Lancashire just like the poor farmers and loom owners back in her homeland.

Bidisha became proficient in spinning yarn in a short time and was able to pull off her daily job. But it was something different that she was interested in. She kept her eyes and ears open for hidden sights that buried secrets and whispers that were shunned before they could even be heard.

She had seen her people, just like the whites who traded cotton, exploit the farmers in Bishnupur. But what she discovered in the mill shocked her. It turned out that people in England were no less cunning. As a matter of fact, as the events unfolded before her eyes and the truth that surfaced, she knew they were the vilest people she had ever imagined could exist. The black spots on humankind.

They not only deceived the poor in both the lands but also the powerful. They mocked His Majesty Mitul Singha Dev for his foolishness of trading his motherland at the price of pennies. And they hushed the voices that dared to speak about their rights and the laws of England. The rich even threatened people who challenged their authority and intimidated them with the rules from the office of the Queen of England.

And just like at times it did, there was a commotion in Oliver's office yet again.

'You don't have to explicitly mention the Queen here. Her Majesty doesn't need that many funds to run the already rich country she rules over,' Sir Oliver murmured, giving his partner a stern look.

Bidisha hid behind the door peeping in now and then. The three partners were engrossed in discussing the increased risk. Her Majesty Queen Victoria had imposed stricter laws for trade and for business owners who imported goods from India and other countries.

One of the partners, Mr Henry Peel, suddenly grabbed his coat and hat and walked out of the office after a heated argument. Bidisha stepped back into her usual safe spot beside the door that everybody overlooked.

'The market demand is increasing and we have now started exporting cotton cloth after the new spinning mill is in place. What else do you want

Oliver? How much more? Should we be caught and subjected to a trial in the court of Her Majesty for you to stop? Don't ruin it all for everyone.'

'Agreed. We are making profits like never before, but let us first hold our ground before abiding by the rash and unfair laws,' Sir Oliver said in a matter of fact tone, loud and clear without caring much for the ears around the office and walked out. 'What about the import tax on silk, opium, spices, tea? The list of commodities being imported from India is endless. Then why this injustice towards the cotton imports?'

'Are you going to be a rebel now? Isn't it enough that England has taken the world by storm and exported cotton everywhere? The days are brighter ahead Oliver,' Gary Brown said, challenging Sir Oliver's decision to trade secretly, sliding his pocket watch back into his coat.

'And so, what? Who has seen the future? Think of what you can do today. It's a matter of time when another 'Luddites' incident uprises and uproots our established business.'

Sir Oliver wouldn't yield to his partners' genuine concern. Luddites, the group of traditional textile workers who had rebelled long back and raided the mills over lack of business for their handmade skills, were already silenced years ago. And just like the condition of the loom workers back in Bishnupur, who were growing poorer, the Luddites had lost any hope of their traditional business reviving. They were forced to work in the mills for pennies after shutting down their handmade textile houses.

Bidisha had gathered information about the new thing she had come across, the exports. She was now aware that, if not for the British loot of cotton and other commodities, Hindustan would earn much more for its priceless natural resources. And in actuality, they would be exporting it to England. And there, Sir Oliver was talking about injustice and exploitation by the Queen over a few changes in the law.

Bidisha was astonished at the level of greed the man harboured within himself. Sir Oliver was rich beyond the avarice and had accumulated wealth enough for his future generations. And yet, he wanted more, even without a family or children to look after.

Bidisha walked out of her dark spot and slowly slid back into her working area before Sir Oliver spotted her. She tightened her white apron on her waist and resumed from where she had left. There were women and children around her who always noticed her long absence between shifts but were too worn out to say anything. The droopy eyes of a small girl, who worked as much as Bidisha did, caught her attention. She didn't look all that well to even stand, let alone work her shift.

Bidisha was aware of the situations of many people who worked in the mill. She had been talking to them and even while some of them refused to spend their energy on the vain talks, Bidisha gathered the information from others. She had grown obsessed with the prevailing conditions around her which she witnessed every day. And the little girl she had learnt, had slogged all her life, though she was hardly 11, for lesser wages than her mother.

The girl's drawing frame was stopped abruptly by the supervisor for her tardiness in her work. Bidisha dreaded what was to come next for the girl. The supervisor was closer to their working area. Bidisha gestured to the girl to start but she was too drowsy to understand. Just then, Bidisha heard the sound of a wooden stick beaten against the floor as the supervisor passed behind her. He paced towards the girl and touched her shoulder asking her to step out with him to the corner.

Bidisha didn't look at them. She had seen far too many incidents already in the past few months.

'No, no. Let me go,' the girl shouted as she struggled to escape the white crook's firm grip.

Bidisha heard the cries of the girl before they suddenly stopped. She knew that the little girl's head was in the water and she would be back in her place in no time. Working harder and on her toes.

The iron cistern was always in place in the corner. Kids, who were too tired, were forced to go through the ordeal the girl went through, before they resumed their work. The supervisor would take the child's legs and dip their head first in the cistern. The girl was lucky not to be beaten by the stick till she turned black and blue like some of the kids who dared to question the man.

Bidisha was not in a position to help any of them. She was aware that by saving them from one misery, she would only make it worse for them. If the master turned up hearing any arguments, the child would have it worse for seeking sympathy and disrupting their discipline during working hours. Bidisha had learnt to let it be and become a silent spectator, just like others. She was used to swallowing the aches in her heart and the pride she thought she once had.

Debesh had made it clear to her that she was lucky to have been looked after by Sir Oliver since she was just another worker in the mill during her stay in Lancashire. It was evident that Oliver had a special concern for her.

And that Debesh could see it clearly, no matter how much Bidisha denied the fact.

He had cautioned her time and again since she accompanied Sir Oliver every day, back and forth, to the mill in his horse carriage. 'Don't ever let a bond of friendship form between you two. That is an illusion. The man cares only about his gains. Do not be seduced by Sir Oliver Watts. Your own life will be in peril,' he had told her many times, in many different ways.

Bidisha had become more docile in the English land, though her focus still was to get out of Lancashire safely and see her mother at the earliest. She had started taking more precautions, something she had never done earlier. Debesh's words were her guiding force as he tried to hold her back from doing anything rash. She had become exactly like her mother and followed her principle—survive and don't bother about right and wrong. The very thing she hated to do.

Sir Oliver never missed a chance to boast about himself, raving about his achievements and showing off his assets. And since they had made it to London after travelling for 5 days, halting each night in different places in the cottages he owned on the way, he was all the more delighted to flaunt his holdings. It was Oliver's grand plan to stay for a month in his majestic palatial mansion in London, which even nobles from the landed gentry couldn't afford.

Built with sandstones, the gothic mansion stood in the middle of a deer park she was told, that was spread over a hundred acres. Bidisha failed to contemplate what it meant. The property had everything a small town would have for its people—formal gardens, a lake, space for pheasant shooting and even a dairy with a farmhouse. Oliver Watts was indeed no less than a duke though he didn't own any such title.

And when she got to see Oliver's majestic mansion in London, she could only stand baffled. This one was grander than the Lancashire mansion, something she hadn't thought was possible. The large windows with elaborate tracery ran up to the high roofs that were well supported by the ribbed vault as if it was holding the heart of the mansion safe above its cage. Bidisha was marvelled at the level of detailing the exterior of the building exhibited. The intricately carved rooftop finials, the decorative gables and eaves, the patio terrace on either side of the entrance and the elaborate plasterwork motifs, everything made her inners churn as she loathed the man who hoarded wealth that was beyond her imagination.

They had crossed the London slums and seen the street urchins on the way. They could use someplace and maybe a bit of Oliver's grace to feed their hungry stomachs that were drawn flat into their backs. While the sturdy grandeur of his palatial mansion promised to protect its own glory for ages to come even after its owner's death, it could never serve the people in need. The homeless would still freeze to death in harsh winters while a lonely man would roam like a ghost in his palace.

And in all the days she spent in the place, she couldn't help but hate the white giant all the more. Statues of Hindu Gods in the mansion, some even abandoned in the storage along with jade and ivory ornaments, screamed his hankering for wealth accumulation without any appreciation. The silver hilt of scimitars set in gems and *talwars* studded with yellow topaz were all, undoubtedly, a part of his loot from India.

If only she had the wherewithal to survive in England on her own and make it to the shores of her motherland without any help from the madman, he would have died his deserving death a long time ago.

And to add to Bidisha's fury, it so appeared that Oliver had conspired to keep Debesh away from her for months since they landed in Lancashire.

Back in Lancashire, Oliver had assigned Debesh jobs that would force him to stay out late at night. Either he accompanied Sir Oliver to towns nearby for days to finish some business or Debesh was sent off in Oliver's stead all alone. The latter scenario was more recurring than the former. And as a result, often, she wouldn't get to see Debesh for days.

With the maidens turning their faces away from her and nobody else to share her heart with, Bidisha's days were nothing more than filled with unfulfillment. And it was no different in London except that she found herself learning ballroom manners, which was, at times, unexpectedly fun activity on the dance floor. Like the darkness in the woods under the bright sunlight, her mind wavered back and forth even as she stood in one of the most coveted mansions in the city.

This would have been one of her most exciting experiences had she been in Bishnupur and dressed up all ladylike. But now was a different situation and she was in an unwanted place where her life was filled with loads of mess.

Debesh had started teasing her since it all started after Oliver had witnessed her planting a kiss on Debesh's lips. His idea, however, seemed too lame to give an ear to. At times, she would laugh it off but sometimes her heart ached. Because the idea came from him, Debesh, it hurt her the most. He had started avoiding her even when Sir Oliver didn't keep him engaged. And that didn't sink well with her. However, the more he tried to stay away from her, the more she craved to be closer to him.

Her foolishness had no bounds. What she had started to mask her ache for Trinabh gave her more soreness than she could handle. Her mind was clouded and she was confused. Either way, she wasn't able to let go of Trinabh. And deep down it scragged her from the inside. She was colluding her own love with the superficial touch and company of another man. Wasn't it clear that Trinabh had the same kind of feelings for her? And yet, the confused and corroded woman that she had turned into was beating her soul down to shreds.

Moreover, she didn't have the slightest information on what was happening back in the palace. And Trinabh, she just hoped he was doing well after what she had done. Whenever she brought up talks about Bishnupur, Oliver stalled her off saying none had any information from the palace, even though she knew that more ships had reached England from India after their arrival. She had seen them, the English, and heard them exchanging information on recent developments in the kingdom, her homeland. But the information was denied to her. Debesh had promised her to get some news but there was no success.

Helplessness had engulfed her and she was now just walking the path paved for her, no longer looking for another chance to rebel and revolt.

And while they were in London for a month, as a new development, she was asked to attend the ball, which was nothing more than an unknown fascination for her. Though it was a puzzle as to why Oliver was generous enough to take Debesh and her to the ball, she didn't give it a second thought. The white giant always did things with his personal gains in mind and his motives were unknown to her despite staying close to him for months.

'Don't forget you're representing me. And what you two are wearing today are the best clothes in London. You better pull your act to suit your attire. I hope you both have learnt your ballroom etiquette well,' Oliver crowed as he pulled his coat and took his hat from the maiden.

It was time to enter the magnificent mansion Oliver had brought her to along with Debesh. And just as they all got out of the chariot, she was reminded to mind her manners by Oliver who gave her a stern expression as her sparkling silk gown crumpled at the bottom showing the lace of her petticoat. Soon after she adjusted her silk, Bidisha slid her arm into Debesh's as they took their steps together towards the mansion. Sir Oliver stood beside her, gesturing her to take his arm too. She readily accepted the invitation and slid her arm into his, walking in the centre, arm in arm with two gentlemen, as they stepped into the bustling grandeur of London's most happening ballroom.

Oliver was all smiles as he greeted the gentlemen and the ladies as he entered the ballroom with Bidisha and Debesh. She decided to go along the flow since she had no choice whatever Oliver was planning to accomplish by taking them to the ball.

Brocade silks in bright hues invited them into the enormous room. The rich fabric was dropped down from high roofs and draped around the pillars. The table covers and the upholstery, every big and little thing, in fact, was covered in plush silk.

The poor Maharaja in Bishnupur, she realized, had accepted the cheap velvet from the Goras while they brought back rich silk from her homeland.

Oliver greeted the elite in the ballroom as they walked in together.

It was the pleasant floral scent that hit her nostrils as the candles around in the room burnt to brighten the mood of the guests. The soft velvety petals of the flowers arranged on the round tables calmed her, a soothing sight in the middle of all the bling in the room. The sweet fragrance from the cakes in the dinner spread immediately tantalized her taste buds. And the rhythmic music played by the band brought some solace to her soul.

But her fine spirit could hardly last.

The riches that she hadn't even seen in the Bishnupur palace had made their home in a faraway land. The *hookahs* in burnished gold, jewelled daggers gleaming with rubies the colour of human blood and the swords that were displayed on the walls with pride with scatterings of deep green emeralds, everything screamed Indianness. It was all a part of what Oliver had hoarded. And the glimpse of the magnificent coats of elephant armour displayed at the entrance had given her an idea of what she could expect inside the huge private ballroom owned by one of the officers in East India Company, who had successfully looted the kingdom he had overlooked for years. Though the Company was no more ruling India, Queen Victoria's reign had done nothing good to her motherland either.

And in the dark of the night, like many others who had slid down their sophistication, a man pressed his lips to a woman's behind the beautiful curtains. It hadn't missed her how the men's eyes were fixed on the women's cleavage that showed above their dropped shoulder dresses.

Bidisha suddenly gasped and clutched Debesh's hand as her eyes caught something that she hadn't expected to see. She looked away at once as her heart thudded though she let go of his hand as soon as she had caught it.

'What?' Debesh asked as he looked in the same direction.

'Nothing', Bidisha said as she fidgeted in the chair as she shook her legs, 'Don't look.'

Debesh cleared his throat and let out a breath.

And she bit her lips as she looked down in shame. He had seen the two, the man in the alcove who had put his mouth on the woman's chest and she seemed to be moaning in delight out in public. In the shades of the drapes. Nothing but the drapes. The fact that she had witnessed such an act with Debesh made her flinch in dread, disgust and embarrassment.

'Go on. Why don't you both give it a try? Your first dance together...' Oliver dared them as he gave a gentle nudge to both Debesh and Bidisha on their back.

'What? No,' Bidisha murmured as she rubbed her palms together and stepped away from the two.

But Debesh took her hand and pulled her closer. She slipped her hand into his even as her cheeks warmed up. And then they joined the other couples trying to match their steps together. Her breathing went haywire as she moved in tune with Debesh. She quivered as his hand touched her waist and took a deep breath at his firm grip. His gaze burnt her into a sweat even though she avoided eye contact. And as they moved around on the shiny smooth floor, her heart slipped out of her chest as their bodies aligned together. But his eyes didn't waver away from her once even as she mustered the courage to glare at him in the middle of their dance. But she couldn't last long in his arms and moved away from him bringing their twirl to halt taking Debesh by surprise.

And just a few steps away, she was before Oliver. He had been a different person at the ballroom acting formal and dignified even with Bidisha and Debesh which wasn't true at other times. To her surprise, he extended his hand before her like a gentleman and escorted Bidisha straight away to a seat farther away from the group of women delicately indulged in their conversations. And Debesh followed them.

Perhaps her sophisticated dress alone wasn't enough for her to be part of their inner group. Just like she was always told she was a filthy half-breed who could never be part of their white society though she resembled them in many ways in her appearance. And perhaps, looked even better with the sharp features she had inherited from her mother. But her blood, for them, was stained with brown and was not all white!

And just as she settled down on the elegant table, Oliver took Debesh away for introductions.

Bidisha dreaded the ambience. The restricted demeanour she was expected to exhibit throughout the evening confined her to her seat. The men who had brawled with their eyes a while ago for her attention had gone missing too.

She was poor in her etiquette and poorer in her skills of their language. The crash course the maiden had offered for her survival in her first-ever ball did not serve of much use to her. Her fingers played restlessly with the ringlets in her hair and occasionally, felt the feathers on her head that matched her pastel blue gown.

Bidisha stared at the glossy floor and then the shiny ceiling. Looked into the mirrors that mocked her and the exuberant chandeliers that were too high to even look down on her. And then she stared some more at the artifice of the people around her.

She was taught not to leave the place unless a gentleman invited her for a dance or dinner. Bidisha was supposed to stick to her seat until the hostess introduced her to men. Nobody could dare talk to a lady, which she was on that day and the night of the ball, without a proper introduction. Not any man even as they admired her from afar.

Sir Oliver was unlike himself, and not the frowning merchant she knew him to be. The man who stood before her was a stranger she hadn't seen before. He was busy moving around, swaying on the dance floor with ladies he had seemingly known all his life. Women who were dressed in rich ensembles, fancy white gloves and decked with fine jewellery, adorned his arms. His gentle moves, elegant gait, long steps that were careful enough not to step on a lady's train, everything was out of the ordinary.

This man was neither the selfish one she had met for the first time in her homeland nor the merchant she had sailed with. The rough and mean monger she knew was tactfully replaced by a gentleman.

Bidisha was agonized by the lack of company. In addition, her bust hurt from the corset and she struggled to breathe. The fancy pair of drawers she wore under her elaborate gown and the silk stockings were testing her patience. The bulky petticoat under her gown was a lot of weight to carry around. She would prefer a handmade, heavy sword instead.

'You must go to the dressing room. I am told women are particular about fancy and expensive underwear. You must have the best of everything and hold up my status as a woman accompanying me to the last ball of the season,' Sir Oliver had instructed her.

It was clear that she was a show. A means to flaunt his wealth, hold his status up and exhibit his power over the rest. And the horrendous man had even spoken about women's innerwear without a tinge of shame on his face.

She couldn't care less about the formal etiquettes that had bound her to the seat anymore.

'Why can't a girl move around freely without an escort'?

Bidisha sighed as she stepped close to a huge window away from the crowd, behind the silken drapes as she untied the soft curtains that were bound to the white pillar. The cold breeze kissed her cheeks. The night sky twinkled with slivery spots over her head. The colourful withering leaves she had seen while entering the building were hidden in the darkness.

Her undying charm that people envied back in Bishnupur was masked in a room full of more elegant women. Though Sir Oliver had paraded his richness by adorning her with expensive clothes and fine jewellery, there were hardly any men in the room who were interested in her. They were all after rank and nobility. Sir Oliver had not only fooled himself by bringing her to the ball but had also insulted her existence.

Instead, another woman of his social strata would have been a better choice. But she was to stand beside him for reasons he alone knew.

Bidisha closed her eyes and took in the calmness of the night as the cool air engulfed her. Her silky gown glittered as the wind swayed it along. She took off her gloves carefully sliding them away from the jewel that adorned her hands and fingers. The diamonds on her bracelet came to life under the moonlight. But her heart, there was an unknown twitch inside.

Bidisha's mind was running wild with thoughts of her mother and Trinabh. Her home, the jungle she lived in beckoned her. If only she could just gallop to her roots far away from this unknown place and two-faced people, the so-called ladies and gentlemen.

At least, if she could go back to Lancashire and resume her routine, it could keep her occupied and away from the heart-wrenching thoughts she was unable to escape from at that moment.

Oliver had instructed the maidens and the male helpers to prepare for the winter while they left the place for London. The maidens had started hoarding firewood in the storehouse and barn when Oliver had asked

Bidisha to prepare for the London trip. She wished she stayed back and worked her worries out.

Instead, here she was, watching the rich indulging in dancing in the up-class society hand-in-hand with unknown men and women. And none of it and nobody there in the ballroom seemed familiar to her.

And to add to it all, she hadn't eaten her fill since she first landed in that country. It was just roasted meat and tasteless bread most of the time. But the cake was an exception which she relished although it was served once in a while. She couldn't survive on that foreign land's food any longer.

If only she could go back to her life in hiding with her mother!

'May I please make it into your thoughts if you don't mind?'

'Debesh!' Bidisha let out a sigh. 'I have had enough of those manners already. Stop it. And no, you stay away from my head for now. It's already chaotic in there. I won't be able to handle one more person infiltrating my thoughts.'

Debesh leaned on the steel railing and loosened his cravat as if it chocked him. He took a deep breath.

Bidisha looked at him and he stared back at her. His face was hung and her's drooped down. And then, they let out a chuckle.

Debesh turned away from her. 'What are we actually doing?'

'Playing dress up, I think.' Bidisha moved closer to him.

'What do you think is happening in the palace. In Bishnupur?'

'Just hoping everything is good. And everyone is well.'

'That is surprising to hear. Don't you hate everyone there in the palace?' Debesh looked at her.

'Hate? Whom? Don't assume things Debesh.'

'What made him think I hated the royals? Was I so obvious?'

Yeah, she hated them, most of them in the palace. But except for one. She was sure of that.

'I am talking about the people of Bishnupur. And I hope you remember I have a mother too.'

She had to find a way to stop her heart from pinning for someone out of her reach. It wouldn't end well for anyone. Her, in particular. She couldn't afford to lose her heart to Trinabh. Bidisha had to take care of herself and battle the odds to survive instead of making the same mistake her mother once made—falling for a man out of her league.

'Aren't you cold?' Debesh looked at her bare and beautiful shoulders.

Bidisha rolled her shoulders, aware of the touch of a cool breeze on her skin and the heat of his gaze. Her fingers fiddled with the bertha made of lace on her deep flounce. The glint in his eyes deepened as his gaze settled on her lips. The look on his face and in his eyes caused her face to flush.

'Shouldn't I set my foot back? No, I should take a step closer to him. Help myself to set my heart free from Trinabh's captive, from the fondness of his touch and his warmth. Surrendering my soul to a royal won't do any good.'

Debesh took a step towards her but she stepped back despite her resolve. He advanced further, his chest almost brushing over her silk-clad bust. Bidisha took another step back as she anticipated what was to come- a kiss or a hug perhaps. But she was not sure if she was ready for that. Debesh suddenly grabbed her by her waist and pulled her closer.

His palm slid over her back and she was saved from clamouring into the glass behind her. But there was a sudden thud in her chest. She was squeezed in the man's arms. Pressed against his armour-like body. Bidisha's muscles were tensed as she went still.

The fingers of his other hand traced her collar bone, going up to her neck. Bidisha fisted her palm clutching the soft cloth of her ball gown. She wouldn't back and would hold her ground. He nuzzled her neck before she could react. Her face flushed hot and she turned away from him unable to bear what was to follow.

But in the next instant, he pulled his hand and stepped away from her. This, she hadn't expected. Just a little nudge from him and she would have given in. Bidisha had made up her mind to go with the flow. He was taking it slow but forward.

'Why did he stop? But what am I trying to do? I don't really...'

Bidisha held his lapels and pulled him closer and kissed him on his lips. Debesh held her by the waist. His hands were all over her back. He bit her lower lip softly. Bidisha let out a moan as her eyes closed. His lips parted and just then, there was a thud again.

Bidisha and Debesh looked back, startled at the sudden commotion. The window glass behind her had shattered all of a sudden.

'Did Oliver really bang it that hard?'

'Oh! Did I interrupt the two of you?' Sir Oliver turned away from them, his hands clasped behind his back. 'But I think this isn't quite a suitable place for a lady and a gentleman to...'

Sir Oliver left his sentence incomplete before he walked inside the hall leaving the two in the dark behind the curtain. Debesh looked at Bidisha and then at Sir Oliver.

'We shouldn't have...' Debesh confessed, turning away from her.

'Hmmm... Not the right place,' Bidisha affirmed standing next to him.

'No. What I am saying is... This is not right. Not in this place or any other. This is not good for any of us. I got carried away. We should stop, Bidisha.' Debesh looked into her eyes and then away. 'Let us not do anything rash like this again.'

Bidisha listened to him without uttering a word even as her head spun knowing where he was headed. Her mind raced with thoughts, about her life and his. But she stood next to him, heeding every word that came out of his mouth. She wasn't sure if his words were a relief to her or a burden that would bring her plan crashing to the ground. But she was stopped from becoming one of those ladies in the ballroom whom she had loathed a while back, and that, for now, was consolation enough.

She had given in to Debesh in the starlit night. Bidisha didn't know how far they would have gone if not for Sir Oliver. However, she knew even Debesh was torn trying to do the right thing, just like her.

The London visit was more for business and relationship building, peppered with fun balls and other social events. They were back in Lancashire before the end of the fall. And as she had seen the vibrant moor on the way, which once was full of swaying purple heather, was now crowded with dry red hay. Just like her heart that was withering in longing for home and loving warmth. And as they prepared for the winter, Bidisha tried to keep her heart warm along with her body.

'Isn't Sir Oliver trying to keep us both away like you keep saying?' Bidisha smirked as she tied her apron over her plain grey dress. 'How are we together in the mill today?'

Debesh leaned on the machinery and crossed his legs. 'I was thinking the same. Not that it bothers me much, but I think this is the first time we are together for work since we came to Lancashire.' He leaned forward and whispered, 'He just can't stand me beside you. Oliver must be really in love with you. Don't you think so?'

'Yes, and that is the reason, he has been giving me a tough time in the mill asking me to slog every day.' Bidisha pushed Debesh aside clearing her work area, ready to start her day. 'Isn't your job easy in the city, away from all the vibrations under the feet, pollution and sound?'

Bidisha was quick to sense a man's intentions towards her. Their lustful eyes, their uncontrollable hands and their expressions gave away their darkest thoughts to her. Every man was different in the way they conveyed their ill intentions towards her. Some would directly talk to her about their need to be with her and how they could not only make her wealthy enough but also please her in ways she wouldn't have imagined. The very thought disgusted her.

But Sir Oliver... She had not felt anything like that around him. Even Debesh was quick enough to display his affection for her and they had even kissed, although the memory made her cringe.

She was in her workplace, after all, and looking at the workers flowing in like ants in lines to take their places and start before they were beaten for being late. Bidisha wanted to get rid of Debesh from that place too. She didn't want to face the same fury from the supervisors as the kids she had seen many times in the past months. She looked around intently if any supervisor was noticing her lame actions as she indulged in banter with Debesh. She felt sorry for the women and children who stood in their designated places, exhausted even before they began their day.

'That I wonder too. He has put all his faith in me. I get to learn a lot about the business and meet people. It was difficult to talk to them earlier. But don't you think I can speak their language well now? But I am telling you, he has something in his heart for you.'

'Can you leave me alone now? And stop boasting about your work and your growth.'

'Are you really worried about your work?' Debesh came closer to her from behind, his white ruffled shirt crushing into Bidisha's back.

Debesh was making it all the more difficult for her. He himself was not sure about his swaying emotions for her. He wanted to be loyal to his master, Yuvaraja Prabir, assuming he had feelings for Bidisha. But in reality, she could say Debesh was struggling too, to give up on her. Just like she was struggling to give up on Trinabh.

'Yes, I am worried sick. Not about my work but that you'll put me in trouble.' Bidisha pushed him just enough to move him back. 'And didn't you make it clear that we should maintain our distance from each other?'

'I am sure we should. And right now I am not trying to do anything that we shouldn't be doing.'

'So please then, can you stay away from me...'

'I just wanted to distract you? I bet you won't stop me.'

'What nonsense! Debesh, out from here. There are people around. And if you are not already aware, some supervisors like to keep their employers happy by punishing the employees. If they see us talking and wasting time like this, I am done. You may excuse yourself now.'

'I don't see anyone here yet.' Debesh reached for her waist again and his face came so close to hers that it would be difficult even for a feather to pass through.

'Fire, fire, fire!' The shouts broke their conversation.

Debesh took his hand off of her and she moved away. But in the next instant, he grabbed her hand again and he looked around. Bidisha tightened her grip as she saw the furious flames consume everything that came in its way. The sudden breaking out of fire didn't make sense but she had to think on her feet and save her life along with Debesh.

'Get out. Run.'

'Fire! Fire!'

The workers ran around trying to find a safe passage to the exit. Bidisha, on the contrary, let his hand go and ran away from him. Debesh followed her.

'Bidisha, not there. The exit! Run towards the exit!'

She grabbed the kids, four of them, who were too scared to step out of their hiding. The kids had ducked under a wooden table nearby shivering and crying. She helped them form a chain and moved them through the narrow space between the machine and the wooden planks that were ablaze. Debesh was quick to move them away one by one. The kids were brought out to safety and were saved from a disastrous fate. But the fire was fast closing in on them.

'Bidisha, hurry now. Come out.'

She tried to make it through, but the space had further narrowed, leaving her little room to pass. She kicked the plank hard, but the pile was too tough to move much. She kicked harder. The fierce flames rose high. But she made it out.

'Your skirt!' Debesh shouted as he tried to douse the fire with his bare hands in a lame attempt.

The furious flames threatened to burn her alive as they got even more violent. But Debesh ripped her dress off. And held her sweaty palm as he pulled her along. They didn't look back as they ran out together, hand in hand, struggling to breathe. Her vision was impaired by the thick smoke that stung her eyes. She jumped over the rolls of cloth, black and charred. And just when she made it to the door along with Debesh, the fire ate up the last of the cotton yarn on the spinning machine.

Bidisha coughed. Her hands were black and her skirt was torn. Her stockings were burnt and her knees were burnt. She raked her fingers through her hair moving them away from her face as she bent down to cover her legs with what was left of her skirt.

Debesh ran to her, his relief that she'd made it out of the fire shining on his face, and pulled her in his arms. He held her tightly almost choking her. She hugged him back even as she tried to catch her breath.

'For a moment, I thought I would never see you again. When do you become so foolish to put yourself in danger for the sake of others?' Debesh said as he loosened his grip on her when he realized that she wasn't comfortable.

Just then, a fire engine reached the spot. The horses had finally pulled it to the place after a long wait. And in no time the pumpers, who pumped out the water manually, doubled their speed and the water moved through the pipe. But Bidisha was sure the water in the main wasn't enough. They needed more and she couldn't see any backup engines behind. To her relief, though, she saw two more fire engines following. There was one more far behind, being pulled by men. People helped refill the main, as it was called, where the water was stored, running back and forth to the nearby lake with buckets and cisterns.

Bidisha grabbed a few cisterns from where the fire was put out. The metal containers that were accessible amidst the fire were finally put to good use and the water was utilized to doze off the fire. She had always hated to see the kids struggle with their faces under the water as punishment. Cisterns were not supposed to be used for a heinous purpose like that.

The fire engine was helpful to stop the fire from spreading to the other mills in the proximity. But a major part of Oliver's mill had turned into smoke. All that was left was ashes and the remnants of the metal. With walls barely holding high and the hot metal roof collapsing on the machines, everything was levelled before their eyes. The workers sat on the ground far away, all exhausted. Children stood in groups, staring at the place they once worked at. The girls cried and their mothers held them dearly, thanking the lord almighty for sparing their lives.

The fire had swallowed up the mill without any mercy and with authority. It hit Bidisha hard, looking at the sight before her eyes, thinking that a small accident couldn't have caused a fire of such magnitude.

The grounds outside the mill was bustling and crowded with people before the fire incident as they were walking in for their shift. Any spark of fire could be easily noticeable. Nobody would delay in putting it off. A fire like that in the broad daylight when there were no candles lit around wasn't a possibility. Not by any accident. Wasn't that clear? Bidisha sensed something awful happening. Someone was definitely fooling around.

Bidisha had been keeping her eyes and ears open at all times, whether at home or in the mill for as long as she could remember. But she hadn't noticed anything out of place and she hadn't seen this accident coming. Was it really an accident? But it couldn't be. It wasn't possible. Something was amiss and she couldn't see what.

Debesh walked towards her, his shirt plastered to his chest, wet and dripping after helping with the water.

'Where is Sir Oliver?' Bidisha asked looking around.

'There. He is settling the bills while trying to bargain, saving some shillings while cutting down the pence of the poor.'

'Is that even possible at a time like this? Is he even worried about what happened to his mill?' Bidisha gaped at Oliver. 'And here I was, wondering if he was safe or burnt to his bones. He simply can't stop surprising me. Rather, shocking me.'

'Let us worry about you. You have burns on your legs. It must hurt you.'

'It is nothing much. I will take care of it after reaching home.'

Truth be told, it did. It burnt like hell. And she had been putting off that pain for a while and when they were at it, talking and seeing the scalded skin, small patches but a few of them, she wanted to howl in pain like a kid. And she did, but only on the inside.

He gently caressed her cheeks. 'You look beautiful even with the dirt and smoke on your face.'

Bidisha smiled. 'And you look tempting when you are all wet.'

'No more hiding your pain behind that smile. Let me treat those wounds.'

CHAPTER FOURTEEN

Sir Oliver had succeeded in keeping Debesh away from Bidisha as usual, depriving her of the only shoulder she had to lean on in a foreign land. On a particularly arduous day, as she tried hard to cope with the cold weather, Bidisha's emotional stress kept disrupting her focus and, therefore, her day's work in the barn. Her mind and her heart had been arc rivals all her life and it was no different when she was put to test yet again. The mind wanted her to get done with the day's jobs but the heart had taken over reminiscing her life in Bishnupur.

She kept convincing herself that the anxiety was only fleeting and she would stop worrying about her mother once she got herself involved in the work.

But she could not ignore the fluttering in her heart for an unattainable man due to some encounters she had. She shouldn't be fretting much about it. She would only hurt herself if she continued to treasure Trinabh's memories. Rather, she should let it go and try to move ahead. But it was way too hard than she had imagined it to be. If only she could give in and embrace Debesh with all her heart that night in the ballroom, it would have been much easier. Perhaps she wasn't giving her best to take her mind off Trinabh.

But who was she lying to? The truth was that no matter what she did, her heart would ache for Yuvaraja Trinabh. No matter how much she tried to bury her feelings, her heart was not going to be able to forget the sense of his touch. His voice pierced her ears every night and his face showed up whenever she closed her eyes.

Bidisha couldn't wait to go home but she had to push herself and survive the days, each of which passed like an eon. She practiced her sword to vent out her frustration every night before she went to bed. However, no matter what, it was hard to take her mind off the worries of her home, her mother and the man whose thoughts wouldn't stop bothering her even when he was seven seas away.

If only she could share her emotions and her feelings for Trinabh with someone. But she couldn't. She shouldn't. It was forbidden. She was a lowly life of a fugitive mother and he was the future king. She couldn't even share her heart with the man himself though she loved him.

The more she thought of letting go of those emotions, the more it brought her pain.

Perhaps the feeling that couldn't be expressed hurt the most.

It was becoming increasingly difficult to read her own mind and connect with her own heart, which betrayed every practical decision she had made on her way.

It was yet another day and yet another job she did every day in the barn. The chickens clucked and their features fluttered as she closed the pen doors before letting the goats out of their dwelling. Bidisha was assigned work at the barn to tend to the animals. She had been doing it ever since the unsettling fire incident at the mill happened. But strangely, Sir Oliver didn't react the way she had expected him to, over his huge loss. Bidisha had assumed that he would either go mad after the disaster, or he would work harder to make up for the losses.

But he had surprised everyone around him. He had taken things lightly, had cut off his ties with his partners, strangely, and even went steady with the insurance authorities, the people who would pay him for his loss. Oliver, astonishingly, didn't press too much on them to pay him what he believed he deserved.

She was perplexed at the very idea that someone would give him a huge sum of money as compensation for the tragedy. She hadn't heard of such a thing before for it did not exist back in Bishnupur. People in England were far more blessed. And yet they had to rob and loot others.

The goats bleated as they all huddled for the sunlight on the hay. Bidisha could feel the biting cold pierce through the layers of the thick winter coats she had managed to get with help from Debesh.

She hunkered down along with the goats she had let out in the barn. Sir Oliver, who preferred goat milk and fresh meat at the snap of his fingers, had given her special instructions to care for the animals during winter. None of the maidens wanted to be part of that job since the cold could freeze the bones in the barn. She was told that snowfall would make it worse for her.

Bidisha, however, had no idea what that worse meant. Their present situation itself was worse than the worst winter she had ever experienced.

It was particularly cold in the afternoon and she wasn't planning to stay in the barn for long. She needed to get back to her room and warm herself up. Her gloves and muffler were simply not enough.

Just then, the huge barn door creaked open. It was Debesh, covered in layers of wool and coats. His hands were in the pockets of his long black coat, Sir Oliver's, but a snuggly fitted one.

'What are you still doing in the barn? Isn't it too cold in here?' Debesh complained, his thick brows forming a frown.

'I only have to move the goats back to their shed and then I can head back to my room.' Bidisha said, rubbing her palms together. 'But you're back early today!'

'Yes. Sir Oliver got the information that it might snow today. That's...'

'Really?' Bidisha looked at him disbelievingly.

'You're reacting like a child!' Debesh said, as he took off his greatcoat and wrapped it around Bidisha before settling down next to her.

'And you got one more new coat again?'

'He bought new winter wear for himself and so he gave some of the old ones to me. I need to survive outside in the killing winter.'

Sir Oliver had invested a great deal in his clothing that particular winter, which even the maidens were astonished about. Moreover, he had given away a few pieces of his old greatcoats and surtouts to Debesh. It didn't make sense to both Bidisha and Debesh.

When she first landed in Lancashire Bidisha had assumed that her life would be hell in the hands of a white whom she had also tried to kill. And Debesh, he had cautioned her time and again to watch her back in a foreign land. But things turned out to be decent and Oliver had even sheltered them.

But as time passed, she was taken by surprise as Oliver showered favours on Debesh, be it lending him his own clothes or expensive shoes. Moreover, Oliver even took Debesh to places on business. All this was way too much to handle.

And now Oliver insisted that Debesh wear them while accompanying him to the cities, so that he looked presentable when he met people of great status. Oliver was not only teaching him the etiquettes of the people of his social status, he was also helping him improve his language proficiency.

'Will you be alright without the coat? You just returned home. It must be cold outside too.'

Bidisha pulled the coat covering herself, feeling the warmth of the coat and his.

'Yes, it's bone-chilling. But still better than what it is like to sit in the rear seat. I have been riding with Sir Oliver in his sheltered couch box for the past few days. I am fine.'

'I never once got to sit inside his carriage. It looked so grand, with soft red velvet seats and a golden framework. Ah! I wish I can sit inside at least once before we leave.'

'There's a lot of time before we can even think of going back. It'll be possible only when it's summer.'

'Did Oliver say anything about sending us back? About Bishnupur? Is there any news? From anyone about anybody in the palace?' Bidisha rushed on, as she held his hand and shook it like a child as her eyes twinkled in anticipation.

'When the leaves turn green and the flowers start to bloom. The white snow they keep talking about melts into water and flows down the rivers. Then comes the day when you can talk about home. Until then our hearts need to be frozen like the waters here will do soon.'

'Unbelievable! When did you start talking like that? You're rambling some lame poetic lines. Couldn't you just say we can go home in summer?' Bidisha laughed blowing into her hands and rubbing them hard.

'Do you think I came up with those lines?'

'Not you? Then who?'

'You won't believe it. It was Sir Oliver who narrated those lines and more when I asked him the same question. I can hardly remember the first few words before this.'

'What is it with him these days? He's behaving strangely. Feels like the person we had seen in Bishnupur all those years was somebody else.'

'I feel the same way. He has been different in many ways. Today, we went to the insurance office. They were asking him so many questions and it seemed like they wouldn't pay him much since everything that happened that day felt out of the ordinary, as per their investigations. And yet, Sir Oliver wasn't worried much. It was money that he was losing after all.'

'First of all, I don't understand this thing called insurance. Had His Majesty known about such a concept, he would have done everything possible under the sky to make money through that scheme,' Bidisha said as she directed the goats into their pens.

Debesh gave her a hand. 'It's not like what you think. Sir Oliver paid them a fixed amount and pays them every year. Though I didn't understand much, you could also lose all the money you have paid, in case nothing goes wrong. They wouldn't return you the amount you paid them earlier.'

'Then, is Oliver blessed that way or is it a curse his mill was burnt?'

'Hard to say. *Goras*, we can't understand them easily.'

Bidisha was now used to the chilling weather and had started to enjoy the snow at times. It was just another day and she was in a reasonably good mood too. She shovelled the snow and cleared the pavement at the noon. But she couldn't take her eyes off of the beautiful front yard that was laced with white like a fairyland. The snowflakes that landed on the drifts sparkled in the sunshine. She had been seeing the same icicles and the dripping water from the tree barks for months. And yet every day, every time, they sparkled a joy within her. It lightened her heart and took away the burden of the guilt she felt towards her mother and Yuvaraja Trinabh.

As the snowflakes showered from the sky, Bidisha looked up and revelled when they touched her face as if it was her mother's love that was being showered from afar. She held the snow dearly in her palms for as long as she could, till it started to sting her skin.

The last news, about Yuvaraja Trinabh, she had received just days back had left her shattered. With his sword hand thumb gone, people and officials alike had started questioning him about his calibre and his ability to become a crown prince. Hearing the news that he was now considered an incompetent man with no skills as a warrior, crushed her heart.

She let the snowmelt in the warmth of her hands as the thoughts about Yuvaraja's struggle to prove his worth to become the crown prince haunted her.

She would have rejoiced over his downfall had it been the situation when she knew nothing about the seemingly demonic Trinabh who was considered to be stone-hearted. But he was the one who was against his father, the king, for favouring the whites in his rule. And he was the only hope Bishnupur had when it came to fighting against the injustice of the British.

Her heart twitched the next moment when his eyes flashed before her eyes. She would never forget those concerned eyes when he had asked her to run away despite being in pain and losing his thumb.

Bidisha wanted to punish herself for taking everything away from him. But she had to see to her mission through too. Bidisha had to make it back, no matter what. But then, she could, to punish herself the least, let the snow freeze her hands as painfully as it was capable of.

'You're doing it again.' Debesh paced towards her, removed his gloves and held her hand, clearing the snow and blowing some warm air on her palms. He slid a pair of gloves on her hands. 'Bidisha what are you doing this for? Even I feel remorse for letting Yuvaraja Prabir down, for leaving him back alone to suffer among the animals in the palace who are ever ready to hunt him down. I know you're worried about your mother. But what good will this do to her?'

'It's not like what you think Debesh. I was just enjoying the—'

'I know you too well now.

'Enough of your banter. Come inside, I need to talk to you both.' Oliver walked past them and inside the house, crunching the snow under his feet.

'How did it go today? Tell me we are soon going home, Debesh.' Bidisha looked at him, her hands in his, gazing at him, trying to read the answers in his eyes.

'We might after all. As soon as the weather clears, we shall leave.' Debesh looked at her, his face beaming with joy.

There was a ray of hope, finally. After all the failed attempts and after hearing the refusals to take the two back to their land, someone had finally agreed. Bidisha had been keeping her whims in check but soon she'd be able to swim her will in the vast ocean of her life. She had failed her mother and made an even bigger clanger of her life. But going back home meant she could find another way. And take care of her mother.

The cork popped just as Bidisha stepped in after Debesh. Sir Oliver was in the mood for wine in the middle of the day. The cold wind kissed her cheeks just before she closed the door behind her.

'You're red!' Debesh whispered as he removed his coat and hung it next to the door, near Oliver's greatcoat and hat.

Bidisha hushed him away in gesture as she removed her coat and took it inside with her to the scullery.

'Let us have this drink together. Bidisha, would you mind bringing in some cheese and sausages?' Oliver asked politely with a smile on his face. 'Debesh, come on, help me with the glasses here. Let's celebrate. Isn't it what you wanted all along?'

Bidisha placed the tray on the table. And a plate full of Oliver's favourite kedgeree, a weird dish with a mix of haddock, rice, boiled eggs, curry powder and whatnot, for he loved Indian spices. He had already asked the maiden to prepare it and Bidisha struggled even to bring it out from the kitchen as it smelt terrible. And then she brought the Haggis, a pudding made of minced beef and animal organs, which made her nauseate. Though Oliver liked everything to be served in an orderly fashion for his every meal at home, it was oddly different at that moment with him being away from the table and eating random dishes at the odd time and that too with wine.

Nothing on the table looked appetizing for her except for the cheese that she loved. But then, by the time she served Sir Oliver, she didn't even want to look at the table with the unappetizing food all over.

On the other hand, Debesh had developed quite a taste for the strange kedgeree over time. Perhaps, he relished the spices, which he missed dearly in Lancashire.

She walked away from the table. Bidisha opened a window to let the air in as the fire sizzled in the hearth and the smoke escaped into the room. The cool breeze gave her sudden goose pimples. She picked the poker and displaced the kindling accumulated under the log. The fire crackled. She warmed her palms, her body relieved of the cold while she tried hard to pay attention to the whispers between Oliver and Debesh.

'Come on, Bidisha, let's toast. Pick up your glass. Consider this as one of those days you would want to get drunk and let yourself lose for the possibilities.'

Bidisha's cheeks warmed up at the thought of it. She had done that before, on the ship. Letting go of everything. And then she had kissed Debesh in presence of Oliver. She had the urge to hide her face. Bidisha paced towards the window to close it. The room had enough air already and the fire was behaving too.

She clanked her glass with theirs and gulped the wine.

'Good! That's good.' Oliver sighed. 'And now it's time we talk about the important things.'

'Bidisha, cheese. I didn't see you eat any of it.' Debesh held the platter before her.

'What's the hurry? Why don't we talk first?' Oliver said as he settled on the couch with his wine, interrupting the conversation between Bidisha and Debesh.

She gave him an understanding look and Debesh placed the platter back on the table. Oliver usually didn't entertain others during his meals. It was against his dignity to sit next to someone lower than his status. It was understood, when he hesitated to offer something to Debesh and Bidisha. How could he share the same food with them? This was just a courtesy invitation. Nothing much. Debesh was aware of the English etiquettes but he'd gotten a little carried away in his happiness. Bidisha held herself back. It was only a matter of a few more weeks before spring. And then the sky would be clear for them to sail. She would act wisely and behave accordingly till then. She had promised Debesh. And now she was reminding him the same.

Bidisha leaned on the wall, next to the warm hearth, and Debesh sat on a stool nearby. They had never really behaved like other servants at home though they were cautious not to offend Sir Oliver. And for some reason, Oliver never insisted they follow suit. Perhaps he didn't expect much from them. Or, maybe Debesh was right about his infatuation with her. But Bidisha never saw Sir Oliver's inclination towards her. He had never expressed anything to her. And she had not observed him showing any kind of signs either.

Bidisha stoked the fire with a bellow, later wiping her hand on her apron and staining it with ash.

'So. Tell me how are you planning to handle the situation back home, Bidisha? You know, after what happened with Yuvaraja Trinabh.' Oliver crossed his legs as he swirled his glass and then sniffed the wine.

Oliver was unusually different. He looked happy and contained. Perhaps because he was getting rid of the burden, of two humans, from another land. Well, that could be the reason. Yes, that was the reason, she concluded.

'If we can keep it under shadows and nobody knows about our travel, I should be able to escape.' Bidisha said, frowning, not looking at Sir Oliver.

If only Debesh had listened to her and gone back his way to the palace, she wouldn't have to feel responsible for his present condition. Just like they received the news about the palace and Yuvaraja Trinabh, the royals must have heard about them too. A couple of ships had left for Bishnupur from Lancashire after their arrival and the informants would have given the information to the Maharaja and Rani Maa.

'Do you think that's possible? And what about Debesh? Everyone in the palace is aware that you are here in Lancashire with Debesh, as you must have already guessed; you are smart enough to deduce that, after all. Do you think the queen will ever let him go? Debesh is a fugitive just like you because he chose to accompany you. Bidisha, you...' Oliver's tone was harsh as he implicated Bidisha for Debesh's condition.

'Sir, Yuvaraja Prabir knows the truth. He will take care of things. Please do not worry about me,' Debesh interrupted Oliver.

Oliver stood up and strode towards the table and poured more wine for himself. 'And you want me to believe that, Debesh? We all know the status of Yuvaraja Prabir in the royal court. Will anybody heed to his words?'

Bidisha already saw what was to come. Looking down on Yuvaraja Prabir in the presence of Debesh wouldn't do any good to Sir Oliver.

'Sir, please. We do have time to think through it. I am sure Debesh and I can work together on that. There will be a way for us. There should be,' Bidisha said, seeing Debesh heading towards Oliver.

'The Yuvaraja will do anything for his people. And I am the most important among them. His person. Sir Oliver, you have no idea about his strength. I hope you'll not say anything against him.'

'Please. Go ahead. Tell me your plan, Debesh. How do you think you can escape the situation? You don't value your safe stay here in Lancashire. You would rather venture into unknown territory without a plan,' Oliver reprimanded, his eyes now fixed on Debesh.

Bidisha, who had wedged herself in the middle of the two men gaped in surprise over the sudden shift in the man's temper.

'I have everything carved in my mind. And I don't want to talk about it to anyone. Least of all to you, Sir Oliver.'

'Debesh, get a hold of yourself. Watch what you are saying.' Bidisha tried to stop him, her hands on his chest as he took another step toward Sir Oliver.

Oliver's hands went to his head and he was trying to hold himself back she could see it, as Bidisha turned around, her back pushing into Debesh's chest, trying to hold him off.

Oliver's eyes blazed like the fire behind him in the hearth. Scarily though, Bidisha saw him glaring at her instead of Debesh.

'What are you holding him away for? Bitch.'

Oliver pushed Bidisha with a force she hadn't expected. Her apron ripped off and she hit her head on the wall before she slumped to the floor. Everything around her stopped. And then she groaned in pain. Her eyes closed.

'Bidisha,' Debesh rushed to her, 'Are you alright?'

She sat up on her knees and held her head. Her eyes were squeezed shut. Bidisha held Debesh's hand and clasped it in pain. Tears were trickling down her cheeks.

Debesh left her and thwacked Oliver in his face. 'You dare hurt her!' Then he punched him in the stomach.

The weakling that Sir Oliver was, he was already on the floor, his hands pressed on his stomach and his knees bent. His nose was bleeding. He grunted like a pig as he rolled on the carpet in pain.

Bidisha held herself upright, her forehead throbbing. She walked towards Oliver and kicked him hard. 'Never call me a bitch again.'

If only she was as alert as she was around crooks, Oliver wouldn't have had a chance to even touch her.

Debesh grabbed her hand and walked out of the door.

'What changed today, Debesh? I held myself back for months and you blew it away in seconds.'

'Nothing changed. I have no idea what Oliver is up to. I could never imagine that he'd hurt you. I thought he...' Debesh stopped, shaking his head. 'I think I made a huge mistake. I shouldn't have lost my mind like that. We are still on his land. But Oliver dared to lay hand on you. I couldn't just watch him do that!'

'We could have escaped. I have been telling you. Only if we had escaped to a dock and slid into a ship, we'd be home long back.'

'Or, in hell, for our foolishness.'

'And what now?' Bidisha asked holding her head. 'And yes, he was right. What about you, even if we successfully make it back to Bishnupur? Will Rani Maa ever leave you alone after helping a convict run away? Especially the one who hurt her son and cost him his throne.'

Bidisha was concerned. She had been for a while now. The more she thought about it, the more she got worried. She wasn't scared for her own self. She would hide away in another place, another jungle far away along with her mother. But the very thought wrenched her heart. All that she had done would be for nothing. Instead of the freedom she wished for her mother, she would push her further deeper into hiding. Worse, she had already put her mother's life at risk. But that was the last resort.

However, she couldn't talk for Debesh. He would straightaway walk into Yuvaraja Prabir's arms. And both, His Majesty and Rani Maa knew that very well. Moreover, she was afraid that Sir Oliver was right. Debesh would be implicated in helping a fugitive. But no matter how hard she tried to come up with a plan, knowing Debesh wouldn't prefer to stay away from Yuvaraja Prabir any longer, she failed miserably.

All the joy of the day had diminished into nothingness in her heart. Now, she only felt numb in her chest and her mind.

CHAPTER FIFTEEN

Oliver's house was lit with candles placed in beautiful lamps, holders and mesmerizing glass chandeliers. But all the brightness in the room couldn't light up her gloomy heart. Debesh had ruined it for them. Rather, the two together had made a huge blunder by annoying Oliver. And she had been restless all day wanting to hurl out her agitation at Debesh.

Bidisha's persistence was fast coming to its limit. She was lonely and had no one to share the burden of her heart. She wanted someone by her side, someone she could put her trust in, someone to lean on and open her heart to, confide her feelings in, a shoulder to cry.

The maidens had all left her back to guard Oliver's home as usual as they planned to indulge in the gossip surrounding the great lords and ladies of the town. However, her heart and mind screamed in unison to pick up the sword and let her frustrations out. It was getting difficult by the day to hold Sir Oliver's interests before hers.

She walked into her room and pulled out her sword from its sheath. The maidens who were lost in their frantic laughter looked at her bedazzled as she walked out of the cottage with the steel in her hand and fire in her eyes.

Just as she stepped on the white bed of melting snow, the soft rays of the sun caused the metal in her hand to sparkle. The sword whistled as she swung it. She took a few calm steps further towards the frozen water of the stream. Bidisha took a deep breath as she took her stance to fight the man in her head. She stared into the space ahead of her trying to visualize him before her eyes.

And then she was quick to position an attack straight on her opponent's imaginary head. But he blocked it. Just as she had expected. He was a warrior after all and his image was no less than his real self. She saw his sword coming for her leg. She jumped up in the air as she made eye contact with him in her head. And then Bidisha indulged in the duel. She advanced on him. And then blocked his sword before her chest. She retreated even as her hand moved in swift actions. Her breathing became faster and her body warmed up as her frustration grew.

The maidens had followed her and were now gaping in shock.

And then Debesh showed up out of nowhere. He had rushed out in the morning without even telling Oliver. And now he had returned at an unexpected time. He mostly returned home late at night. But it was only dawn. The birds had just started to fly back to their nests in the clear sky after days.

The grin was back on the women's faces. She had never seen them showing up like that before Sir Oliver. Never. Looked like their preference in men was just like hers.

Debesh paced towards her. And the maidens walked back to the mansion but turned around again and again for a glimpse of him.

'It's soon going to be dark. And where is the lantern?' Debesh asked looking around.

Bidisha continued with the duel. She snapped and ripped her invisible enemy apart.

'Is everything alright? You do this whenever you want to fight someone whom you can't in reality. Who is it this time?' Debesh stepped into her zone risking an accidental cut she could make in her furious mood.

'I am glad you asked it. It's you.'

She advanced on him with her sword while he was unarmed.

'What's up with you?' Debesh walked back dodging her attack.

'Didn't you say we would make it home safely? But now we are in waters all because of you. Why did you have to punch Oliver? Do you think he is gonna forget it and send us back?'

'A lot is going on with Oliver than you know, Bidisha. Let me first explain it to you. Hold your sword.'

'What could possibly be going on with Oliver the great?' Bidisha charged even as he rolled on the ground and bounced back up moving away from her sword.

'He has been acting crazy around me after the fire incident in his mill. And when he hit you the other day, I could only vent it all out on him.'

She was overwhelmed with the unknown the future had in store for her. Just when things seemed to be falling in place, her hopes had actually fallen apart.

'What do you mean by crazy? And, why didn't you tell me anything about it earlier? Bidisha acted with all her strength and the blade almost made it to his neck.

Debesh dodged her every move 'What are you up to? Bidisha, stop.' Debesh ducked and escaped the sword.

Bidisha's moves were getting faster and she was barely cautious.

'Bidisha, watch. Stop it, I said. Do you wish to kill me tonight?'

'Yes, I do. Unless you give me a clear answer.'

She kicked him straight in his gut and he was on the ground in an instant.

'Ufff!' Debesh let out a sigh. 'Something is up with you today.'

She pushed him down again as he attempted to get up, her hand on his chest and her sword on the ground. Bidisha held her long black skirt just a little high enough to move freely, the white lace of her petticoat flashed. Debesh's eyes widened as she straddled him. He looked petrified, his eyes plastered on Bidisha.

But unlike her action, her face said a different tale. It was obvious, she was more than just an angry girl.

'Do I have your attention now? Shall we talk about us?' Bidisha asked, her tone like her steel, as she pressed him further against the ground.

'Wha... What are you trying to say? What... What about us?' Debesh's hands were still on the grass, next to his ears as if he was surrendering to her.

'I know it very well that you are pretending to be unaware of what's going on between us. And, I also am sure you feel something for me too. Now tell me...'

'Hold on. Why are you bringing that up now, in the middle of this conversation?'

Debesh closed his eyes and pressed his fingers to his temples. He took a deep breath and held her arms. In an instant, he flipped her off of himself and under him. She heard material ripping, and realized it was her dress. Debesh's firm grip had pulled her sleeves, tearing the fabric in the upheaval and exposing her shoulder.

Bidisha gulped. The rage within her had turned into something she couldn't relate to. Her ears burned and her cheeks warmed up. He looked at her shoulders before his gaze shifted to her face.

'Do you want to make out with me? Is that why you are acting like this?'

Bidisha used all her strength and forced him off her.

'You think so shallowly of me? I expected more from you. Now I wonder if I even want to ask you what I wanted to earlier.' Bidisha pulled her dress together, covered her legs and held the lace on her shoulder in place.

The two sat next to each other in the dark. Bidisha's resolve to get answers from him was gone. However, she was not one of those who would stall till things fell in place on their own. Bidisha liked to make things happen, seek answers, take action. She wouldn't wait for anything.

She mustered courage though her heart pounded inside the wilderness of her chest. And her thoughts raced faster than she could speak. 'I can see it; we both want to be with each other. But something is holding you back. Don't you want to talk about it and get over with it?'

'It is not as simple as it looks. It's not like I love you and...' Debesh stopped and stood up.

'So, you admit that!' Bidisha asked as she pulled his arm and forced him to sit down again. 'Let us talk it out today. It's important for me.'

'Now that you have brought it up, yes, let us be clear about everything between us. But I can't believe, we are sorting matters of the heart and our feelings like it is an issue of business or royal politics.'

'When someone falls in love with a man like you, a stone-faced hound, bound to his master's loyalty, what else can be done?'

'First, stop calling me a hound. I am loyal but I am not a dog who has blind faith in his master. Yuvaraja Prabir is more than a master to me. And second, if I go soft, I'd have girls and the maidens in the palace after me all the time.'

'Yeah, that I can see even here. But I wonder why those three women never sneak around Oliver.' Bidisha tossed a stone on the frozen layer of the river.

'Because they know exactly what and who Oliver is. A stonehearted man who values nothing but wealth.'

'I would have killed that bastard if not for that boar. Why do the heavens even want to save a soul so black who neither values others' lives nor cares for someone's feelings?'

'So it was really you...' Debesh said with a smirk. 'I wonder what was cooking between you and Yuvaraja Trinabh. But now it's clear, he agreed to solve your problem in the court.' Debesh gave her a long stare before he continued, 'How can you be so calm about this whole thing? As if you were gone missing when Oliver discovered about it on the ship.'

'What else can I do about it when we are here in his country and his home? The more I think about it, the more I find myself helpless. If only we were in Bishnupur, things would have been different. Nothing feels good anymore. It has been like that for a while. But today it is awful. But that doesn't mean I will let you slide away without giving me an answer. You can try and change the topic all you want. But you can't leave from here without answering me.'

'Why do you keep asking the same question when you know my answer very well? Don't you know the Yuvaraja has a special place for you in his heart?' Debesh looked away from Bidisha.

'I want to hear it from you, Debesh. I don't care about what Yuvaraja Prabir wants or what Oliver wants. I want to know how far you can go to be with me.' Bidisha's voice was feeble as if the words came out with fear.

'What answer do you want when the question itself is wrong?'

'Will you give me a straightforward answer?'

'Why don't you accept the Yuvaraja Prabir? Don't you see he loves you like there's no other person on this earth? He has always been lonely all his life. I have never seen him worry about someone else to this extent. You say you want to be with me. But don't you see that I have nothing to give you?'

'Why do you think I want something in return?'

'Are you telling me that you are fine to wander along with me all your life? I can't even give you a roof on your head.'

'I've never had one before. And like you can see, I am doing alright. And I don't need a house in the future either.' Bidisha said, wanting to get into his head, trying to understand him even though she herself wasn't sure of her needs and her wants, 'I am happy to live in your heart all my life.'

'If you must really hear my answer, then listen. No, I can't be with you, I can't confess that I love you, I can't say out loud that in my heart, I want to be with you all my life, every day of my life.' Debesh looked into her eyes. 'Do you hear me now? I can't utter any of those words. I will never give up on Yuvaraja Prabir. My duties towards him come before anything or anyone. So, don't ever ask me again.'

His words came as an assurance of what she already knew. And it also put her heart at ease knowing she wouldn't be the one to betray him with her unwilling act of love. She had something for him that she couldn't understand herself but it wasn't love she was aware of. And yet her heart ached at his rejection.

'Will you not stop me even once, Bidisha? I am giving up on you. Do you understand?' Debesh looked into her eyes in anticipation and longing, 'I want to beg you to hold me tight. Stop me and not let me go, Bidisha.'

'But I know you wouldn't ask me to do that no matter how much you want to. Your loyalty lies with Yuvaraja Prabir.'

'And you wouldn't do that even if I ask you to. Your heart longs for Yuvaraja Trinabh.'

'You know me too well, Debesh. You are making it easy for me to let go of you.'

'Because I know your heart beckons someone else.'

'Would you stop me from going to the man I want to? And ask me to stay with a man you want me to stay with?'

'How can I force you to, Bidisha, when you have nothing for Yuvaraja Prabir? Maybe it's his fate to lose everyone he has loved.'

'Except for you. I know you won't leave his side for anyone or anything. Not even for your life.'

Debesh gave a half-hearted, sad smile, 'You and me, maybe we are just a disaster. We know each other well and yet we don't want to be together.'

'I can't live with you and I can't live without you. That's my fate,' Bidisha declared as her eyes welled up even as her gaze was stuck on him.

'I can see it in your eyes. Your affection for me could be my destiny I thought. But I was wrong.'

Debesh looked at her for a long second, moved closer, held her by her waist, pulled her in and pressed her against his chest. His eyes were set on her lips as his thumb ran over her lower lip.

Bidisha raised her eyebrows before she threw her head back. All the words she wanted to hurl at him were choked inside of her. And the heart that had lost hope and slumped into darkness moments ago now raced just like her frantic mind that was both confused and scared.

His hand traced her jaw from her lips and then down to her nape. Bidisha broke into a sweat. The warmth of his breath and his touch took her mind to a faraway fairyland. Away from the harsh reality, she had faced just a while back.

Before she realized it, his other hand was wrapped around her waist. And his moonlit face came closer. She closed her eyes. His lips touched her moist quivering one and he kissed her softly at first. Her skin ruptured into goose pimples and the cold breeze didn't make it easy. Debesh took her in, his grip stronger on her waist. That heartless, rustic man had evoked a storm of sensations within her.

Bidisha's long fingers ran through his hair and she grabbed a tuft of hair as his callous mouth parted her lips. Her other hand traced his back inside his shirt. The touch of his bare skin and the feel of that warm man warmed her heart, overpowering all her worries.

All she wanted to do a while ago was to talk to him. But here she was, giving in to her long-entrapped desire, forgiving and forgetting his words. And before she knew it, she kissed him back.

Bidisha dreaded the possibility that she might go too far, far enough that she won't be able to return. She felt a pang at that thought. But she wanted to give in, be in that moment for as long as it was possible so that she could hold on to him. A tear trickled from the corner of her eye although the joy expunged the thought of their hearts departing. She moaned as their tongues collided with passion.

But she jerked and let her grip loose. If he couldn't be with her, by her side, then he didn't have the right to tease her emotions, fuel her desire and then get away from her, leaving her heart scalded for life.

Debesh pulled his hands back and moved away from her. His eyes were moist and hers welled up with tears. He held her hands and caressed her fingers as his gaze locked with hers.

'This will be our first and last time,' Debesh said, firming his hold.

'Don't you remember our first time on the ship?' Bidisha gave him a reluctant smile, her chest tightening as she looked at the shiny teardrop rolling from his eyes.

'That wasn't even a peck. I call it nothing.'

Bidisha sniffed as Debesh stepped away and then she cried her heart out. Debesh stopped but walked away without even looking back. Bidisha had never shed tears like that before. She deserved to be thrown away. How could any man accept her when she wasn't honest with her own feelings?

She pushed herself to love him but didn't succeed. And he pushed himself to stop loving her but couldn't. Whatever they had for each other, the two couldn't be together. Both were at fault. Both hadn't been faithful to each other and their own feelings.

'You don't understand, Debesh. It wasn't like what it sounded like. I never meant to hurt her. It was just that... Come on now. Let it be. After all that I have done for Bidisha and you, can't you let my one mistake slide? And I got a really bad one for what I did. Where do you think you both are going?' Oliver pleaded, one hand on Debesh's shoulder and the other pointing to the purple blotches on his nose.

Bidisha had tried speaking to Debesh about staying back till the time they could arrange for their travel. But he had made up his mind. He wouldn't take the chance of staying in the shelter of a man like Oliver. Whether or not Oliver kept his word and sent them back home as promised, Debesh had decided to find another way out of Lancashire.

He had been making trips back and forth to meet people he had come in contact with in the past months. Debesh had tried everything at hand but the three ships that were to depart, come summer, were all owned by Oliver. There was no chance of getting on board unless they sneaked in. However, it would be worst for them this time if they are discovered travelling on the ship illegally. And it was highly impossible to stow away for months on the ship in hiding. That wasn't an option at all.

And then there he was, the great Sir Oliver Watts, trying to convince Debesh to stay back a week after the drunken incident.

'Or was it? Did Oliver really act on impulse under the influence of alcohol?' Bidisha wondered.

He looked alright that day. And he had hardly had a couple of glasses of wine to be under its effect. Oliver had been enraged and he knew what he was doing.

Debesh didn't answer Oliver for a long while and Bidisha didn't urge him to either. And it was a surprise to her that Oliver wanted them to stay back. Didn't they travel illegally on his ship? He was even trying to offload them ever since he discovered them on the ship?

But it didn't look like that anymore.

'Why do you want us to stay, Sir? Debesh has finally managed to find a place for us to stay till we arrange something for our travel.' Bidisha questioned, her voice firm and clear.

'I was too angry after what happened. For what Debesh did to me. How could he break my nose? Don't I mean anything to you both?' Oliver sounded low as if he was hurt not just on his nose but in his heart too.

That was the first time she had seen Oliver in their petty servants' cottage. She folded her clothes, her three pairs of dresses and her only coat to protect her from the cold. Bidisha was getting ready to move away from Oliver's house.

To find their way home.

Debesh walked out of his room, with a small cloth haversack in hand, his luggage that would go places from now on along with him and perhaps to Bishnupur someday soon.

'You have no gratitude towards me. You two would be begging on the roads and lay frozen on the streets like those homeless filths out there. I took you both in, cared for you, provided shelter, work and dignity here in a foreign land. And you are turning your back on me.' Oliver followed Debesh, held his elbow and turned him around. 'And you, Debesh, do you know what all I have to go through for you. The things that I have done.'

Bidisha stood right behind them, with her bag in hand. The other servants looked at Oliver like they were seeing a ghost. Unlike his usual dignified demeanour, Oliver had dropped his guard.

'You were born in filth and have lived in it. You simply can't live without it, can you? That is why you're kicking the fortune I planned for you and want to squander in the trash with that filthy whore.'

Debesh turned and punched Oliver's stomach sending him down on his knees in pain. And before he lost his mind and beat him to death, Debesh grabbed Bidisha's hand and walked out of the door. The fresh snow, white as the clouds, was coming down in lumps. It had been like that since last night. And the wind was picking up speed.

'Wait... Wait... Debesh... I am sorry. Don't leave me.' Oliver limped after them, clutching his stomach, as he groaned and struggled to catch up with Debesh's pace, crunching in the knee-high snow.

Bidisha was unable to get a grasp of the situation. There was no way they could be of any worth to Oliver. After the way he had behaved with her and the names he had called her, it was clear that he didn't harbour any feelings for her as Debesh had assumed. She didn't see any reason for him to stop them.

'I gave up everything for you. All my fortune. I lost everything that I had worked on for years. And you, Debesh, you not only beat me up but you are also ready to leave me to die of heartbreak and don't even want to look back at me.'

Bidisha was baffled.

'Heartbreak?'

Debesh dropped his haversack, turned around and caught Oliver by his ruffles, his eyes throwing daggers at him. 'Sir Oliver, don't you dare question my actions and intentions. I could put up with your doings all these days, since the time the mill disaster happened, only because I wanted to repay for your kindness. You spared our lives on the ship, took us in and sheltered us. I am forever indebted for what you have done for Bidisha and me. But I realize now that your intentions were not as good as your deeds. What you're asking in return for your generosity, I can never do that for you.'

'What are you both talking about?' Bidisha picked the bag up and stepped carefully as the snow scrunched rising over her black boots. 'Debesh, what is going on?'

'Hear me out today, Bidisha,' Oliver barked. 'I love Debesh. Do you hear me? He is mine. Stay away from him.'

Bidisha was perplexed as she gaped at Oliver's scary face. One part of her understood what Oliver meant. But the other part of her didn't want to acknowledge what the words meant.

And the next moment, she was choking. It was Oliver. He had her neck. His flaming eyes closed in on her. Bidisha struggled to breathe. But then she struck at his elbow. Broke the tension in his hand. Oliver lost his grip. She twisted his arm even as she coughed. Clasped it at his back. Turned him away from her. She firmed her grip on his nape. Bidisha took a deep breath and shoved him into the snow face down. Oliver bawled even as he struggled to lift his head out of the snow. Her hand was still firm on his nape when she kicked his rump before she let him go.

'Come on if you have it in you. I haven't fought in a long time,' Bidisha challenged him.

Debesh placed his hand on her shoulder. 'Are you alright? I... I wanted to tell you earlier. About Oliver.'

Bidisha's lips formed a thin line as she picked up her bag and stared at Oliver who grunted lifting his head but his hands were still inside the snow.

The cold wind whooshed in her ears and the snowflakes didn't stop from creating havoc in their path further. Her cloak was hardly of any help against the freezing wind. Her fingers and toes were numb, and her head felt heavy as she struggled to gain her balance.

'No... No... You can't leave. I can't lose you too.' Oliver trembled as he stood up. 'I have lost my whole family and...and...my mill in the fire. Not you... Don't leave me alone, Debesh.'

'Oliver, come to your senses.' Debesh shook him hard.

'Debesh, you know...I...I burnt down my own mill for you. Turned my lifelong efforts and my dream into ashes. Debesh, the moment I first saw you on my first visit to the palace as a young boy, I realised what I wanted. And you were the one who showed it to me. You were the reason for my visits to Bishnupur from then on, not the trade or the money. Debesh... Debesh...listen. I...I...forgive you for hitting me. And I submit myself to you. Take me.'

Bidisha dashed in as Debesh jerked back listening to Oliver. She tried to decipher the psyche of the savage of a man as her blood rushed in rage.

'I have heard of men longing for men. And women wanting to be with women. But I have never seen someone like you who would put the lives of innocent women and children at stake. How could you? And for what?' Bidisha asked attempting to read the hidden truth behind his frightening visage.

'It was all because of you. You, witch. You... You have possessed his soul. And seduced him. He would have become mine for the wealth I would give him in the future. But you... You ruined it all. You were loose on your fangs that day. Trying to stick your tongue in his throat. I did it to see you burn alive—'

'You take those words back.' Debesh's eyes were blazing hot as he lifted Oliver by his ruffles.

'I don't care what you have to say about me, Oliver. I have heard worse things. But, unfortunately, you take poor lives for play.' Bidisha fumed even as the chill took over her as the blasted blizzard worsened.

'It's not a play. It's the strength. I am strong enough to put my life above everybody else. You...you are only talking about the good-for-nothing workers in my mill. I have dared to burn my own family for denying me the right to my inheritance only because they discovered I had fallen in love with Debesh as a young boy.'

Her insides rumbled. She closed her eyes as she felt nauseated.

Tears trickled from the corner of her eyes at the very thought of his family burning alive in the fire. Bidisha tried to get her mind out of her gruesome imagination.

'How could he?'

But a wave of dizziness assaulted her as the coldness of the man shook her from the inside. And she blacked out.

CHAPTER SIXTEEN

It was one of the darkest nights of Bidisha's life and the whiteness of the snow didn't do much to brighten her path on a no-moon night. The battering gusts weren't pleasant to the ears nor to her body, which was already worn out. The skies wouldn't stop pelting snow. And every flake deadened her hope of finding a warm place.

Bidisha's legs screeched her to stop even as she trod the path, hand-in-hand with Debesh. They were close to the last shelter that was left to be checked.

Unlike London, they were told, Lancashire hardly had any shelter homes. Though the neighbourhoods were demolished to accommodate the railroads that were being planned throughout England, the promised number of boardings for the abandoned and the homeless were still not in place. This was the last place they were left with after being rejected by three other shelter homes. Everywhere they stepped in was crowded and full. Though the two had enough money to sustain lodging in a good bed and breakfast, they had to save to buy a place and silence on the ship.

With no hope left from Oliver, Bidisha had to find another way to reach home safely. Being a person of colour made it much worse for Debesh. In the previous shelter home, a penny lodging, a place where a night's shelter and bread is promised for the homeless for just a penny, Debesh was shown the door. Instead, a family of four whites were given entry for an extra penny per person because they had a child who could freeze to death outside. But Bidisha saw it—the look on the man's face when he saw Debesh. While Bidisha would be easily mistaken as a native unless she spoke, Debesh didn't stand a chance.

The warmth of the shelter house hit Bidisha like bliss from the heavens just as they opened the wooden door. But the sight before her demolished the last of her faith. Debesh quickly shoved the small haversack into her hand and rushed to the queue. He took out pence from his pockets and waited patiently for his turn to buy them a night of warmth, if not much comfort and good food. Her eyes were fixed on him as he moved up a place in the queue of men with their faces hanging down to the floor. The place looked much better though there were not many women and children around. At least there was no one surpassing the queue and stepping on people's feet in the crowded group in front of the desk.

The man behind the table could close it anytime; she had seen it happening to them all night. If not for that place, they would either have to spend the night on the streets or, go to an expensive stay and lose money when they didn't even have a chance at landing a job yet. However, finally, Debesh handed the pennies to the man and Bidisha let out a sigh as she rubbed her cold palms together.

'Coffin beds it is,' Debesh said with a smile on his face as he ran back to her. 'We need to hand over these leather blankets in the morning before leaving.'

Bidisha gave the bags to Debesh and covered herself with the black blanket. 'As long as we are warm. Anything will work. Even animal skin.'

Bidisha and Debesh walked into a huge hall where hundreds of people sat on benches squeezing into one another as they had their tea and bread in silence. And it occurred to her that, without the onlookers with sticks in their hands to maintain the discipline, the hall would have easily turned into a fish market. Bidisha and Debesh too followed the queue and joined the others on the bench sticking to each other.

The warmth of the teacup in her palms was a welcome change that night. The tea warmed her and the bread, though not enough, brought enough relief that she could think backwards as Oliver's words beset her mind.

They entered a narrow room with rows of barren hardwood coffin-like boxes on the floor against the wall on either side. They went to the beds with their allotted numbers.

With no place to waste, the boxes were almost attached. So much so that the body temperature and the warmth of each other's breath alone would be enough to save lives in situations like these.

However, Bidisha was not someone who was used to people. Not so many in a room where she slept. And mostly men. There were only three women in the room of forty coffins. But she would make do, though it was daunting.

'Fourpence for this doss will do. No mattress is fine too,' Bidisha said out loud as she thought hard of the situation that could have been far worse.

'Better than sleeping in the wet doorway or in the alley with the dogs, freezing just like them in the frozen dirt. You are better off here in Lancashire. I have seen it in London and you wouldn't want the same here,' a man said, his face haggard, a white beard that had almost turned brown and his clothes nothing better than oily rags.

'Better, you say?' Another man rose from one of the forty coffins, just like the dead rising, raving as his alcoholic breath filled the small space. 'This is a bloody hole, filthy and disgusting. The only promise of this place is hot boiling water that I have access to make my tea anytime.'

Debesh moved the man away politely as he advanced towards the other gentleman with aggression. 'Sir, please rest. We can talk it out in the morning.'

'When are you going to tell me what happened between Oliver and you?' Bidisha whispered.

'Do I look like I want to talk about it to you? Or, anybody else. I would never fan a sin like that. Do you hear me?' Debesh shouted. 'Don't ever bring that up again, Bidisha.'

People in the room glared at them.

'If you have a lovers' tiff to resolve, you can go out of the shelter and bark in the streets all you want. Not in here,' a man shouted.

'Lovers' tiff?'

She was quick to grab her place at the end near the wall. At least she would have one free side with no man breathing her air. But, on the other hand, she'd be next to Debesh, just two thin wooden boards apart, who had her heart for a while before smashing it hard. Bidisha had a lot to talk to Debesh—about their work till they left Lancashire, their stay and food, and, most importantly, about their sail in summer.

Howbeit, she got into her hard coffin box, covered herself with the leather and went to sleep. The snug bed was warm but gave her little room to turn around or even stretch her legs. Bidisha stared at the ceiling. With the lousy grunts and sundry noises around her making it to her ears, she could only think about the calm of the nights in the jungle.

Debesh removed his shoes and stepped into his coffin bed.

Bidisha chuckled.

'What? Did you remember something funny?'

'No, I imagined you in that box—your shoulder pushing hard to fit into it and then people carving you out from it in the morning in an attempt to save their little wooden box.'

'It's not that difficult. Look.'

Debesh leaned back and she heard a 'thug'.

'Ugh,' Bidisha said, looking at Debesh's face that was clenched in pain as he hit his head on the board, though he didn't utter a sound.

He rubbed his head looking away from her and then slid down as he stretched his legs that spilled outside the box, resting his calves on the board. And then he fidgeted till he finally squeezed in his shoulder.

Bidisha let out a chortle though she tried hard not to.

Months had passed and Christmas was gone too. There was no reason for Bidisha to celebrate just like their mates in the shelters, hostels and lodgings for the homeless. Finding a warm place at night and the hustle to find a place on the ship were the only things that occupied her mind.

Most of her day passed in the mill and trying to earn her living. They had enough gold and silver crowns to make it back home. But Oliver was the problem. He had used his money, influence and every other dirty means to stop them from getting what they wanted.

Every person who could help them with a place on the ship was now aware of Debesh's and Bidisha's identity even before they met them. Rumours were that Bidisha was a slave from India and had been looking out for a way to escape after stealing from her master, Sir Oliver Watts. And though they had a sketch of Debesh's appearance, they were instructed to deal with him differently by just denying him any ticket.

There were attempts to detain her and she went into hiding once again. The worst she had expected after running away from a similar situation back home. Debesh and Bidisha had decided to stay low and carry on with their life until it was time. But Oliver had seen to it that Bidisha wouldn't be able to talk to people about taking them onboard to India without the risk of getting arrested.

No matter how much Debesh tried in secret, the other passenger, Bidisha's identity was too strong to miss. The owners and masters of the ship, Oliver's acquaintances mostly, had her physical description flawlessly written and documented.

But she couldn't let Oliver do that to her. Bidisha had the right to live on her land and not on a foreign land against her will. She would make it to her home even though a tough time awaited her there, given what she had done to Yuvaraja Trinabh. She was ready to face anything on her land.

Bidisha would face the queen for harming her son. She would bow down before the man she had loved even though she had committed the crime unintentionally.

But she wouldn't crawl her way to death in her old age on a nobody's land away from her mother. She had waited for long enough and with patience. However, she wouldn't do that anymore. The waiting. And for nothing.

While Debesh hesitated and even held her back, she couldn't care less even if she nettled Oliver further. She had to take charge and do something about her situation.

She snuck out of the mill on the pretext of working overtime elsewhere after her work every day till she finally located and met with Oliver's mill partners.

Gary Brown and Henry Peel had agreed to arrange a safe passage for both Debesh and her, in exchange for the truth behind the fire accident in the mill. The men had been loathing Oliver since he had nothing much to lose even though he too had to endure some losses. On the other hand, the two lords weren't able to sustain the huge financial blow that had crushed them to their knees.

The news that Oliver had sabotaged their business for his personal gains was not only a shock, it also brought out the beasts in them, exactly what Bidisha had hoped for.

However, Bidisha couldn't come to terms with whether she should talk about Oliver's interest in Debesh as a life companion since Debesh was enraged at the very thought of it. Bringing it up would mean hurting Debesh who thought the relationship between the two men was a sin. Moreover, it was not her truth to reveal and she wouldn't be able to forgive herself for using it for her gains. Hence she had decided against the idea of disclosing that part of the truth.

Both, Gary Brown and Henry Peel had promised her that Oliver would meet his fate for duping them. He would be arrested and enquired. And that was enough for Bidisha.

Bidisha rolled her locks with her fingers as she sipped her tea. 'I don't know what are we getting into but Oliver has left us no choice. Tomorrow, we will go see him.'

'We will. And teach him the lesson of his life,' Debesh declared, taking a morsel of bread.

'We don't have much time left. The ship will leave in two weeks.'

'Yes, but I am warning you. Do not try to do anything behind my back. We will get out of this together. I promise.'

Bidisha didn't reply. She had been looking out for ways that Debesh would never approve of, including her deal with Gary and Henry. But how could she sit back and do nothing?

'You two there,' the monitor shouted as Debesh and Bidisha sat in a huge penny sit-up room having their meals along with the other inmates at the shelter.

She glared at him and then looked at Debesh. 'The strict discipline[1] they maintain at all times annoys me to the core.'

It felt like a punishment of sorts, to spend the night on a bench without having a wink of sleep while monitors saw to it that no one closed their eyes. She always cribbed about such ridiculous rules in the penny sit-up homes.

Bidisha was too tired from the day's work. And it had been months since she last slept well. There were days the two would chance upon coffin beds and other days they would have to make do with sit-up accommodation. The grim faces around her, seated in long silent rows, agitated her reminding her of the helpless people back home.

All this would be over if only Oliver hadn't muddled in their affairs before the first ship sailed three weeks ago. They would have been on their way home.

But she wouldn't let the same happen again and miss the last ship. Their next chance then would be several months later and she couldn't take any of it anymore. She was longing to embrace her mother and sleep in her own bed, in the ruins so dear to her.

The night passed but her mind was still stuck. Her eyes were drooping shut when a monitor started shouting for tea and bread. Had she been in Bishnupur, she would have drawn her sword out and his head would be on the ground. But she hadn't held her sword in her hands in months. It was not allowed there in Lancashire, to carry the sword openly everywhere. Debesh had promised her to keep it safe for her along with his sword. He had hidden it in Oliver's backyard. A place he knew nobody would go to. When the time came, he would get it out and they would board the ship.

Bidisha sipped on her water-like tea and ate the last morsel of her dry white bread. She gulped it all with water in a rush to step out and head to

Oliver's mansion along with Debesh.

The warmth of the morning sun and the freshness in the breeze brightened her spirit, just like it had always done in the jungle. But the sight before her was nothing like the jungle. The crowded buildings, lodgings and shelters stood everywhere she looked. The old and the sick walked out like zombies, the living dead, as they were known, with no sleep all night, and they took their steps without aim.

But she could feel her home when she closed her eyes after the harsh and gloomy winter was gone.

'Let us get done with it and get out of this land as soon as possible.' Debesh came out behind her and marched like he was going for a war.

It indeed was, after almost a year of struggle.

'We have to take care of Oliver. Or, we will soon be zombies like them.'

After a long wait, they could finally make it into a horsebus. Whenever she saw them on the road, she was fascinated at how just two horses were capable of pulling a huge carriage with 8 to 10 people. And ironically, the rich, like Oliver, had their small but luxurious carriage drawn by 4 horses.

People were cramped in the horsebus, 5 on either side facing each other. Debesh and Bidisha were too as they sat next to each other in the little available space. The woman on her other side kept pushing Bidisha to make more room for herself on the wooden bench.

The next moment Debesh's elbow brushed her bosom as he tried to adjust in the seat. He pulled his hand away immediately. Bidisha blushed. Just as he was about to settle, the two horses cantered and Debesh lost his balance resting his hand on her upper thigh. Bidisha suddenly stood up in faze and hit her head to the roof as the wheels of the horsebus rolled.

She stumbled and as she struggled to find her footing, she fell forward. She thought she would land on the man sitting in front of her but Debesh caught her just in time. And she had landed in his lap, her face pressed against his neck. His hands held her waist firmly to stop her from the fall.

Debesh's gaze was fixed on her, and Bidisha gulped. The next moment, she pushed the woman away and settled between Debesh and the odious person. Bidisha rubbed her palms as she felt Debesh's eyes still on her. She looked up straight at the row of men staring at her. Bidisha clenched her face in embarrassment and then glared at them forcing them to look away.

The man she was hoping to hug in distress sat right beside her but the kind of awkwardness that lingered in the air suffocated her. And for no specific reason, Bidisha was overwhelmed. She was not the kind of woman to easily break down over nothing. But her heart became heavy at that moment.

Bidisha pressed her fingers on her brows as her eyes welled up. And then her fingers trembled as they moved to her nose in an attempt to hide her face from Debesh. She was reminded of her lost septum ring and it brought her mother's face before her eyes. She wanted to hug her and cry on her shoulder. Howbeit, she didn't know where to turn as her chest tightened and a lump formed in her throat.

Debesh took her hand in his even though he looked away from her. His hold was firm and affirming. Bidisha gently squeezed his hand back when she saw his eyes were moist too.

A horse carriage waited in front of Oliver's property and she could hear loud voices coming from inside. Just like Bidisha had anticipated, Oliver was at home, since it was early in the morning. But the carriage didn't belong to him. Debesh and Bidisha walked past it and towards the entrance.

The cottage behind the mansion had been her house for months, but she couldn't really connect with the place. Neither the people nor the place had left any kind of an intimate impression on her. And when she had returned to get over with some unfinished work to teach Oliver a lesson, all that she was filled with was rage and anger. If things went well, she would present Oliver's head to Maharaja Mitul Singha Dev on his next visit to Bishnupur. But then it wasn't a guarantee that he'd come to India now, after what Oliver had done to his mill.

And now that she had even informed his partners about his scheme, he would be taken care of. She contemplated if she should come back just before boarding the ship and kill the bastard. His head would rot by the time they reached but she could present some other evidence. It would work; if not for a pardon for her mother, at least the Maharaja would spare her and she could leave somewhere far away from Bishnupur with her mother.

The door was open and there were men inside whom she had never seen before. She held her grey floral dress just a little as she stepped up closing in on the door.

'Did I hear it right?'

'Yes, Sir. The king, he is no more. And the fight for the throne will get interesting now. One has been a weakling all his life and the other is left with no thumb.' The man said, pulling his red collar with a wide smile on his face.

'I didn't expect this. Well then. That's the end of Maharaja Mitul Singha Dev.' Oliver stood up, his pipe in his hand. 'Let's see what's in store for Bishnupur now.'

Bidisha dropped her bag on the ground.

Debesh slumped on the bench next to her. Whatever safety Yuvaraja Prabir was accorded in the palace was because of the Maharaja's affection towards him. Now, with the Maharaja gone, Debesh shuddered to even think of the fate that awaited his beloved Yuvaraja.

Oliver heard the sound and looked around to face the intruders in his conversation. 'Oh! Look who is here. And what perfect timing. I have news for you two. Aaa...hmmm... Guess you've already heard it.'

'What really happened in the palace?' Bidisha asked as she clutched her skirt.

'Come, my dear. Come in. We shall talk.' Oliver slipped his hand on her shoulder, a smile on his face.

Bidisha shrugged his hand and moved away.

Oliver's lips curled down as he put his hands up in the air. 'Alright! Would you like to come inside Debesh? I understand it's devastating for you considering that Yuvaraja Prabir is all but alone hereafter.'

Debesh stomped his leg against the wood on the floor as he rose. His jaw was clenched with rage, his eyes were hardened and narrowed into slits as he took his hands to Oliver's neck.

'You watch your mouth before I kill you. He, Yuvaraja, still has me. I will never let him be alone. You hear me?' Debesh bared his teeth as his grip around Oliver's neck tightened and he pushed him to the wall.

Bidisha rushed to him, as Oliver struggled to breathe. Bidisha pulled Debesh's hands in an attempt to relive Oliver. Just when she had managed to loosen his grip, Debesh pushed her hard.

Bidisha backed, unable to resist the force. She slammed into a man behind her who held her in support. The man was kind enough to help her to her feet too. Together they stepped back due to the impact. The men had barged out hearing the commotion. Three of them together tried hard to save Oliver from Debesh.

'Who is this man?'

'Get him off of Oliver.'

Bidisha ran towards Debesh and punched him hard in his stomach. Debesh immediately let go of Oliver's neck growling in pain.

The men held him, pulling him away from Oliver who coughed and fell.

'Let him go, Debesh.' Bidisha stepped forward and hugged him.

'I... I need to go back, Bidisha. Yuvaraja... He... He is waiting for me,' Debesh murmured, looking more lost and hopeless than she had ever seen him.

His lips had gone pale and beads of sweat formed on his forehead as he gaped into nothingness.

'We both have to go, Debesh. We will.'

Bidisha had the strong urge to see Trinabh, ask him if he was doing alright, if he needed her, a shoulder to lean on, even as her mind blamed her for all the fiasco.

If only she hadn't slit his thumb. If only she hadn't left him behind to suffer. If only, she would have thought about her step one more time, as her mother had always told her. But it was done.

Debesh hugged her back. His neck rested on her shoulder. She stood blank in his arms.

Her only hope had died even before she could ask for help. Prove her worth to him. Make a settlement. Kill the bastard Oliver and ask him to lift the sobriquet of 'royal fugitive' off of her mother's head. Free Mokshita from the false conviction of killing her own love. Let her lead a free life, among the people, away from the jungle.

But that wouldn't happen anymore. The Maharaja was gone. And Rani Maa would only seek her revenge on Bidisha for the downfall of her son.

And Trinabh, why would he ever help the one person who was the cause of his fall?

Moreover, would he be able to rise to the power, gain authority and even be in the position to even think of doing anything for anyone? A handicapped prince would have to face many more challenges to attain the thrown. She had taken away his glory from him. Perhaps, she had taken away everything from him. It was her time to pay for it.

And just like that, Goddess Bipottarini Devi had deprived her of the only chance she had to free her mother from her suffering. Bidisha's eyes were dry. Maybe the pain had not reached her heart yet. It was all in her mind. Yet.

Debesh pushed away from her, out of her arms, and held Bidisha by her shoulders. He peered into her empty eyes.

'I shouldn't have handled you the way I did. How could I push you like that? I am ashamed of myself for behaving—'

'Let's talk to Oliver,' Bidisha said as she turned around, freeing herself from Debeh's hold and walked inside behind the goras as they helped Oliver to settle.

Oliver stared at Bidisha and then his glare shifted to Debesh, turning into a pitiful gaze as he held his eyes on him for a long second. Debesh's arms crossed over his chest that rose high with every breath as his eyes darted back at Oliver.

'Are you even telling the truth?' Bidisha inquired the envoy, her tone even and her eyes gloomy.

She was parched, her legs frail and her hands trembled as she went closer to the man who had brought the lamentable news from her land.

'Yes. Of course, it is true. And the rumour is that it was Rani Durga Moni Devi who committed the heinous act of murdering the Maharaja.'

Bidisha trudged to the chair and flumped into it, her head in her hands. Tears rolled down her cheeks.

'What happened to you? I didn't know you cared for His Majesty's life,' Debesh asked as he sat next to her, his hand on her back, stroking her softly.

'I didn't. But all that I went through was for nothing.' Bidisha wiped her tears and walked out of the living room.

The men stared at her but then continued with their banter with Sir Oliver.

She was there to confront the moron who had ruined her hopes of going back to her mother at the earliest. But she was not sure if she really could face her mother anymore. Bidisha had not even considered her mother's advice when Mokshita wanted to stop her from going to the palace. And then she had left Bishnupur without considering the consequences, chasing after the mirage, Sir Oliver. In the end, she had put her mother in insurmountable pain.

Bidisha had taken away the only person her mother lived for, her daughter, herself.

She had broken her mother's trust, ditched the queen who had promised to help her and carelessly played with Debesh's feelings. Above all, she had put everyone's life at risk the moment she slit Yuvaraja Trinabh's thumb.

In her head now, she could see the gushing blood that had spilled on her saree followed by Trinabh's face. His words, 'run', she could hear them clearly again. She had put the man she loved, Yuvaraja Trinabh, on the test of fire.

Bidisha kneeled on the grass, her heart heavy like the rock she had placed her hand on. She had been strong for a long time, years perhaps. But not anymore. Her eyes pricked and her hands went to her face as the sparkle in the water poked her eyes. And just like the water in the stream in front of her, her tears gushed. Her shoulders shook and her sobs overpowered the burbling sound of the water.

The warmth of a hand touched her shoulder. 'Bidisha...' Debesh said, filling her in his arms as he dropped the swords he had retrieved from the backyard.

She let it all out then, her face buried in his chest. Debesh embraced her as she convulsed in his warmth.

[1] It was a strict rule in the penny sit-up homes. No body was allowed to sleep and so they had monitors to maintain discipline.

CHAPTER SEVENTEEN

Dawn had set in killing the darkness of the unsettling night. Birds chirped, flocking out from the nests. The briny cool breeze brought vigour to Bidisha as she looked at the blooming crimson flower on the faraway horizon. The warmth of the rays snogged her with a new day's essence.

The day she had been looking forward to had finally arrived. Bidisha, along with Debesh, desperately waited on the shores near the harbour to board the ship. They had together watched the laborious work by the men and women who slogged all night as the guards and officials barked commands to load the ship. The poor and helpless people loaded the ship with the merchants' goods and all the supplies required for the voyage that would last months. Perhaps, some messily gift for the royals like velvet, liquor, perfumes, tableware and such eye candies to please them.

Bidisha's hair wiggled over her face and the waves hitting the shore touched her feet as she walked up and down on the sand barefoot.

In contrast to how she had felt on board while sailing to Lancashire, this time Bidisha looked forward to stepping on those planks that were weathered under the sun. She couldn't wait to feel the perfumes of the sea that the wind would bring to them on deck. The ever-changing beautiful clouds above her and the blues of the sea would lead her home this time and not away.

'Who are you waiting for?' Debesh fidgeted, his eyes set on the narrow pathway leading to the dock.

'Me? Nobody. Hmmm... for Oliver, yes...' Bidisha flapped her hands as she grinned nervously, pacing away from Debesh in an attempt to hide her anxious face from him.

'Isn't Oliver coming from the other side? You have been watching the opposite direction all along.'

'I am... I am just nervous.' Bidisha blabbered, 'What if Oliver does not keep his promise? Only his instructions can get us inside the ship.'

'And you want me to believe you. What are you waiting for?'

Bidisha's eyes flickered as she trudged on the sand heading towards Debesh, who looked as worried as her.

'I couldn't trust Oliver with this and so...ummm...I did something.'

'What? I told you—'

'It's all good. Don't worry. I... I met with Oliver's partners, Gary Brown and Henry Peel, and requested them to arrange the tickets for us,' Bidisha told him, as she scrubbed the sand off of her feet.

'And what did you give them in return? They wouldn't have done anything for nothing.' Debesh glared at her. 'Do you know what it means for them to catch and surrender you to their queen's law? I had warned you, Bidisha. It's not that simple. What would you do if they had got you arrested?'

'I know. But I had to take a chance. To go home. I just had to tell them the truth. And they have promised me to manage our tickets.'

'What? What do you mean by truth? What did you tell them?' Debesh closed in on her, his lips pressed and his brows pulled together.

'I only had to tell them about the fire incident. Of course, they had questions. Why? How?' Bidisha recounted her meeting with them to Debesh. 'Don't you think I am capable enough to stall those off? I didn't speak a word about you. Don't be too worried about it.'

'Can't trust anybody or anything that's happening at present. Not until we make it into the ship.'

Bidisha's ears pricked up when she heard footsteps approaching. She turned to the sight she had been waiting for. It was Lord Henry Peel. Her lips curled up, 'There he is. In the end, we will be going back home, this way or that.'

'It is done. I can see your anxious eyes, lady. You better board the ship now before it sets the sail. I can't guarantee a bunk but a place on the ship for you and the man is spoken for.' Lord Henry beamed at them in delight at his impossible accomplishment.

'I will forever be indebted, Sir.'

It was indeed difficult to find a place on the ship unless one was truly required on board. Bidisha's tainted reputation made things more complicated if not impossible.

At times, even high acquaintances and influence couldn't get people a place to sail. The resources and food were limited to last for months and an extra mouth to feed meant a threat to the strict discipline. The merchants never entertained men onboard unless they added value to the voyage.

'As you anticipated, Oliver has indeed not shown up. You did good, Bidisha. Or, we would have to stay back once again,' Debesh said with a smile that Bidisha was seeing after months. 'But you risked your life for it and I am not happy about it.'

'Come on now. Let's settle our differences onboard.' Bidisha beamed with joy.

The swords were detained as they arrived from the shore in a boat before stepping on the deck and their passage was allowed.

Henry Peel and Gary Brown had indeed helped Bidisha with a ticket to freedom from the clutches of the foreign land. She took a deep breath as she stood on the deck looking into the never-ending waters, as far as her sight let her. She didn't want to turn back to the sight of the shore she had waited for so long to leave behind.

Debesh came closer to her and slid his hand into hers. 'If not for you, we would never be able to make it.'

'What matters is that we are finally leaving for home, Debesh. I will be able to see Maa soon,' Bidisha said as she spoke about her mother to him for the first time.

Debesh took his eyes away from the sea and looked at her. 'So do you trust me enough now to talk about your mother?'

'Aren't you surprised to hear about her? 'Did you already know about her?'

'Do you think I would believe you if you said you lived in the jungle, in that old ruined temple without anybody but animals?'

Bidisha smiled, firming her grip on his hand.

'But more months to go before we can soak in the warmth of our motherland.'

'I was right. You didn't have any idea about the Suez Canal passage, did you?'

The voice startled Bidisha as she turned to look into the face she dreaded the most at that moment—Oliver. It had to be him. Bidisha looked at him in horror, her hand on her chest and her eyes wide open. Words failed to make it out of her mouth as her breath was caught in her throat.

'You? What... What are you doing here?' Debesh asked as he turned shiftily to face Oliver, his hand still clasped with hers.

'I just wanted to give you a piece of information. That's all.'

'How? How can you be here?' Bidisha mumbled finally, her brows furrowed in angst.

'You mean, why was I not arrested yet despite your adventurous trip to Henry and Gary's den? You're too innocent for that, Bidisha. You don't read people well. You thought those two nincompoops would do that for you? Oh, dear! Well, I am here in front of you.'

'But they bought us tickets. They took the risk to help a person you tagged a thief.'

'Because I asked them to my, dear. Just a small act.'

'I can't believe those crooks played us!' Bidisha said, gauging her options to get rid of Oliver with caution.

She needed to think. Oliver had their fate in his hand. Any action taken in haste would cost her no less than her life as well as Debesh's freedom.

'It was too easy. I bought them, their integrity, their faith and their soul. I gave them my mansion. Anyone would do anything for a place like that. Don't you agree?'

Bidisha clenched her jaw. 'But what are you doing here? And why let us board the ship in the first place? Stop toying with others' lives.'

'You see, that's the thing. I want to settle it once and for all.' Oliver said as he straightened his coat, 'Debesh, I am giving you a choice and you make it now.'

'You can't stand a chance against me. Don't you already know that?' Debesh snarled as if he would take him down any moment.

'But what you don't know is that the people around you are all my men. And the person who owns this ship is my acquaintance.'

7 tall and bulky lads gathered around them. Dressed in rags and a couple of them bare-chested, they were indeed intimidating. But she didn't give in to the fear. Even without her sword, she was much more capable.

'Nothing that you are saying makes sense. What are you up to?' Bidisha said stepping forward, closing in on Oliver, her eyes fierce and her hands fisted even as the sweat dripped into her clothes.

'Do you think I want to go back to India? Hell no. I need to get back to my home. But the thing is, I can't go alone. I need Debesh. I really do. I mean, I want him. I simply can't imagine my life without him. I tried. I tried hard. But it's not possible to live without him. So, I am here to take him.' Oliver stared right back at her. 'And take only him.'

'Who said you can Oliver? Don't you understand? Just leave the ship while you still can. If you try anything here against my wish, you'll not have a chance to return. You will neither go to Bishnupur nor your home.'

'Not so soon. Don't conclude yet, Debesh. Hear me out first. You can either let Bidisha leave alone today so that she reaches Bishnupur safely in a matter of 100 days. Yes, that's what I wanted to tell you. A new short route. So, think about it. In just 100 days...' Oliver walked towards Debesh, their eyes locked. 'Or you resist and I will see to it that she doesn't live anymore. Neither here in Lancashire nor Bishnupur.'

'You touch her and I will show you stars in the daylight,' Debesh warned as he grabbed Oliver's lapels.

'And you touch me, she'll never be able to stay in this ship today. Or board any other ship for that matter...' Oliver threatened and puffed from his pipe.

'I don't understand why we are even talking about this. Bring what you got Oliver. Let's see the end today. Because I am not leaving this ship and I will not let anyone harm her.' Debesh moved Bidisha aside and took his position, glaring at Oliver and his men.

She was pulled into the realm of agony and distress that showed up on her forehead as her brows furrowed. Bidisha closed her eyes in dubiety as her mother's longing eyes bore into hers. She wanted to touch her but Mokshita vanished just as quickly as she had appeared.

It was not her life to choose to sacrifice for Debesh's safe passage or she would have, wouldn't she? But she was her mother's life and she was her mother's freedom, which she needed to protect and uphold.

However, she was not so selfish to put Debesh's will at stake. The palace was the place where he belonged and Yuvaraja Prabir was the person he wanted to serve. And nobody could take that away from him. Not by forcing him. She would fight for what she had to do, for her mother and Debesh.

Bidisha squeezed her eyes as she shook her head. She fisted her hands and rolled her shoulders before she opened her eyes to scowl at Oliver.

She let go of Debesh's hand and stepped forward. 'Don't forget who I am, Debesh. It's our fight for our journey back home. And we will fight it together.'

'If that's what you want. Let us do it your way then.' Oliver backed as the circle of his men came closer to Bidisha and Debesh.

Bidisha looked each one in the eye as the crooks took cautious steps shrinking the distance between them. She moved towards Debesh, her back touching his, each protecting the other. She ripped her long dress. She had to get through what was before her. And she would do just that and make herself more movable. The men signalled to each other and they ran towards them together.

Bidisha lunged, slid her leg out and kicked him in the shin and into his loins throwing him out of her way as he crumbled on the floor. She tightened her fingers and punched another man in his face as she rose. Bidisha bolted, two men following her. She hung on the spar, swirled over, kicking into a scoundrel who fell over the other.

Her hands were weak; eating bread for months had done her no good. Bidisha struggled to gain her balance.

Another pair of hands grabbed her legs and attempted to pull her down. Bidisha's hands slipped off the spar and her head slammed onto the rusting rod on the floor. Bursts of light appeared before her eyes. His hand came in, punching her hard in the face and her mouth filled with the taste of blood. And then he was on top of her. But, just in time, Debesh kicked him in the chest sending him crashing into the wooden board. The man lay dead, his neck twisted. Perhaps broken.

Debesh gave her a hand and she jumped back up. She held her head in her hands, eyes shut.

'Aaugh!' Bidisha growled the next instant wiping her mouth, blood on her hand.

She struggled to find her footing on the wood. Debesh held her as she swayed, her head pounding.

'You killed my brother,' a loud howl pierced her ears.

When she opened her eyes, she looked into the face of a man holding a pistol in his hands. Bidisha's heart thudded inside her ribs, her insides shook and her palms became sweaty. Debesh shielded her.

'Is this my end?'

'Down, you fool.' Oliver paced towards the man. 'Didn't I warn you not to hurt Debesh?'

'He... He killed my only brother.' The last of the standing crooks shouted.

'I will pay you a hefty compensation. Just tell me what you want.' Oliver extended his hand. 'Now give that pistol to me.'

Bidisha gulped, sucking in some blood from her wound.

'Wish I could see Trinabh once before I met my death.'

'No. Not money in exchange of blood.' The man almost pressed the trigger when Oliver jumped over him.

The bullet was out and Debesh growled baring his teeth that pulled her out of her trans. Blood oozed from his arm.

Oliver was on top of the man trying to snatch the pistol. Bidisha's eyes flared. Like a crouching tigress, she steadied her body and her mind into the moment. She pounced on him and snatched the pistol from his hand. As Oliver moved in haste, Bidisha pulled the crook up and sent a blow with her knee straight into his gut and toppled him off the deck. The man went down flying into the waters.

She glared at Oliver who was still on the floor, gasping, his eyes shut. Debesh walked towards Bidisha and snatched the pistol and pointed it at Oliver.

'No.' Bidisha shouted moving it away. 'We need his word. We need him alive.'

Oliver opened his eyes, his face red under the sun and shock on his face at the sound of a bullet that was fired at the hull.

'What? Didn't you want to kill him Bidisha? He's the reason we are here in the first place. In this hell of Lancashire.'

'Yes. But don't forget, if he dies, we will never be able to reach Bishnupur.'

Debesh fidgeted, holding his wounded arm. 'Listen, you creep. I am either going back to the palace or hell even. But never with you. I am not stepping down from this deck. Not back on this shore again.'

He was right before her eyes. The scoundrel she wanted to kill to prove her loyalty to the king. She had the opportunity. They could still make it home. At least she could try rather than abandoning the ship and going back to the hell of a shelter home again.

She wished the Maharaja was still alive. She could take advantage of the man's death, and comfort His Majesty's ego. But he was no more and Oliver's head meant nothing.

'Oliver, I don't want any more trouble.' Bidisha bent forward and glared at him as Oliver still sat on the deck looking at Debesh. 'Talk to the captain, get us out of Lancashire and you better leave before I change my mind and the ship sails.'

Oliver smiled. 'The man I love the most in this world wants to kill me. And the woman I hate the most wants to save me.'

'This man has no right to live,' Debesh debated, without even heeding Oliver's words.

'Debesh, let me take care of this.'

'Are you still not able to see, Bidisha? This man burnt his own mill putting the lives of so many workers at stake. And he is so dangerous that he saw his dream burn before his eyes. He has destroyed himself obsessing over me. He will not stop.' Debesh paced up and down, his face contorted with rage. 'Moreover, I know he will someday follow us to Bishnupur. And I can see very well how this is going to end. He will not only hunt you down but also go after Yuvaraja Prabir because he knows I would never part my way from my Yuvaraja.'

Her head exploded with rage, that she almost let out on Debesh. 'First, let's get done with our purpose.' Bidisha dragged Oliver inside the cabin, away from Debesh.

'You must treat your wound before it gets infected, Debesh,' Oliver said, looking back, his voice calm but his body limp as he walked with Bidisha to see the captain.

Just then, a man with a long golden moustache came to stand before them. 'You. Woman. Clear this deck and dump all the bodies in the sea. I like my ship to be mess-free.'

'Let them have their way, Captain. Please allow them to sail in your ship,' Oliver said with a grim face but making firm eye contact with the chubby man who gave his full attention to Oliver.

'I didn't know this would be so easy. What came over you all of a sudden, Sir Oliver? 'What are you scheming now'

Bidisha was flummoxed. She couldn't construe the motive behind the shift in his attitude. She was scared, to say the least.

'If you would have asked me the same question a while ago, my answer would have been different. And you know that very well, Bidisha. But now, I can see hatred in Debesh's eyes. So much so that he wants me dead. I don't have an answer to that question anymore.'

His words didn't sit well with her. She took him from top to toe in an attempt to read his weird behaviour.

'Woman. I don't want any more gore and death on my ship. You and your man there can leave now. Given the shambles you have made on the deck, I wouldn't budge to your tears. Don't even try. Out now,' the captain voiced and shut the cabin door right on her face.

'I swear, Captain, it won't happen again once this man is out of the ship. We...We just want to go to our home.'

Her eyes moistened as she clenched her dress in her trembling hands trying to hold back her tears. She couldn't fathom the fact that Oliver could ruin her last chance to make it home despite getting a chance to board the ship.

Bidisha dragged herself out of the cabin with a heavy heart after she was unable to convince the Captain. Outside, she looked at Debesh. His hand was covered in blood, face pale as he leaned back on the wooden bench under the hot sunlight. Bidisha ran and hugged him, her hands over his shoulders while he sat up straight in shock. She cried and he soothed her.

'It's my turn now, Bidisha. Don't you worry. I will take care of it all,' Debesh said, even as he whimpered in pain.

Oliver walked up to them, his eyes red and moist. 'I was just a man after money. But you, Debesh, you awoke the evil in me. You made me do things I never intended to. And even when I did, I never realized what I was doing just to get you by my side. It saddens me to even think about it. How could I fall so hard for a person? I lost everything because of you. And for you. The moment I met you for the first time in the palace years ago as a humble young man, this hidden side of me became very aware. You were the person who showed me that I wanted to be with a man. You are my first love, Debesh.'

Bidisha stood up as anger consumed her. All she could see was an animal standing before her. She growled at him through clenched teeth and attacked without a second thought. The meek man that Oliver was, he couldn't take her strong punch. His back hit the gunwale.

'Only because I am in love with a man and not a woman, I... I have to face this fate...' Oliver grunted panting.

'Then what do you think about Debesh and me? Why are we not together? Do you think it's all that simple?'

'I am worried for Debesh. He will be killed if he goes back to the palace. He is the only support Prabir has. And he is a huge obstacle for Her Highness. The queen wouldn't leave him alone. You know it too well.'

'You worry for your life first, Oliver. You either make it happen for us or die on this very ship.'

Bidisha struck him in the face. But this time Oliver didn't hold himself back. He slapped her in reflex.

It all rushed into her veins. The rage. Her hand in his gut. He let out a growl as he coughed. She thwacked his jaw. And her tears rolled down. 'You ruined everything. I am not going to spare you, Oliver.' And then there was another blow on the other side. Blood spewed out from his mouth.

She had bruised him, just like he had her heart. And her hand went up again for another one. But Debesh held it.

'You don't have to. I will take care of him. I know, Bidisha, you have killed animals before but he is a beast who doesn't deserve an easy death.'

Bidisha's hand went straight to the pistol that Debesh held. But he pulled it away from her. 'I should have shot him earlier but he will meet his fate no matter what. He has earned it with his evil deeds and I will pay him in full.'

The instant Bidisha's hand made to Oliver's neck, Debesh's hand was on her waist as he pulled her back in one swift move.

She swung her fist to oppose Debesh but he dodged.

'Listen to me, Bidisha. He is mine to kill.'

She threw a punch. He grabbed her arm, pulled her in close. Their breath tethered. 'And we stop here,' Debesh said.

'Lovers' tiff over the third wheel's death, I guess,' Oliver said, the smile on his face showing his bloody teeth.

'Are you worried for him now that his death is imminent?' Bidisha asked as she struggled to free herself from Debesh's grip.

'No, I am worried for you,' Debesh said swirling her away from Oliver, clenching his arm in pain.

Bidisha slumped on the bench. She didn't make an effort to move any further. The weight of grief for not being able to sail crushed her down. Her lips trembled as she rested her head in her hands. Tears trickled down on her lap as her dress soaked the grief that cascaded from her heart.

Her mother had never asked for any of this. No matter how uncomfortable or even disgusting it might seem to be.

Sometimes the best thing you can do is wait because the stronger you try to fight the adversity, the harder it could strike back.

She should have known better.

Everything had worked just the opposite. Bidisha let her tears roll. She had not only made it difficult for her mother when she left her back all alone but also, she had to lead a life in hiding even here in Lancashire, away from her home.

She didn't want to live a lonely life in the jungle and had desired a normal life. But little did she know what it meant to be in the crowd and live in a place surrounded by people. With no one to guide her, her worst fears had come true in the past year. She had made mistakes that would haunt her for life.

The most terrible thing of all was to make the same mistake her mother had committed. Chase the wrong man and that too with a purpose in her mind, unlike her mother who had truly fallen for a white. She had left behind a caring soul who loved her enough to uphold her safety even when he was in pain and distress because of her.

How could she not see it that she would never be able to embrace Debesh's feelings for her even if he would have accepted her presumptuous love for him? She had tried to plan her love for convenience and to solve a problem with it. There couldn't be another person more shallow than her.

'I knew the Captain would do exactly the opposite of what I ask him to do...' Oliver muttered even as he struggled in pain. 'And look, you'll be thrown out of the ship soon.'

Bidisha was too anguished to heed Oliver's prattle.

Debesh fumed. 'And why would he do that? Just stop spewing venom from that mouth of yours or I won't be able to hold myself back.'

'That's because he is more than just a connection, or an acquaintance to me.' Oliver let out a peal of laughter, 'We were once in a relationship. Years back. When I returned from Bishnupur after seeing you for the first time. I wanted it. To be with a man. But I guess my heart beats only for you and I broke up with him.'

'I don't want to hear any of your nonsense anymore. Let me just shut you for a while,' Debesh said as he paced towards Oliver.

'You know what, I was holding myself back but I guess I will let you know a secret,' Oliver said as he wheezed, leaning on the hull, his body weak from all the beating it had taken.

'Do you think we want to hear you anymore?'

Oliver reached for the gunwale for support. 'What if it has to do with your mother, Bidisha?' Oliver raised his eyebrows and smirked.

Bidisha's heart thudded against her ribs as she suddenly jerked her head out of her hands. And Debesh stopped punching him.

Oliver laughed. 'I was taking a chance. Bidisha, if at all you reach Bishnupur alive, it will give you the shock of your life, especially after months of dreaming about hugging your mother. And if at all you were supposed to die today on this ship, I want to tell you this fascinating truth when you will take your last dying breath. That would make you suffer in your death and even in hell. But I think this is much better, you dying every minute of the day, every day worrying about what could have happened to your mother back home. Something even I would like to do. But was done by someone else in the palace.'

Bidisha stood up, her stare piercing through his eyes, 'Stop blabbering and tell me what happened, you dratted bull!'

'You will know it when you reach home, Bidisha. I mean, if you reach home.'

Bidisha scowled as she tried to keep the anxiety from her voice even as her stomach churned. There was a blissful expression on Oliver's face. She was enraged. She ran towards him.

'Tell me what you know. What happened to my mother?'

'Come on, kill me. Show me your rage. Even if you do, I wouldn't tell you a thing.'

'I have never killed anyone for sport or revenge. Not even an animal. I had planned to kill you earlier but you would be the first one I would be killing in cold blood. But for the sake of my mother and her upbringing, I wouldn't stain my hand with your dirty blood,' Bidisha said as she held his lapels in a firm grip, 'But I will not let you go till you tell me everything that you know.'

'Do you think you are capable of that? You don't want to kill me, you say,' Oliver paused and smiled, 'But I will make sure you live your life with the burden of my death on your heart.'

And in the next instant, he leaned back and toppled down into the waters.

'No!' Bidisha screamed, her eyes widening as she saw him sink into the waters. 'You can't die. You mutt! Tell me what you know.'

Debesh pulled her back when she was about to jump in behind Oliver and hugged her tight. 'Let me go, Debesh. Leave me. He can't just die like that.'

Debesh tightened his grip on her. 'Let him go, Bidisha. Didn't you see, the ship has started sailing already. We are leaving. We are going home. Everything will be alright. I promise. Your mother too.'

Oliver had taught her a lesson in his death.

'The claws that are not visible are the most dangerous ones. They not only deceive the opponent but also leave deeper scars.'

She couldn't contain her joy as the prow pierced the waters moving forward. The rough waves buffeted the ship. Masts and sails afforded a measure of emergency propulsion. It was the grace of the captain that she was able to dream of seeing the light of the day in Bishnupur for real.

The sailing boat blossomed in the blue ocean, with white sails that complimented the sky and clouds. The rest of the solid oak with warm browns spread under her feet reminded her of home. The rich timber brought her peace akin to that given by the flowering meadow. And yet for the next few weeks, she wouldn't be able to breathe in the fragrance of the wilderness but of the open briny sea.

'I know your eyes are on me,' Bidisha said as she looked up at the sky.

Debesh smiled, his eyes still locked on her, as he gently moved a lock of hair away from her face. 'I am aware you know that. But you look different today. Graceful but not flattering, delicate but not fragile, like wildflowers, naturally blossomed to face the wilderness.'

'Are you possessed? What's that coming out of your mouth?' Bidisha brushed him off as she took a step to walk away inside the cabin.

Debesh held her hand and turned her around. Bidisha squinted when he held her arms taking her in with his soft gaze. He pulled her closer and planted a kiss on her forehead. His eyes moistened and her mind convulsed in confusion.

'Will you ever confess your love for me?' Bidisha asked as her heart ached for him.

'Is it necessary for me to tell you that?'

'I thought that would put you a little at ease. Perhaps.'

'If only I could. I know, the feeling of loving someone secretly is painful. But the happiness you get is above that pain.' Debesh took her hands in his calloused hands. 'I would never want the burden of my heart to be passed on to the one I love.'

And just like that, he left her and walked inside to take his place in the cramped bunk for a sleepless night, biding his farewell formally to whatever was between them.

Her heart was heavy and ached as she even thought of what she had done by fueling his feelings for her aimless pursuit to forget the man she had truly fallen for.

Their bond would never get a name and yet it would be the strongest one. Some encounters turn to become fleeting moments while others linger in hearts for life even if the people involved don't spend their life together. Bidisha and Debesh's relationship was one that would linger long.

She knew Debesh was preparing for the times that would come soon. She didn't have an idea of what was in store in their future but she wondered if she could ever talk to him with the same ease once they stepped out of the ship in Bishnupur.

Bidisha was hungover Debesh whom she had decided to leave back and his decision was no different. But to pursue Trinabh was not in her bounds. Her heart was ripped between the two men. And she had turned into a woman whom the world had always despised and shamed.

True love for her had turned out to be a ghost that everybody spoke about but only a few daring ones had encountered. Because true love was in the deeper part of the unreachable realm, in the darkest of the nights surrounded by dangers with scary glowing eyes lurking over. Not everybody would dare to go after it.

But what about her. Hadn't she seen it already? Twice.

'Wasn't it all planned by destiny? Should I go against it? Or, can I have a chance to play along and chase it in the wilderness of the darkest of nights? Can I afford to risk everything for my true love?'

After what felt like forever, they could see the land she was proud to be born on. And she could finally tell that.

The wait to see her mother would soon be over. And all the anticipation that had carved holes in her longing heart would come to an end. She had prayed every single day for the safety of Mokshita Maitra. And had made a promise to herself that she wouldn't spare any person who had dared to harm her mother. The only hope that had kept Bidisha going was that Oliver's words were just a hoax to startle her and agitate her mind. Her mother would just be fine to embrace her daughter after a long time. And she would accept any punishment for putting her mother through all the battles she had always cautioned Bidisha about.

On the other hand, her eyes twinkled at the thought of Trinabh standing before her. She hoped, he would look at her the same way he did before. But even then, she knew it was too good to be true and that they could never be together.

However, the moments they had spent together were the ones she would cherish all her life. She wished she could at least see him from afar every day and feel like she had lived a life with him when they both would have aged.

But more than anything, knowing that he was doing well even if not a part of her world would bring her peace and solace. His hand in hers was all she had yearned for all those days they were apart. She had died inside for him every fleeting night when she had wished to be with another man just so she could forget Trinabh.

Howbeit, his arms would be where she would want to rest in the last moments of life. It was selfish to say without thinking about anyone else but she was waiting for her love to show up before she could let him go back to his life.

After all those months, she had wondered if he had longed for her or just forgotten her as a non-existent being. But either way, will she ever be able to be with Yuvaraja Trinabh? And just like she had always been scared, she might after all not be able to be with any man despite her best efforts to correct her wrongdoings. But there she was, longing for him more than ever.

But the sudden hue and cry around broke her moment of calmness. The Captain, along with a few men, surrounded her. And just like that, even before she made sense of what was happening around, her hands were tied behind her back.

'What... What is going on?' Bidisha struggled to let herself loose from the tight hold of men.

Before she knew it, she was gagged. A ripping pain shuddered through her as she growled. But even before she could do anything they tied a black cloth on her eyes so tight she thought her eyes would rupture in the sockets.

Bidisha had hoped to escape the scene as soon as she set her feet on the sand. But her blood went cold at the very thought of what was to come, although her mind couldn't make complete sense of it all.

Even Debesh's struggling voice was lost soon as her mind's undying chaos took over. And in no time, she was moved, forced to pace down the wooden plank. Her feet, she was sure, touched the sand along with men who held her hands with a crushing grip. She could hear Debesh scuffling next to her.

Her heart thudded against her chest. Nothing that was happening to her made any sense.

Why would the Captain detain Debesh and her?

She heard a scuffle right next to where she was forced to kneel. It was Debesh, she could tell, who was possibly trying to fight back. But she didn't see a point. Even if he succeeded to free himself away from the crooks they had travelled with, all the way from Lancashire, his blindfold wouldn't allow him to go far.

And just as the scrimmage settled, a pair of hands opened her blindfold. She squinted at the sudden strike of bright sunlight directly on her eyes. The sight before her gave Bidisha a nerve-wracking jolt.

It was Rani Maa, sitting in a regal chair under the shade of a silken umbrella over her head. And Yuvaraja Trinabh stood next to her, his hands crossed on his chest, his eyes locked on hers.

There was an eloquent silence. And the love was found missing.

For she didn't understand how to phrase her feeling, it was a love departing reunion.

To Be Continued...

Just when Bidisha thought she'd figured out Yuvaraja Trinabh, he has deceived her in the most unimaginable way.
Is he the same man who, even when in intense pain, had protected her from the wrath of his men? Or was this the true Yuvaraja Trinabh, who was capable of trapping her?
What does this return to her homeland mean for Bidisha? Has she fallen into a trap bigger than the one she escaped? Or does Yuvaraja Trinabh have a card up his sleeve to protect her?
What is Yuvaraja Prabir up to? Does he have feelings for Bidisha like Debesh claims about his master or is there more to it than what eyes meet?
Get answers to all your burning questions in the sequel to edge-of-the-seat historic drama.
Reign of the fallen, the second book in <u>The Sting of Love duology</u>, releases this **December**.

Leave Your Feedback

Your opinion on this book would mean the world to me.
Please leave your feedback on **Amazon** and **GoodReads**
Here's how you can connect with me
https://www.facebook.com/MedhaNagurAuthor/
Instagram @medhanagur
Twitter @NagurMedha

About The Author

Once upon a time, a Computer Science lecturer, Medha Nagur now writes riveting novels based on the intricacies of human relationships and the subjects that make a man less of a machine. She portrays the philosophy of life through stories laced with love, romance, drama and suspense. A writer who refuses to be boxed in one particular genre, she loves to surprise readers with her thought-provoking and emotionally intriguing human life sagas. Much like her characters, she learns from her mistakes and likes to challenge her limits.

She lives with her husband and two kids in Bangalore. It's also her workstation where she mastered the art of storytelling when her younger child was too young to let her sleep through the night. At times she likes to feel the grass on her bare feet when she travels deep into nature's womb for warmth and comfort while vibing to her favourite numbers.

Glossary

1. **Panjabi-** Indian style kurta for men
2. **Purdah-** Simply a curtain or the practice in certain Muslim and Hindu societies of screening women from men or strangers, especially by means of a curtain
3. **Athpourey saree-** Athpourey is one of the adorable saree draping styles from Bengal
4. **Jomidaar-** A zamindar (Pronounced Jomidaar in West Bengal) in the Indian subcontinent was an autonomous or semiautonomous ruler of a province who was originally known as bhumipati
5. **Misti-** Sweets and desserts
6. **Pallav-** The loose end of a saree also called as aanchal, pallu, pallav, seragu, or paita
7. **Gondhoraj Maachh-** Fish flavoured with kaffir lime
8. **Matka-** Clay pot
9. **Izzat-** Honour, reputation, or prestige
10. **Bajuband-** Gold armlet or armband, an ornament
11. **Resham-** Silk
12. **Sarbath-** Juice
13. **Darbar-** Royal court
14. **Byaktigata darbar-** Private court or Royal court with the close-knit or the important people
15. **Gadda-** Mattress
16. **Phulkori singara-** A Bengali samosa like dish made with cauliflower with a thinner outer cover and different flavours as compared to samosa.
17. **Begun bhaja-** Crispy eggplant fries enjoyed as a snack, side or appetizer
18. **Aloo chorchori-** Potato stir fry
19. **Chingri malai-** Prawn curry made by cooking large tiger prawns or big freshwater prawns in a super-subtle, super-creamy coconut-milk sauce
20. **Shorshe bata ilish maach-** Bengali-style mustard-based Hilsa fish curry
21. **Tok maach-** Fish curry cooked in tamarind sauce
22. **Nolen gurer payesh-** Rice pudding with date palm jaggery
23. **Luchi-** Bengali puffed deep fried bread
24. **Hookah-** Hookahs are water pipes that are used to smoke specially

made tobacco

25. **Sharaab-** Wine, or other alcoholic drinks
26. **Aftaba-** A vessel for water, like an aiguière with handle and long spout, made in Persia and northern India, commonly of metal, and decorated with enamels or gems and stones.
27. **Jomidaar Boro Bari-** Zamindar's huge bungalow or house
28. **Khichodi-** Dish made with rice and moong lentils
29. **Kaada-** Medicinal herbal concoction
30. **Chaddar-** Blanket
31. **Mard-** a sulky mood or fit of petulant bad temper
32. **Kapula-** Traditional footwear made from shoots of plants and animal skin or 'pakpa'
33. **Bellow-** Fireplace accessory used to stoke the fire by blowing air
34. **Silver crowns-** English coin, its value was five shillings
35. **Penny sit-up-** The penny sit-up for a price of a penny allowed the person to sit on a bench all night in a warm building strictly monitored for discipline. The homeless were not allowed to dose or sleep.

www.ingramcontent.com/pod-product-compliance
Lightning Source LLC
Chambersburg PA
CBHW031255160726
47993CB00001B/168